THE SELECTED STORIES OF ROBERT BLOCH, VOL. I—III

LAST RITES

Volume Three

THE SELECTED STORIES OF ROBERT BLOCH

LAST RITES

U-M
Underwood-Miller
Los Angeles, California
Columbia, Pennsylvania
1987

The Selected Stories of Robert Bloch, Vol. I — III
Vol. III LAST RITES

0-88733-055-X (set)
Limited signed edition 054-1 (set)

Printed in the United States of America

All Rights Reserved

FIRST EDITION

Underwood-Miller
515 Chestnut Street
Columbia, PA 17512

Library of Congress Cataloging-in-Publication Data

Bloch, Robert, 1917–
  Last rites.

  (The selected stories of Robert Bloch ; v. 3)
  1. Science Fiction, American. 2. Horror tales,
American. I. Title. II. Series: Bloch, Robert,
1917–   Short stories. Selections ; v. 3)
PS3503.L718A6 1988   vol. 1   813'.54 s   87–34265
ISBN 0-88733-055-X (set)   [813'.54]
ISBN 0-88733-054-1 (lim ed. : set)

CONTENTS

LAST RITES

TALENT

IT IS PERHAPS A PITY that nothing is known of Andrew Benson's parents.

The same reasons which prompted them to leave him as a foundling on the steps of the St. Andrews Orphanage also caused them to maintain a discreet anonymity. The event occurred on the morning of March 3rd, 1943 — the war era, as you probably recall — so in a way the child may be regarded as a wartime casualty. Similar occurrences were by no means rare during those days, even in Pasadena, where the Orphanage was located.

After the usual tentative and fruitless inquiries, the good Sisters took him in. It was there that he acquired his first name, from the patron and patronymic saint of the establishment. The "Benson" was added some years later, by the couple who eventually adopted him.

It is difficult, at this late date, to determine what sort of a child Andrew was; orphanage records are sketchy, at best, and Sister Rosemarie, who acted as supervisor of the boys' dormitory, is long since dead. Sister Albertine, the primary grades teacher of the Orphanage School, is now — to put it as delicately as possible — in her senility, and her testimony is necessarily colored by knowledge of subsequent events.

That Andrew never learned to talk until he was nearly seven years old seems almost incredible; the forced gregarity and the conspicuous lack of individual attention characteristic of orphanage upbringing would make it appear as though the ability to speak is necessary for actual survival in such an environment from infancy onward. Scarcely more credible is Sister Albertine's theory that Andrew knew how to talk but merely refused to do so until he was well into his seventh year.

For what it is worth, she now remembers him as an unusually precocious youngster, who appeared to possess an intelligence and understanding far

1

beyond his years. Instead of employing speech, however, he relied on panto-mime, an art at which he was so brilliantly adept (if Sister Albertine is to be believed) that his continuing silence seemed scarcely noticeable.

"He could imitate anybody," she declares. "The other children, the Sis-ters, even the Mother Superior. Of course I had to punish him for that. But it was remarkable, the way he was able to pick up all the little mannerisms and facial expressions of another person, just at a glance. And that's all it took for Andrew — just a mere glance.

"Visitors' Day was Sunday. Naturally, Andrew never had any visitors, but he liked to hang around the corridor and watch them come in. And after-wards, in the dormitory at night, he'd put in a regular performance for the other boys. He could impersonate every single man, woman or child who'd come to the Orphanage that day — the way they walked, the way they moved, every action and gesture. Even though he never said a word, nobody made the mistake of thinking Andrew was mentally deficient. For a while, Dr. Clement had the idea he might be a mute."

Dr. Roger Clement is one of the few persons who might be able to furnish more objective data concerning Andrew Benson's early years. Unfortunately, he passed away in 1954; a victim of a fire which also destroyed his home and his office files.

It was Dr. Clement who attended Andrew on the night that he saw his first motion picture.

The date was 1949, some Saturday evening in the late fall of the year. The Orphanage received and showed one film a week, and only children of school age were permitted to attend. Andrew's inability — or unwillingness — to speak had caused some difficulty when he entered primary grades that September, and several months went by before he was allowed to join his classmates in the auditorium for the Saturday night screenings. But it is known that he eventually did so.

The picture was the last (and probably the least) of the Marx Brothers movies. Its title was *Love Happy*, and if it is remembered by the general public at all today, that is due to the fact that the film contained a brief walk-on appearance by a then-unknown blonde bit player named Marilyn Monroe.

But the Orphanage audience had other reasons for regarding it as memo-rable. Because *Love Happy* was the picture that sent Andrew Benson into his trance.

Long after the lights came up again in the auditorium the child sat there, immobile, his eyes staring glassily at the blank screen. When his compan-ions noticed and sought to arouse him he did not respond; one of the Sisters (possibly Sister Rosemarie) shook him, and he promptly collapsed in a dead faint. Dr. Clement was summoned, and he administered to the patient. Andrew Benson did not recover consciousness until the following morning.

And it was then that he talked.

He talked immediately, he talked perfectly, he talked fluently — but not in the manner of a six-year-old child. The voice that issued from his lips was that of a middle-aged man. It was a nasal, rasping voice, and even without the accompanying grimaces and facial expressions it was instantaneously and unmistakably recognizable as the voice of Groucho Marx.

Andrew Benson mimicked Groucho in his *Sam Grunion* role to perfection, word for word. Then he "did" Chico Marx. After that he relapsed into silence again, mute phase. But it was an eloquent silence, and soon it became evident that he was imitating Harpo. In rapid succession, Andrew created recognizable vocal and visual portraits of Raymond Burr, Melville Cooper, Eric Blore and the other actors who played small roles in the picture. His impersonations seemed uncanny to his companions, and the Sisters were not unimpressed.

"Why, he even *looked* like Groucho," Sister Albertine insists.

Ignoring the question of how a towheaded moppet of six can achieve a physical resemblance to Groucho Marx without benefit (or detriment) of makeup, it is nevertheless an established fact that Andrew Benson gained immediate celebrity as a mimic within the small confines of the Orphanage.

And from that moment on, he talked regularly, if not freely. That is to say, he replied to direct questions, he recited his lessons in the classroom, and responded with the outward forms of politeness required by Orphanage discipline. But he was never loquacious, or even communicative, in the ordinary sense. The only time he became spontaneously articulate was immediately following the showing of a weekly movie.

There was no recurrence of his initial seizure, but each Saturday night screening brought in its wake a complete dramatic recapitulation by the gifted youngster. During the fall of '49 and the winter of '50, Andrew Benson saw many movies. There was *Sorrowful Jones*, with Bob Hope; *Tarzan's Magic Fountain*; *The Fighting O'Flynn*; *The Life of Riley*; *Little Women*, and a number of other films, current and older. Naturally, these pictures were subject to approval by the Sisters before being shown, and as a result movies depicting or emphasizing violence were not included. Still, several Westerns reached the Orphanage screen, and it is significant that Andrew Benson reacted in what was to become a characteristic fashion.

"Funny thing," declares Albert Dominguez, who attended the Orphanage during the same period as Andrew Benson and is one of the few persons located who is willing to admit, let alone discuss the fact. "At first Andy imitated everybody — all the men, that is. He never imitated none of the women. But after he started to see Westerns, it got so he was choosey, like. He just imitated the villains. I don't mean like when us guys was playing cowboys — you know, when one guy is the Sheriff and one is a gunslinger. I mean he imitated villains all the time. He could talk like 'em, he could even look like 'em. We used to razz hell out of him, you know?"

It is probably as a result of the "razzing" that Andrew Benson, on the evening of May 17th, 1950, attempted to slit the throat of Frank Phillips with a table knife. Probably — although Albert Dominguez claims that the older boy offered no provocation, and that Andrew Benson was exactly duplicating the screen role of a western desperado in an old Charles Starrett movie.

The incident was hushed up, apparently, and no action taken; we have little information on Andrew Benson's growth and development between the summer of 1950 and the autumn of 1955. Dominguez left the Orphanage, nobody else appears willing to testify, and Sister Albertine had retired to a rest home. As a result, there is nothing available concerning what may well have been Andrew's crucial, formative years. The meager records of his classwork seem satisfactory enough, and there is nothing to indicate that he was a disciplinary problem to his instructors. In June of 1955 he was photographed with the rest of his classmates upon the occasion of graduation from eighth grade. His face is a mere blur, an almost blank smudge in a sea of preadolescent countenances. What he actually looked like at that age is hard to tell.

The Bensons thought that he resembled their son, David.

Little David Benson had died of polio in 1953, and two years later his parents came to St. Andrews Orphanage seeking to adopt a boy. They had David's picture with them, and they were frank to state that they sought a physical resemblance as a guide to making their choice.

Did Andrew Benson see that photograph? Did — as has been subsequently theorized by certain irresponsible alarmists — he see certain *home movies* which the Bensons had taken of their child?

We must confine ourselves to the known facts, which are, simply, that Mr. and Mrs. Louis Benson, of Pasadena, California, legally adopted Andrew Benson, aged 12, on December 9th, 1955.

And Andrew Benson went to live in their home, as their son. He entered the public high school. He became the owner of a bicycle. He received an allowance of one dollar a week. And he went to the movies.

Andrew Benson went to the movies, and there were no restrictions. No restrictions at all. For several months, that is. During this period he saw comedies, dramas, Westerns, musicals, melodramas. He must have seen melodramas. Was there a film, released early in 1956, in which an actor played the role of a gangster who pushed a victim out of a second-storey window?

Knowing what we do today, we must suspect that there must have been. But at the time, when the actual incident occurred, Andrew Benson was virtually exonerated. He and the other boy had been "scuffling" in a classroom after school, and the boy had "accidentally fallen." At least, this is the official version of the affair. The boy — now Pvt. Raymond Schuyler, USMC — maintains to this day that Benson deliberately tried to kill him.

"He was spooky, that kid," Schuyler insists. "None of us ever really got close to him. It was like there was nothing to get close to, you know? I mean, he kept changing off so. From one day to the next you could never figure out what he was going to be like. Of course we all knew he imitated these movie actors — he was only a freshman but already he was a big shot in the dramatic club — but it was as though he imitated all the time. One minute he'd be real quiet, and the next, wham! You know that story, the one about Jekyll and Hyde? Well, that was Andrew Benson. Afternoon he grabbed me, we weren't even talking to each other. He just came up to me at the window and I swear to God he changed right before my eyes. It was as if he all of a sudden got about a foot taller and fifty pounds heavier, and his face was real wild. He pushed me out the window, without one word. Of course I was scared spitless, and maybe I just thought he changed. I mean, nobody can actually do a thing like that, can they?"

This question, if it arose at all at the time, remained unanswered. We do know that Andrew Benson was brought to the attention of Dr. Max Fahringer, child psychiatrist and part-time guidance counselor at the school, and that his initial examination disclosed no apparent abnormalities of personality or behavior patterns. Dr. Fahringer did, however, have several long talks with the Bensons, and as a result Andrew was forbidden to attend motion pictures. The following year, Dr. Fahringer voluntarily offered to examine young Andrew — undoubtedly his interest had been aroused by the amazing dramatic abilities the boy was showing in his extracurricular activities at the school.

Only one such interview ever took place, and it is to be regretted that Dr. Fahringer neither committed his findings to paper nor communicated them to the Bensons before his sudden, shocking death at the hands of an unknown assailant. It is believed (or was believed by the police, at the time) that one of his former patients, committed to an institution as a psychotic, may have been guilty of the crime.

All that we know is that it occurred some short while following a local rerun of the film *Man in the Attic*, in which Jack Palance essayed the role of Jack the Ripper.

It is interesting, today, to examine some of the so-called "horror movies" of those years, including the reruns of earlier vehicles starring Boris Karloff, Bela Lugosi, Peter Lorre and a number of other actors.

We cannot say with any certainty, of course, that Andrew Benson was violating the wishes of his foster parents and secretly attending motion pictures. But if he did, it is quite likely that he would frequent the smaller neighborhood houses, many of which specialized in reruns. And we do know, from the remarks of fellow classmates during these high school years, that

"Andy" was familiar—almost omnisciently so—with the mannerisms of these performers.

The evidence is oftentimes conflicting. Joan Charters, for example, is willing to "swear on a stack of Bibles" that Andrew Benson, at the age of 15, was "a dead ringer for Peter Lorre—the same bug eyes and everything." Whereas Nick Dossinger, who attended classes with Benson a year later, insists that he "looked just like Boris Karloff."

Granted that adolescence may bring about a considerable increase in height during the period of a year, it is nevertheless difficult to imagine how a "dead ringer for Peter Lorre" could metamorphose into an asthenic Karloff type.

A mass of testimony is available concerning Andrew Benson during those years, but almost all of it deals with his phenomenal histrionic talent and his startling skill at "ad lib" impersonations of motion picture actors. Apparently he had given up mimicking his associates and contemporaries almost entirely.

"He said he liked to do actors better, because they were bigger," says Don Brady, who appeared with him in the senior play. "I asked him what he meant by 'bigger' and he said it was just that—actors were bigger on the screen, sometimes twenty feet tall. He said, 'Why bother with little people when you can be big?' Oh, he was a real offbeat character, that one."

The phrases recur. "Oddball" and "screwball" and "real gone" are picturesque, but hardly enlightening. And there seems to be little recollection of Andrew Benson as a friend or classmate, in the ordinary role of adolescence. It's the imitator who is remembered, with admiration and, frequently, with distaste bordering on actual apprehension.

"He was so good he scared you. But that's when he was doing those impersonations, of course. The rest of the time, you scarcely knew he was around."

"Classes? I guess he did all right. I didn't notice him much."

"Andrew was a fair student. He could recite when called upon, but he never volunteered. His marks were average. I got the impression he was rather withdrawn."

"No, he never dated much. Come to think of it, I don't think he went out with girls at all. I never paid much attention to him, except when he was on stage, of course."

"I wasn't really what you call close to Andy. I don't know anybody who seemed to be friends with him. He was so quiet, outside of the dramatics. And when he got up there, it was like he was a different person—he was real great, you know? We all figured he'd end up at the Pasadena Playhouse."

The reminiscences of his contemporaries are frequently apt to touch upon matters which did not directly involve Andrew Benson. The years 1956 and 1957 are still remembered, by high school students of the area in particular, as the years of the curfew. It was a voluntary curfew, of course, but it was nevertheless strictly observed by most of the female students during the period of the "werewolf murders"—that series of savage, still-unsolved crimes which terrorized the community for well over a year. Certain cannibalistic aspects of the slaying of the five young women led to the "werewolf" appellation on the part of the sensation-mongering press. The *Wolf Man* series made by Universal had been revived, and perhaps this had something to do with the association.

But to return to Andrew Benson; he grew up, went to school, and lived the normal life of a dutiful stepson. If his foster parents were a bit strict, he made no complaints. If they punished him because they suspected he sometimes slipped out of his room at night, he made no complaint or denials. If they seemed apprehensive lest he be disobeying their set injunctions not to attend the movies, he offered no overt defiance.

The only known clash between Andrew Benson and his family came about as a result of their flat refusal to allow a television set in their home. Whether or not they were concerned about the possible encouragement of Andrew's mimicry or whether they had merely developed an allergy to Lawrence Welk and his ilk is difficult to determine. Nevertheless, they balked at the acquisition of a TV set. Andrew begged and pleaded, pointed out that he "needed" television as an aid to a future dramatic career. His argument had some justification, for in his senior year, Andrew had indeed been "scouted" by the famous Pasadena Playhouse, and there was even some talk of a future professional career without the necessity of formal training.

But the Bensons were adamant on the television question; as far as we can determine, they remained adamant right up to the day of their deaths.

The unfortunate circumstances occurred at Balboa, where the Bensons owned a small cottage and maintained a little cabin cruiser. The elder Bensons and Andrew were heading for Catalina Channel when the cruiser overturned in choppy waters. Andrew managed to cling to the craft until rescued, but his foster parents were gone. It was a common enough accident; you've probably seen something just like it in the movies a dozen times.

Andrew, just turned eighteen, was left an orphan once more—but an orphan in full possession of a lovely home, and with the expectation of coming into a sizeable inheritance when he reached twenty-one. The Benson estate was administered by the family attorney, Justin L. Fowler, and he placed young Andrew on an allowance of forty dollars a week—an amount sufficient for a recent graduate of high school to survive on, but hardly enough to maintain him in luxury.

It is to be feared that violent scenes were precipitated between the young man and his attorney. There is no point in recapitulating them here, or in condemning Fowler for what may seem—on the surface of it—to be the development of a fixation.

But up until the night that he was struck down by a hit-and-run driver in the street before his house, Attorney Fowler seemed almost obsessed with the desire to prove that the Benson lad was legally incompetent, or worse. Indeed, it was his investigation which led to the uncovering of what few facts are presently available concerning the life of Andrew Benson.

Certain other hypotheses—one hesitates to dignify them with the term "conclusions"—he apparently extrapolated from these meager findings, or fabricated them out of thin air. Unless, of course, he did manage to discover details which he never actually disclosed. Without the support of such details there is no way of authenticating what seems to be a series of fantastic conjectures.

A random sampling, as remembered from various conversations Fowler had with the authorities, will suffice.

"I don't think the kid is even human, for that matter. Just because he showed up on those Orphanage steps, you call him a foundling. Changeling might be a better word for it. Yes, I know they don't believe in such things any more. And if you talk about life forms from other planets, they laugh at you and tell you to join the Fortean Society. So happens, I'm a member.

"Changeling? It's probably a more accurate term than the narrow meaning implies. I'm talking about the way he changes when he sees these movies. No, don't take my word for it—ask anyone who's ever seen him act. Better still, ask those who never saw him on a stage, but just watched him imitate movie performers in private. You'll find out he did a lot more than just imitate. He *becomes* the actor. Yes, I mean he undergoes an actual physical transformation. Chameleon. Or some other form of life. Who can say?

"No, I don't pretend to understand it. I know it's not 'scientific' according to the way you define science. But that doesn't mean it's impossible. There are a lot of life forms in the universe, and we can only guess at some of them. Why shouldn't there be one that's abnormally sensitive to mimicry?

"You know what effect the movies can have on so-called 'normal' human beings, under certain conditions. It's a hypnotic state, this movie-viewing, and you can ask the psychologists for confirmation. Darkness, concentration, suggestion—all the elements are present. And there's post-hypnotic suggestion, too. Again, psychiatrists will back me up on that. Most people tend to identify with various characters on the screen. That's where our hero worship comes in, that's why we have Western-movie fans, and detective fans, and all the rest. Supposedly ordinary people come out of the theater and fantasy themselves as the heroes and heroines they saw up there on the screen; imitate them, too.

"That's what Andrew Benson did, of course. Only suppose he could carry it one step farther? Suppose he was capable of *being* what he saw portrayed? And he chose to *be* the villains? I tell you, it's time to investigate those killings of a few years back, all of them. Not just the murder of those girls, but the murder of the two doctors who examined Benson when he was a child, and the death of his foster parents, too. I don't think any of these things were accidents. I think some people got too close to the secret, and Benson put them out of the way.

"Why? How should I know why? Any more than I know what he's looking for when he watches the movies. But he's looking for something, I can guarantee that. Who knows what purpose such a life form can have, or what he intends to do with his power? All I can do is warn you."

It is easy to dismiss Attorney Fowler as a paranoid type, though perhaps unfair, in that we cannot evaluate the reasons for his outburst. That he knew (or believed he knew) something is self-evident. As a matter of fact, on the very evening of his death he was apparently about to put his findings on paper.

Deplorably, all that he ever set down was a preamble, in the form of a quotation from Eric Voegelin, concerning rigid pragmatic attitudes of "scientism," so-called:

"(1) the assumption that the mathematized science of natural phenomena is a model science to which all other sciences ought to conform; (2) that all realms of being are accessible to the methods of the sciences of phenomena; and (3) that all reality which is not accessible to sciences of phenomena is either irrelevant or, in the more radical form of the dogma, illusionary."

But Attorney Fowler is dead, and we deal with the living; with Max Schick, for example, the motion picture and television agent who visited Andrew Benson at his home shortly after the death of the elder Bensons, and offered him an immediate contract.

"You're a natural," Schick declared. "Never mind with the Pasadena Playhouse bit. I can spot you right now, believe me! With what you got, we'll back Brando right off the map! Of course, we gotta start small, but I know just the gimmick. Main thing is to establish you in a starring slot right away. None of this stock-contract jazz, get me? The studios aren't handing 'em out any more in the first place, and even if you landed one, you'd end up on Cloud Nowhere. No, the deal is to get you a lead and billing right off the bat. And like I said, I got the angle.

"We go to a small independent producer, get it? Must be a dozen of 'em operating right now, and all of 'em making the same thing. Only one kind of picture that combines low budgets with big grosses and that's a science fiction movie.

"Yeah, you heard me, a science fiction movie. Whaddya mean, you never saw one? Are you kidding? How about that? You mean you never saw any science fiction pictures at all?

"Oh, your folks, eh? Had to sneak out? And they only show that kind of stuff at the downtown houses?

"Well look, kid, it's about time, that's all I can say. It's about time! Hey, just so's you know what we're talking about, you better get on the ball and take in one right away. Sure, I'm positive, there must be one playing a downtown first run now. Why don't you go this afternoon? I got some work to finish up here at the office — run you down in my car and you can go on to the show, meet me back here when you get out.

"Sure, you can take the car after you drop me off. Be my guest."

So Andrew Benson saw his first science fiction movie. He drove there and back in Max Schick's car (coincidentally enough, it was the late afternoon of the day when Attorney Fowler became a hit-and-run victim) and Schick has good reason to remember Andrew Benson's reappearance at his office just after dusk.

"He had a look on his face that was out of this world," Schick says.

" 'How'd you like the picture?' I ask him.

" 'It was wonderful,' he tells me. 'Just what I've been looking for all these years. And to think I didn't know.'

" 'Didn't know what?' I ask. But he isn't talking to me any more. You can see that. He's talking to himself.

" 'I thought there must be something like that,' he says. 'Something better than Dracula, or Frankenstein's Monster, or all the rest. Something bigger, more powerful. Something I could really be. And now I know. And now I'm going to.' "

Max Schick is unable to maintain coherency from this point on. But his direct account is not necessary. We are, unfortunately, all too well aware of what happened next.

Max Schick sat there in his chair and watched Andrew Benson *change*.

He watched him *grow*. He watched him put forth the eyes, the stalks, the writhing tentacles. He watched him twist and tower, filling the room and then *overflowing* until the flimsy stucco walls collapsed and there was nothing but the green, gigantic horror, the sixty-foot-high monstrosity that may have been born in a screenwriter's brain or may have been spawned beyond the stars, but certainly existed and drew nourishment from realms far from a three-dimensional world or three-dimensional concepts of sanity.

Max Schick will never forget that night and neither, of course, will anybody else.

That was the night the monster destroyed Los Angeles. . . .

THE WORLD-TIMER

HE MAY or may not have been human. It was hard to tell, because in a psychiatrist's office, you get all kinds.

But he *looked* human—that is to say he had two arms, two legs, one head, and a slightly worried expression—and there was no reason for the receptionist to turn him away.

Particularly since he was here to give free samples.

"I'm from the Ace Manufacturing Company," he told the girl. "An old established firm. You've heard of us?"

The receptionist, who dealt with an average of ten salesmen a day, nodded politely and proceeded to file her nails.

"As the name indicates, we used to be a specialty house," the salesman continued. "Manufactured all the aces used in decks of playing cards. But lately we've branched out into pharmaceuticals."

"How nice for you," said the receptionist, wondering what he was talking about, but not very much.

"Not ordinary products, of course. We have the feeling that most pharmaceuticals are a drug on the market. So we've come up with something different. As our literature indicates, it's more along the lines of the lysergic acid derivatives. In addition to the usual tranquilizing effect, it alters the time sense, both subjectively and objectively. Mind you, I said 'objectively.' I'm sure you employer will be interested in this aspect, which is to say the least, highly revolutionary—"

"I doubt it. He's always voted Republican."

"But if I could just discuss the matter with him for a few moments—"

The girl shrugged and cocked her head toward the inner sanctum of Morton Placebo, M.D.

"Nobody rides that couch without a ticket," she told him. "The standard fee is $50 an hour, first class, or $30, tourist. That's with three on the couch at the same time. He says it's group therapy, and I say it's damned uncomfortable."

"But I'm not a patient," the stranger persisted. "I merely want to discuss my pharmaceuticals."

"You can't discuss your hemorrhoids without paying the fee," the receptionist drawled. "Doctor isn't in business for your health, you know."

The salesman sighed. "I'll just have to leave a few samples and some literature, I guess. Maybe he'll look it over and see me when I call back later. I'm sure he's going to be interested, because these little preparations will alter the entire concept and structure of psychotherapy."

"Then he won't be," the girl decided. "Dr. Placebo likes psychiatry just the way it is right now. Which is to say, at $50 an hour."

"But he will take the free samples?" the salesman persisted.

"Of course. He'll take anything that doesn't cost money. In fact, he told me it was the free-fantasy which attracted him to the profession in the first place."

She reached out her hand and the representative of the Ace Manufacturing Company placed a little packet of three tablets on her palm.

"The literature is inside," he said. "Please ask the Doctor to study it carefully before he experiments with the dosage. I'll stop by again next week."

"Don't you want to leave your card?" asked the girl, politely.

"Of course. Here you are."

He handed it to her, turned on his heel, and made his exit.

The receptionist studied the card curiously.

It was the Ace of Spades.

Normally, Dr. Morton Placebo wouldn't have paid much attention to a salesman's sample; largely because the very idea of paying was anathema to him.

But, as psychiatrists are so fond of saying—and, quite frequently, demonstrating—the norm is an abstraction.

And Dr. Placebo was always interested in anything which came to him without charge. Perhaps his receptionist hadn't been far wrong when she'd analyzed his reasons for entering a psychiatric career. All psychotherapists have their quirks.

According to his eminent disciple and official biographer, Ernest Jones, the great Sigmund Freud believed in occultism, telepathy, and the magic of numbers. The esteemed Otto Rank developed a manic-depressive psychosis; Wilhelm Reich's rationality was impugned on occasion; Sandor Ferenczi suffered from unbalance due to organic brain damage.

Compared to these gentlemen, Dr. Placebo's problem was a minor one; he was a frustrated experimenter. Both his frustration and his stinginess had their origin in his childhood, within the confines of the familial constellation.

In plain English, his father was stingier than he was, and when the young Morton Placebo evinced an interest in laboratory experimentation, the old man refused to put up the money for a chemistry set. Once, during his high school years, the young man managed to acquire two guinea pigs, which promptly disappeared. He was unable to solve the mystery — any more than he could account for the fact that his father, who always carried peanut butter sandwiches in his lunch-pail, went to work during the following week with meat sandwiches.

But now, at fifty, Morton Placebo, M.D., was fulfilled. He had his own laboratory at last, in the form of his psychiatric practice, and no end of wonderful guinea pigs. Best of all, the guinea pigs paid large sums of money for the privilege of lending themselves to his experiments. Outside of his receptionist's salary, and the $25 he spent having the couch resprung after a fat woman patient had successfully reenacted a birth-fantasy, Dr. Placebo had no overhead at all. With the steady stream of salesmen and their free samples, there was no end to the types of experimentation he could indulge in.

He'd use pills which produced euphoria, pills which produced depression, pills which caused a simulation of schizophrenia, pills which had remarkable side effects, pills which tranquilized, pills which stimulated; pills which resulted in such fascinating manifestations as satyriasis, virilescence and the sudden eruption of motor reflexes in the *abductor minimi digit*. He kept copious notes on the reactions afforded by LSD, *peyotl* extracts, cantharadin, yohimbine and reserpine derivatives. Whenever he found himself with a patient on his hands (or couch) who did not respond to orthodox (or reformed) therapy, Dr. Placebo — purely in the interest of science, of course — reached into his drawer and hauled out a handful of free pills.

Thus it was that he was grateful when he received the samples from the Ace Manufacturing Company.

"The literature's on the inside," his girl told him. He nodded thoughtfully and stared at the glassine packet with its three yellow pills.

"*Time Capsules*," he read, aloud.

"Alters the time sense, both subjectively and objectively," the receptionist said, parroting what she remembered from the salesman's pitch.

"Subjectively," snapped Dr. Placebo. "Can't alter it objectively. Time is money, you know."

"But he said — "

"Never mind. I'll read the literature." Dr. Placebo dismissed her and thoughtfully opened the packet. A small wadded-up piece of paper fluttered out onto the desk. He picked it up, unfolded it, and stared at the message.

NSTRCTNS

Nclsd smpls fr prfssnl s nly. ch s cpbl f prdcng tmprl dslctn prmnntly nd trnsltng sr nt nthr cntnm r tm vctr.

There was more to it, much more, but Dr. Placebo didn't bother attempting to translate. Apparently this literature was written in the same foreign tongue used by general medical practitioners when they scrawl their prescriptions. He'd better wait and get an explanation from his friendly neighborhood drugstore.

He gazed at the samples once again. *Time Capsules.* Catchy name for a pharmaceutical product. But why didn't the Ace Manufacturing Company print its literature in English? He scanned the last line of the literature.

Dnt gt yr vwls n n prr.

Made no sense. No sense at all.

But then, neither did most of his patients. So perhaps the pills would do some good. He'd have to wait for a likely subject.

The likely subject arrived at 3 P.M. Her name was Cookie Jarr, which was probably a polite euphemism for "sexpot." But what's in a name?

Sexpot or Jarr, Cookie was obviously quite a dish. She sprawled, in obvious *déshabillé*, on the couch, and like the professional stripper she was, proceeded to bare her psyche.

After a dozen or so previous sessions, Dr. Placebo had succeeded in teaching her the technique of free association, and now she obediently launched into a form of *monologorrhea*.

"I had a dream under very peculiar circumstances the other night . . . I was sleeping alone . . . and in it I was a geek. . . ."

"One moment, please," murmured Dr. Placebo, softly. "You say you were a geek? One of those carnival performers who bites the heads off of chickens?"

Cookie shook her auburn locks impatiently. "Not chickens," she explained. "I was very rich in this dream, and I was geeking a peacock." She frowned. "In fact, I was so rich I was Marie Antoinette. And they dragged me out for execution, and I looked at the executioner and said, 'Dr. Guillotine, I presume?' and he said, 'Please, no names — you must be the soul of indiscretion.' So then I woke up and it was four in the morning and I looked out of the window at this big neon sign that says OK USED CARS. You know something, Doc? I'd never buy an OK USED CAR. And I'd never eat at a place that says EAT. Or one that says FINE FOOD. And I'd never be buried in a funeral parlor approved by Duncan Hines. Do you think I'm superstitious? They say it's bad luck to walk under a black cat."

"Perhaps," said Dr. Placebo, sagely. "And then again, perhaps not. We must learn to relate, to adjust. Life is just a bowl of theories." He gazed at her piercingly. "The dream sequence is merely symbolism. Out with it now — face the truth. Why did you really wake up at four in the morning?"

"Because I had to go to the bathroom," Cookie snapped. "No, really, Doc, I'll level with you. It's the love bit. That damn Max keeps getting me down, because he's so jealous of Harry, only that's ridiculous because I don't like Harry at all, it's really Fred, on account of he reminds me of Jerry, the guy I'm crazy about. Or almost as crazy about as Ray." She paused, biting her lip. "Oh, I hate men!" she said.

"Ummm-hmmmm," said Dr. Placebo, doodling on a scratchpad with which he was ostensibly taking notes but actually drawing phallic symbols which looked suspiciously like dollar-signs.

"Is that all you got to say?" demanded Cookie, sitting up. "Fifty bucks an hour I'm paying, and for what? My nerves are killing me. You got any happy pills, Doc?"

"Happy pills?"

"Tranquilizers, or like whatever. Remember that stuff you gave me last month?"

"Oh, the cantharides."

"Yeah." Cookie smiled happily. "That was the greatest!"

Dr. Placebo frowned; his memories did not coincide with Cookie's, particularly when he recalled the frantic aftermath of that episode when he had to drag her bodily from the ninth floor of the local YMCA. But the experimental urge was strong. Few men could look at Cookie without feeling the urge to experiment.

"Well, there's something new," he said, cautiously.

"Give."

"It's called a Time Capsule. Alters the subjective time sense and — er — all that jazz." He found himself lapsing into the idiom with Cookie; she was the sort who inspired lapses.

"Meaning what?"

"I'm not quite sure. I imagine it slows down the reflexes."

"Relaxes you, huh? That's for baby."

"You'll have to take it here, under test conditions."

"The mad scientist bit? You are gonna hypnotize me and get fresh, is that it?"

"Nothing of the sort. I merely mean I must observe any side effects."

"Stuffy really turns you on, eh?" Cookie bounced up happily. "Well, I'm for kicks. Spill the pill for me, Bill."

Dr. Placebo went to the water cooler and filled a paper cup. Then he carefully extracted one of the yellow capsules from its cellophane container. He handed it and the water to Cookie.

She gulped and swallowed.

Then she lay back on the couch. "Wow, I'm in Dizzyville," she whispered. "Everything's like round and round—no squares—"

Her voice trailed off, and for a very good reason.

Now it was Dr. Placebo's turn to gulp and swallow, as he stared down at the empty couch.

Cookie had disappeared.

"Where is she?" Ray Connors demanded. "Come on, where is she?"

Dr. Placebo sighed. He felt a horrible depression, quite unlike the shapely depression which had been left in the couch by Cookie's body.

"She—she canceled her appointment this afternoon," he said, weakly.

"But I drove her over," the mustached young man insisted. "Went downstairs to do a bit of business—I'm booking a flea circus out in Los Angeles and I had to see about renting a dog so the troupe could travel in comfort—and then I came right back up to your office to wait. The receptionist told me Cookie was inside. So what happened?"

"I—I wish I knew," Dr. Placebo told him, truthfully. "She was lying right there on the couch when she vanished."

"Vanished?"

Dr. Placebo nodded. "Into thin air."

"Thin air, fat air, I don't believe it." Connors advanced on the pudgy little psychiatrist. "Come on, where you hiding the body?"

"She vanished, I tell you," Dr. Placebo wailed. "All I did was give her one of these sample pills—"

He indicated the packet on his desk-top and Connors picked it up. "This says *Time Capsules*, not *Vanishing Cream*," he snorted. "Look, Doc, I'm not one of your loony patients. I'm an agent, and you can't con me. So you got sore at Cookie and pushed her out of the window—*this* I can understand. Why don't you admit it and let me call the cops? We could get a big spread on this." He began to pace the floor rapidly. "Real headline stuff—JEALOUS HEADSHRINKER SLAYS BEAUTIFUL PATIENT. Why, we'll push the Finch trial right off the front page! Think of the angles; exclusive interview rights, sob stories to all the women's magazines, a nice big ghostwritten bestseller, a fat movie deal. Doc, you've got a fortune in your lap and you don't know enough to cross your legs! Now for ten percent, I'll handle everything, you won't have to worry—"

Dr. Placebo sighed softly. "I told you," he murmured. "She swallowed one of these pills and disappeared."

"Fiddlesticks," said Connors. "Or words to that effect." And before Dr.

Placebo could stop him, he walked over to the couch, sat down, ripped a pill from the cellophane confines of the package, and popped it into his mouth.

"No—don't!" cried the Doctor.

Connors shrugged. "You see? I swallowed one and nothing happens. I'm still here." He leaned back. "So how about it, Doc, you gonna level with me? Maybe you didn't push her out of the window. Maybe you carved her up and stuck the pieces in your filing cabinet. Hey, that's an even better angle—MAD BUTCHER CARVES CHICK! Or RIPPER GETS FLIPPER WITH STRIPPER. For ten percent of the gross, I'll fix it so you—"

Young Mr. Connors fell back on the couch and closed his eyes.

"Hey, what was in that last drink?" he mumbled. "I can't see."

Dr. Placebo advanced upon him nervously. "That pill," he gasped. "Let me phone Dr. Glutea down the hall—he's a GU man, maybe he has a stomach pump—"

Connors waved him away. "Never mind," he whispered, faintly, "I *can* see, now."

This was strange, to say the least, for he still had his eyes closed. Dr. Placebo bent over him, not daring to touch his rigid body.

"Yeah, I can see. Stars. Nothing but stars. You running one of those science fiction movies, Doc?

"Sure, I'm hip now. There's the world. Or is it? I can see North America and South America, but where are all those funny lines?"

"What funny lines?"

"Like in all the geography books—isn't there supposed to be latitude and longitude?"

"That's just on maps."

"I dig. This isn't a map, Doc. It's for real . . . but it can't be . . . no . . . no. . . ."

"Please, Mr. Connors, pull yourself together!"

"I'm pulling myself apart . . . oh, Doc, if you saw what I see . . . like crazy, the world inside a big egg timer up in the sky . . . sort of an hourglass, you know the bit?"

"Go on," murmured Dr. Placebo.

"There's sand or something running out of the end, into the other half of the timer . . . and now . . . a big claw, bigger than the whole world . . . reaching out and squeezing . . . squeezing the guts out of the Earth. . . . squeeeeee . . ."

"Go on," repeated Dr. Placebo. But it wasn't necessary, for Connors had already gone on.

The couch was empty.

The little psychiatrist blinked and shook his head. He walked over to the desk and, indulging in a symbolic funeral, buried his face in his hands. "Now what?" he groaned. "Physician, heal thyself."

Then he sat up and took stock of the situation. After all he *was* a physician; moreover, a skilled analyst. The thing to do was to consider the problem logically. There were several obvious courses of action.

First of all, he could call the police. He'd simply explain what had happened, they would simply not believe him, and he'd simply go to the gas chamber.

Secondly, he could tell his receptionist. She was a sweet young thing, and madly in love with him as a father image. Her reaction was predictable; she'd pop him into her car and they'd drive off to Mexico together, where they'd live happily ever after until she ran off with a bullfighter. No, the gas chamber was better. But why wait, when there were even faster methods?

Maybe he could adopt some of Connors' ideas to his own use. Perhaps he could jump out of the window, or cut himself up into little pieces and hide in the file cabinet. Merely a logical extension of filing one's fingernails.

No, he was irrational. He needed time to think. Time to think —

Dr. Placebo stared at the cellophane envelope which still rested on his desk where Connors had tossed it after taking the capsule. *Time Capsule.*

"Alters time sense both subjectively and objectively." Suppose it were true? Once again he picked up the cryptic literature and studied it closely. All of a sudden he found himself translating fluently. Only the vowels were missing.

INSTRUCTIONS

Enclosed samples for professional use only. Each is capable of producing temporal dislocation permanently and translating user into another continuum or time vector.

It was plain English, all right, and even the last line of the literature made sense now. He read it slowly.

Don't get your vowels in an uproar.

Excellent advice. Advice from an area where the time sense was altered, where linguistics were attuned to another tempo, where others marched to a different drummer.

Cookie had vanished suddenly, Connors slowly. Why the difference? Perhaps because Cookie had taken the capsule with water and Connors swallowed his dry. Took a while for the gelatin coating to dissolve.

Funny, Connors seeing those hallucinations. All very symbolic — the Earth in an egg timer and somebody squeezing it; the sands of time running forth. Running where? Running out, that's where. In another minute *his* time would run out; the receptionist would run in and ask where his patients were.

He had lost his patients. He had lost his patience. It all came back to the same thing—call the police, run off to Mexico, or jump out of the window, or kill himself and stuff his dead body in the file. Sort of a necro-file. Maybe he deserved to die, if he was capable of making puns like that. It would rise up from the grass over his grave to haunt him, for the pun is mightier than the sward—

No time for that now.

No time.

But a Time Capsule—

He picked up the cellophane container gingerly.

Why not?

It was a way out. Way out, indeed—but a way.

For one idiotic instant, Dr. Placebo took a good hard look at himself. A fat, foolish little man, driven by greed, who had never known love in all his life except as a professional father image. A man surrounded by sensualists like Cookie and opportunists like Connors. What was he doing here in the first place?

"I am a stranger and a Freud, in a world I never made."

It was a terrible realization, a bitter pill to swallow. But swallow it he must. There was no other choice. Fingers trembling, he extracted the last Time Capsule from the packet and raised it to his lips. He swallowed.

There was no sensation. He floated over to the water cooler and poured a drink. It gurgled down his throat. And then came the kaleidoscope, engulfing him.

Five minutes later his receptionist walked into the empty office. She inspected it, panicked, but eventually recovered and did what any sensible girl would do under the circumstances—called the Bureau of Missing Persons.

There was no answer. . . .

There was, of course, no kaleidoscope. Nor did Dr. Placebo find himself entrapped in a cosmic egg timer whirling in outer space. No huge hand stretched forth to menace his reason and he knew that he had not died.

But there was a dizzying sensation and he waited until it ceased before he allowed the autonomy of his nervous system to resume sway and blinked his eyes open once more.

Dr. Placebo was prepared for almost anything. If, indeed, the Time Capsule had been efficacious, he knew that he could have gone an infinite distance forward or backward in temporal dimensions. Long conditioning through attendance at monster movies led him to expect either the titanic vistas of *papier-mâché* cities of the far future or *papier-mâché* dinosaurs of the distant past. In either era, he knew, nothing would bear the slightest resemblance to the world he had lived in, except that the women of the future or the prehistoric age would still wear lipstick and mascara.

There was just one thing Dr. Placebo didn't expect to see when he opened his eyes — the familiar walls of his very own private office.

But that's where he found himself, sitting upon his own couch. And most uncomfortably, too, because he was wedged between Cookie and Connors.

"Oh, here you are," Cookie greeted him. "Where'd you go, Doc?"

"Nowhere. I've been here all the time. Where did *you* go?"

"Never left the couch."

"But you weren't here when I showed up," Ray Connors interrupted. "Then I saw you and I lost the Doc."

Dr. Placebo shook his head. "That's not the way it happened at all! First she disappeared and then you disappeared. I stayed right where I am."

"You weren't right where you are a minute ago."

"Neither were you."

"What does it matter? We're back, now," Connors said. "I told you those pills were fakes."

"I'm not so sure. We didn't travel in space, obviously, because we're in the same place we started. But if the capsules affect objective time —"

"So each of us passed out and lost a couple minutes. Big deal." Cookie sniffed and swayed to her feet.

She glanced curiously at the calendar on the desk. "Hey, Doc," she called. "What kind of month is Jly?"

Instantly, Dr. Placebo was at her side. "You're right," he groaned. "It does say 'Jly.' And that's not my writing on the notepad. Who is this 'Dr.' My'?"

"Maya," said a soft voice. "We don't write the vowels but we pronounce them. Indoctrinated associative reflex."

Placebo turned to confront the newcomer to the room. She wa a tall, plump, gray-haired woman with a rounded face and shoe-button eyes. She wore a plain smock and a bright smile.

"You must be the new patients," she observed, glancing at the trio. "Armond did his job well." She glanced again at the startled faces before her. "I had hoped for a random sampling, but you actually exceed my expectations."

"We're not patients," Dr. Placebo exploded. "I happen to be a practicing psychiatrist. And expectations be damned — we want explanations!"

"Gladly given." The woman who called herself Maya moved into the chair behind the desk. "Please sit down."

The trio retreated to the couch.

"First of all," Dr. Placebo began, "where are we?"

"Why, here, of course."

"But —"

"Please." Maya lifted a plump hand. "You don't deny that you are here, do you? If so, you're more disturbed than I thought. Believing yourself to be a psychiatrist is dangerous enough without any further disorientation."

"I *am* a psychiatrist!" Dr. Placebo shouted. "And this used to be my office."

"It still is, in another temporal vector. But when you swallowed one of Armond's little capsules, you entered a parallel continuum."

"Hey, how about making with like English?" Cookie demanded. "I don't dig."

"This must be one of those crazy planets," Connors muttered. "And she's an alien." He stood up and approached the desk. "So take me to your leader."

"Leader? There is no leader."

"Then who runs things around here?"

"Things run themselves."

"But who's the boss?"

"We all are."

Maya turned back to the girl. "I note your saying that you don't dig. Allow me to reassure you—in our society there is no need for physical labor. I'm sure you'll find a worthy niche here for whatever you are qualified to do."

"Wait a minute," Connors interrupted. "Nobody books this chick except me. I'm her agent."

"Agent?"

"Yeah, her manager, like. I find her work and collect my ten percent."

"Ten percent of what—the work?"

"No, the money."

"Ah, yes, money. I'd forgotten about that."

"You'd forgotten about money?" Dr. Placebo asked, excitedly. "Very peculiar symptom indeed. Rejection of the economic incentive—"

But Maya ignored him. Again she addressed herself to the girl. "Might I inquire just what sort of work you perform?"

"I'm a stripper."

"I see," Maya said, though it was obvious she didn't. "And just what do you strip?"

"Why, myself, of course."

"Oh, an exhibitionist." Maya smiled. "That's very nice. We have lots of them around. Of course, they don't get any recompense for it here, outside of their own pleasure."

"You mean they do it for fun?" Cookie demanded. "Standing up there on a bare stage with the wind blowing up your G-string and letting a lot of meatheads watch you break your fingernails on your zippers—this you call kicks?"

"I've had it," Connors announced, leaning over the desk. "The way I figure it, there's just two answers to the whole kockamamie deal. Either you're squirrelly or we've been kidnapped. Maybe both. But I'm calling the fuzz."

"Fuzz?"

"Law. Coppers. Police."

"There is no police force. Unnecessary. For that matter, no method of outside communication."

"You don't have a telephone?"

"Unnecessary."

"Then, lady, you'd better start hollering for help. Because if you don't send us back where we came from in thirty seconds, I am going to lean on you."

"Why wait?" Cookie bounded to her feet, raced over to the window, and flung it open. She leaned out.

"Help!" she yelled. "Hel — "

Her voice trailed off. "Holy Owned Subsidiary!" she whispered, faintly. "Sneak a preview at *this!*"

Connors and Dr. Placebo moved to her side and stared out at *this.*

This was the city below them, a city they knew as well as they knew the month of the year.

But the month was July, and the city was oddly altered. The buildings seemed familiar enough, but they were not nearly so high here in the downtown section, nor were there so many of them. No traffic hummed in the streets below, and pedestrians moved freely down the center of the avenues. The sides of the structures were not disfigured by billboards or painted advertisements. But the most dramatic difference was a subtle one —everything was plainly visible in clear bright sunlight. There was no smoke, no soot, no smog.

"Another continuum," Dr. Placebo murmured. "She's telling the truth."

"I still want out," Connors said. He balled his fists. "Lady, I'm asking you in a nice way — send us back."

Maya shook her head. "I can't possibly do so until next week. Armond must return and prepare the antidotes."

Cookie frowned. "You still insist we got her just because we swallowed some kind of Mickey Finn? You didn't smuggle us aboard a spaceship or whatever?"

"Please, my dear, let me explain. As I understand it, in your time vector you employ a variety of drugs — heroin, *cannabis indica*, various preparations such as marijuana and *peyotl* which affect the time sense."

"I never touch the stuff," Cookie snarled. "I'm clean, see?"

"But there are people who use these concoctions, and it does affect their time sense. Their subjective time sense, that is. A minute can become an eternity, or a day can be compressed into an instant."

"I buy that," Connors said.

"My friend Armond has merely extended the process. He perfected a capsule which actually produces a corporeal movement in time. Since it is impossible to move into a future which does not yet exist, or into a past which exists no longer, one merely moves obliquely into a parallel time stratum. There are thousands upon thousands of worlds, each based upon the infinite combinations and permutations of possibility. All coexist equally. You have merely gone from one such possible world to another."

"Merely," Cookie muttered. "So Connors was right. You kidnapped us. But why?"

"Call it an experiment. Armond and I worked together, to determine the sociological variations existing in several continuums. You will remain here a week, until he returns. During that time, let me assure you, no harm can possibly befall anyone. You'll be treated as honored guests."

Ray Connors stepped closer to Cookie. "Don't worry, baby—I'll protect you," he said. "You know I only got eyes for—*wow!*"

Wow stood in the doorway. She was about eighteen, with baby-blue eyes, but any resemblance to infancy ended right there.

"This is Lona," Maya told him. "She will be your hostess during your stay here."

Lona smiled up at Connors and extended her hand. "I already have my instructions," she said. "Shall we go now?"

"Over my dead body!" Cookie screeched. "If you think for one minute I'm gonna let you fall out of here with that hunk of *Bastille*-bait, you got another—"

It was her turn to react, when the tall young man entered. He too was about eighteen, but big for his age.

"I'm Terry," he said. "Your host during the coming week. If you'll be good enough to accompany me—"

"I'm good enough," Cookie told him.

"Now wait a minute," Connors interrupted. "If you go off with this gorilla, how'm I gonna protect you?"

"You better worry about protecting yourself, buster," Cookie told him, eyeing the clinging blonde. She turned to the waiting Terry. "Off to Funville," she said, and swept out.

"Shall we go?" Lona asked Connors. "A week is so little time, and I've so much to learn—"

"That's the spirit," Connors said. "Come on."

As they exited, Dr. Placebo glanced at Maya. "And what is in store for me—something out of LOLITA?"

The plump woman frowned at the unfamiliar reference. "Why, you'll be my guest. Stretch out on the couch and make yourself comfortable. I expect there are a few questions you'd like to ask."

Dr. Placebo was beyond resistance. Meekly, he sank down on his own couch—which wasn't really his own couch any more—and Maya promptly joined him.

"Really," spluttered the little man. "This is hardly approved psychotherapeutic procedure."

"I'm not a psychotherapist," Maya told him. "I'm your hostess."

"Need you be so hospitable?" Dr. Placebo protested.

"My feet hurt," Maya explained, kicking off her shoes and wriggling her toes. "Besides, is there any rule that says you have to conduct a sociological experiment standing up?"

"This is an experiment?"

"Of course. Why did you think Armond brought you here?" She stared at him levelly.

"I was going to ask about that. There are so many things I don't understand."

"Look into my eyes. Perhaps I can tell you better in that way than by questions and answers."

"Hypnosis? Telepathy? Rubbish!"

"Three labels, in as many words. Just forget that you're a scientist for a moment and open your mind. Look into my eyes. There, that's better. Keep looking. What do you see there?"

Dr. Placebo stared fixedly. His breathing altered oddly and his voice, when he spoke, seemed to come from far away.

"I see—*everything*," he whispered.

There was the world he came from, and there was *this* world. But these were only two in a coexistent infinity of possible states of being, each subject to an individual tempo, and each ruled by the Law of the Universe, which men call *If*.

There was a world were the dinosaurs survived, and the birds who ate their eggs perished. There was a world in which amphibians crawled out upon the land and found it uninviting, then swarmed back into the sea. There was a world in which the Persians defeated Alexander, and Oriental civilization flourished on the site of what would never be Copenhagen.

Dr. Placebo, guided by some power of selection emanating from Maya's will, sampled a dozen of these possibilities in rapid succession.

He saw worlds which had developed in a manner very similar to his own, with just a tiny difference.

A world in which a few tiny birds wheeled and took flight at the sight of sailing vessels, so that Columbus never noticed them and sailed on his course to the coast of Mexico where he and his men were quickly captured by the Aztecs and enslaved. So quickly did the inhabitants of Central America learn the arts of their prisoners that within a hundred years they built ships and weapons of their own, with which they conquered Europe. . . .

A world where it didn't rain along the Flemish plains one night early in the nineteenth century — and next morning, Napoleon's cavalry charged to victory across a dry field instead of tumbling into a sunken road. After winning Waterloo, there was no Bourbon restoration, no ensuing Republic, no Commune, no rise of Communist theory, no German nation or Russian Revolution, no World Wars. And Napoleon VI was emperor of all the Earth. . . .

Dr. Placebo saw the world in which the Hessians overheard the sound of oars one Christmas Eve at Trenton, and hanged George Washington. He saw the world where an ax slipped, and a young rail-splitter named Abe Lincoln lost his left leg and ended up as the town drunk of Magnolia, Ill. He saw a world in which an eminent scientist suffered a minor toothache and neglected to investigate the queer mold which he'd observed, with the result that two of the men who might have subsequently developed atomic power installations died of disease instead, because there was no penicillin to save them, and a whole continent subsequently plunged into war and . . .

Faster and faster the worlds whirled; the one in which Adolf Hitler was just a man who painted houses and Winston Churchill painted landscapes full-time instead of on Sundays . . . a world in which a real detective named Sherlock Holmes wrote a highly successful series of stories about an imaginary London physician whom he called Arthur Conan Doyle . . . a world ruled by great apes, and a somewhat similar world ruled by a teenage aristocracy who were proud of their blue genes.

"Possible," murmured Maya's voice, from a great distance. "All possible. Do you understand, now?"

Dr. Placebo sensed that he was nodding in reply.

"Good. Then, *this* world."

The panorama of impressions expanded, on a multileveled basis, so that Dr. Placebo was aware of sweeping generalization and specific example simultaneously. And slowly, a picture evolved. Dr. Placebo sensed and surveyed it with growing horror.

"But it *can't* be!" he heard himself muttering. "No Freud — and Havelock Ellis entering a monastery at twenty-two — no psychiatrists — no wonder you all became disturbed."

"*You're* disturbed," Maya's voice told him, calmly, "We're not. Look again."

Dr. Placebo looked again.

He looked at a world in which society was conditioned by biological principles, with Kinsey-like overtones; a world which lived in accordance with certain basic postulates. And as the examples expanded, Maya's voice provided accompaniment.

"As in *your* world, the sexual drive in the human male reaches its height between the ages of 16 and 26, whereas in the females the sex urge is highest between 28 and 40. The only difference is that in *our* world this biological fact is accepted, and acted upon.

"Accordingly, our young men, at 16, are permitted to establish relationships with women of 28 or older, for any period of time up to 10 years. During this decade of association, there is no procreation — and, of course, no domestic or emotional responsibilities.

"At 26, the males are permitted to establish another relationship, again for a decade or so, with the females aged 16 and upwards. During this time, reproduction is encouraged, for the females are young and healthy and the males are fully mature; they lavish affection upon their offspring, who are — of course — turned over to the care of the state when they reach the age of 6.

"As both males and females reach 40 or thereabouts, they can again change their partners and seek permanent or temporary companionship within a domestic relationship but without reproducing.

"Thus the sex drive is fully satisfied during its period of maximum intensity, the reproductive urge is given full sway at a time likely to be most beneficial to both parents and offspring, and the social needs of later life are gratified without the rancor, tensions, frustrations, and naggingly permanent obligations which are the fruit of most monogamous marriages in your world. Simple enough, isn't it?"

Dr. Placebo sat up. He was once again in full possession of his faculties, all of which were strained beyond credulity.

"It's absurd!" he shouted. "You're going against all natural instinct — "

"Are we?"

Maya smiled. "Our society is actually founded on a realistic basis — pure biology. In the animal kingdom, 'fatherhood' as we know it does not exist. The male may protect its spawn for a time and feed the pregnant female, but it does not safeguard or exhibit affection for its young over any extended period of time, except in your 'moral' textbooks for children or the cinematic fantasies of your Mr. Disney. In many species, the male does not even secure food for the female, let alone 'support a family.' This is an artificial concept, yet your whole society is based upon it and everyone seems to believe that it's 'natural.'

"And when your poets and writers and philosophers envision an 'ideal' society, it is merely an extension of the same basic misconceptions with an attempt to put a little more of what you call 'justice' into them — even though one of your own writers, Archibald MacLeish, in his play, *J.B.*, so wisely observes, 'There is not justice; there is only love.' Ours is a world founded on love, and it begins by setting aright the biological basis of love."

"Monstrous!" Dr. Placebo exploded. "You've destroyed the fundamentals of civilization — the home — the family — "

"The so-called home and so-called family have destroyed the fundamentals of *your* civilization," Maya told him. "That's why you therapists flourish, in a sick world of emotionally-twisted youngsters who grow up as overly-frustrated or overly-aggressive adults; a world of prurience and poverty, of sin without atonement and atonement without sin, a world of bombs without balms. Don't look at your prejudices and your theories; look at the *results*. Are the people of your world truly happy, Doctor? *Are* they?"

"I suppose your way is better?" Dr. Placebo permitted himself a slight sneer.

"See for yourself," Maya suggested. "Look into my eyes —"

Dr. Placebo found himself staring and sharing; it was all a matter of viewpoint, he told himself.

He saw a world in which there was no transference of aggression, due to sexual problems; a world devoid of jealousy and fear and secret guilts.

There was, to begin with, a complete change in the pattern of courtship; the element of rivalry, of competition, was almost eliminated. Male and female paired first for mutual pleasure, without the necessity of seeking the almost impossible combination of perfect lover, ideal helpmate, good provider, wise companion, and social prize which dogs most young people in their choice.

Later on, male and female paired for the purpose of reproduction; children born of the union of these matings were given a healthy environment of genuine love during the years when they were most lovable — and most subject to lasting psychological impressions. Then, at the time when they became encumbrances in a complex social order, they were turned over to well-organized state establishments for education and proper development.

Finally, male and female allied on the basis of fully matured judgments; as companions with mutual tastes and interests. Their early sexual drives fully satisfied, their reproductive drive fulfilled, their responsibilities in these areas ended, they were free to seek permanent or temporary liaisons on a fully realistic basis of compatibility.

Inevitably, there were other — and far-reaching — results.

For one thing, a change in personality values — the notion of what constituted a "good" or a "bad" individual differed greatly from those prevalent in Dr. Placebo's world.

Less time was wasted, by young and old alike, in false and exaggerated emphasis upon presumably "masculine" or "feminine" attributes. A 16-year-old boy could *honestly* prove his masculinity, with full approval and satisfaction, on a biological basis, instead of spending most of his energy on football, juvenile delinquency, surreptitious indulgence in alcohol and narcotics and the assumption of an outward brutality designed to impress the female. A 16-year-old girl could fulfill her biological function in maternity instead of retreating into narcissism, virginity fantasies, or a rebellious and unsatisfactory promiscuity.

The young man found sympathy and understanding with an older woman during his initial relationships, and learned to appreciate these qualities. The young woman found steadiness and strength in an older man, and was not impressed by reckless exhibitionism and irresponsible behavior. When the age-patterns of later relationships were reversed, an even greater mutual understanding prevailed; in the final maturity, there was a peace and a satisfaction born of genuine love and respect. In this world, men and women actually *enjoyed* one another's company, and there was no rivalry.

As a result, there was no fear of the domestic situation; it was not a lifelong trap in which both parties became enslaved to a consumer economy because they had to "preserve" a so-called home at all costs. Because there was no set and permanent family status, the element of economic competition virtually vanished; there was no need to pile up great accretions of consumer goods for conspicuous consumption or as substitutes for genuine satisfactions. And there was no "inheritance." The state regulated employment and recompense but did so benevolently — for there was no familial tension-source to spawn the guilt, hate, frustration and aggression which resulted in individual crime and mass warfare. Hence an "police state" proved unnecessary. Simple miscegenation had done away with national, racial and religious strife. And the limited 12-year breeding span had done away with population pressure; there was abundance for everyone. Social and economic freedom followed as a matter of course.

Perhaps most important of all, there was a great increase in creativity and the development of aesthetics.

Dr. Placebo began to realize why, when he looked out the window, there were no advertising displays — why there was no need of automotive traffic or "quick communication" devices, or any variety of artificial stimulants, escape devices, or gilded carrots designed to keep the donkeys in perpetual harness as they tugged their cartloads of woe along the road of life.

There was actually plenty of time to *live* in this world; no claws were squeezing; within this hourglass lay no danger of an eruption or explosion.

All this Maya showed him, and much more. Until at last, Dr. Placebo hurled himself upright again and tore his gaze away.

"Fine!" he commented. "Wonderful! Now I know why you found a youthful hostess for Ray Connors and a young host for Cookie. And maybe it does work, at that."

"I'm glad you think so," Maya said. "Because that was Armond's plan, you see."

"I don't see," Dr. Placebo confessed.

"For some time Armond and others have used the capsules to visit worlds in other time vectors. Most of them were either too alien in their patterns or too dangerous to explore, but yours seemed most similar to our own.

"Somewhere along the line, your world went wrong in the areas of social-sexual relationships, but we have studies your mores and folkways and decided to make a radical experiment. Armond believed *we* could, if necessary, live in *your* world—but of course, we wouldn't want to. He then determined to discover if *you* could live in *our* world. That's why he went down to hand out a limited number of sample pills—in hopes of getting a representative assortment of specimens here for observation. One week should be long enough to determine your reaction—"

Dr. Placebo stood up.

"One minute is all it takes," he announced. "At least, as far as I'm concerned."

"You are a wise man, Dr. Placebo," Maya said. "It didn't take you long to see how sensibly we live, how sanely we have ordered our lives."

"That is correct," Dr. Placebo murmured, and then his voice swept upwards shrilly. "And that's just why I want out of here! I'm a psychiatrist, and a highly successful one. What place have I in a world where nobody is emotionally disturbed or maladjusted? Why, I'd starve to death in a month! I tell you, all this sanity is crazy—"

Suddenly he doubled up and fell back upon the couch.

"Why, whatever is the matter?" Maya cried.

"Ulcer," Dr. Placebo groaned. "Kicks up on me every once in a while. Purely psychosomatic, but it hurts like hell."

"Wait just a minute," Maya soothed. "I'll get you some milk."

And in exactly a minute, she was back with a glass. Dr. Placebo drank it slowly and gradually relaxed. It was good milk—damned good milk, he reflected bitterly, and no wonder. In a lousy, perfect world like this, the cows were probably more contented that any back on Earth. . . . It figured!

"All right," said Ray Connors, pausing in his restless pacing to face Cookie and Dr. Placebo. "I got to talk fast because there's not much time. For a whole week I've been figuring out how to get a chance to see you two alone here in the office without Maya or any of the rest of these squares butting in. Because I got a billion-dollar idea by the tail and all I need is your help."

"How's Lona?" Cookie inquired.

"The chick?" Ray Connors smiled. "Okay, okay. But that's not important."

"Isn't it?" Cookie frowned. "You know, this guy Terry is the greatest. He's so—so *sweet*. Treats me like I was some kind of princess—"

"Never mind that jazz," Connors interrupted. "We got no time."

"Your idea?" Dr. Placebo inquired.

"Okay, now hear this. This is a square setup, dig? Both of you must have noticed what I did—everybody gets along with everyone else, there's no muscle, no sweat. Strictly Loveville."

"Yeah, isn't it wonderful?" Cookie sighed. "That Terry—"

"I'll say it's wonderful!" Connors exulted. "The whole setup is a pushover for a couple of hip operators like us. I started to figure things out, and you know, I think the three of us could really do it?"

"Do what?" inquired Dr. Placebo.

"Why, take over, of course!" Connors eyed him elatedly. "Look, we each got our own racket, and all we need to do is start working. Cookie here knows how to turn on the glamour. Me, I'm the best combination agent and flack in the business. You're a skull-specialist, you know about psychology and all that crud. Suppose we just team up and go to work?"

"Remember that old gag about Helen of Troy, or whoever—the gal whose face launched a thousand flips, something like that? Started a big war over her, didn't they? Well, we got Cookie here. Suppose I started beating the drums, working up a little publicity, spreading the word about how this chick is the hottest dish in the whole pantry? And you coach me on the psychology, Doc.

"You know the way they got things rigged here—young gals with middle-aged guys, middle-aged guys with young gals, old folks at home together. Well, it would be the easiest thing in the world to upset the whole applecart. Get the kids excited about Cookie, and the old daddy-types, too. Teach 'em something about sex appeal. You know what'll happen. Inside of a month we can start opening up schools—regular courses to give all the chicks lessons on how to really land a man and hang onto him. Give 'em all the techniques on how to play hard-to-get. And that means the works—we bring out a line of cosmetics, fashions, beauty-parlor treatments, promote jewelry and perfume and luxury items.

"We'll have the men flipping, too. They don't use money in this crazy system, but we ought to be able to take our cut in land and services. I tell you, they're so innocent it'll be like taking candy from a baby. Inside of a year we can work our way up so that we'll be running the whole world! Think of it—no police, no army, nothing to stop us! Wait until we bring in advertising, and jukeboxes, and hotrods, and pro football and falsies—"

"You intend to transform this world into a reasonable reproduction of our own, is that correct?" asked Dr. Placebo.

"Reasonable is right," Connors snapped. "What's to stop us?"

"I am," said Cookie. "I don't buy it."

"You don't—what?"

"I like it just the way it is," she murmured. "Look, Ray, let's face it. I'm pushing thirty, dig? And for the past fifteen years I been knocking around, getting my jollies in just the kind of a world you want to turn this into. Well, I had it, and no thanks. What good did it ever do me? I ended up a second-rate stripper, tied to a second-rate nogoodnik like you and spending all my extra loot on Doc's couch.

"I don't need to be Helen of Troy here. I'm just Cookie, and that's good enough for Terry — and believe me, he's good enough for me. I never had it so nice as this past week, believe me. Why louse it up?"

"Okay, so who's begging? You think you're the only chick I can promote? I got Lona. She's plenty square — one of those real sick, goodhearted types — but I can twist her around my little finger. So I'll slap a little makeup on her, teach her a few tricks, and we're off and running." Connors wheeled to face Dr. Placebo.

"How about it, Doc? You want in, don't you?"

"You're quite sure you can do all this?" Dr. Placebo murmured. "It's a big program for one man to tackle."

"Yeah, but we got a natural. No competition. No opposition. Nobody that's hip. They'll never know what hit 'em. In fact, they all love each other so damned much they don't suspect anyone could ever pull a fast one, and they'll cooperate just for asking."

Connors walked over to the open window and gazed out at the sunlit city.

"Look at it, Doc," he said. "All laid out and waiting for us to carve. Like the old saying, the world's our oyster."

"That's right." Dr. Placebo moved to his side, nodding thoughtfully. "And the more I think it over, the more I believe you. You could do it, quite easily."

"I damn' well *will* do it," Connors asserted. "And if you and Cookie chicken out, I'll make it alone."

Dr. Placebo hesitated, shrugged, and glanced at Cookie. She nodded. He put his hand on Connors' shoulder and smiled.

"A good idea," he muttered. "Make it alone, then."

And with an agile dexterity somewhat surprising in an older man, he pushed Connors out of the window.

The press agent fell forth into the world that was his oyster; Dr. Placebo and Cookie leaned out and watched as he landed in the oyster-bed below.

"Nice work, Doc," Cookie commented.

He frowned. "That's the last time I'll ever do anything like that," he sighed. "Still, it was necessary to use violence to end violence."

"Yeah. Well, I got to be running along. Terry's waiting for me. We're going to the beach. See you around, Doc?"

"I hope so. I intend to be here for a long, long time." Dr. Placebo turned, staring past the girl, as Maya entered the room.

"Your conference is over?" the plump woman inquired. "Your friend left?"

Cookie nudged Doc in time for him to match her sudden look of consternation.

"A terrible thing just happened," she gasped. "He fell out of the window!"

"Oh, no—" Maya gasped and rushed to the open window, staring down. "How awful! And just when he could have joined you in returning home—"

"Home?"

"Yes. Armond is back. The week is up, and he'll be able to supply you with time capsules now. You're free to return to your own world."

"Do we have to go?" Cookie's voice quavered. "I—I want to stay here. Terry and I talked things over, and we hit it off so good together, I was hoping I could just sort of like settle down."

"And what about you?" Maya confronted Dr. Placebo.

"Why—uh—I agree with Cookie. Since that first day, I haven't had the slightest twinge from my ulcer. Something about the milk you serve, I suppose."

"But what about your profession?" Maya asked. "You said yourself that there's no need for a psychiatrist here. And, of course, there's no way of making money."

"I've been thinking about that," Dr. Placebo said. "Couldn't I assist you in your sociological experiments?"

Maya permitted herself a small smile. "Standing up or lying down?" she demanded.

"Er—both." A slow blush spread over the bald expanse of Dr. Placebo's forehead. "I mean, each of us is past forty, and under the existing order of things—well—"

"We'll discuss that later," Maya told him, but the smile was broader, now. She turned to include Cookie in her glance. "Actually, I'm very happy about your decisions. And I shall inform Armond that the experiment was a complete success. I take it your deceased friend intended to stay, also?"

"He did," Cookie answered, truthfully. "He intended to make his mark here." She glanced down at the sidewalk below. "And in a way, I guess he succeeded."

"Then you can adapt," Maya said.

"Of course, we can adapt," Dr. Placebo nodded.

"All right, I shall inform Armond. And we can go into the second stage of the experiment."

"The second stage?" Dr. Placebo echoed.

"Yes. And we'd best hurry because there isn't much time."

Just how Maya got her information, we, of course, shall never know. Perhaps Armond read the papers during his visits to Earth, or maybe he just used his eyes and ears.

At any rate, Maya knew the truth—the truth behind the vision of the green claw squeezing the sands of time from the hourglassed Earth. She knew that time is running short for this world.

Hence the second stage of the experiment; the stage in which not one but thousands of Armonds will descend in mortal guise or disguise, to pass out millions of time capsules.

Some will come as salesmen, some as pharmacists, some as physicians. Naturally, techniques of distribution will vary; it will be necessary to disguise the capsules as vitamin tablets, tranquilizers, or simple aspirin. But Dr. Placebo and Cookie will both cooperate with their suggestions, and Armond and his crew are both knowledgeable and efficient.

So, sooner or later, chances are you will be handed a capsule of your own.

Whether you elect to swallow it knowingly or not depends upon whether or not you're willing to swallow the concepts of another world.

If not, of course, there's always a simple choice.

You can stay right where you are, and let this world swallow you. . . .

FAT CHANCE

THEIR NAMES WERE John and Mary, and they lived in a little white frame house with a picket fence all around the front lawn. They owned a fintail car and a TV set with a 21-inch screen, and a power mower and a freezer. John went bowling once a week, on Thursday nights, and Mary subscribed to three of the better women's magazines and cut out all the recipes. They had been married for fourteen years now, and in every respect they were a typical middle-class American couple.

So, naturally enough, John wanted to kill Mary.

Perhaps this is an oversimplification. In John's defense it must be stated that he was perfectly willing to put up with most of his wife's little ways. He did not object to her pin-curled presence at the breakfast table every morning, or to her habit of using baby talk when she addressed the canary, or the way she appropriated his electric shaver to use on her legs. He had no complaints about her cooking, or the way she ran the household and spent his money. He had long ago realized that she was not a stimulating companion or conversationalist and he was willing to accept the fact that her domestic habits, in the kitchen, parlor, or bedroom, were dull indeed. All this he resigned himself to putting up with, as most typical middle-class American husbands inevitably do. But there was just one thing he couldn't endure, one crime he could not forgive.

Mary was getting too fat.

She had begun putting on weight a few years after they were married. Eight years ago she had been "pleasingly plump" but presentable. Six years ago she began having trouble finding "her" size in the dresses she selected. Five years ago she had embarked on what proved to be an endless series of ineffectual diets, all of which failed to remedy the situation because in the end they required that she cut down on her intake of calories. Three years ago she had apparently resigned herself to the situation—she was fat, and she admitted she was fat. Not *too* fat, of course; just plain "heavy."

Of course Dr. Applegate warned her about stuffing herself; there were examinations and explanations about the way she reddened upon the slightest exertion, about the high blood pressure and the strain on her heart. But the fatter Mary became, the less she felt like exerting herself and the easier it was to just stay home and watch television. Besides, as she told the doctor, John was away almost every night at the store—his pharmacy stayed open until ten, except on Sundays—and there was nothing for her to do. And she didn't really eat a lot; just nibbled now and then to calm her nerves.

Dr. Applegate had a few words to say about compulsive appetite and John had quite a lot to say about her sloppy appearance, but these things only seemed to make Mary more nervous. So, of course, she ate.

Now she was positively gross, but John didn't bother to talk about it any more. He knew it wouldn't do any good. She was fat as a pig.

That's when John began to have these dreams about butchering hogs.

It might very well have ended with that—after all, John was so typically middle-class and middle-aged, and he could have so easily developed a few interests of his own. An ulcer, perhaps, or a coronary condition, or a woodworking shop in the basement.

It took something out-of-the-ordinary to bring him to the actual point of murder.

Her name was Frances.

Actually, Frances Higgins was extraordinary only in John's eyes; to others she was only a tall, well-preserved woman on the wrong side of thirty, with rather pretty auburn hair. John saw her slimness and was dazzled. He had frequent opportunities to be dazzled, because Frances Higgins was Mary's best friend.

They had gone to school together (incredible, that fat, candy-chewing, Welk-watching Mary had ever attended business college!) and continued the acquaintance after Mary married and Frances went on to a career as private secretary for a prominent downtown attorney.

Neither John nor Frances realized that they were embarking on an affair. One does not associate passion with middle-aged pharmacy proprietors, or with private secretaries who keep rubber plants in the office. Both of them were quite unprepared for the overwhelming consequences—the compulsive need to constantly see one another, touch one another, and be with one another at any cost to self-respect or self-control.

"I can't stand it, darling!" she told him. "Visiting you and Mary, seeing you together. And then thinking of you and Mary together when I'm *not* there—"

"I know," John sighed. "How do you think it is with me? I don't *want* to be with Mary; I hate the sight of her. Even before I found you, I hated her. Now I can't bear it. And if what you say is true about a divorce — "

Frances nodded sadly. That had been one of the first things they'd thought about; the possibilities of divorce. Frances had not been fool enough to reveal her true feelings about John when she sounded Mary out on the subject. Instead she had chosen the devious method; she had gone to Mary, as her best friend, and hinted that there was something she ought to know. It appeared as though John had been, as she put it, "stepping out of line a little." There were nights when he absented himself from the drugstore without Mary's knowledge. She refused to mention the sources of her information, but people were talking. And while it might not be really "serious" one never knew; perhaps Mary ought to prepare herself just in case and think about the future. A friendly warning —

Mary shrugged. Yes, she knew John had been restless lately; a wife can always tell. And she and John had been so very close through all the years. But for that very reason, she had no intention of leaving him, now or ever. Let him have his fling, poor dear. Sooner or later, it would blow over.

"But what if he came to you and demanded a divorce?" Frances had persisted. "What if he just walked out on you, cold, and left you for another woman?"

"He wouldn't do a thing like that," Mary answered. "He just *couldn't*; John isn't that type at all." Then her apologetic air had suddenly given way to grim resolution. "But if he did, he'd be sorry, believe me! There are laws, you know. I'd see to it that he paid — I'd get everything I've got coming to me. By the time I was through with him, he and this little tramp, whoever she is, would be good and sorry they ever started anything."

Frances had reported the conversation to John the following evening and they both agreed, sadly but logically, that Mary meant what she said. Moreover, she had the power to execute her threat. A divorce would mean an irreparable financial loss to John, perhaps even the loss of his business. And as for Frances, her elderly employer (who never, under any circumstances, ever handled a divorce proceeding) would fire her handily. Love in a garret is all very well for moon-struck teenagers, but both John and Frances had reached a time in life where they enjoyed the creature comforts both of them had striven for over the years. And, being human, they felt the equal necessity of protecting their present status as respectable members of the community.

So divorce was out. And the only apparent result of Frances's conversation with Mary was that she began to gorge herself still more heavily. Dr. Applegate's latest diet was tossed overboard and Mary stuffed herself night and day. John would come home and find her consuming candy from the store—indeed, she insisted that he constantly supply her with more each time he put in his appearance from a night of work behind the counter.

"Cheer up," John told Frances, although he didn't really believe she would follow his suggestion. "The way the old sow is going now, she'll eat herself to death in a few years."

"A few years!" Frances looked at herself in the mirror behind the soda fountain. Then she looked at John. She didn't say anything, but then she didn't have to. John knew what she was thinking. A few years was all they had left, really. A few years of being together as they wanted to be together, or a few years of this endless aching, this ceaseless torment of furtive, fear-filled meeting interspersed with interludes of mocking, maddening pretense. And meanwhile Frances would have to live on in her little cell-like apartment, while John stayed with the fat pig.

That's what Frances called her now. "The fat pig." A year ago she would never have dreamed of describing anyone that way, let alone her best friend. But a year ago she hadn't really know John, hadn't wanted John. So now it was easy for her to say what she really felt. "I can't go on like this. I won't go on! It isn't right. It would be different if she felt anything for you, darling, anything at all. But she doesn't. I've talked to her, and I know. To Mary, you're just property. Another household appliance, something she owns, a convenience that supplies her with food and shelter and performs menial chores around the house for her comfort. When I hinted you might be running around, she wasn't even jealous—just *angry*. The way you get angry at some gadget when you suspect it might be going out of order and cost you something to repair.

"I can't bear to think of you putting up with her any longer; the way she just sits around all day and all night feeding her fat face—why all the time I was talking to her, even when she started to get excited, she kept eating those damned macaroons out of a big box and watching the Arthur Godfrey show. She isn't any good to you. She isn't any good to herself. Nobody would miss her if she died tomorrow."

She stared at John. He lowered his eyes and didn't answer.

"Look, darling. I've been thinking. You're a druggist. Isn't there something you could give her that—"

John shook his head. He continued to avert his gaze as he answered. "I won't lie to you. I've been thinking about that, too. And it wouldn't work. Just because I *am* a pharmacist. Don't you realize that's the very first thing the police would think of if they ever became suspicious? And they *would* become suspicious, because of the medical report. A doctor would have to be called, he'd have to sign the death certificate, and he'd know right away. Contrary to what you may be thinking, there just aren't any drugs that will do the trick without detection; at least nothing I could get out of stock here. And I couldn't order anything special or obscure without accounting for it.

We have to make out reports, they check on us, we're inspected. No, that's out."

Frances put her hand on his arm—her cool, slim hand, with the long fingernails which could claw so deeply when she clung to him.

"All right," she said. "All right. But you've got to do something. I can't take much more of this. In fact, I'm going away."

"Going away?"

There was such anguish in his response that her own voice softened. "Don't be alarmed, darling. It's just a vacation. I've got two weeks coming this year, you know. At first I wasn't even going to take them, but I decided I'd better. All this had made me so nervous lately. There's an aunt and uncle of mine out in Portland—they've asked me to visit them."

"When?"

"Next week. I've got plane reservations for Monday."

John blinked. "But that means I won't be seeing you again, not for almost three weeks."

The nails dug into his arm. He could feel them even through his suitcoat. "Maybe longer than that," she said. "Darling, I meant what I told you. I can't stand living this way any longer. It's up to you, now. Either you find some way out for us, soon, or this is the end."

"But I can't—"

"You must! I don't care if you hit her over the head with a club and lock her in the deep-freeze. All I know is that I've had it. From now on, it's all or nothing." She relaxed her grip. "I didn't tell you this, darling, but my aunt and uncle have been urging me to move out there. They say the climate is wonderful in Oregon and I'd have no trouble finding another job in Portland. When I visit them, I'm going to investigate the possibilities. Maybe that's the best thing to do, after all."

"No!" John muttered. He stood up taking a deep breath. "You're coming back here, you've got to promise me you'll come back."

"Do I?"

"Yes. And I'll make you a promise, too. I'm going to think of a way. I don't know how, but I'll think of one. When you come back she'll be gone."

John kept his word. From that moment on, he thought of a way. He thought of a hundred ways during the next few days before Frances's departure. He thought of them by day while he sold bobby pins and aspirins and band-aids in the store, and he thought of them by night as he watched Mary eating doughnuts in the living room, belching in the bathroom or snoring stertorously by his side in bed.

He didn't see Frances again during the weekend, but he saw a lot of Mary. There was, he reflected grimly, quite a lot of her to see. She tipped the scales at about 240 now. All weekend long she kept babbling about still another new diet Dr. Applegate wanted her to try. And all weekend long, John kept thinking about ways of killing her. A hundred ways.

But none of them were any good. None of them would work. Oh, he could *murder* her all right, but the point was to get away with it. Get away with it scot-free, get away with Frances, sell the damned business and move to Oregon after everything was over. That part would be easy. But the method, the method —

One Sunday night it came to him, just like that. And there was nothing particularly surprising in the phenomenon, because it had been there all the time. Frances had told him; he was a pharmacist and he had access to poisons.

Not obscure poisons, not undetectable poisons, but that didn't matter; he didn't need anything special, as long as he made sure he administered a lethal dose. Of course a physician would examine Mary's body before writing out a death certificate, but there wouldn't be any trouble.

Because the physician would be Dr. Applegate. And Applegate, in addition to being the family doctor, was the man who had come to John when he needed some extra, but also extra-legal, prescriptions for narcotics. Now he would come to John's aid in *his* hour of need. And he would not demur, he would not question, he most certainly would not talk. If he did, then John would talk too, and Dr. Applegate would be up on criminal charges.

It was really very simple, now that he realized how to solve the medical aspects of his problem. Mary's few friends all knew that she was grossly overweight, that she had put a strain on her heart. So the death certificate would testify, and nobody would ask any embarrassing questions.

All that remained to be considered now was the exact *modus operandi* to employ.

John thought about it all that day Monday in the store. It kept him from thinking about Frances's departure that morning. On the other hand, he was really quite glad that she had left, under the circumstances. It meant she'd be out of town during the time of the tragedy; there'd be no strain of having to simulate grief, attend the funeral, and avoid any accidental betrayal of her true feelings in John's presence. Better still, her absence would rule out any evidence of collusion.

For his own part, it would be ideal for him to dispose of Mary immediately; the funeral and the subsequent winding-up of her affairs would occupy him during the next two weeks and keep him from brooding about Frances's absence. Yes, all in all, this was the ideal time.

And the method?

He had the whole pharmacopoeia at his disposal, everything from acetanilide to zinc phosphide. Yet in the end, John decided upon the simplest toxic agent of all, the old standby of Borgia and bourgeoise alike — plain arsenic. It was fast, reliable, deadly, and that's what he wanted; it didn't in the least matter if the symptoms of arsenic poisoning were apparent to a physician under the circumstances. More to the point, John could easily remove the necessary quantity from his stock without fear of its loss being noted.

Administration of the dosage would be no problem, either. He'd put it into some chocolates; bring Mary a box of candy from the store, as she expected. With her sweet tooth, she'd gobble down one or two — probably just one, because of the taste, but that would be enough. More than enough. Her resultant agonies would be painful to witness, but John had no intention of being present. He'd take her the box tonight but neglect to give it to her until tomorrow when he left again for work. That should give her something to do while she watched her daily soap operas. Of course, there was always the off-chance that Mary, after swallowing a piece of the candy, would manage to get to the telephone before collapsing. But even then there was little risk; she would either call him or Dr. Applegate. *He* knew how to react, and as for Applegate, John intended to have a chat with him this evening in private before heading for home with the chocolates. It might prove to be a bit messy, but he knew he could convince the physician to cooperate.

As it turned out, he had little difficulty with Applegate. The only really messy part of the entire business was in actually introducing poison into the candy.

There were so many things he hadn't anticipated; opening the box itself and removing the plastic wrapper without damage, so that it could be re-sealed without detection — carefully melting the chocolate coating and re-moving a portion of the creamy fondant to make room for the poisonous powder — then remelting the coating and smoothing it over until each indi-vidual piece of candy could survive inspection.

But finally he was finished, and the telltale evidence of his labors obliter-ated so that Willie Hayes, the assistant pharmacist, would notice nothing tomorrow morning when he opened the store. John made a mental note; he must remember to dispose of the remainder of the chocolates tomorrow night, the moment he was sure Mary had succumbed. If he took care of a few details like that, the rest was just a matter of routine.

The routine of going home, after his brief but satisfactory interview with Dr. Applegate. The routine of greeting the old sow as she grunted up at him from her chair before the TV set; of kissing her fat forehead and asking her the same stupid questions about the same stupid daily routine; of using the bathroom and turning out the lights and settling down in bed next to that repulsive mountain of flabby flesh (for the last time, he exulted silently, the last time) and composing himself for sleep.

Sleep did not come easily, because anticipation stood in its path; antici-pation of the morning, when he'd give her the box of candy and leave for work. He'd let Willie handle the evening shift tomorrow, as was usual on

Tuesdays, and come home for supper early. No sense in waiting too long; suppertime would be long enough. She ought to open the box right after lunch, and then —

No, John did not sleep. He merely planned. He planned what he'd do after he found the body and phoned Applegate, planned how he'd break the news to the neighbors and send a wire to Mary's sister in Omaha. While he was at it, he might just as well be practical and consider what undertaker to select. A decent funeral would be expected, but there was no need of being unduly lavish. Mary had two thousand dollars' worth of life insurance. He could probably pick out a nice coffin for about four hundred; the whole deal would run a little under a thousand. Then, with the extra thousand, he could think about something for Frances, later on. On their honeymoon, perhaps. Say a year from now, or a little less. He could sell the business, sell the house here, move out to Portland or some other city. He'd always wanted to see the West Coast anyway; he'd never been there. Maybe Frances and he could take a plane over to Hawaii. That would be nice. Oh, it was all going to be nice, after tomorrow —

The odd thing was that he felt no guilt, no fear, no remorse. It had been Frances who actually came out and suggested the murder, of course, but now he realized that he had been killing Mary for years, in the deepest, darkest dungeon of his own mind. He was completely prepared to accept the act; he welcomed the role of murderer as familiar.

Everything seemed familiar, everything was normal. In the morning he rose and shaved and dressed and Mary had his breakfast ready as usual. She made the usual pretense of passing up the meal — "just coffee and orange juice, that's enough for me today" — but he knew she'd fry herself the usual three eggs as soon as he was out of the door. And when, at the door, he produced the box of chocolates as an afterthought, she could not conceal her squeal of delight. Hogs always squeal.

John managed to conceal his own elation long enough to peck at her cheek and escape.

Escape. Today was the day he would *really* escape! Escape forever.

Forever is a long time, and before the afternoon was over, John was thinking only of escaping the store itself by five o'clock.

He wanted to get home and get it over with. He didn't actually look forward to seeing what he'd see when he got there, or doing what he'd have to do during the subsequent evening hours. But the whole point was that it was something which *must* be done, and the sooner, the better.

So he drove home, as usual, at five-thirty, parked the car in the driveway, and went inside.

The kitchen was deserted, and he could hear the idiot drone of the TV set from the parlor beyond. Naturally that's the way it would be; she'd settled down to watch the afternoon programs, opened the box of candy, popped a chocolate into her mouth, and probably never managed to leave the easy chair.

John tiptoed through the hall. He saw her then, slumped in the big chair, with just the back of her head showing—the back of her head and her big fat neck with those repulsive rolls of heavy flesh. Frances had a slim neck; a pale white adorable neck, with delicious little hollows made for kisses.

John was glad he could think of her under the circumstances because it proved he wasn't frightened, he wasn't going to lose his nerve, even at a time like this. A time like this, when he walked into the parlor to see his wife's dead body—

His wife's dead body turned and stared at him. And then it rose from the chair. Mary was standing in front of him, big as life. Hideously big, hideously alive. She grinned at him.

"Early tonight, aren't you?" she said. And then, "John, what *are* you staring at?"

It took a moment for him to answer, and when he did he couldn't help himself, he had to blurt it out.

"Wh-where are the chocolates I brought you?"

The stupid grin loomed closer. "Surprise! I didn't eat any of them! Remember that new diet I told you about? Well this time I'm sticking to it. I'll lose at least twenty pounds, you'll see. I was telling Frances—"

"Frances?"

"Yes, Frances, silly! Remember she was supposed to leave yesterday? Well, she didn't. She left today. She stopped by here this afternoon, on her way to the airport. And since she was going on a trip, I gave her the box of candy to eat on the plane."

"You gave her—"

"Sure." Mary giggled. "I figured it was a sort of a farewell present. . . ."

THE FINAL PERFORMANCE

THE NEON INTESTINES had been twisted to form the word EAT.

I squinted up at it, the sand stinging my eyes, and shifted my overnight bag to the left hand. As I opened the sagging screen door a trickle of perspiration ran down my arm.

Two flies accompanied me into the restaurant. One of them headed for a pile of crullers on the counter and the other alighted on the bald head of an elderly fat man who leaned behind it. The man looked up and the fly buzzed away.

"Evening," he said. "What'll it be?"

"Are you Rudolph?" I asked.

He nodded.

I slid onto a stool. "Fellow named Davis sent me."

"From the garage?"

"That's right — the place up the highway. My car conked out on me coming through the mountains. He had to phone Bakersfield for a new connecting rod. They're bringing it out first thing tomorrow morning, and he figures he can get it installed before evening. But tonight I'm looking for a place to stay. He told me to try here — said you used to run a motel."

"Not any more. Isn't enough traffic along this route."

"I noticed a couple of cabins out in back."

"Closed up." The fat man reached under the counter and came up with a half-empty bottle of beer. He took a long gulp; when he set the bottle down again it was empty. "Look, you could hitch a ride into Bakersfield and come back tomorrow."

"I thought of that, but I hate to leave all my belongings. Everything I own

45

is in that car—guess it broke down because it was overloaded. You see, I'm moving to Hollywood, and I packed all my books and—"

"Hollywood?" The fat man blinked. "You in show biz?"

"I'm a writer."

"Television?"

"Short stories and books."

He blinked again. "That's better. TV is lousy, I can't understand what they think they're doing out there. Now you take a guy like that Ed Sullivan—" He broke off abruptly and stared at me. "Book writer, you say. Ever run into Arnie Pringle?"

"No, I can't say that I have."

"Before your time, I guess. Probably dead by now. He used to write my act."

"You were in show business?"

"Are you kidding? Rudolph the Great. Twenty years top billing, Pantages, Albee, Keith-Orpheum time. Why, I've got three press books full of—"

I rose from the stool.

"Here, where you going?"

I shrugged. "Sorry, but if I'm hitching a ride into Bakersfield I'd better get out there on the highway before dark."

"Never mind that. Guess we can fix up a cabin for you. Put some clean sheets on the bed." He swayed along behind the counter, and it suddenly occurred to me that he was just a little bit drunk.

"Look, I wouldn't want to put you to any trouble," I told him.

"No trouble. My pleasure." He jerked his head toward the swinging door behind him. "Rosie!" he yelled.

Rosie came into the room.

She was a tall girl, blonde and amply proportioned, her hair done up in a ponytail. She wore a blue sleeveless smock and her legs were bare.

"Rose, this is Mr. —"

"Chatham. Jim Chatham." I nodded at her and she wrinkled up her nose at me. It took a moment before I realized she was smiling.

"Had a little trouble with his car," Rudolph said. "Davis is fixing it up at the crossroads. He needs a place to stay overnight. You think you can find some clean bedclothes for Number One?"

She nodded at him, still looking at me.

"Better take him out with you. Let him have a look."

"All right." Her voice was soft, deeper than I'd expected.

"Keys in my desk, right-hand drawer."

"I know. I'll get them."

She turned and left the room. Rudolph reached under the counter into the cooler and brought out another bottle of beer, a full one this time. "Care for a brew?" he asked.

"Later, perhaps. Let me get settled and then I'll come back for dinner."

"Suit yourself." He bent to open the bottle, then raised it to his lips.

Rosie came back into the room; she carried a bundle of sheets wrapped around a pillow. "All set?" she asked.

I picked up my bag and followed her outside. The sun was setting and the desert wind was cool. Joshuas cast their shadows along the path leading to the cabins in the rear, striping the sand and the backs of her bare calves as she walked along before me.

"Here we are." She halted and opened the door of the tiny cabin. The interior of the little shack was dark and stifling hot. She switched on the light. "It'll cool off in a minute with the door open," she said. "I'll make up the bed for you."

I put down the suitcase and slumped into the single chair next to the gray-filmed window. She went to work, bending over the bed. She had fine breasts. As she moved around to tuck in the sheet, her leg brushed mine.

All at once, for no reason at all, my mind was filled with corny dialogue. *What's a nice girl like you doing in such a godforsaken hole? Let me take you away from all this. . . .*

Suddenly I noticed she had stopped working. She stood there with the pillow in her arms, staring at me.

"I heard you talking to him," she said. "About being a writer. What are you going to do out in Hollywood, work for the movies?"

"I doubt it. Probably just keep turning out stories the same as usual. But the climate's better."

"Yes, the climate." She nodded and wrinkled her nose at me. "Take me with you."

"What?"

"I said, take me with you."

"But Mrs. Rudolph—"

"His *first* name is Rudolph. Bitzner."

"Mrs. Bitzner, then—"

"I'm not Mrs. Bitzner either."

"Oh, I just thought—"

"I know what you thought. Never mind that. Just take me with you. All I'd do is ride along. There wouldn't be any trouble." She let the pillow fall on the bed and moved closer. "I wouldn't be any bother at all. I promise."

I stood up, but I didn't reach for her. I didn't have to reach for her, because she came right into my arms, and she said, "Please, please, say you'll take me. You've got to. You don't know what it's like all alone out here. You don't know what he's like. He's crazy—"

She had this trick of talking without opening her mouth, keeping her lips puckered up, waiting to be kissed, and she wrinkled her nose and I could see the tiny freckles on the bridge, and her skin was marble-cool in all this heat.

And it's one thing to sit back and make sophisticated remarks about cheap waitresses named Rosie (*Rosie, for God's sake!*) and another thing entirely to feel a waiting, willing woman stirring hard against you and whispering, "Please . . . promise me you will . . . I'll do anything. . . ."

So I opened my mouth to answer, then let it remain open in bewilderment as she stepped back quickly and picked up the pillow again. Then I heard him scuffling along the path and understood.

"Rosie!" he yelled. "You almost finished? Customers!"

"Be right in," she called.

I stepped over to the doorway and waved at Rudolph.

"Everything all right?" he asked.

"Everything's fine."

"Come and eat, then. You can wash up inside."

I glanced back at Rosie. She was bending over the bed and she didn't look at me. But she whispered, "I'll see you later. Wait for me."

That's what kept me going through the long evening.

I followed Rudolph, and I cleaned myself up a bit in the filthy washroom, and I shared a steak and french fries with the two flies and their cousins. The customers were in and out for the next couple of hours, and there was no chance to talk to Rudolph or even catch a glimpse of Rosie out in back. Then, finally, it was nine o'clock and the place was empty again. Rudolph yawned and walked over to the door, switching off the EAT sign.

"This concludes the evening's performance," he said. "Thanks for the use of the hall." He went over to the swinging door. "You fixing yourself something?" he yelled.

"Yes, just a hamburger. How about you?" Rosie asked.

"Never mind. I'll have myself another beer." He looked at me. "You ready for one now?"

I shook my head and stood up. "No, thanks, It's about time I turned in."

"What's your hurry? Stick around. We'll go in back and chew the fat awhile. To hell with the beer — I've got some hard stuff there."

"Well, I—"

"Come on. Got some things that might interest you. Man doesn't get much chance to talk to anybody halfway intelligent around here."

"All right."

He ran his wrist across the gray stubble around his mouth.

"Tell you what, I'll check the register first. You go right on back, through that door on the end. I'll be along."

So I went back, into the little room on the side of the restaurant which served as a parlor. I saw the overstuffed couch and the easy chair and the desk, the lamp, the TV set, but I didn't do any more than glance at them.

Because I was staring at the walls — the walls of another world.

It was the world of the Twenties and the early Thirties, a world that belonged to the half-forgotten faces which peered out at me from a thousand photographs reaching from floor to ceiling. Some of the pictures had peeled and faded, just as my memories had peeled and faded in the long years since early childhood. But I could still remember the familiar countenances, and I had at least heard of most of the names scrawled in autograph fashion beneath the unfamiliar ones. I moved around the room, moved around the mementos of what had once been a world called vaudeville.

Here was a skinny, gangling kid called Milton Berle and a buxom young woman named Sophie Tucker. Here was a youthful Bert Wheeler holding an apple and a smiling Joe Cook holding an Indian club and explaining why he would not imitate the Four Hawaiians. There was an entire section of faces in burnt cork — Cantor, Jolson, Lou Holtz in the pre–Sam Lapidus days, Frank Tinney (way before my time), and one mournfully humorous countenance which needed no spurious blackface; the signature read, "To Rudolph from Bert Williams."

And there were the teams and the acts — Moran and Mack, Gallagher and Shean, Cross and Dunn, Phil Baker and Ben Bernie, Smith and Dale (Dr. Kronkheit, I presume), and a surprisingly handsome young couple who signed themselves "George and Gracie." And there was an incredible Jimmy Durante — with hair — and Clayton and Jackson.

"See? It's like I told you, I knew 'em all." Rudolph had come up behind me, carrying a bottle and glasses. "Here, let me fix you a snort and I'll show you my press books."

He made me a drink, but he didn't get around to the press books. Instead he sprawled out on the sofa, uncorked the bottle again, and uncorked himself.

I don't know how long he rambled on about the old days and the old ways; about the Six Brown Brothers and Herman Timberg and Walter C. Kelly and Chic Sale. At another time, under other circumstances, I might have hung on to his every word. But right now I was hanging on to other words — "I'll see you later. Wait for me."

So I really didn't listen to him, to Rudolph the Great who used to do Orpheum Time until vaudeville died and then wandered out here into the desert to do a twenty-year layoff as Rudolph Bitzner. Twenty years — why, Rosie couldn't be much over twenty herself! And here was this fat old man wheezing away on the couch, drinking out of the bottle now and slobbering. He was getting ready to pass out. He had to pass out soon, he *had* to. . . .

"Have 'nother drink?" He sat up, blinking at the bottle. "Oh, 's empty, well whaddya know?"

"That's all right," I told him. "I've had enough."

"Well, I haven'. Got more 'round here someplace. Rosie!" He yelled her name, then lowered his voice as he turned to me. "She's out front. Told her to clean up the joint. Won't come near me when I'm drinking, anyhow, you know?" He chuckled. "Don't matter—I locked the door before I came back. Got the key ri' here, so she can't get away. Never get away, not from me."

He swayed to his feet. "Know what you're thinkin'—just an old lush, that's all, just an old lush. But wait till I show you the press books. Then you'll see who I was. Who I *am*." He stumbled back against the sofa. "Rudolph the Great. Tha's me. Keep in practice. Jus' as good as I ever was. Better. Why, I could go on Sullivan's show nex' week. . . ."

Then the color drained from his face and he fell back on the couch. I never did get to see those press books. By the time I put his feet up on the sofa he'd started to snore. I took the keys from his pocket and went back into the restaurant. She was waiting for me in the dark. And we went out through the dark to my cabin, and she clung to me in the dark, and that's the one thing I want to remember, *have* to remember now.

Afterward she told me about herself. She'd been ten when she'd come to Rudolph—her parents stopped by on their way to Texas and dropped her off while they filled a fair date. They were a couple of ex-vaudevillans themselves: the Flying Keenos. They knew Rudolph from the old days and they accepted his suggestion to leave her in his care while they traveled on, because they were down on their luck.

"Only they never came back," she said. "They never came back. And he tried to find them. He wrote to *Billboard* and everything, but they just disappeared. So I stayed on. Rudolph—he wasn't so bad then, you know. I mean, he didn't drink so much or anything. He sent me to school on the bus, bought me clothes and things. Treated me just like he was my father—until I was sixteen."

She started to cry, very softly. "He isn't even in love with me, not really. It's because of living out here all alone in this crazy desert and knowing he's getting old. Before it started he used to talk about making a comeback on TV. He said it was just like vaudeville, he'd always known there'd be a revival. Then, that summer when I was sixteen, he decided the time was right and he took me with him out to L.A. He went around and saw some agents, had a few auditions. I never did find out what really happened. But when we came back here in the fall he started to drink right away, and that's when—"

That's when she tried to sneak off, and he caught her, and he closed up the motel so she couldn't see anyone or attempt to hitch a ride. He kept her inside the restaurant, didn't even allow her to go up to the crossroads for supplies, wouldn't let anyone come near her.

There were times when she thought of running away in the night, but something always stopped her. She realized she owed him something for all the years he'd taken care of her, and he needed her now. He was just an old man, not quite right in the head, and he seldom bothered her any more. Most nights he just drank and passed out. She'd resigned herself to putting up with it until this evening. Then, when she saw me—

"I know. You figured you *could* get a ride, and maybe I'd even take care of you out on the Coast for a week or so, long enough for you to find a job. That's it, isn't it?"

"No!" She dug her nails into my arms. "Maybe I *did* think something like that at first. But not *now*. Believe me, not *now*."

I believed her. I believed her voice and I believed her body, even though it was incredible that I should be lying here in the desert night with this stranger whom I'd known forever.

"It's all right," I said. "We'll go away. But I'd feel better if we told him. Maybe if I talked things over with him, explained, I could make him understand."

"Oh no — you can't do that! He's crazy jealous. I didn't want to tell you, but one time he caught this truckdriver talking to me outside — just talking is all — and he took after him with that big butcher knife. He would have killed him if he caught him, I know he would! And he beat me up so that I couldn't even get out of bed for three days. No, he mustn't even suspect. Tomorrow afternoon, when the car is fixed. . . ."

We made our simple plans. The restaurant was closed on Sundays, and it would be better if I didn't attempt to take a meal there — just went straight to the garage and saw to it that Davis got the car fixed as soon as possible. Meanwhile Rosie would have her suitcase packed and ready. She'd encourage Rudolph to drink — not that he generally needed any encouragement from her. Maybe he'd even pass out. If not, she'd go so far as to cut the phone wire, if necessary; just so she could slip out to me with the assurance of getting a head start.

So we talked it all over, calmly and sensibly, and she slipped out of the cabin, and I lay there and tried to sleep. It was almost dawn when I closed my eyes, and the bats were out, flying against the gaudy desert sunrise.

I slept for a long time. When I left the cabin and cut across to the highway, it was almost two o'clock. I walked the mile to the crossroads garage and found Davis working with the car up on the rack. We talked for a while, but I didn't listen to what he said, or to what I said either. From time to time somebody drove up for gas and Davis would have to stop and give them service. The car wasn't ready until a little after five; it was already getting dark.

I paid him and drove off. The motor hummed smoothly, but I almost stripped gears as I shifted. I was nervous, that's all, just nervous. I didn't feel any guilt and I didn't feel any fear. Certainly I didn't feel any horror.

That came later.

That came when I parked in the deepening shadows on the side of the darkened restaurant and went up to the door. This was it. If something had gone wrong —

But nothing could go wrong. I squared my shoulders and took a deep breath, then rattled the doorknob. That was the signal; she'd be waiting to hear me.

Nothing happened. A few flies buzzed against the glass awaiting entry. I rattled the door again softly. It was locked.

Then the figure emerged from the back room.

I recognized Rudolph.

He moved briskly; there was no shuffle in his gait and no stagger either. His face was gray and puffy, but his red-rimmed eyes weren't blinking. He stooped and unlocked the door, motioning for me to come inside.

"Good afternoon," I said. There was nothing else I *could* say, not yet, not until I knew what had happened.

He nodded, moving behind me to lock the door again. I could hear the click of the key and I didn't bother to look around.

That's when the horror came.

Horror is something cold and sharp, biting against the back of your neck.

"Let's go into the other room," Rudolph said. "Rosie has something to say to you."

"What have you done to her?"

"Nothing. She just wants to talk to you. You'll see."

We went down the aisle past the counter, the flies buzzing in our wake. Then we were in the back room and they were all waiting for me there — George and Gracie, Frank Tinney, Lou Holtz. They were all staring, as I stared, at the open torn heap. For a moment, in the dim light, I thought it was Rosie lying there.

But no, Rosie was sitting on the sofa and she was looking at the suitcase too. She didn't say a word when I came in because there was nothing to say now.

I could feel Rudolph's breath on my neck, right behind me. And I could feel the coldness, too, the sharpness, the horror. All at once it went away. I heard the knife clatter to the floor.

"You can thank her for that," Rudolph murmured. "I could have killed you, you know. I wanted to kill you. But she talked me out of it. And now she has something to say to you. Go ahead, Rosie, tell him."

He left me standing there in the doorway and walked over to where Rose was sitting. He slid down on the sofa beside her and put his arm around her, smiling. Rosie looked up then, but she didn't smile.

The shadows crept across the walls, across the faces of Williams and Bernie and Jolson, across his face and hers. But I wasn't watching the shadows. I was listening to the girl.

"You see how it happened," she murmured. "He walked in while I was packing. He found out."

"All right," I said. "So he found out. I wanted to tell him in the first place. And now that he knows, he can let us go."

I was already moving before I finished my last sentence, crossing the room in two strides and scooping up the big, broad-bladed butcher knife from the floor.

"Look," I said. "I've got the knife now. He can't hurt us and he'd better not try. We can walk out of here whenever we please."

She sat there, turning her head to stare at the knife. And he stared, too, tightened his arm around her and stared and smiled while she said, "No. I've changed my mind. I'm not going with you."

"But I don't understand—"

"We talked it all over before you came. I can't go. He needs me so. It's right that I should stay. I belong with him. Can't you see that?"

I shook my head. There was something wrong with her words, something wrong with the way she stared and he smiled. And all at once it came to me as I looked into his fat face off in the shadows. "Maybe I can see," I said. "Rudolph the Great. You were a hypnotist, weren't you? That's the answer, isn't it? You've hypnotized her, that's what you've done—"

He started to laugh.

"You're wrong, mister," he said. "Tell him how wrong he is, darling."

And then she was laughing, too, in a high, hysterical titter. But there was no laughter in her face, and her words, when they came, were soft and somber.

"He's no hypnotist. I know what I'm doing, believe me. I'm telling you to get out. Just get out, do you hear me? Go away and don't come back. I don't want to go to the Coast with you. I don't want you pawing me in some dirty cabin. I know what you are. You're a—"

She began to curse me then; the filth and the foulness poured out of her mouth and she bobbed her head at me in rage, while he just sat there and smiled.

Finally she was finished. "All right," he said. "Have you heard enough?"

"I've heard enough," I said. "I'll go." And I dropped the knife again. It rolled across the floor, and a thin ray of light from the dying sunset streaked the dulled and darkened blade.

I turned to go, and neither of them rose. They just sat there, arms entwined, and stared at me. The shadows blotted out their faces, then pursued me all the way down the hall.

The car stood waiting for me in the twilight. I climbed in, switched on the ignition, pulled away. I must have driven two or three miles before I remembered to turn on my lights. I was in a daze. There was nothing but the shadows, the strange shadows. Shadows in the room, on their faces, on the dulled and darkened knife. *The dulled and darkened knife. . . .*

Then it hit me, and I speeded up. I found a phone just ahead in a filling station outside Pono and put in my call.

The state troopers arrived in fifteen minutes, and I told my story as we roared back to the restaurant in their patrol car.

"He must have done *something* to her," I said. "That knife blade was dark with dried blood."

"We'll see," the sergeant told me.

But at first we didn't see, because Rudolph must have heard us coming, and that's when he used the knife on himself. We found it sticking out of his chest there on the floor in the back room, and he was quite dead.

Rosie still sat there on the sofa, staring at us. It was the sergeant who discovered she'd been strangled.

"Must have happened a couple of hours ago," he told me. "The body's getting stiff."

"Strangled? A couple of hours? But I was just here. We were talking—"

"See for yourself."

I walked over and touched her shoulder. She was stiff and cold and there were purple marks on her neck. Suddenly she toppled forward, and that's when I saw how the knife had been used—saw the huge, foot-long gash extending from the back of her neck down across the shoulders. The wound was incredibly deep; I couldn't understand why. Not even when the sergeant called my attention to the blood on Rudolph's right hand.

It wasn't until I saw the press books that I really knew. Yes, we found his press books, and I finally saw them there at the last, finally found out what must have happened in his dark room, in his dark mind, when he walked in and discovered her getting ready to leave.

That's when he'd strangled her, of course, strangled her to death in a crazy rage. But he was sane enough to realize I'd be coming by to get her and that he'd have to find a way to get rid of me.

So he used the knife then and cut the hole, cut it wide and deep. Wide and deep enough so that she could bow and nod and turn her head when he had his hand behind her. Of course I'd heard her talking to me, but the press books explained all that.

He wasn't lying about his notices; they were raves.

And he wasn't lying about hypnotism either. Rudolph the Great hadn't been a hypnotist. He was just one of the best damned ventriloquists in the business.

Hobo

HANNIGAN HOPPED THE FREIGHT in the yards, just as it started to roll. It had already picked up speed before he spotted an empty in the deepening twilight, and in Hannigan's condition it wasn't easy to swing aboard. He scraped all of the cloth and most of the skin from his left knee before he landed, cursing, in the musty darkness of the boxcar.

He sat there for a moment, trying to catch his wind, feeling the perspiration trickle down under the folds of the dirty jacket. That's what Sneaky Pete did to a man.

Staring out of the doorway, Hannigan watched the lights of the city move past in a blinding blur as the train gained momentum. The lights became links in a solid neon chain. That was also what Sneaky Pete could do to a man.

Hannigan shrugged. Hell, he'd been entitled to drink a few toasts to celebrate leaving town!

Unexpectedly the shrug became a twitch and the twitch became a shiver. So all right, he might as well be honest. He hadn't been celebrating anything. He'd drunk up his last dime because he was scared.

That's why he was on the lam again—he had to get out of Knifeville. That wasn't the name of the town, of course, but Hannigan knew he'd always remember it that way. There wasn't enough Sneaky Pete in the world to drown the memory.

He blinked and turned away from the dwindling chain of light, trying to focus his vision in the dimness of the empty boxcar.

Then he froze.

The boxcar wasn't empty.

Sprawling against the opposite side of the wall was the man. He sat there nonchalantly, staring at Hannigan — and he'd been sitting there and staring all the time. The farther reaches of the car were in total darkness, but the man was just close enough to the opposite door so that flashes of light illumined his features in passing. He was short, squat, his bullet-head almost bald. His face was grimy and stubbled, his clothing soiled and wrinkled. This reassured Hannigan. It couldn't be the Knife.

"Brother, you gave me a scare!" Hannigan muttered. The train was passing over a culvert now and the rumbling cut off the man's reply. When the lights flashed by again he was still staring.

"Going South?" Hannigan called.

The man nodded.

"Me, too." Hannigan wiped the side of his mouth with his sleeve; he could still taste the Sneaky Pete, still feel it warming his churning guts. "I don't care where I end up, just so's I get the hell out of that burg."

They were rolling through open country now and he couldn't see his companion. But he knew he hadn't moved, because now, in counterpoint to the steady clickety-clack of the cars, he heard the steady cadence of his hoarse breathing.

Hannigan didn't give a damn whether he saw him or not — the main thing was just to know he was there, hear the reassuring sound of another man's breath. It helped, and talking helped, too.

"I suppose you hit the iron for the same reason I did." It was really the Sneaky Pete talking, but Hannigan let the words roll. "You heard about the Knife?"

He caught the man's nod as a farmhouse light flashed by. The guy was probably drunker than he was, but at least he was listening.

"Damnedest thing. Killed four bums in a week — you see what it said in the papers? Some skull doctor figured it out. This loony just has it in for us poor down-and-outers. I was down in Bronson's jungle yesterday. Half the guys had hit the road already and the rest were leaving. Scared they might be next. I gave 'em all the Bronx salute."

The stranger didn't reply. Listening to his rasping gasps, Hannigan suddenly realized why. He was blind drunk.

"Loaded, huh?" Hannigan grinned. "Me, too. On account of I was wrong. About giving those guys the Bronx, I mean." He gulped. "Because today — I ran into the Knife."

The man across the way nodded again; Hannigan caught it in a passing beam of light as the cars rolled on.

"I mean it, man," he said. "You know Jerry's place — down the alley off Main? I was crawling out of there this afternoon. Nobody in sight. All of a sudden — zing! Something whizzes right past my ear. I look up and there's this shiv, stuck in a post about three inches from my head.

"I didn't see anyone, and I didn't wait to look. I ducked back into Jerry's and stayed there. Drank up my stake and waited until it was time to hop this rattler." He was twitching again, but he couldn't help it. "All I wanted was to get out of there."

Hannigan leaned forward. "What's the matter, you a dummy or something?" He tried to catch a glimpse of the man's features, but it was too dark. And now he needed the response. He began to edge forward on his hands and knees as the train lurched over the bumpy roadbed.

"How do you figure it?" he asked—knowing that he was really asking himself the question. "What gets into a guy's skull that makes him kill that way—just creep around in the dark and carve up poor jokers like us?"

There was no answer, only the hoarse breathing.

Hannigan inched forward, just as the train hit the curve. A light flashed by and he saw the man topple forward.

He saw the blood and the gaping hole and the blinding reflection from the blade of the big knife stuck in the man's back.

"Dead!" Hannigan edged away, shivering, then paused. "But he can't be. *I heard him breathing!*"

Suddenly he realized he could still hear the breathing now. But it was coming from behind him, coming from close behind. In fact, just as the train went into the tunnel, Hannigan could *feel* the breathing—right against the back of his neck. . . .

A Home Away from Home

THE TRAIN WAS LATE, and it must have been past nine o'clock when Natalie found herself standing, all alone, on the platform before Hightower Station.

The station itself was obviously closed for the night—it was only a way-stop, really, for there was no town here—and Natalie wasn't quite sure what to do. She had taken it for granted that Dr. Bracegirdle would be on hand to meet her. Before leaving London she'd sent her uncle a wire giving him the time of her arrival. But since the train had been delayed, perhaps he'd come and gone.

Natalie glanced around uncertainly, then noticed the phone booth which provided her with a solution. Dr. Bracegirdle's last letter was in her purse, and it contained both his address and his phone number. She had fumbled through her bag and found it by the time she walked over to the booth.

Ringing him up proved a bit of a problem—there seemed to be an interminable delay before the operator made the connection, and there was a great deal of buzzing on the line. A glimpse of the hills beyond the station, through the glass wall of the booth, suggested the reason for the difficulty. After all, Natalie reminded herself, this was West Country. Conditions might be a bit primitive—

"Hello, hello!"

The woman's voice came over the line, fairly shouting above the din. There was no buzzing noise now, and the sound in the background suggested a babble of voices all intermingled. Natalie bent forward and spoke directly and distinctly into the mouthpiece.

"This is Natalie Rivers," she said. "Is Dr. Bracegirdle there?"

"Whom did you say was calling?"

"Natalie Rivers. I'm his niece."

"His what, Miss?"

"Niece," Natalie repeated. "May I speak to him, please?"

"Just a moment."

There was a pause, during which the sound of voices in the background seemed amplified, and then Natalie heard the resonant masculine tones, so much easier to separate from the indistinct murmuring.

"Dr. Bracegirdle here. My dear Natalie, this is an unexpected pleasure!"

"Unexpected? But I sent you a 'gram from London this afternoon." Natalie checked herself as she realized the slight edge of impatience which had crept into her voice. "Didn't it arrive?"

"I'm afraid service is not of the best around here," Dr. Bracegirdle told her, with an apologetic chuckle. "No, your wire didn't arrive. But apparently you did." He chuckled again. "Where are you, my dear?"

"At Hightower Station."

"Oh, dear. It's in exactly the opposite direction."

"Opposite direction?"

"From Peterby's. They rang me up just before you called. Some silly nonsense about an appendix — probably nothing but an upset stomach. But I promised to stop round directly, just in case."

"Don't tell me they still call you for general practice?"

"Emergencies, my dear. There aren't many physicians in these parts. Fortunately, there aren't many patients, either." Dr. Bracegirdle started to chuckle, then sobered. "Look now. You say you're at the station. I'll just send Miss Plummer down to fetch you in the wagon. Have you much luggage?"

"Only my travel-case. The rest is coming with the household goods, by boat."

"Boat?"

"Didn't I mention it when I wrote?"

"Yes, that's right, you did. Well, no matter. Miss Plummer will be along for you directly."

"I'll be waiting in front of the platform."

"What was that? Speak up, I can hardly hear you."

"I said I'll be waiting in front of the platform."

"Oh." Dr. Bracegirdle chuckled once more. "Bit of a party going on here."

"Shan't I be intruding? I mean, since you weren't expecting me to-night —"

"Not at all! They'll be leaving before long. You wait for Plummer."

The phone clicked off and Natalie returned to the platform. In a surprisingly short time, the station wagon appeared and skidded off the road to halt at the very edge of the tracks. A tall, thin gray-haired woman, wearing a somewhat rumpled white uniform, emerged and beckoned to Natalie.

"Come along, my dear," she called. "Here, I'll just pop this in back."

Scooping up the bag, she tossed it into the rear of the wagon. "Now, in with you — and off we go!"

Scarcely waiting for Natalie to close the door after her, the redoubtable Miss Plummer gunned the motor and the car plunged back onto the road.

The speedometer immediately shot up to seventy, and Natalie flinched. Miss Plummer noticed her agitation at once.

"Sorry," she said. "With Doctor out on call, I can't be away too long."

"Oh, yes, the houseguests. He told me."

"Did he now?" Miss Plummer took a sharp turn at a crossroads and the tires screeched in protest, but to no avail. Natalie decided to drown apprehension in conversation.

"What sort of a man is my uncle?" she asked.

"Have you never met him?"

"No. My parents moved to Australia when I was quite young. This is my first trip to England. In fact, it's the first time I've left Canberra."

"Folks with you?"

"They were in a motor smash-up two months ago," Natalie said. "Didn't the Doctor tell you?"

"I'm afraid not — you see, I haven't been with him very long." Miss Plummer uttered a short bark and the car swerved wildly across the road. "Motor smash-up, eh? Some people have no business behind the wheel. That's what Doctor says."

She turned and peered at Natalie. "I take it you've come to stay, then?"

"Yes, of course. He wrote me when he was appointed my guardian. That's why I was wondering what he might be like. It's so hard to tell from letters." The thin-faced woman nodded silently, but Natalie had an urge to confide. "To tell the truth, I'm just a little bit edgy. I mean, I've never met a psychiatrist before."

"Haven't you, now?" Miss Plummer shrugged. "You're quite fortunate. I've seen a few in my time. A bit on the know-it-all side, if you ask me. Though I must say, Dr. Bracegirdle is one of the best. Permissive, you know."

"I understand he has quite a practice."

"There's no lack of patients for *that* sort of thing," Miss Plummer observed. "Particularly amongst the well-to-do. I'd say your uncle has done himself handsomely. The house and all — but you'll see." Once again the wagon whirled into a sickening swerve and sped forward between the imposing gates of a huge driveway which led toward an enormous house set amidst a grove of trees in the distance. Through the shuttered windows Natalie caught sight of a faint beam of light — just enough to help reveal the ornate façade of her uncle's home.

"Oh, dear," she muttered, half to herself.

"What is it?"

"The guests — and it's Saturday night. And here I am, all mussed from travel."

"Don't give it another thought," Miss Plummer assured her. "There's no formality here. That's what Doctor told me when I came. It's a home away from home."

Miss Plummer barked and braked simultaneously, and the station wagon came to an abrupt stop just behind an imposing black limousine.

"Out with you now!" With brisk efficiency, Miss Plummer lifted the bag from the rear seat and carried it up the steps, beckoning Natalie forward with a nod over her shoulder. She halted at the door and fumbled for a key.

"No sense knocking," she said. "They'd never hear me." As the door swung open her observation was amply confirmed. The background noise which Natalie had noted over the telephone now formed a formidable foreground. She stood there, hesitant, as Miss Plummer swept forward across the threshold.

"Come along, come along!"

Obediently, Natalie entered, and as Miss Plummer shut the door behind her, blinked with eyes recently unaccustomed to the brightness of the interior.

She found herself standing in a large, somewhat bare hallway. Directly ahead of her was a large staircase; at an angle between the railing and the wall was a desk and chair. To her left, a dark, paneled door — evidently leading to Dr. Bracegirdle's private office, for a small brass plate was affixed to it, bearing his name. To her right was a huge open parlor, its windows heavily curtained and shuttered against the night. It was from here that the sounds of sociability echoed.

Natalie started across the hall toward the stairs. As she did so, she caught a glimpse of the parlor. Fully a dozen guests eddied about a large table, talking and gesturing with the animation of close acquaintance — with one another, and with the contents of the lavish array of bottles gracing the tabletop. A sudden whoop of laughter indicated that at least one guest had abused the Doctor's hospitality.

Natalie passed the entry hastily, so as not to be observed, then glanced behind her to make sure that Miss Plummer was following with her bag. Miss Plummer was indeed following, but her hands were empty. And as Natalie reached the stairs, Miss Plummer shook her head.

"You didn't mean to go up now, did you?" she murmured. "Come in and introduce yourself."

"I thought I might freshen up a bit first."

"Let me go on ahead and get your room in order. Doctor didn't give me notice, you know."

"Really, it's not necessary. I could do with a wash — "

"Doctor should be back any moment now. Do wait for him." Miss Plummer grasped Natalie's arm, and with the same speed and expedition she had bestowed on driving, now steered the girl forward into the lighted room.

"Here's Doctor's niece," she announced. "Miss Natalie Rivers, from Australia."

Several heads turned in Natalie's direction, though Miss Plummer's voice had scarcely penetrated the general conversational din. A short, jolly-looking fat man bobbed toward Natalie, waving a half-empty glass.

"All the way from Australia, eh?" He extended his goblet. "You must be thirsty. Here, take this — I'll get another." And before Natalie could reply he turned and plunged back into the group around the table.

"Major Hamilton," Miss Plummer whispered. "A dear soul, really. Though I'm afraid he's just a wee bit squiffy."

As Miss Plummer moved away, Natalie glanced uncertainly at the glass in her hand. She was not quite sure where to dispose of it.

"Allow me." A tall, gray-haired and quite distinguished-looking man with a black mustache moved forward and took the stemware from between her fingers.

"Thank you."

"Not at all. I'm afraid you'll have to excuse him. The party spirit, you know." He nodded, indicating a woman in extreme décolletage chattering animatedly to a group of three laughing men. "But since it's by way of being a farewell celebration — "

"Ah, there you are!" The short man whom Miss Plummer had identified as Major Hamilton bounced back into orbit around Natalie, a fresh drink in his hand and a fresh smile on his ruddy face. "I'm back again," he announced. "Just like a boomerang, eh?"

He laughed explosively, then paused. "I say, you *do* have boomerangs in Australia? And blackfellows? Saw quite a bit of you Aussies at Gallipoli. Of course that was some time ago, before *your* time, I daresay — "

"Please, Major." The tall man smiled at Natalie. There was something reassuring about his presence, and something oddly familiar, too. Natalie wondered where she might have seen him before. She watched while he moved over to the Major and removed the drink from his hand.

"Now see here — " the Major spluttered.

"You've had enough, old boy. And it's almost time for you to go."

"One for the road — " The Major glanced around, his hands waving in appeal. "Everyone *else* is drinking!" He made a lunge for his glass but the tall man evaded him. Smiling at Natalie over his shoulder, he drew the Major to one side and began to mutter to him earnestly in low tones. The Major nodded in sudden, drunken placation.

Natalie looked around the room. Nobody was paying the least attention to her except for one elderly woman who sat quite alone on a stool before the piano. She regarded Natalie with a fixed stare that at once emphasized her role as an intruder on a gala scene. Natalie turned away hastily and again caught sight of the woman in décolletage. She suddenly remembered her own desire to change her clothing and peered at the doorway, seeking Miss Plummer. But Miss Plummer was nowhere to be seen.

Walking back into the hall, she peered up the staircase.

"Miss Plummer!" she called.

There was no response.

Then, from out of the corner of her eye, she noted that the door of the room across the hallway was ajar. In fact, it was opening now, quite rapidly, and as Natalie stared, Miss Plummer came backing out of the room, carrying something in her hand. Before Natalie could call out again and attract her attention, she had scurried off down the hallway.

Natalie crossed before the stairs, meaning to follow her, but found herself halting instead before the open doorway.

She gazed in curiously at what was obviously her uncle's consultation room. It was a cosy, book-lined study with heavy, leather-covered furniture grouped before the shelves. The psychiatric couch rested in one corner near the wall and near it was a large mahogany desk. The top of the desk was quite bare, save for a cradle telephone, and a thin brown loop snaking out from it.

Something about the loop disturbed Natalie and before she was conscious of her movement she was inside the room, looking down at the desk-top. Now she recognized the loop, of course: it was the cord from the phone.

And the end had been neatly severed from its connection at the wall.

"Miss Plummer!" Natalie murmured. "That's what she was carrying—a pair of scissors. But why—"

"Why not?"

Natalie turned just in time to observe the tall, distinguished-looking man enter the doorway behind her.

"It won't be needed," he said. "After all, I *did* tell you it was a farewell celebration." And he gave a little chuckle.

Again Natalie sensed something strangely familiar about him and this time it came to her. She'd heard the same chuckle over the phone from the depot station.

"But you're playing a joke!" she exclaimed. "You're Dr. Bracegirdle, aren't you?"

"No, my dear." He shook his head as he moved past her across the room. "It's just that no one expected you. We were about to leave when your call came. So we had to say *something.*"

There was a moment of silence. Then, "Where *is* my uncle?" Natalie murmured, at last.

"Over here."

Natalie found herself standing beside the tall man, gazing down at what lay in a space between the couch and the wall. An instant was all she could bear.

"Messy," the tall man nodded. "Of course it was all so sudden, the opportunity, I mean. And then they *would* get into the liquor —"

His voice echoed hollowly in the room and Natalie realized the sounds of the party had died away. She glanced up to see them all standing there in the doorway, watching.

Then their ranks parted and Miss Plummer came quickly into the room, wearing an incongruous fur wrap over the rumpled, ill-fitting uniform.

"Oh my!" she gasped. "So you found him!"

Natalie nodded and took a step forward. "You've got to do something," she said. "Please!"

"Yes." But Miss Plummer didn't seem concerned. The others had crowded into the room behind her, and stood staring silently; Natalie turned to them in appeal.

"Don't you see?" she cried. "It's the work of a madman. He belongs in the asylum!"

"My dear child," murmured Miss Plummer as she quickly closed and locked the door and the silent starers moved forward. "This *is* the asylum. . . ."

THE UNPARDONABLE CRIME

SHERRY HEARD THE MUSIC before she was halfway up the stairs. It was long-hair and loud, and all at once she got the shakes so bad she thought she'd go out of her skull.

What she needed was a fix, but Sherry was through with Fixville. For the first time in three years she'd play it cool. All she had to do was get Roger to take her back and do the script with her.

That wouldn't be any sweat. She remembered how it had been when they were together—no matter what kind of stuff she pulled on Roger, she could always twist him around her little finger.

Only now she had to make her little finger stop trembling, and go up to the door and knock. Sherry managed it but she had to pound for a long time before he heard her over the music. Then the hi-fi went off, and he opened the door.

He just stood there for a moment, staring at her like she was a stranger, and she could feel the shakes coming back again, crawling around in her stomach to form a big hard question mark. She knew what the three years had done to her, but she'd been so careful with the makeup and her hair especially. *I haven't changed that much,* she told herself. *He's the one who's changed.*

Even in the dim light, Roger looked much older. His hair was gray, and his face was gray, too. There was this big scar on his forehead, and for a second she wondered where it came from; then she remembered what Santo's boys had done to him just before she and Santo went away together.

He remembers, too, she thought. *I ought to cut out of here.* And then she realized just where she'd have to go if she did cut out, and she smiled and said, "Hello, darling! Aren't you going to ask me in?"

"Sherry." There was no surprise in his voice, no emotion at all. When she remembered the way he used to speak her name, in the big bed, with all the mirrors — but she could make him do it again. She *had* to.

"Come in."

She followed him into the apartment. It wasn't bad, by Mexican standards, and compared to that rathole she'd been padding in this was the greatest. But too damned dark to suit her, considering what she was going to do.

"How's about some electricity?" she asked. "When a gal hasn't seen her husband for three years, she kind of likes to get a good look at him."

Only, of course, she meant it the other way around. As he went over to switch on the lamp, she took a quick inventory. Her hair was loose across her bare shoulders — not quite as long as it had been back in Bel Air, but long enough. And the cleavage was good; in spite of everything, there wasn't any sag. And to hell with *everything*, she told herself. *Forget it. Make like it never happened.*

Sherry sat down on the sofa, crossing her bare legs and letting her dress ride up. She didn't have to worry — the needle marks were all on her thighs.

Roger took a chair on the other side of the room. She smiled at him, but he didn't say anything. Her stomach started to crawl again.

"Aren't you surprised?" she murmured. "Aren't you even going to ask why I came here?"

"The script," he said. "Milton's script."

"Isn't it wonderful, darling? The moment I saw it, I knew how excited you'd be."

"I didn't read it," Roger told her. "I sent it back."

"You *what?*" Sherry's stomach stopped crawling; she didn't feel anything.

"I'm out of the picture business, my dear. You're responsible for that — among other things."

Jesus, what could she say? He was still carrying the torch that bad, after three years. Well, in a way, maybe that would help.

"But honey, it's perfect for us. It's not just a comeback deal. You know how big Milton is now — he got the Award last year."

"Nice of him to think of us."

Sherry wondered, as he said it, if he remembered that she and Milton used to ball around together before Santo came along. And a damned good thing, too — otherwise she'd never have been able to pitch him for a look at the script when she ran into him on vacation last month down at Acapulco.

"Roger, you can't just sit out the rest of your life in this godforsaken hole!" She leaned forward, glancing around the room. "Why, you don't even have a television set — what do you do with yourself?"

"I play records. I walk in the Plaza. There is a woman who comes once a week to clean for me. Everything is very simple."

"Everything is crazy!" Sherry stood up. "Look. You get on a plane. You come back and you do the picture. Milton says there's no problem on financing—he'll put up a third, and the bank will go for the rest of the bundle. We'll take equal cuts. It can't miss, darling."

Roger nodded. "I thought that's why you came," he said. "You're in a bind. What's the matter, did Santo walk out on you?"

He doesn't know, she told herself. But then, how could he know that Santo had walked out six weeks after they'd run off together, while Roger was still in the hospital from that clobbering job Santo's boys had done on him for a farewell present. She hadn't known Santo would pull a trick like that, but then he was a spic and a hood and cruel. She found out just how cruel when he left her stranded in Mexico City; stranded and knocked up.

But Roger didn't know about that. And he didn't know about Murray, and that greasy doctor who almost killed her and then had the nerve to come pawing around afterwards. He didn't know about Art and Phil and all those nameless, faceless men in the bars; about Jerry, who put her on the fix and then on the turf, or about Tony and Dino and, now, Luis. When she thought about Luis the crawling began again, and the only thing that kept her from flipping was that Roger didn't know.

"Santo was a mistake," she said. "I admit it. When I heard about how his goons jumped you I walked out."

"You didn't come back to me," Roger muttered. He wasn't angry about it, just making a statement.

"I couldn't come back, don't you understand?" Roger was a director, he wasn't expected to come on strong, but Sherry was an actress. She still knew how to build a scene. "I"—and she let her voice catch—"I was too ashamed."

"But you're not ashamed any more," he said, just as quietly. "Now that you're in a bind."

He'd topped her. But she had to keep crowding, had to. "I don't know what you're talking about! I've had all kinds of offers. I can make pictures down here if I want to."

It was the truth, too. But Sherry felt the cold crawling as she thought about the kind of pictures she could make. Luis had suggested it just last night—only it wasn't a suggestion, it was an order. He'd made her promise before he gave her the fix. He'd tried to put her down easy by telling her he'd be in it himself with her; just he and one other man, the first time. And there would be no way out stuff—no whips, or anything like that. Not the first time—

Roger was shrugging. "Then you have no problem," he was saying. "I advise you to make a deal."

All right, Sherry told herself. *This is it.* She stood up, very slowly, and she wasn't trembling now. She never trembled when she was doing an important take.

"I have only one problem, Roger," she murmured. "You." She paused for a beat. "That's why I came back. Because I couldn't forget. Have you forgotten, Roger?"

He didn't move, just sat there staring at her with that poker face of his. But she saw that his knuckles were white, gripping the arms of the chair.

Sherry took a step forward. "Have you forgotten the way it was when you'd come home from the studio at night — and I'd be waiting, like this —"

She was right where she wanted to be now, in the circle of lamplight which was like an amber spot. And she made it all in one quick gesture, just as she'd planned; her hand reaching around and pulling the zipper, while her shoulders shrugged and the dress fell over her breasts, across her thighs, down to her knees, to the floor. Just in time she remembered to pull in her belly.

"This is why I came back, Roger." She said it, knowing now that her words wouldn't matter; they never had mattered, once she had made the gesture and he carried her into the big bedroom with the mirrors. And the way he stared at her now she knew she was right — the three years didn't matter to him, nothing mattered but the sight of her waiting and willing and wanting —

Sherry moved toward him, the long hair tumbling across her naked back. She smiled, and held out her arms, knowing how the gesture would lift her breasts, knowing his response.

Then she stopped.

Because Roger started to laugh.

Roger started to laugh, and he couldn't stop. He couldn't stop until he choked. And she was choking, too, choking with what had crawled up inside her when she heard him. She turned around and reached for her dress.

And all the while he was gasping and wheezing at her, trying to get the words out between spasms. "That's right — put it on and get out of here! I thought you'd pulled every trick in the book on me, but I was wrong. You lied, you stole, you cheated, you whored. And I used to take it and come back for more. But this time you've gone too far, Sherry. This time you've committed the unpardonable crime!"

Sherry didn't understand. All she understood was that she had to go. Had to go back to Luis and get a fix for tonight, before he took her down to that dirty basement under the *cantina* to make the movies.

She fastened the zipper and turned around to say something to Roger, but he was laughing again. The scar on his forehead had turned red and he couldn't seem to stop. Sherry wanted to ask him what he meant by that crack about the unpardonable crime, but she knew it wouldn't do any good. Nothing would do any good except to get out of here, away from the laughing and the staring — to get out of here and find a fix.

Then all at once she *was* out, running down the stairs, and the laughter followed, though Roger never moved.

Roger didn't move for a long time. It took quite a while before he stopped laughing and the scar faded. Then he stood up and shook his head. "The unpardonable crime," he murmured, chuckling softly. "Mopery. The act of indecently exposing oneself to a blind man."

He walked across the room, took his red-and-white cane out of the closet, and went out to dinner.

CRIME MACHINE

"LET HIM ALONE," said Stephen's father. "It's a phase they all go through. He'll snap out of it."

Stephen didn't really believe he was ever going to snap out of it, but he was grateful that his folks let him alone. He wasn't worried what they thought, just as long as they allowed him to watch the viddies.

Because his father was rich and connected with the university labs, Stephen had his own viddie set. While his parents indulged their normal tastes and watched the adult mush on the wall downstairs, Stephen stayed in his room and his own world.

It was a wonderful world for any thirteen-year-old — the world called the Good Old Days. There were all kinds of viddie shows about the golden pioneer era of seventy-five years ago, the marvelous time when heroes like Dion O'Bannion and Hymie Weiss walked the Earth.

Stephen watched a show called *Big Jim* — about Big Jim Colosimo and his lovable friends. He watched *The Enforcer*; that was the one about Frank Nitti. He was a man of action, like the heroes of *Johnny Torrio* and *Legs Diamond*. The *Legs Diamond* show was very exciting, because Legs was the one who always danced his way around the bullets in a gang war. That was how he got his name.

Stephen learned a lot about the people who had lived in the romantic past. He knew about flashy gambling men like fancy Arnold Rothstein, who was so suave, and wild rascals like Bugs Moran. There was a new show out called *The Great Dillinger*, and that was pretty good. But the best of all was Stephen's favorite — *Scarface Al*. No wonder it was right up there on top with all the kids; its hero was Scarface Al Capone, the Robin Hood of Chicago, who took from the rich and gave to the poor.

Lots of times Stephen found himself humming the theme song, which went:

> *Al Capone, Al Capone,*
> *A mighty man who*
> *walked alone —*
> *Wherever daring deeds*
> *are known,*
> *Men sing the praise of*
> *Al Capone.*

Stephen liked the way the machine guns came in on the end of the last line.

But then he liked everything about Al Capone; the way he got his scar — defending his sister from the crooked Prohibition agents; the way he disguised himself as "Mr. Brown" when he was fighting the wicked cops and the thieving politicians of Chicago. Stephen knew all about Al Capone, riding in from his hideout in Cicero to bring justice to Chicago and save pretty girls from the evil Vice Squad men.

Stephen joined the "Scarface Al Club" and ate enough cereal to get himself the complete prize outfit — the artificial scar to wear, the bulletproof vest and everything.

He might have been a very happy boy if he hadn't found his uncle's subjectivity reactor.

It was a big machine, resembling nothing quite so much as the genetic control, which his uncle had also invented. The genetic control was a large box in which a woman could sit and be bombarded by radiations which would eradicate recessive and undesirable traits in her ova, thus leading to the reproduction of healthy offspring. This apparatus, marketed under the popular name of "Heir Conditioner," was an immediate success because it was a failure. Nothing really happened, but the woman who used it felt better; in that respect it resembled a face cream and had the additional advantage of being much more expensive.

The machine which Stephen found — the subjectivity reactor — was a failure because it was a success. Not an immediate failure, for it was never manufactured or marketed, but a gradual failure. His uncle had devised it while still a young man, many years ago, and it too was a large box which contained a variety of mechanisms. Under their stimulus, the subject became capable of materializing, in tangible three-dimensional form, his immediate thought patterns.

The gradual failure came about because his uncle had experimented upon himself, and pretty soon his home was overflowing with tangible three-dimensional forms to which his wife objected; most particularly to the redheads.

Consequently the subjectivity reactor was carted off to the storage building behind the university labs where Stephen's uncle and father both worked, and no one ever mentioned that it was also capable, by virtue of the same principle of materializing thought, of acting as a time machine.

Stephen himself found it out by accident one day when he was playing around, exploring the deserted warehouse premises. He noticed the boxlike apparatus and crawled inside, pretending for the moment that he was a hero like Pretty Boy Floyd, hiding out from the dirty old Feds. He didn't pay much attention to the blinking lights and whirling mirrors which became self-activating the moment he stepped inside and closed the door; he was wishing he had a gat to protect himself in case that archfiend J. Edgar Hoover showed up. He'd show him!

"All right, copper — you asked for it." And he'd reach in his pocket and pull out his gat, like this, and —

Stephen felt the weight before he saw it. And then he *did* pull his hand out of his pocket and he *was* holding a gat. A real roscoe, a genuine equalizer. Stephen stared at it, his thoughts whirling faster than the mirrors.

The gun — when did it come from? He'd just thought about it and it was here; how could that be? Actually, he hadn't even thought, just *wished*. The way he wished he had been around back in the Good Old Days, the way he was wishing now. He'd give anything to see real live American History in the making, like that morning of St. Valentine's Day in the garage on Clark Street. . . .

The mirrors revved faster and suddenly they disappeared. Everything disappeared. It was like a viddie dissolve, so Stephen wasn't frightened. He knew the next scene would come up right after the commercial. The next scene came up when the blurring stopped and he found himself sitting in the same box, the mirrors still whirring and he heard the noise outside. Stephen blinked, tugged at the door of the compartment, opened it, and saw the machine guns spit.

He knew where he was now. He'd seen it a dozen times on viddie, imagined it a thousand more. The garage, at eleven o'clock in the morning; the two executioners disguised in the uniforms of the hated police were mowing down the seven finks.

Stephen, in the subjectivity reactor, had materialized at the very instant the firing started. For thirty seconds Stephen stared at the finks as they writhed and fell. And during those thirty seconds the finks became men. Men who wriggled and flopped after the bullets struck, until the two swarthy hoods in uniform stepped up and completed their work with revolvers. There was blood on the wall and floor, and a terrible, acrid odor. The two men noticed it, too, and commented harshly in Italian. One of them laughed and spat on the floor.

Stephen wasn't laughing and he felt that unless he got out of here right away he'd do more than spit. He started to close the door and it was then that the executioners looked up and saw him.

"What the hell—" said the short one, and raised his revolver. His taller companion slapped it out of his hand.

"Wait," he said. He stooped, picked up the machine gun, and faced Stephen in the doorway of the compartment. "Awright, kid, how you get in here? Where you come from?" He raised the muzzle of his weapon. "C'mon, talk!"

Stephen talked. It was hard to, with the choking in his throat as he watched the machine gun muzzle that was like a cruel mouth—almost as cruel as the mouth of the man who held it. It was hard to explain, too, and he wasn't sure he understood the situation himself. Certainly the shorter assassin didn't understand, because he nudged his companion and said, "He's nuts! Hurry up and give it to him—we gotta get outa here!"

The big man with the machine gun shook his head. "Shaddup and listen. Dincha hear? This thing goes through time. It's a time machine. Aincha never heard?"

"*Porko Dio!* No such thing—"

"No such thing now." The big man nodded. "But maybe they invent it later on. That's where this kid comes from. How else you figure he got here if not like that?"

"So?"

"So you wanna get outa here, right?"

"Sure, to St. Louis. That's where Al said we'd get the payoff—"

"You know what kinda payoff we end up with." The big man made a nasty noise in his throat. "But suppose we *really* get out. Suppose we go back with the kid here."

He took a step forward. "Awright, kid, whaddya say?" He stared at Stephen.

Stephen stared back, into his face and the face of his companion. Here was his chance to take two real live gangsters back into his own world, his own time. It was something he'd always dreamed of. Only he had never dreamed they really looked and talked like this. And he had never dreamed the reality he glimpsed over their shoulders; the torn, huddled, oozing reality on the garage floor. Now he knew all there was to know about the Good Old Days.

The big man raised his weapon. "Hurry up! We ain't got all day. Whaddya say?"

Stephen knew he himself didn't have all day, or even another minute. Fortunately, thanks to the viddies, he knew what to say and how to say it. His hand squeezed the trigger inside his coat pocket. First the small man went down and then the big man.

As the big man fell there was a short, staccato burst from the machine gun. Several bullets punctured the shell of the compartment. But by this time Stephen had slammed the door of the subjectivity reactor and hurled himself to the floor in quivering panic, wishing with all his being that he was back where he belonged. . . .

He might have had a hard time explaining the presence of the gat if he hadn't wished so strongly that it would disappear. As it was, he emerged from the subjectivity reactor completely unscratched. To all intents and appearances, Stephen was unchanged by his experience.

The thing of it was that from then on he never watched *Scarface Al* any more.

"He's growing up," his mother said proudly.

"What did I tell you?" his father said. "I knew he'd get over it. All it takes is time."

When he said, "All it takes is time," he suddenly remembered Stephen's visit to the old storage building. That night he made a trip there himself to confirm his suspicions.

And there, as he expected, he found the subjectivity reactor — and the telltale impressions left by the machine gun bullets.

Funny thing, they didn't penetrate with half the force of the old Colt .45s. Stephen's father stooped until he found the holes near the bottom of the machine. Stephen's father remembered the day *those* shots had been fired.

Sometime he'd have to tell Stephen. Tell him how it was when *he* was a boy, when the machine had first been invented. Like father, like son.

Stephen's father gazed at the Colt bullet holes and smiled reminiscently. He too had had his viddie heroes in his youth. Only *his* personal favorite happened to be the *real* 1870 Wyatt Earp.

UNTOUCHABLE

RACE WAS BORED WITH INDIA.

"Nothing moves here, you know?" he griped. "Where's all the action?"

He gave everybody a hard time on location, and finally Simon took him on. Simon had always been able to handle him, and maybe that's why he was directing the picture; a lot of people just wouldn't work on a Race Harmon production any more.

"Look, sweetheart," he said. "I know it's been a drag. First the heat, then the rains, and then everybody coming down with the trots. Miller called me last night about the budget figures — the way he screamed, I could have heard him loud and clear from Bel Air without a phone."

"Let him suffer," Race muttered, then took a gulp of his drink. "I should bleed for him, shacked up in that air-conditioned office with the blonde throw-rug and a chick to match? Why doesn't he get off his butt and fly over here? We'll see how he likes being cooped up with a bunch of dumb niggers — "

"Please!" Simon frowned. "That's one of the things I wanted to warn you about. They're *not* niggers. Why, some of those technical people we hired out of the studios down in Bombay could run rings around any crew in Hollywood. The trouble is, they hear you talking on the set and they resent your attitude. Just remember, you're not home now."

"You can say that again! Where I come from, we call a spade a spade, whether he wears shoes or not. And that's the way it's gonna be, so kindly lay off the jazz, huh?"

Race poured himself another drink.

"Another thing," Simon said. "Aren't you hitting the sauce a little hard lately?"

"Got to get my kicks somewhere, Pops. This is a nothing unit here, you know? When we came out, I thought I had it made with Gladys, only she's got eyes for that Method swish, that Parker. So I gave a little play to this script girl of yours, Edna what's-her-name—"

"Messy." Simon sighed. "You didn't have to break into her trailer."

"All right, she made a federal case out of it." Race emptied his glass and thumped it down. "What am I supposed to do for some action? I'm hurting bad."

"Control yourself. We'll wrap up our location shots and be out of here in two weeks."

"Two weeks? Look, Dad, this is Race Harmon you're talking to, not Barry Fitzgerald. I may have to make the scene with some of that dark meat. Noticed all these chicks in the sarongs, or *saris*, whatever you call 'em, parading down by the river. Why I spotted one yesterday, she couldn't be a day over fifteen, but she had a pair of—"

"Race, that's murder!" Simon shook his head. "I saw you talking to that girl, and so did everyone else. You're lucky you left it at that—one false move and there'd have been a riot. I only hope they didn't hear about it up at the palace."

"So what?"

"Can't you understand? These people are *not* ignorant savages. You've met the Nizam; he's an intelligent man. If you want me to lay it on the line, I think he's a damned sight more civilized than you are."

"He's a nigger."

"Well, you'd better not make any such statements tonight," Simon said. "Don't forget, we're invited to the palace for dinner."

"I'll eat here."

"You'll come to the palace." Simon's voice was firm. "It's important, Race. We're guests here in the Nizam's territory. We've rented his land, hired his people. We can't afford to offend him. I want you to show up sober and on your best behavior. Is that clear?"

"I dig you, Pops." Race waved his glass. "Okle-dokle, it's a take. Who knows? Maybe he'll give us a little of that old Southern hospitality—"

The Nizam's hospitality was lavish and unmistakable. There were twenty at table, including Race, Simon, and the principals of the cast. The only representative of the Nizam's household was a bearded Sikh whom he introduced as his major-domo.

"Actually, Rass Singh commanded the palace guard," the Nizam explained. "But since I am no longer the official ruler of this territory, he too has been deposed. We have bowed to progress, or at least, to governmental decree."

"They took away your title, huh?" Race paused and emptied his champagne glass for the fourth time since starting dinner. "I suppose they got to your harem, too."

"Harem? But I am not a Moslem, my dear fellow."

The Nizam was plump, middle-aged, bespectacled, and he wore a conservative gray tweed suit. But his complexion was unmistakably swarthy, and people with unmistakably swarthy complexions didn't go around calling Race Harmon "my dear fellow." Even if they *did* serve damned good champagne.

"Come off it!" he said, holding out his glass for a refill. "Everybody knows you rajahs have a ball. I'll bet the joint is full of—whaddya call 'em?—concubines. Yeah, concubines. That's the bit."

"Sorry," the Nizam answered. "I'm afraid I can't oblige you, Mr. Harmon."

"Never mind the double-talk," Race told him. "Bring on the dancing girls!"

"*Devi-dasi?* But they are confined to their temples."

"So take me to your temple!" Race laughed, then broke off as he realized none of the others were joining in.

The Nizam stared at an imaginary spot on the table linen before him. "Perhaps it would be wise, Mr. Harmon, if I explained the customs of my country. Nonbelievers are not welcomed in our places of worship. There is a certain—prejudice, shall we say? You see, there is still ignorance amongst my people. They even resent the notion of a stranger approaching a *pariah*, such as the water-carriers in the village. It would be most embarrassing if an outsider were to exhibit any—any—"

"So you heard about that, eh?" Race waved his glass. "I get the message. Hands off, is that it? Yankee, go home!"

"Please, Mr. Harmon—"

"Never mind. You heard about old Race, huh? That's why you locked up the harem."

"I assure you, I have only one wife. At the moment she happens to be in *purdah*. She is untouchable."

"Untouchable?" Race grinned. "Sure, they're all untouchable, aren't they? Well let me tell you something. Nobody upstages me. And if I want a little poontang, I'm gonna get it, understand?"

"Poontang?"

"What's the matter, don't you niggers understand plain English?" Race stood up, ignoring Simon's frantic gestures. "Ah, forget it. Where's the head?"

The Nizam glanced at his major-domo. Race watched them, fuzzily alert for any indication of anger. That's what he was waiting for; just let the nigger blow his top and he'd *really* let him have it.

But there was no anger, merely a quiet exchange of glances and a nod.

Then the bearded Sikh rose and gestured politely, and Race followed him out of the room and down a long, dim corridor.

For a moment there was silence in the dining hall behind; then everybody started talking at the same time.

Covering up, Race thought. *The civilized bit.* Well, if they wanted to be polite to niggers, that was their business. He knew what *he* wanted to do. What had that snotty spade said about his wife? She was in *purdah,* whatever the hell that was. And damned lucky, too, because right now, if he could find her —

"Here we are, sir." The bearded man bowed and stepped aside. Race entered a modern bathroom.

Three minutes later he stood before the mirror, shaking the cold water out of his eyes and toweling off his face. He'd sobered somewhat, just enough to feel a sneaking distaste about rejoining the others in the banquet hall. Maybe the best idea was to just cut out of here.

He stepped into the deserted hall, moving slowly past a row of closed doors. That is, they had all been closed when he'd followed the major-domo. Now one of them was slightly ajar. As he passed he was aware of a heavy, musky scent drifting into the corridor.

Race halted and peered into a darkened room. Moonlight filtered from barred windows. Beneath the windows was a couch. On the couch was a girl. Her sole garment was a *sari* and she wore no ornaments, but such artifices were unnecessary. She was young and lovely, and when she rose in wide-eyed wonder the *sari*'s transparency disclosed an undulating outline in the moonlight.

"Hot damn!" Race muttered, as he stepped inside and closed the door behind him.

"Sir —"

The girl moved back toward the couch.

"Sir —"

Race grinned and reached for her.

"Please, sir — it is not permitted. I am untouchable —"

Her knees pressed against the couch and she fell. Race held her there, his hands ripping the soft silk, feeling the incredible warmth of the body beneath. For a moment she writhed in resistance, until his lips found the fiery crater of her mouth, its tongue erupting like molten lava.

"Untouchable, huh, baby?" Race whispered. "Well, we'll see about that —"

He left her sobbing, without a word. What the hell was there to say? He knew she wouldn't talk, and neither would he. If anybody back at the banquet hall asked where he'd been so long, he'd tell them he got sick, heaved his cookies. Nobody would ask any questions.

But sometime, just before they pulled out of here for good, he'd find a way of letting the Nizam know what happened. That uppity nigger thought he was so damned smart, handing out a line of jazz about keeping his hands off all the chicks. It would be a real gasser to see his face when he found out somebody had scored with his wife.

Well, he'd played it cute, but Race had the last laugh. It was all he could do to keep from busting out right now when he walked back into the banquet scene.

He got a real break because nobody even seemed to notice when he came in. They were all standing around some guy in a white suit at the head of the table.

Then the Nizam looked up and saw him.

"Feeling better, Mr. Harmon?" he asked.

Race nodded, trying to hold back the grin.

"That is good. But if you felt ill, you could consult with Dr. Ghopura, here."

Race blinked. "You called a doctor for me?"

"No — it just so happened that he arrived a few moments ago. I asked him to fly in from Bombay."

"It is useless, of course," the little doctor said. "If what you told me is true, the patient will surely die. All I can hope to do is ease the suffering in the terminal phase. I only pray you have kept her isolated."

"Wait a minute!" Race's throat was dry. "Your wife — she's sick — ?"

"My wife is in *purdah*, Mr. Harmon, in Bombay. We are speaking about a poor untouchable from the village whom I discovered the other day. I brought her here immediately to avoid panic and the spread of contagion, for the disease is invariably fatal."

"What disease?"

"Cholera."

The Nizam shrugged and turned away. "Doctor, if you will come with me, please? Her room is right down the hall — "

Everything started to whirl. Just before he fell, Race thought he saw the Nizam exchange a smile with his major-domo, but he could not be sure. All he was sure of was the pain flooding his head and throat. It was a hot pain — hot and throbbing, like the mouth and tongue of the untouchable.

METHOD FOR MURDER

ALICE WENT INTO THE STUDY when Charles called her.

It wasn't really a study, just his workroom. The place where he wrote all his silly mysteries and suspense novels, or whatever they were called.

Alice didn't like the study because it was filled with books, and because it was filled with Charles.

With a contract to deliver four novels a year, he spent most of his time in here. And when he wasn't working, all he could talk about was his writing. It was like an obsession with him; his characters were more real to Charles than she was.

Right now he was showing her some little pen-and-ink sketches of the people in his next book; he had written capsule biographies of each character, too, and described each one in great detail. Charles explained everything very carefully and Alice nodded her head just as though she were listening, though she never listened to him any more.

Then she saw Dominick.

Dominick had a long, thin face, matted hair, and a scraggly beard. And there was something strange about the way his mouth twisted.

"That's because he's giggling," Charles said. "Remember that picture Richard Widmark played in years ago? He giggled when he killed. It's a good tag, that giggle. Helps to make a character come alive."

Alice stared at the picture, and now she listened to him.

"Funny thing," Charles was saying. "Somehow, the villains are always more real to me than the heroes. I suppose that's why I write the sort of things I do. Perhaps it's a subconscious identification with the monster role. Dr. Jekyll, playing Hyde-and-seek." Charles giggled, a bit, himself.

Alice stared at the picture.

"Who is he?" she asked.

"Dominick?" Charles was flattered by her interest, that was obvious. And he was quite taken with Dominick; that was obvious, too. "Dominick is a strangler who has escaped from an asylum for the criminally insane. He takes refuge in this —"

He went on and on. When he'd finished, Alice knew all there was to know about Dominick. And all she needed to know about everything else. She made sure of it by asking questions.

"Just one thing more, darling," she concluded. "Is it a high or a low giggle?"

Charles blinked, like a partially animated stuffed owl. "Why, a high giggle, I suppose." He squinted. "Yes, of course, it would be a high giggle. Quite hysterical, in fact."

Alice nodded and went away, and her husband started to type. Aside from mealtimes and odd moments, devoted to cat naps, Charles typed steadily the next three days.

He came out of the study just once during the third day to tell her he'd lost his sketch of Dominick.

Alice looked up from her knitting. "Then draw another," she said.

Charles went into his blinking routine again. "Good idea," he said. "You know something, my dear? Dominick is taking over. That's always a good sign — when the villain takes over the book. Lends a certain three-dimensional quality to the menace."

He went back to his work and Alice resumed her knitting. In a few hours he burst out of the study again. This time he wasn't blinking. He was staring.

"Alice!" he cried. "Something's happened!"

"So I gather." Alice put her knitting aside. "But what?"

Charles shook his head. "I don't know," he said, in an unsteady voice. "It's Dominick. He's alive!"

"I'm so glad, dear."

"You don't understand. I'm not talking about the book. He's actually alive, there in my study. He peered in at me through the window about five minutes ago — I thought it must be an hallucination. Then he opened the window and came inside." He faltered. "I know it sounds crazy, but —"

Alice stood up.

"Where are you going?" Charles murmured.

"Into your study, of course."

"But you can't — he's dangerous —"

Alice sniffed and marched into the study. She stared around the room while Charles cowered in the doorway behind her.

"I don't see anything," Alice said. "Where is he?"

"Right over there," Charles pointed a none-too-firm finger. "Right over there, in that chair."

"Nothing in that chair," Alice told him. She walked over to the chair and pressed the seat-cushion down with her hand. "See?"

"But he moved—he got up and walked over to the corner, there, when you came close. Don't you see him?"

Alice gazed at the corner and shook her head.

"Can't you even hear what he's saying?" Charles was almost begging her now. "Listen, he's explaining it all. He says he's a creature of my creative force, born of my psychic energy. He is a materialization of my imaginative faculties—"

Alice went over to Charles and put her hand on his forehead. "You have a fever, darling," she said. "Come up to bed."

She led him from the room, ignoring his backward glances. By the time he reached the bedroom he was trembling. She helped him undress and pulled the covers over him.

"You'll be all right in the morning," she nodded.

"No!" Suddenly Charles sat bolt upright in bed. "Don't leave me! He's here—here in this room—listen to him giggle! He's going to kill me—"

Charles tugged at her arm. "You can't leave me alone with him—"

"I must," Alice answered. "I have to call the doctor."

Dr. Anderson came right over, but he found nothing wrong. "That's because he left when he heard you come in," Charles explained. Dr. Anderson nodded understandingly, administered a sedative, then drew Alice aside out in the hall. She told him what had happened and he gave her the name of this Dr. Richter.

In the morning she passed the name along to Charles. "But I have no intention of consulting a psychiatrist!" he snapped. "It was just temporary exhaustion. I'd been pressing too hard. Now let me get up; I've got work to do."

That afternoon, when she heard the sudden outcry from the study, Alice didn't even wait for the door to open. She put down her knitting and called Dr. Richter.

This time Charles offered no objections. He got ready to keep his appointment for late afternoon, and at Alice's suggestion he took a cab down to the psychiatrist's office. Obviously he was in no condition to drive.

After he left, Alice made another phone call and in a short while another cab pulled up in front of the house. Van Thornton came in. Nobody saw him, because of the wooded grounds all around the house—Charles's books really brought in a great deal of money, Alice told herself.

And then she stopped reflecting, and just reacted, in Van's arms. It was he, and not she, who finally pulled away.

"What did I tell you?" he said. "I'm doing great—absolutely great!"

"The moment I saw that picture, I knew," she giggled. "It all seemed to come to me in a flash—I said to myself, that's just the way Van would look if he wore a beard. And then everything fell into place, the whole plan, all at once. Maybe I've learned something about plotting from listening to that fat slug all these years."

"Well you won't have to listen much longer, baby!" Thornton squeezed her arm. "Not the way I'm playing.

"Remember how they used to kid me down at the Troupers—all that jazz about being a Method actor? Well, now you're seeing how it pays off when you play for real." He chuckled, low and throaty—the sound was quite different, Alice noted, from the hysterical giggling of last night. Thornton *was* a good actor; he'd picked up everything she told him.

"It's going to work, doll," he muttered. "I know that, now. You and me, the perfect team!" Then he sobered. "So what's next on the program?"

Alice sat down and picked up her knitting. "Here's the way I thought it should go," she began. . . .

And that's the way it went. Charles had an appointment with Dr. Richter every afternoon, now. In between times he just sat around in the living room. He wouldn't go near the study any more, because he was afraid. Several times he saw Dominick staring in at him through the windows, and after that he avoided work. Sometimes, at night, he'd wake up with a scream, claiming he heard giggling in the hall.

Dr. Richter had it all down in his notes. But that didn't help Charles any. "The man's an idiot!" he snapped. "You know what he had the nerve to hint to me? Oh, he didn't dare come right out and say it, but I know what he was driving at. Schizophrenia. That's his diagnosis. I'm indulging in an imaginary projection of my own character. Writing is like acting, in a way, he says. A certain role takes hold, captures the imagination—"

Alice sighed. "I thought we agreed not to talk about that any more. You're just overtired. Stretch out on the sofa and relax."

"I can't relax," Charles whined. "Could *you*, knowing that at any moment you might look around and see—"

"There, there, darling." She made all the right sounds and all the right gestures and he lay down. Within a few minutes he dozed off, because he was really very tired.

Charles was sound asleep when she started to scream. He blinked, sat up, jerked to his feet, his eyes bulging and rolling as he stared at Dominick's hands around her throat. By the time he was halfway across the room, Dominick was gone, and Alice shrank away from him as he approached.

"Don't!" she whimpered. "Don't touch me! You've already done enough!"

"I? What do you mean—?"

"Look!" She gestured toward her throat. The livid marks were plainly visible in the lamplight.

"Dominick," he whispered. "He tried to strangle you."

She began to sob. "There is no Dominick. *You* did that."

He could only blink at her.

"You got up off the couch and grabbed me. And then you started to choke me, and you giggled and giggled—"

Charles wasn't giggling. He was shaking. Shaking all over. Both his chins wobbled.

Alice went to the phone. "I'm going to call Dr. Richter," she said.

"But it's eight o'clock—he's not in his office—"

"This is an emergency," she told him. "He'll see you."

"Couldn't he come out here?"

Alice shook her head and her lips formed a grim line before she spoke. "I don't want him to see *me*," she said.

Charles sat down on the sofa. "I don't want to go," he whispered. "I don't want to go."

But in the end, he went.

He went, and Alice waited. She didn't knit now; just sat very quietly, glancing at her wristwatch from time to time.

Now Charles would be reaching the office. Now he would be talking to Dr. Richter, telling him what happened. She could see it now—like a scene from a play. And the psychiatrist calming Charles, explaining the workings of his imagination, how a character can become real when you live with it day after day, how a part of you begins to believe that you are that character. Oh, it was all very convincing and it was all a lot of nonsense. Dr. Richter must be a very stupid man, even for a psychiatrist.

Alice wondered if he was realizing his own stupidity, now. For now must be the time when it was happening. The time when Dominick would appear. He would walk down the deserted corridor and into the psychiatrist's office, opening the door very quietly as he tiptoed in. He would creep up behind Dr. Richter while Charles lay on the couch, and then his hands would swoop down and he would strangle him. Strangle him very swiftly and very expertly, using his thumbs to crush the windpipe. And Charles would watch, paralyzed with fear; too paralyzed to even scream. The screaming would come later, after Dominick left. With luck, Charles would keep right on screaming—even after they found him there with Dr. Richter's body. Even after they read Dr. Richter's notes about the schizophrenia, and came to question her, and put Charles away. They had places for people who couldn't stop screaming.

But Alice caught herself; she was thinking too far ahead, and she must concentrate on now. Now was when Thornton should be driving out. Now was when she ought to turn on the radio and wait for the ten o'clock news. Now was when she should hear Thornton's key turning in the door. He had his key, of course.

And here he was, right on schedule. Still wearing that nasty beard and those black gloves she'd had the good sense to insist on. He looked positively horrible.

Alice had the radio turned up, and she had to almost shout at him over it, but he heard her and immediately went to the desk in the corner where she'd laid out the alcohol and the cold cream. He peeled off his gloves and started to remove the beard. Then he got rid of the makeup.

It was good to see his own face again. Alice wanted to see his face before she asked him how things had gone. Somehow it would ease the situation—make things seem a little less awkward. She and Thornton would really be talking about another person; a person who no longer existed. Just as Dr. Richter no longer existed—

Alice started over to the radio, to turn it down so that she could speak, and he stood up and made a restraining gesture with his hand. Then she realized what the voice on the radio was saying.

"We interrupt this broadcast to bring you a special news bulletin—"

And here it was, she didn't have to ask Thornton after all, because the radio was telling her. Brutal slaying . . . prominent psychiatrist and his patient found strangled . . .

And his patient?

Alice snapped the switch and faced Thornton.

"Charles is dead, too?"

Thornton nodded. "Both of them are quite dead. Richter first, then Charles. It was very easy. Much easier than I'd imagined."

Alice felt the anger rise. "But that wasn't the plan—don't you understand? The whole point was to establish Charles as a schizophrenic. So they'd convict him of Dr. Richter's murder and put him away."

"It's better this way. Much better."

Alice was almost ready to hit him. "How can you say that? Don't you see—now they'll be looking for a killer. We haven't got a madman any more. Thornton, what if they come looking for you?"

He stared at her for a moment and he seemed quite bewildered. Then, "Thornton?" he said. "I don't know anyone named Thornton."

She wanted to scream at him then, scream that they still had their madman and there was a Method in his madness. But there was no time, because his hands came up around her throat, and he started giggling.

The Living End

When Herbert Zane received the Nobel Prize in Science, his acceptance speech was simple.

"All that I am," said Herbert, "I owe to my wife."

Which was quite true, because Herbert hated his wife.

Fifteen years ago, at the time of their wedding, he had been very much in love with Hilda. During the early months of marriage he had spent all of his nights and a good part of his days in demonstrating his affection — but somehow those demonstrations had never quite come off. His most painstaking and elaborate experiments in amour always failed completely. All of Herbert's profound knowledge of anatomy and physiology did not come to his aid; while he could evoke miracles of response from a guinea pig in the laboratory, he got no reaction from Hilda in the boudoir.

Finally Herbert faced up to the facts, as scientists must do; his most devoted research in the field of physical passion had brought him, quite literally, to a dead end. Turning his back on Hilda, he dedicated himself entirely to the pursuit of his profession.

Hilda didn't object to him turning his back to her — as least, not within the confines of their double bed — but she became increasingly impatient with his open neglect by day.

As a result she began to nag him, and because of *that*, Herbert's indifference was transformed into actual hatred.

Some men answer nagging wives with a sharp rejoinder; Herbert was more interested in scientific retorts. Other husbands might take refuge in the bottle; Herbert preferred the test tube. So it really was because of his hatred that he spent so much time in the laboratory and became such an eminent scientist.

By the time he won the Nobel Prize, the two of them scarcely exchanged a word; she didn't ask what he planned to do with the money and he didn't tell her. It wasn't until all the new and complicated apparatus was moved into the basement that she opened her mouth in a question.

"What's all this stuff for?" she asked.

"Gravity."

"You're going to experiment on gravity? Is that what you need these fancy machines for? Why couldn't you be sensible and buy a dishwasher and a new vacuum cleaner—"

Herbert shook his head impatiently. "Gravity is just a part of the problem," he muttered. "Sterols, too."

Then he went downstairs and stayed there. He spent four months and forty thousand dollars. He started with a hypothesis, evolved a theory, developed working experiments, and came up with an ultimate achievement.

It was a very ultimate achievement indeed—for Herbert Zane perfected nothing less than an elixir of immortality.

And when he came up with it (in a small, one-ounce bottle) he still had nothing to say. There was no sense even trying to explain anything to Hilda. He couldn't tell her that during the long years in the laboratory he cursed the idea that he was wasting his life tied to a stupid shrew. He couldn't tell her he drowned his curses in dreams of the day he might finally be free of her and then—as is the way with scientists—attempted to translate his dreams into reality. He'd experimented endlessly, with fruit flies and frogs, with roaches and white rats. Now, finally, he'd succeeded. And there was nothing to do but exercise his scientific patience and wait.

Herbert knew he could never give his gift to the world; mankind as a whole wasn't ready for immortality. If the news ever leaked out, there'd be bloodshed. Granting perpetual life to a favored or wealthy few would mean war and revolution, and extending it to everyone would bring overpopulation and perpetual famine.

So he decided to drink the elixir himself and then just sit back and sweat it out until Hilda died of old age. After all, there'd be plenty of time to enjoy himself in the future—he had all eternity ahead of him.

And someday, perhaps, he *could* reveal his great achievement. Herbert had visions of himself sitting before a cabana at Antibes, gazing into the frank, open eyes and cleavage of a voluptuous and understanding blonde— someone like Brigitte Bardot's granddaughter, perhaps.

Softly and tenderly he'd murmur of how he'd investigated physiological deterioration, which he felt was linked with the pull of gravity upon the internal organs and cellular structure of the body. He'd whisper his belief that once they lost the proper tonus, it was possible for various sterol compounds to form, which in turn led to the degenerative processes of senescence. Gently he'd impart the thrilling news that if a biochemical means could be found to counteract these processes, the regenerative function of the individual cells would remain unimpaired and the result would be perpetual life. Then, as he lifted her to her feet and led her into the cabana, he would reveal the greatest news of all—he had found the biochemical solution.

And as she stared up at him, eyes and cleavage widening, she would gasp, "But *cherie*, is it that you mean to tell me you will live forever? *How old are you?*"

"One hundred and five," Herbert would boom triumphantly, as he hurled himself upon her—

Oh, it was a great dream, and an even greater reality. Because it *was* reality, it need never end. If he liked, he might confer immortality upon Brigitte Bardot's granddaughter or Kim Novak's great-great-stepniece, if they particularly pleased him and he preferred to do so. But perhaps not; no sense in building up a perpetual harem when he had free choice of all the billions of women yet unborn. It might be that even the most beautiful and passionate females would grow tiresome in time. Right now he was sure of only one thing; he was already tired to death of unbeautiful, unpassionate Hilda. Not really "tired to death," of course, because once he drank his elixir he would never die.

So Herbert Zane emerged from his laboratory, an ounce of immortality in his hand, and settled down to wait. He planned to drink off the potion that very night, but first—

First there was his duty as a trained and dedicated scientist. Even if he had no intention of ever revealing his discovery to the world at large, he must still set down his findings in accurate, orderly form. There were all his notes and observations of experiments to transcribe, starting from the day he first conferred immortality on two fruit flies (whom, in a burst of unscientific sentimentality, he immediately had christened "Adam" and "Eve").

Going into his study, Herbert placed the precious bottle of elixir at his left elbow, stacked his notes on the desk at the right of the typewriter, and went to work. It was a tedious process, and Herbert was already at the point of physical and nervous exhaustion. Somewhere along the line, he fell asleep.

And somewhere along the line, while he slept, Hilda must have tiptoed in to stare at him, peer over his shoulder, and then read what he had written.

Because Herbert was awakened by her whoop of joy.

"Oh, darling!" she wheezed, all three of her chins quivering with the intensity of her delight. "I couldn't resist peeking, and now I understand! You went and did it, didn't you, without even breathing an itsy-bitsy word to me, and here all along I thought you were just being mean! But it was a secret, wasn't it, and you wanted to surprise me!"

"Huh?" Herbert inquired.

"I'm talking about *this!*" And Hilda lifted the tiny one-ounce bottle containing the elixir of immortality. "You made it just for *us*, didn't you — just for we two, so we can always be together. Oooh, isn't he the sweetums boy — "

"Hey, what do you think you're doing?" Herbert gasped.

Hilda uncorked the bottle and lifted it to her lips. "I'm taking my half, of course, silly," she informed him. "Ladies first! Well, here's looking at you — "

But she wasn't looking at him, and that was her mistake. With a snarl of mingled rage and apprehension, Herbert sprang at her and wrenched the bottle from her fingers. As the precious liquid began to spatter, he thrust the bottle between his teeth and drained it dry at a single gulp. A fiery essence coursed through his veins, flowed through his fingers as they closed about Hilda's fat neck. Everything turned red before him — including her astonished face. Then she stuck her tongue out at him. By the time he realized what this meant and relaxed his grip, her face wasn't red any more. It was quite purple. And Hilda herself was quite dead.

Herbert didn't panic.

Quickly, he considered the situation. Hilda was dead, and nothing could change that now. The best thing to do was to get rid of all the evidence. First he broke the bottle, then he burned all his notes and papers. Then he got ready to drag Hilda's body down into the basement and stuff it into the furnace. It was a gruesome project, but he had no choice. Besides, he was immortal now — and the stakes were worth it. He was fighting for eternity. The sight of Hilda's flabby corpse unnerved him, but he'd be able to forget about it in time. And there would always be plenty of time —

That's what he was thinking as he started to drag it down the cellar steps. That's what he was thinking as the doorbell rang and the neighbor lady stepped into the kitchen, unannounced, to ask Hilda for a cup of flour.

She didn't get her flour, but she did get a glimpse of Hilda on the steps — and ran out, screaming.

Herbert ran out, too, but he didn't scream. Not even when the squad car caught up with him, three blocks down the street. Not even when he was questioned, booked, indicted, and tried for murder. Immortals are proud people.

Herbert Zane didn't scream at all. Not until the very moment, after the verdict was brought in, when the judge said, "I sentence you to imprisonment for life — "

IMPRACTICAL JOKER

THERE'S ONLY ONE TROUBLE being a practical joker — after a while, it gets so that people don't really believe what you say.

Teddy had a hell of a time convincing Mac that he meant what he said about quitting. He told him about it during the supper break, while the relief bartender took over, and at first Mac just couldn't get it through his head.

"I really mean it," Teddy said. "This is my last night. Tomorrow I'm pulling out for Canada. See, here's the plane ticket. Picked it up this afternoon."

When Teddy showed him the ticket for Toronto, Mac finally realized he wasn't kidding. But he still didn't understand.

"I don't get it," he told Teddy. "I thought you liked it here."

"You know how it is," Teddy said. "A guy gets itchy."

"Is it the dough?" Mac fiddled around with his coffee cup. "You been good for business, I was gonna give you a raise anyhow, first of September. I could maybe go another fifteen a week. That's good wages for a night bartender."

Teddy shook his head. "It isn't money," he said. "I'm just fed up with working. Besides, it's so damned hot in here. Honest Mac, I don't see how you ever stood it, summer nights like this."

Mac grunted at him. "Guy's got to stand a lot of things if he wants to build a business. But the way the Fun House is going now, next year we can go for air conditioning. Whaddya say, Teddy? Stick it out for a while — another couple of weeks and there won't be any more heat waves. You got yourself a good following here. What's the sense of kicking it and starting out all over again?"

"You don't get me, Mac." Teddy chose his words carefully. "I'm not going

95

to start over again. I'm quitting the bartending racket for good, as of tomorrow."

"Tomorrow?" Mac spilled some of his coffee into the saucer. "You can't do that to me. Tomorrow's Saturday — I'll have one hell of a time getting a man for tomorrow night. You know I can't put a dog on for Saturday, it's our biggest rush."

"Tough." Teddy fingered his ticket. "But I already made my reservation." He leaned forward. "I know this puts you on the spot, Mac. By rights you're supposed to have at least two weeks' notice. But did you ever happen to figure that maybe I'm on the spot too?"

Mac blinked at him. "You mean you got to leave town, is that it?"

Teddy shrugged. "I never robbed any banks," he said. "You know me better than that. A whole year I been here and never got my hand caught in the register."

He paused, letting it sink in. Mac began to nod. "It's a dame, isn't it?" he murmured. "That Ella, maybe. You got her in trouble, huh?"

Teddy made a production out of looking at the floor. "I'm not saying anything, Mac. Not a word. All I can tell you is I'm sorry about the rush act, but I want out. I want out bad."

Mac stood up then and put his big hand on Teddy's shoulder. "All right," he said. "I guess we can manage OK. But stop around in the morning, will you? We'll check the take like we always do, and I'll settle for this week."

"Sure," Teddy said. "Ten o'clock, same as always."

Then Mac went away, and that was that. Promptly at eight the relief man left, and for a few minutes Teddy had the joint all to himself.

It was nice to be alone in the Fun House. This was the time Teddy always liked best — the little break between the late afternoon customers and the evening regulars. There was nobody around to make trouble for you, nobody hollering for a shot or spilling their beer or trying to get you to listen to some dirty joke you already heard maybe a hundred times and couldn't even laugh at the first time. There was no one shoving nickels into the jukebox, or yelling for you to turn on the television.

Come to think of it, tonight he'd get a break — the lousy ball games weren't on, according to the schedule. And he could turn down the volume on the juke. Chances were, there wouldn't be too much business anyway. Maybe he could take it easy and relax.

Teddy turned and faced the mirror. The minute he saw himself he knew that he wasn't going to take it easy. He couldn't relax. Not when he looked in the mirror and remembered who he was. Teddy Baer. A fat-faced little guy with ginger-colored fuzz all over the top of his skull. He looked like Teddy Baer, all right. No wonder they always called him by that nickname, ever since he was a kid, instead of Donald. Not that Donald was such a hot name, either, but it was better than Teddy.

Teddy Baer.

Funny, he hadn't minded it for a long time; got used to it, he guessed, because wherever he went some wise guy would think of his last name and then take a good look at him and come up with that Teddy Baer crack. Very clever.

But Teddy went along with the gag, and maybe that's what helped him get started as a practical joker. What's a little guy to do, especially if he's too fat to be handy with his dukes? He might as well grin and bear it. And the jokes helped too—if you had to take it, once in a while you got a chance to dish it out.

No, he hadn't really minded his nickname until Ella came along. He remembered how she used to come in at first, all alone, and sit way down at the end of the bar. At first he spotted her for a neighborhood tramp, but he learned different. She never tried to give anyone the business, and when a couple of the regulars tried to move in they got a very fast brush. Ella just liked to sit down at the end of the bar and drink maybe two–three beers on a hot night. Along about the second week she started bringing in a book with her and sitting in a booth.

That's when Teddy found out she was a student, up at Columbia. She'd come from some hick town in Indiana, and she was going to be a biologist. He might have figured it was something like that; she didn't look like a pushover. Not Ella, with that clean, scrubbed look that comes from not wearing any makeup. She always smelled kind of fresh, and her voice was so soft, and she had a way of looking up at you when she talked like a kid trying to please a grown-up.

What the hell was the use of kidding about it; Teddy was nuts about her. He'd known a couple of dames in his time, what bartender hasn't, but they were just the usual line of pigs. That's all a bartender usually gets to meet, seeing what his hours are and where he does business. But this Ella was a different proposition.

At least, he always thought so, until after he took her out a few times on his off-nights, and got around to telling her he was serious.

Mac had an idea that Teddy had given her the business, and that's just what Teddy wanted him to think.

How could he tell him the truth? How could he tell him that Ella had tried to let him down gently; told him that it would never work, because she had a career to think of and he was—let's face it—just a bartender? And then, when Teddy kept after her, when he was practically down on his knees begging her, she'd laughed. Laughed at him, because he was a funny old Teddy Baer, and it was all a joke; he was a practical joker, couldn't he take a joke on himself?

Teddy took it, all right.

He even took it when Ella started to come in after that with her friends from the school. He noticed she never showed up alone any more, and that bothered him plenty, but he made up his mind to take it. Ella was always very friendly and polite, and she never made fun of him, so he took it just for the pleasure of seeing her once or twice a week.

But lately, she'd stopped coming around for almost a month—and then, last Saturday, she came in with this guy. This young punk, this tall snotnose with the crewcut and the wise-guy glasses. The minute Teddy saw him, he knew. And he watched the two of them sitting together in the booth, all evening. It was Saturday, and on Saturday nights Teddy never served the booths. But he could see them, laughing together, and drinking martinis. Beer wasn't good enough for her any more. No, she had to drink martinis, one of those snotty college-type drinks.

The two of them had been so busy playing footsie in the booth that when they went out the guy had even forgotten his satchel. Briefcase is what it really was, and Teddy noticed it right after they left.

He could have run out the front door and maybe hailed the guy before he got away, but he didn't. Let the punk come back. Donald Thomas, his name was, stamped in gold letters right on the briefcase. That was a coincidence for you. This guy's name was Donald, too. But nobody was calling him Teddy. Nobody was making corny remarks about him or handing him a hard time. He was tall and young and going to college and he had a future ahead of him. A future, and Ella.

So let him come back and look for his lousy briefcase.

Teddy had put it away under the bar, not even bothering to try and open it. Full of schoolwork, probably. Well, it couldn't be too important, or he'd have remembered and come back for it on Monday.

Chances were, he intended to pick it up again on Saturday night. Teddy had a hunch he'd come in then. Him and Ella.

But he wouldn't be around to see them.

Just when he made up his mind to clear out, Teddy couldn't remember. Maybe it had been last Saturday night, when Ella left with the guy.

That was the time the headache had started, anyway. He'd had a headache ever since. At first he thought it was something he ate, maybe he'd better cut down on the fried food for a few days. Then he figured it must be the heat. This last heat wave was murder, and it kept hanging on and hanging on. And no air conditioning. Of course the fans helped a little, but when you got a lot of traffic and had to rush around behind the bar, you wilted fast. And how many times had he been forced to listen to that crack about, "It's not the heat, it's the stupidity?"

It was the stupidity, all right, but he wasn't going to take much more of it. Or the heat, either.

He couldn't take much more of it. Running back and forth behind the bar, sweating his eyeballs off, and all the while this pounding in the back of his head. It was like something had tightened up inside him, all his neck muscles, when he saw Ella and that guy together for the first time. And he'd been seeing them ever since — when he went to his room at night and laid down on the hot bed, closing his eyes. That's when he could see them best. Ella and Donald. Ella and Donald sitting together. Ella and Donald laughing. Ella and Donald kissing. Ella and Donald —

No, he couldn't tell Mac the truth about that. Let him think he'd gotten her into trouble. Just too damned bad it *wasn't* that way. He wished it was, now. If he had a chance to do it all over again, she'd never be able to laugh at him. Because the first time he got her alone, he'd have his hand over her mouth, and he'd shove her down, the lousy pig, and —

Teddy turned away from the mirror. He didn't like to look at himself when his face changed that way. It was like seeing a stranger. A stranger with a splitting headache, a stranger with a head ready to bust because there was too much inside it. Something had to give, something had to spill out.

Maybe he was ready to flip. Lots of guys flipped in hot weather like this; guys who didn't have his kind of trouble to think about, either.

Well, he wouldn't have the trouble much longer. He was getting out while the getting was good. Getting out fast, before tomorrow night, before there was a chance of seeing Ella again. He knew he couldn't take any more.

That's why he'd insisted on quitting after tonight. And Mac had let him. Tomorrow evening he'd be up where it was nice and cool. So now, why not forget about it?

Teddy glanced at the clock. A little after eight, time to clear the decks for action. The bar was clean. He'd already done a bottle check, and there was plenty of ice. Let's see; the relief bartender had washed up the glasses, and checked the pressure on the taps. Teddy opened the refrigerator. Must be almost five cases on ice — that ought to hold them for tonight, even if it was hot. Unless some damned queer came in and asked for ale. Those lousy queers and their ale! There wasn't anything Teddy hated worse, unless it was the smart young punks who never told you they wanted a beer but always said, "Give me a brew." There was a smart, sophisticated remark for you! "Give me a brew." Teddy could spot that kind a mile off. They were the ones who never told you the exact size of anything, either; they made a gesture with their hands and said it was, "Yea big."

Teddy would like to give them all something "Yea big"; jam it right down their throats. Yes, them and the guys who came in to cry over the way the horse ran out, and the guys who came in to cry over the way the wife ran out, and the guys who came in to cry over the way the dough ran out. He hated them all. And he hated the laughing-boys and the women who wanted their martinis "Very, *very* dry, please," and the old moochers who tried to peddle papers but got mad if anybody actually took one, and wanted you to hand them out a free shot, too. He hated the tramps, and he hated the lonely guys who tried to pick them up, and he hated the married couples who said this was their fifteenth wedding anniversary and expected you to pop, and he hated the soldiers and the sailors and the goddam Marine Corps and —

Jesus, who didn't he hate?

It was the heat, it was the headache. He'd better grab a quickie and ease up.

Teddy poured out a drink. Come to think of it, he'd been drinking a lot this last week; usually he never even touched the stuff, and when somebody was buying he settled for a cigar. But the sauce had kept him going, particularly when he couldn't sleep. And seeing as how this was the last night, he might as well help himself to something off the top shelf. Mac wouldn't care; he owed him a few shots. Besides, the hell with Mac.

But he had to stop that kind of stuff. As the drink went down — hot, but then the whole place was like an oven anyway — Teddy tried to argue himself out of it.

He was Teddy Baer, and he was on duty tonight for the last time. Teddy Baer, just a ton of fun, always good for a laugh, the best back-bar joker in the business. He could tell a story, he could pull a rib, he could give a hotfoot with a straight face. All during this last week, Teddy had been doing more and more of just that.

It sort of helped him to take his mind off things, cutting up a little. Usually he averaged maybe one hotfoot a week, and then only when somebody asked him to as a special gag, and he was sure it wouldn't cause any trouble. But this past week he'd given seven. And on his own, too. A couple of the guys got pretty sore, but Teddy managed to cool them down. He didn't mind cooling them down, or even buying a couple on the house, because seeing them jump made it worth it.

After he knew he was really going to quit, he even took to watching out for some of the customers who liked to give him a hard time. He told them off, but good; always making with the big smile, of course, and being careful not to go too far out of line. But there were a couple of old biddies he scored on, and one guy got in dutch with his wife because Teddy made some crack about "Who's the new girlfriend?" The guy was a salesman, and he'd been in before with some stenographer from his office. Teddy liked the look that came over the guy's face when he saw that his wife had caught on. The two of them had gone out quarreling.

Best of all had been last night, when Teddy pulled the old dribble-glass routine on those smart alecks up in the front booth. Bacardis they wanted yet, and then when he brought them they had to make some remarks about how he used dark rum instead of light. Teddy noticed they were all dressed up for an evening on the town, so the next round came to them in the dribble-glasses. He made a point of whispering to everybody at the bar, so they'd understand it was all a gag, and they sure laughed loud enough. He knew if they all laughed together, the people in the booth wouldn't have guts enough to get really sore; people are like that, they want to pretend they're good sports. But those damned Bacardis sure spoiled the party dresses the two dames were wearing, and he bet the cleaners wouldn't be able to get the stains out, either.

Teddy laughed so hard himself that for a minute he'd almost forgotten how he really felt; but only for a minute. The laughing made his head hurt worse. It was like he blacked out for a second, and when he came to and looked again he could see the Bacardis slopped all over the tablecloth in the booth, oozing red like blood.

Teddy shook his head now. He was going to cut out that kind of stuff, remember? He turned around and checked the signs behind the cash register. There were a lot of those comical sayings stuck up along the mirror — wooden plaques, mostly. He started to read them.

IN GOD WE TRUST — ALL OTHERS PAY CASH.

FREE DUCK DINNER — TOMORROW.

DON'T GO AWAY MAD — JUST GO AWAY!

There were others, too; Teddy had bought a whole snag of them, with his own dough, just to help out on the "atmosphere" of the Fun House. Sort of build up the gag idea. He wondered if he ought to take them along with him. Oh, what the hell, let Mac keep them. They'd be like a souvenir. Mac was really going to miss him; a lot of the regular gang would miss him. They'd be sorry to hear he was going away. All but Ella. Damn Ella! Damn her to —

Teddy stiffened. Customers were coming in the door, two of them. The night was starting.

He put on his Teddy Baer smile for them. And he put on his Teddy Baer voice, and he brought them their beers and he gave them their change, ringing up the lousy thirty cents just as if they'd ordered champagne. Even when they slopped suds all over the bar, he just wiped it clean without a word.

He was a bartender, by God, and this was his last night. He'd show them what a professional could do.

By this time another guy had come in, a rye-on-the-rocks, and a middle-aged couple, one vodka martini and one gin-and-tonic. Then there were two Buds and a Rheingold, and a young whiskey-and-water who left right after he got it down. Guy looked frightened, like he was in some kind of trouble; maybe he had a headache too. But Teddy was too busy to notice, for a while. A couple came in and sat in the second booth. Teddy didn't like the booth trade when he was on alone like this, and the damned jerks were always playing the jukebox, too.

Sure enough, they got their lousy beers and then the creep went over to the juke and plunged a quarter. The last of the big-time spenders.

Teddy might have known what he'd pick. That goddam rock-and-roll, or whatever they called it. Some guy who sounded like he was sick at his stomach and heaving all over his guitar. Made you sick too, listening to it. Teddy was glad he had the volume turned down as far as it would go.

But now what? The creep was putting in a beef about the volume. Couldn't the juke be turned up a little?

"Yes, sir."

Teddy went back behind the bar and turned the box on full-blast. The noise almost blew the top of his head off, but he didn't care. Let 'em live a little. The next beer was going right over the guy's pants. He wouldn't be getting up to drop another quarter so soon, not with a wet fly.

Teddy grinned when he thought about it, and the face across from him grinned back over the bar. It was a regular, name of Jensen, and he had two other guys with him.

"Set 'em up," Jensen said. "Straight shots all around."

"Celebrating?"

"That's right. You're looking at the proud father of a baby boy. Born just three hours ago. Weighs seven pounds, nine ounces."

"Good for you!" Teddy said.

Yeah, good for him. Teddy knew all about Jensen—he was a flunkey in a department store, a shoe-dog. Probably made all of fifty bucks a week; he never bought anything but beer. And here he was, playing big shot and buying shots for a couple of moochers. Why in hell was he so happy, just because he'd brought a brat into the world? Lousy kid'd eat him out of house and home, he'd spend a fortune just raising him up, and chances were he'd turn out to be another hard-luck working stiff, just like Jensen. Sure, that called for a celebration, all right. Big deal.

"Say, you ought to be buying cigars," said one of the other guys.

"That's right." Jensen was all set to reach into his pocket and pop for smokes, but Teddy shook his head.

"No—allow me," he said. He turned and took the box off the shelf behind him. The trio selected their cigars.

"Gee, thanks a lot," said Jensen.

"Man doesn't have a kid every day," Teddy said. "Not unless he's shacked up with a harem."

Jensen chuckled and started to make some crack about harems and how he could use a little of that right now, but Teddy spotted another customer. The middle-aged couple had left; probably the juke got on their nerves just like it was murdering Teddy. But another pair of regulars had taken their place. Teddy recognized Meyer, from the tailor shop down the street, and one of his pals.

He went over and smiled. "What'll it be, gents?"

Meyer shrugged. "So, the usual." He always said the same thing and he always shrugged. A sad sack, this Meyer character, and something about him got on Teddy's nerves. With that sick puss of his and everybody in the neighborhood knowing that his old lady was down with cancer, Teddy never could give him the needle. Instead, he always pretended to cheer him up with jokes.

Well, he had a special joke for him tonight. The way his head felt now, the way he was sweating under the arms and his feet burning, Teddy didn't feel very much like telling jokes. But for sad little Meyer he had to.

Setting down two beers, Teddy leaned over the bar. "Hey, I heard a good one," he said. "Cohen dies and his wife goes to the undertaking parlor, see? She asks the funeral director for a real classy job—you know how it is with the Hebes, they're great on family stuff." Teddy paused, just long enough to let it sink in. This was a beauty, because he knew Meyer didn't like cracks about the Jews, and he knew he didn't like to think about funerals. But Meyer would have to go along with the gag, and he did. Teddy smiled at him and made him smile back.

"So anyway," Teddy said, "the funeral director does his stuff and when the body is all laid out he brings Mrs. Cohen in to take a look at it. And he says, 'How do you like it?' So Mrs. Cohen looks at Abie and she says, 'Vell—you did a movelous job. A movelous job.' "

Teddy bore down heavy on the accent. He was sure Meyer didn't like dialect stories.

" 'But one thing,' Mrs. Cohen says. 'Just one thing. Mine Abie, he was a very conservative man. A real pillar from sassiety. How come you got him dressed in soch a jazzy bow tie, wit' a striped shoit, yet, and soch a fency-schmency checkered suit? Couldn't he maybe wear some'ting a leetle plainer?'

"So, the funeral director calls his assistant over and he says, 'Sam, I got a job for you.' He explains what the trouble is and Sam says, 'OK, boss, I'll fix it up in a jiffy. Don't go away.' And he wheels the body out, see? In about two minutes back he comes, pushing Cohen in the coffin, and he says to Mrs. Cohen, 'How's this?'

"Mrs. Cohen looks down and there is Abie, wearing a white shirt, a plain tie, and a blue suit. She says, 'Wonderful, just vot I vanted.' And away she goes.

"Funeral director looks at his assistant and he says, 'Great work! I'm proud of you. But tell me something—how did you manage to change all the guy's clothes in just two minutes?'

"The assistant looks at him and says, 'Who said anything about changing clothes? I just changed heads.' "

Teddy was all set to cap it with a big horselaugh, but there was another noise. It came from Jensen and his friends. All three of the damn cigars had exploded at once.

He almost busted a gut looking at their faces, particularly Jensen, who'd gotten his glasses knocked crooked. But the sound hurt his head, and he could feel his ears ringing, and for a minute he almost blacked out again — the way he had the other night.

Jensen was starting to say something, sounded like a squawk, only Teddy didn't pay any attention.

All at once he was staring at the door. He could see Ella coming in. Ella and this Donald Thomas, walking arm in arm and laughing, heading for the rear booth.

Just then the couple in the second booth got up, and the creep was putting another quarter in the juke — wet fly or no wet fly. The first record started, and it blasted his eardrums. He couldn't have heard Jensen complaining even if he wanted to. Jensen and his friends probably realized that, because they turned away and started out the door. Damned soreheads, couldn't take a joke.

Teddy walked over to the rear booth. Now he was glad the juke was on so loud, because it was an excuse not to try and talk — all he did was say, "Your order, please?"

Ella tried to tell him, "Hello" or something like that, but Teddy made believe he couldn't hear her. He just bent over the guy and listened while he asked for a couple of martinis. Very dry. Teddy nodded and turned away quickly.

On the way back, Teddy picked up another beer order from the young couple in the second booth. He decided to serve them first, and this time he managed to pull the spilled beer routine. It looked like an accident, but the guy must have been wise, because he started to get up. Teddy didn't even bother to try and listen to him. He was watching Ella and Donald Thomas over the top of the booth, and he could see the ape grabbing her hand.

For a minute he wanted to smash the guy who was complaining about the spilled beer, so he just turned away again. He felt like turning away from everybody, now. He just wanted to crawl in a corner and die. They were pushing him in a corner, all of them, pushing him with their squawks and their noise and their celebrations. They wanted to push him, push him out of the way, he didn't matter a damn to anyone. He was just a flunkey, a servant, somebody to jump when they called him. Make with the drinks, make with the funny stuff, and then leave us alone. We have our own wives, our own lives, our own babies, our own music, our own pleasures, our love —

Teddy made the martinis. He swung the shaker, gripping it so hard his hand almost broke the glass. If he broke it, he'd cut himself, and then there'd be blood —

The juke pounded, his head pounded, his feet pounded as he served the drinks. It was hard to hear, and even hard to see. Everything was a blur, a hot blur that throbbed. And Donald Thomas gave him a dollar and said something about, "Keep the change, Mac."

His name wasn't Mac, it was Teddy. Mac was the boss, and he was just Teddy Baer. Teddy Baer, the practical joker. Only nobody appreciated his practical jokes. Look, Meyer and his friend were walking out.

The young couple in the second booth were still listening to the records. The kid was trying to dry his pants. Maybe they'd go away, then. He wanted them to go away, everybody. Go away and leave him alone.

Jesus! Now a hillbilly record came on.

"Come sit by my si-ude, litt-ul dah-r-lingg—"

And they *were* sitting side by side, Ella and Donald Thomas; he'd switched places, come over to her side of the booth so he could get closer to her.

Teddy turned his back. A sign behind the bar caught his eye. QWICHER-BELLYACHIN!

And there was the mirror, he could still see them in the bar mirror. That fancy-pants student, with his name in gold on his lousy briefcase!

Suddenly Teddy remembered about the briefcase. He reached under the bar and pulled it out on the serving platform. Might as well hand it back. He fingered the lock. All at once it came open.

Teddy noticed a sheaf of papers and several notebooks.

Something about *Lab.* and something about *Pre-Med.* That was it, the fink was a medical student. Might have known Ella would go for one of them.

Thinking about medical students gave Teddy an idea. The place was almost empty now, except for the couple in the second booth, and they'd be on their way soon. That would leave just Ella and Donald Thomas. Donald Thomas, that big wheel in Medical School.

Suppose, on their next drink, Teddy played a little practical joke? Just one last little joke, for old times' sake?

Maybe that would sort of square things up a bit. A kind of a farewell present on the house—a fast Mickey.

Teddy had a bottle of the stuff in a drawer. He wasn't supposed to, and he'd never used it, but he knew it was there. He'd picked it up, wondering if someday it might come in handy. Well, when would he find a better chance? Let's see if the big-shot medical student would know what hit him. He could use a small amount, make sure it wouldn't work for an hour or so—then ease them out of the joint and close up early. By the time the Mickey got in its licks, they'd be gone and he'd be gone. And when they figured out what happened, tomorrow, he'd be far, far away.

Ella would finally get the connection, though. She'd realize he hadn't left without slipping her a little farewell present.

The more he thought about it, the more excited he got. Teddy felt it coming over him in waves, like the heat did, and like the throbbing in his head. It was the same feeling he got when he watched a guy get the hotfoot.

He'd stare at the flame, looking at it lick away at the leather, and sometimes the idea popped into his head that the flames wouldn't stop. Suddenly they'd catch hold, go leaping up the trouser legs, burst out all over the guy's body, burn him to ashes, burn him while he screamed—

But that was goofy, he mustn't think of such things. Just wait until that other couple left, and then make with the Mickey. And keep the amount small, remember not to go overboard. No sense killing anybody.

Now the couple from the second booth was leaving; the guy was hot all right, and he kept giving Teddy dirty looks. He mumbled something as he passed by the bar, but Teddy couldn't hear him above the racket. The damned fool was going out while he still had two records coming. Well, let him.

And Ella was waving at him from the booth.

Teddy walked over there. It was easier to walk, now that he knew what he was going to do. Easier to smile, too. He bent down and said, "What's your pleasure? Another round?" The guy nodded, but Ella grabbed his arm.

"Teddy," she said. "I want you to meet Donald Thomas, he's a friend of mine."

The guy stuck out his paw—he had one of those lousy signet rings from some fraternity—and he sort of grinned, and he said, "Why don't you tell him, Ella, you aren't ashamed, are you? I'm her fiancé."

Teddy stood up straight, and he heard his voice coming from far away. He'd intended to say something about the guy's briefcase, but instead what came out was, "Congratulations. The next round's on me."

It was hard for him to hear himself talk, with that blast from the box. And walking back was very hard indeed. The only thing that kept him going was remembering what he intended to do with the drinks.

He started to mix, keeping his head down so he wouldn't have to look at them across the bar. The sweat ran down into his eyes, and he put his hand around the shaker. It felt like a throat. A cool throat, something to squeeze and squeeze—

But now the drinks were ready to serve. All he had to do was add the Mickey.

Teddy hesitated, because he knew that he'd changed his mind. He couldn't give them the small dose now. They were going to get a big one. They were going to get it all. Maybe enough to kill them.

Sure, it was risky. Sooner or later, somebody would figure out what happened, where they got it. Then they'd come looking for him. Well, let them come. He was going through with it because this was his only chance.

Teddy wiped the sweat out of his eyes and his hand groped down to open the drawer under the bar. Somehow he bumped the briefcase, and another notebook fell out. A notebook and a shiny thing that rolled.

It must be a test tube—no, what did they call the small bottles?—a vial.

Teddy picked it up. There was a little label stuck on the side, with something written across it in ink. What did it say? *Cult. tetanus bacilli.* Whatever that was.

Wait a minute. Tetanus. Wasn't that the stuff that gave you lockjaw?

Sure, he'd read about it someplace. Tetanus germs. Jesus, that stuff could kill you. Just a drop of it.

All at once Teddy wasn't hot any more. He was cold. And his headache was gone, because he could think very clearly.

Tetanus. Better than a Mickey because it couldn't be traced. You could pick up the germs in bad food, catch it off a glass or something. And it probably took a couple of days to work, too. Even if the law did start nosing around, they'd never figure things out. What the hell, you didn't buy tetanus in a drugstore. All he had to do was slip it to them, and then get rid of the vial and the briefcase.

Fate, that's what it was. Fate, handing him the last laugh after all. He was going to serve a farewell drink, a real farewell drink. What a gag!

Teddy began to giggle as he opened the vial, and he had to tell himself to be careful. Mustn't spill anything now. Oh, this was rich, this was a real hot one. The best practical joke of all. But he must play it straight. Pour it in, two drops for each drink. And recork the vial, there. Now put the glasses on the tray. Carry it over to them, carry it over and try not to laugh right in their silly, staring faces.

"Here you are."

Teddy set the glasses down, watched them reach for their drinks.

"A toast to your future."

He watched Ella pick up her glass, place it against her lips.

And then the damned punk stood up. "Hey, wait a minute," he shouted. "Don't drink that!"

"Donald, what on earth — ?"

"He put something in it, I was watching him in the mirror."

Teddy moved, then. He bent forward, scooping up Ella's drink, and pressed it to her mouth.

But the punk knocked the glass out of his hand and shoved him back into the aisle, back against the bar. Ella rose, screaming, and ran out of the booth, out of the tavern.

Teddy tried to make a break for it too, but the guy grabbed his arm and twisted it behind him so he couldn't get loose. Then he marched Teddy behind the bar. Of course he saw the briefcase there, and the tetanus vial.

"This what you put in our drinks?" he asked.

Teddy nodded, and the guy smiled. "At first I was afraid you were trying to slip us a Mickey Finn."

"What the hell's so funny?" Teddy shouted. "I was going to slip you a Mickey. The whole damned bottle, enough to kill you. But then I found this stuff. What difference does it make—I damned near got away with it, didn't I? So you can wipe that silly grin off your face. I'll still kill you if I get another chance, I'll kill you and her too, I'll kill them all—"

He'd been shouting so loud he hadn't even noticed Ella come back in with the cop, but the cop was there, all right. And now he took Teddy's arm, and he was asking the guy what happened, and the guy was telling him.

"—forgot I left my briefcase, and of course that's where he found it. Fortunately, there's nothing in the vial but water."

"Water?" Ella said.

"That's right, honey. I'd fixed it up for tomorrow night—you know, the fraternity initiation. It was supposed to be a practical joke."

A practical joke. All at once it struck Teddy, and he began to laugh. "You heard what the man said," he told the cop. "It was a practical joke, that's all. I thought I was fooling them, and all the time the joke was on me! The funniest damned thing—of course I knew it was water all along, but they didn't know I knew and I didn't know they knew, and—"

Teddy could see the officer understood. It was just a gag he'd cooked up; everybody knew what a joker he was, always clowning and never meaning any real harm.

The officer said something about hearing Teddy admit he meant to kill Ella and her boyfriend, but of course that was ridiculous. Teddy started to explain, but the officer told him he'd have to come along with him and tell it downtown.

It took Teddy quite a while before he understood, because he was laughing so hard he couldn't hear anything else. He'd just noticed one of those funny signs behind the bar. The one that said, YOU DON'T HAVE TO BE CRAZY TO WORK HERE—BUT IT HELPS.

BEELZEBUB

HOWARD WAS STILL HALF-ASLEEP when he heard the buzzing.

It was a faint, persistent drone, balanced delicately on the very threshold of consciousness. For a moment Howard wasn't sure whether the sound came from the sleeping-side or the waking-side of his mind. God knows, he'd heard plenty of strange noises in his sleep lately; made them, too. Anita was always complaining about how he'd wake up in the middle of the night, screaming at the top of his lungs. But he had reasons to be upset, the way things were going, and besides Anita was always complaining, period.

The drone deepened insistently and Howard knew he was awake now. He could feel the stale heat of the bedroom and the response his body was making to it — the loginess of his limbs and the cold pattern of perspiration forming on them.

Bzzzzzzz.

Howard opened his eyes.

The room was dim, but the California sunshine filtering through the smog was also filtering through the interstices of the window blinds. Just enough to transform the bungalow-court apartment into a small oven with its baking heat. Just enough to give Howard a glimpse of what he didn't want to see — the living room filled with a fan-shaped clutter of clothing and furniture radiating from the axis of the rollaway bed, the cubby-hole kitchen through the open archway, with the caked and crusted dishes heaped in the sink. Yes, and the damned portable typewriter on the table in the corner, its carriage accusingly empty and its untouched keys leering up like rows of dusty teeth.

Rows of dusty teeth — Christ, man, what a writer you are! When you're asleep, that is.

But he wasn't asleep. He could hear that buzzing. Louder now, much louder. Goddam fly. How'd it get in here, with all the windows tight shut? Anita had a thing about opening windows, no matter how hot it was, when she had her curlers in. And she always had the curlers—

Bzzzzzzzzz.

Howard sat up. Noise was too loud to be coming from the kitchen. It had to be here in the room. He turned and glanced at the huddle in the bed beside him.

The sun glinted off the curlers. A ray played cruelly across Anita's neck, accentuating the stringy fold.

That's where the fly was sitting. At first he thought it was Anita's mole. But moles don't move. Moles don't buzz.

It was a fly, all right. He stared at Anita, thinking God how he hated the thing—noisy, rasping at your nerves, always around when you don't want it, demanding attention, intruding on your privacy. Dirty, messy creature, carrying filth—

Somehow his hand had drawn back and now it was coming forward; he wanted to hit it, not too hard, just swat it and destroy it because it had to be destroyed, he had to get rid of it.

Howard wasn't conscious of the blow or its force. Realization of its impact vanished before the overwhelming explosion of Anita's shrill scream.

"Ohhh, you *bas*tard!" And then she was sitting up, striking at him; not once, but again and again, harder and harder, and shrieking louder and louder. "You—you—trying to kill me while I'm asleep—"

It was crazy, she was crazy, and he was trying to explain about the fly, he was only going to swat the fly, but she wouldn't listen, she never listened when she got into one of those hysterical rages. She was crying, sobbing, stumbling into the bathroom; of course she locked the door. There was no sense continuing with the same old scene, no sense pounding on the panel and stammering out apologies. All he could do was find his clothes and get dressed, locate his briefcase under the jumble of *her* clothing. Past nine already, and his appointment was at ten. He had to be there on time.

In his haste, Howard forgot all about the fly. What he had to decide now was whether to spend the next twenty minutes catching a cup of coffee at the drugstore on the corner or run into the barbershop for a quick shave. He settled for the shave; it was more important to show up looking presentable.

Luck was with him. He got the car started without any trouble, made it over to the barbershop. There was a vacant chair. Howard settled back in it, grateful for the hot towels that blotted out the sound of the radio and the sight of the autographed photos on the wall. Why was it that every damned barbershop in this town had to keep the radio blatting at full volume, had to disfigure the wall with faded pictures of faded actors?

And why was it that barbers didn't have enough sense to keep their places clean?

Howard found himself flinging the sheet aside before the barber had finished applying aftershave lotion. "What's the matter with you guys — can't you even keep the lousy flies out of here?"

He hadn't meant to blow up, and come to think of it, there was only one fly, buzzing around the ceiling in Howard's range of vision as he lay tilted back in the chair.

But Howard didn't come to think of it until he was out of the shop, until the damage was done. The way that crummy barber had looked at him —

Oh, well, he wouldn't be going back there again anyway. There were plenty of other barbers around.

Not so many producers, though. At least not so many who wanted to make a deal with him. Howard reminded himself of that as he wheeled up to the studio gate. He put a big smile on his face for the guard who directed him to a parking space, and an even bigger smile for Miss Rogers, the secretary in the outer office of Trebor Productions. But he saved the biggest smile for Joe Trebor.

That took a little doing. First of all, there was the damned half-hour wait in the outer office. Well, that was Trebor for you — an A-OK rat fink. Of course they were all alike, these producers. They all had the same routine. Set up an appointment, then postpone it. Set up another, give you the pressure; "How soon can you make it? Tomorrow morning? Good — ten o'clock sharp, in my office. I'll leave a pass at the gate for you."

So you showed up promptly at ten, carrying the briefcase and taking the best possible care of that extra-big smile so that it wouldn't crack around the edges. And then you sat there like a damned fool in the reception room, crossing and uncrossing your legs in the uncomfortable little chair, trying not to stare at the secretary as she kept putting calls through to the guy you were supposed to be seeing right now. Sometimes you even sat there while the charm-boys finger-snapped their way in and out of the *sanctum sanctorum*; the sharp young agents, hair just a little too long over the back of the button-down collar, trousers just a little too tight in the seat, always a little bit ahead of you as they made their pitch, set their deal — for somebody else.

Howard got into Joe Trebor's office at 10:32. He stayed six minutes.

Three minutes later he was standing before a pay phone in a glass booth, trying to dial Dr. Blanchard's number with a forefinger that wouldn't stop trembling, then interrupting the incoherency he poured into the mouthpiece to take a wild swipe at the insect that soared and swooped insanely within the confines of the phone booth. "It's following me!" he shouted into the mouthpiece. "The damned thing's following me —"

*   *   *

"Do you want to talk about it now?" asked Dr. Blanchard quietly, as Howard sank back into the big, leather-covered chair. Scarcely another twenty minutes had elapsed, but Howard was not quite calm. And of course he wanted to talk about it.

That's why he'd called Blanchard, even though it wasn't his regular appointment day, that's why he'd come running over here to the nice, quiet office where you could sit back and relax and nobody pressured you.

It wasn't like Joe Trebor's office — he was telling the Doctor about that now. About the phony modern paintings on the walls and the big desk with the high executive chair behind it and the low chair in front of it, the one you sat in. When you sat in that chair the producer looked down on you and you had to look up to him. You looked up over that bare desk which told you here was a man too important to waste his time on mere paperwork the way writers did. You looked at the intercom and the phone with the six extension buttons which showed just how busy a producer he was, and at the solid silver water carafe which showed just how wealthy he was. And you looked at the picture of the wife and kids, which was supposed to show you what a solid citizen he was, if you didn't happen to know the stories about the way he interviewed for feminine leads.

But you didn't look directly at Joe Trebor, because he was staring at you. Staring and waiting for you to come up with the storyline. You got the notes out of the briefcase and you started to read, all the while conscious that you were just wasting your time with a showboat operator like this, a guy who kept interrupting to make Mickey Mouse suggestions for changes, a guy who didn't understand the values you were aiming for. All he knew was "storyline" and "How do you go out, what's the curtain, you need a tag here," and "Why don't you change it and play this scene exterior?" Typical fly-by-night producer.

And then the buzzing. The *buzzing*, just when you were trying to build, trying to sell, trying to nail him down. The *buzzing*, drowning out your voice.

And you looked up and saw the fly, perched on the stopper of the silver carafe. It was just squatting there, rubbing its tiny forelegs together, cleansing them. If you put those forelegs under a microscope you'd understand the need for cleansing, because they were covered with filth.

Then you looked at Joe Trebor who was smiling and shaking his head and saying, "Sorry, I don't quite see it. You haven't licked the storyline yet." And as he said it he rubbed his hands together because they were covered with filth, he'd walked through filth, he left a trail of filth wherever he went, and what right had he to buzz at you? And what right did he have to keep flies in his office to bug you when you were telling your story, your story that you'd sweated over for weeks in that lousy one-room apartment, like a furnace, with Anita slopping around in her dirty housecoat and whining why didn't you get up the bread?

And some of this you thought and some of it you must have said because Joe Trebor stood up and he got that look on his face and he was telling you something you couldn't quite hear because of the damned buzzing. So you smiled, holding your lips very tight, not wanting to admit you blew it, but you knew. And you split out and made the phone call to the Doctor and there it was — the fly, the same fly, the little black thing with a million eyes that can see everything, everywhere, right in the booth with you now, buzzing and listening. It saw and it heard and it followed you, through all the filth in the world.

Howard knew Dr. Blanchard understood because he was nodding quietly, calm and relaxed, and there was nothing wrong with his eyes. They weren't like Anita's or the barber's or Joe Trebor's eyes, all accusing him of putting them on. And they weren't like the fly's eyes had been, either, watching and waiting. Dr. Blanchard really understood.

Now he was asking Howard all about it, when the fly had first appeared, how long ago he could remember being conscious of flies. He even knew that talking about such things made Howard a little nervous, because he was saying, "Don't be afraid. There are no flies here. Just go right ahead and say whatever comes to mind. You won't be interrupted by any buzzing — *buzzzing* — *buzzzinnnggg* — "

The buzzing. It was in the room. Howard heard it. He couldn't hear the Doctor's voice any more because the buzzing was so loud. He couldn't even hear his own voice shouting, but he knew he was telling the Doctor, "You're wrong! It's here — it followed me! Can't you see?"

But of course Dr. Blanchard couldn't see, how could he see, when the fly, the black, buzzing fly, was sitting there and buzzing on top of his bald head?

And it buzzed and it stared, and the droning drilled through Howard's skull and the eyes lanced his brain, and he had to run, had to get out of there, had to get away, because they didn't believe him, nobody believed him, not even the Doctor could help him now —

Howard didn't stop running until he got to the car. He was panting when he climbed in, panting and wringing wet with perspiration. He could feel his heart pounding, but he forced himself to be calm. He *had* to be calm, very calm now, because he knew there was no one else to depend on. He'd have to do it all himself. The first thing was to check the car very thoroughly, including the back seat. And then, when he was quite sure nothing had gotten in, to lock the doors. Lock the doors and roll up the windows. It was hot inside the car, but he could stand the heat. He could stand anything but the buzzing and the stare.

He started the engine, pulled out. Calm, now. Keep calm. Drive carefully, right up to the freeway access. And edge out slowly. Get into the left lane and open up. Now. Drive fast. The faster you drive, the faster you get away from the buzzing and the staring. Keep it at seventy. A fly can't do seventy, can it?

That is, if the fly is *real*.

Howard took a deep breath.

Suppose everyone else was right and he was wrong? And there was no fly, except in his own imagination? But it couldn't be; not in his imagination, the one tool, the one weapon, the one area a writer must protect. You can't open your imagination up to a buzzing beast, a creature that crawls through filth, you can't allow the invasion of an insect that incubates in your own insanity, an incarnation of your own personal devil, an evil that torments you incessantly. But if it *was* that way, then of course there was no escape. He couldn't drive fast enough, run far enough, to get away. And there was no hope for him at all.

Bzzzzzzz.

It was there, in the car. At least, he heard it. But the sound might be coming from inside his own shattering skull.

And now he saw it, fluttering against the windshield before him, just below the rear-view mirror. Or did he see it? Wasn't it just a fragment of inward vision? How could there be a real fly in the car, with all the windows closed tight?

But he saw and he heard and it buzzed and it crawled, and his sweat poured and his heart thumped and his breath rasped and he knew it was real, it *had* to be real. And if it was, then this was his chance, his only chance, locked inside the car with it where it couldn't get away.

Howard shifted his foot from the gas pedal to the brake. The car was hurtling down an incline but he knew he had it in control, everything was under control now. All he needed to do was swat the fly.

The creature had paused in its progress across the windshield so that it was poised directly before his line of vision. Howard could see it very clearly now, as his hand moved up. He almost laughed at himself as he stared, laughed at his absurd fantasies. Silly to think of demoniac possession by such a tiny, fragile insect; he could see every delicate veining and tracery of its fluttering wings as he leaned forward. For an instant he even stared into its eyes; its multifaceted eyes, mirrors of myriad mysteries.

In that instant he knew.

But his hand was already swooping out, and all he could do was shriek as the car lurched and the culvert wall loomed —

When the squad car came the fly was resting very quietly on Howard's eyeball.

Its eyes swiveled slowly as the red-necked patrolman bent over the body, pausing just long enough to sense the frustration, the suppressed anger, the seething tension behind the stolid face. Then it rose gracefully and buzzed around the patrolman's shoulders as he straightened. As the patrolman turned away, the fly followed.

The patrolman sighed. "Poor devil," he muttered.

It was, of course, an epitaph. . . .

THE OLD COLLEGE TRY

ADMINISTRATOR RAYMOND'S HEAD was a hive of hornets. He could feel them buzzing in his brain, and before opening his eyes he held out his hand.

The Yorl, who had probably been crouching at his bedside for the past hour, in anticipation of this very moment, thrust a glass of Aspergin into his shaking fingers.

Administrator Raymond gulped it down, and gradually his fingers ceased twitching. The buzzing died away inside his skull, and he was able to open his eyes. In a moment he could even manage to sit up.

The blue-skinned little Yorl smiled at him and said, "Goo morning, Ministrata," then bowed as he offered Raymond his undergarments.

Raymond acknowledged the greeting with a friendly grin. He wondered just how much longer the Yorl would continue to bow if he knew that this was the last day. The new Administrator was arriving, and soon Raymond would go home—back to Vega and civilization. It would be good to see a normal world again—a world where grass was an honest pink and the birds snarled sweetly all the day.

On the other hand (even though that hand might tremble a little) he rather regretted leaving Yorla. He even regretted leaving the Yorls. The dark-visaged, stunted little blue humanoids might seem alien and uncivilized to strangers, but after five years on Yorla, Administrator Raymond was oddly fond of them.

Puffing a trifle, Raymond struggled into his uniform. Damned nuisance, but he had to keep up appearances. After all, today he must welcome the new Administrator. He hoped they were sending out a good one. It took a certain temperament to endure the heat and the solitude of life on Yorla.

And, more important, it took a certain temperament to understand the Yorls.

"Ship has land!" Another Yorl came scuttling in, as usual, without bothering to knock. He grinned up at Raymond. "Bringa pinky."

"Pinky." That's what the Yorls called humans. He must be referring to the new Administrator.

"I'm coming," Raymond told his informant.

The Yorl shook his head. "No botha. We bring him, in your office now."

So they'd organized their own welcoming committee. Good. Raymond smiled as he thought of the new Administrator stepping out of the ship and being confronted with a mob of naked blue Yorls. Must have been something of a shock, particularly if they'd paraded for him with their trophies. Well, he'd just have to get used to it — as Raymond himself had gotten used to it when he arrived, five years ago.

"You go back, tell him I'll be right down," Raymond instructed. The Yorl messenger withdrew, and the other Yorl gave Raymond a shave, a shoeshine, and another glass of Aspergin, in that order.

Then Raymond waddled downstairs to his office and greeted the new Administrator.

He found him standing on his hands in the center of the floor.

"Greetings," he called, from his upside-down position. "You must be Raymond, eh? I'm Philip."

"Pleased to meet you," Raymond said, wondering if he ought to advance and shake Philip by the foot.

"Excuse the informality," Philip said. "Just trying to get back a little circulation. Long trip, and the decompression effect is a bother."

He lowered himself to the floor, but instead of rising, began to do pushups. He was good at it, and Raymond felt himself grow tired just watching the exercise.

"One's duty to keep fit, eh?" Philip said, cheerily. He didn't even pant.

Raymond nodded, staring at the newcomer. Philip upside-down or Philip horizontal was still a remarkably handsome young man. He had blond curly hair, regular features, sparkling blue eyes, white and gleaming teeth, and a superabundance of muscles. His smile radiated enthusiastic vitality. In a word, he looked a bit too good to be true, and Raymond wondered how on Vega a prime specimen like this had ever been relegated to a post as Administrator on remote little Yorla.

Philip bounded to his feet, healthily flushed and perspiring mightily, and held out his hand to Raymond. His grip was as hearty as his voice.

"Good to see you," he said. "By the way, Captain Rand sends regrets. There was a slight mishap when we landed — something went wrong with the auxiliary grav-mech. I don't understand the technical side, but I'm afraid he and the crew are in for about a week of repairs here before they can take off on a return flight."

"A week?" Raymond couldn't conceal his frown. "But I'm all packed—I thought we'd be leaving today."

Philip shrugged. "I know how you feel," he said. "But speaking selfishly, for my own sake, I'm glad of the delay. It gives me a chance to find out a few things from you. In a week you can brief me on this post."

Raymond remembered his duties as a host. "Of course," he said. "Glad to."

"Want to see my papers?" Philip asked.

"Not necessary. Just a formality." Raymond turned and beckoned to his waiting Yorl. "Two Aspergins, hup-hup!"

As the Yorl nodded and backed out of the room, Philip shook his head. "Nothing for me, thanks. Never touch the stuff."

"Better learn," Raymond advised. "This is a fever planet."

"I'll manage," Philip said, confidently. "They gave me all the new shots before I left. Besides, I've never been sick a day in my life." He paused, waiting until the Yorl had disappeared, then lowered his voice. "Odd creatures, aren't they?"

"You'll get used to them," Raymond said. "They make wonderful servants. You'll find you'll never have to lift a finger to do anything. There's a post staff here of twenty—they'll bathe you, dress you, brush your teeth for you if you like."

"I'm afraid I'm not accustomed to such luxuries," Philip told him. "Besides, isn't it a bit—ostentatious?"

"If you mean expensive, forget it," Raymond answered. "It costs Interplan next to nothing in wages. The Yorls aren't greedy. And they actually enjoy working for a pinky. That's what they call us, you know. It's easier than slaving in the mines. You'll find them faithful and loyal if you treat them decently. Once you get used to the blue skins and the language, and accept their customs—"

Philip sat down, cracking his knuckles. "Their customs," he said. "Do you know how they met me when the ship landed? They came running out waving their spears. And on the tip of each spear was a head."

"They meant to do you honor," Raymond explained. "I told them a new Administrator would be arriving. So they got up a group to welcome you and brought out their trophies for display."

"Trophies? You mean they're actually headhunters?"

"Of course not. They prize heads, and preserve them, but they don't go around killing one another just to collect more. After all, they're not barbarians. Besides, Interplan wouldn't tolerate such savagery."

"Then where do the heads come from?"

"Well, as you know, most of the Yorls work in our mines. The labor is hard and they don't particularly enjoy it, but they like our trade goods and the arrangement has worked out satisfactorily for all concerned. So much so that when the Yorl chiefs made their agreements with Interplan, they set up a quota. Every Yorl who signs up for mining is obliged to produce a set amount of ore. If a Yorl fails to meet his quota, if he's caught shirking — his companions merely chop off his head."

"And you say they're not barbarians," Philip murmured.

Raymond shrugged. "This is Yorla, not Vega or Titan. Remember the old saying — when on Rigel, do what the Rigelians do."

"But chopping off one another's heads that way! I should think something would be done about policing them."

"Meaning *I* should have done something as Administrator?"

Philip flushed but made no effort to deny the words.

Raymond sighed. "Maybe I felt the same way when I arrived here, five years ago. Since then I've learned a few things. As I say, the Yorls don't kill for the sake of killing, even though they value their trophies more highly than anything else. They have their own restraints, and it's all a matter of meting out justice."

"But the laws — "

"They have their own laws. Remember, Interplan sent us here to administrate, to supervise the mining operations and trade with the natives. It is not our duty to superimpose our own concepts or customs on this planet. Besides, oddly enough, the system works. We want what the mines produce. The Yorls see that we get it. They eliminate their own slackers and misfits, weed out their own criminals, deal with them promptly and efficiently. Why, we'd need to employ hundreds of men to act as overseers if we tried to keep them in line according to our own methods. This is a simpler, easier, cheaper way."

"But it's not right! In the name of common humanity — "

"Humanity." Raymond sighed again. "The Yorls are not humans. They are *humanoid*. That's the first thing you have to learn, the one thing you must always remember."

A Yorl bowed his way into the room.

"Affanoon, Ministrata," he said.

Philip glanced at Raymond, who nodded briefly. "That's right, it *is* afternoon. You're going to have to accustom yourself to the shorter days here." He turned and confronted the Yorl. "What is it?"

"You go way, tha ri'?"

"That's right. I will be going away, and Mr. Philip will be your new Administrator. But I won't leave for a while, not until the ship is ready."

"We no wish you go."

"Sorry. Interplan makes the rules. And you'll like Mr. Philip, I'm sure."

"So. But first you come long *torga*, this night, we hold *koodoo*, your honna."

"He's inviting us down to the village here for a party," Raymond explained.

"You come long?"

"We'll be there."

"Yaya!" The Yorl grinned happily. "Much fun!"

It may have been much fun according to Yorl standards, and it may have been much fun for Raymond, but Philip didn't enjoy the *koodoo* a bit.

He sat there on the dais, sweltering in the heat of the warm night, and watched the dancers with a strained smile on his face. The pounding of the drums made his head ache. And when Raymond got up to make his speech, explaining how he was leaving and Philip would be taking over, the Yorls had shouted for almost five minutes. It was unnerving. Then there had been the banquet, and the nauseous concoctions he had to pretend to sample. Raymond didn't seem to mind—but then, he kept washing down his food with Aspergin.

Philip didn't like the setup at all. They *were* savages, and no amount of talking would change the fact. Dancing in a huge circle of spears set up in the sand—and each spear surmounted by the preserved and grinning head of a Yorl. The way those heads grinned was actually frightening, but the grins on the faces of the living dancers seemed worse.

And yet he had to maintain outward calm, outward dignity. Even when a hundred little blue Yorls writhed naked before him, chanting and contorting their bodies in gyrations that were positively obscene.

How could Raymond endure the noise, let alone the sight of them? Why, he was actually grinning himself—his fat face flushed and foolish, as if he enjoyed the disgusting spectacle. He was drunk, that was the answer.

Now the dancers had separated into two groups, male and female. They formed two lines, facing one another, and the drums beat in a quickening tempo. The lines advanced, converged, and then the drums went frantic. And now the dance was no longer a dance. It was mass orgy. Why, they were actually going to—

"Raymond!" Philip whispered. "Look! Aren't you going to stop them?"

"What for? They seem to be enjoying themselves."

"But in the name of common decency—"

"I told you they have their own customs. This is being done in our honor."

"Disgusting!" Philip rose abruptly.

"Natural." Raymond blinked. "Where are you going?"

"Back to my quarters. I'm afraid I'm not up to this sort of thing."

"Wait!"

But Philip did not wait. He moved away. Raymond waddled after him, puffing. Philip didn't slow his stride. The older man didn't catch up to him until they reached the Administration Building.

"Come back," Raymond wheezed. "You can't do this. You're insulting them by walking out."

"Insulting them? What did you expect me to do, get down there and wallow with them?"

"If they invited you, yes."

"Are you serious?"

Raymond nodded. "Of course. You can't offend their sense of hospitality." He chuckled. "Besides, it isn't so bad. Maybe their skins are blue, but you'd be surprised how white they look after five years out here."

"Not to me." Philip scowled. "I'm turning in."

"You're angry? Now look, son, let me explain a few things to you about—"

"Never mind. I've heard some of your explanations. And I'm afraid the Company reports are right. Interplan gave me specific orders to come out here and clean up the situation—"

Philip hesitated, then took a deep breath. "I'm sorry I mentioned it, but perhaps it's better that you know just where you stand. They know about you, Raymond. They know how you've been running this operation, and they don't approve of it any more than I do. Lording it over the natives like one of those colonial governors in prehistoric days back on Earth."

"But Interplan sent me out here to supervise the mines. I've done a good job. They get their ore, there's no trouble, the natives are satisfied—"

"Of course they're satisfied! Why shouldn't they be, when they're allowed to run wild; killing each other at will, indulging in every debauchery? You haven't made a move to stop them, have you? In five years you've made no attempt to educate them, no attempt to institute reforms, no attempt to provide them with decent government, decent standards of living. Instead of setting an example for them, you've merely sunk to their level."

"Now wait a minute—"

"I'm not waiting a minute! Starting tomorrow, I'll take over. Officially. You'll stay here until Captain Rand completes his work on the ship, but from now on I'm in charge."

"It isn't that simple. I know the Yorls, I understand them. You can't hope to change them overnight." Raymond blinked at him with his reddened eyes. "Why, you don't even *like* them! And that's the first thing, the most important thing. You've got to learn to like them."

"And I suppose you do?" Philip laughed shortly. "I suppose you think you're being kind to them when you take a staff of twenty servants to wait on you hand and foot as if you were some kind of lord of the manor here? Is it kindness to permit them to murder and rape?"

"They're entitled to their own way of life, their liberty."

"Liberty isn't license."

"You don't understand."

"Oh yes, I do, only too well. Administration and Aspergin don't mix. I advise you to go to bed and sleep it off."

Philip turned on his heel and marched down the corridor to his room. A Yorl squatted beside the door, and as Philip approached, he rose hastily and bowed.

"You wanna—" he began.

Philip took a second look, then realized that the Yorl was not a *he* after all, but a young female. He flushed as he guessed the nature of the unfinished question; flushed first with shame and then with indignation.

"No!" he shouted. "Get away from me! Go to Raymond."

Obediently, the Yorl trotted off along the corridor.

Philip entered his room and slammed the door. Immediately a second Yorl—this one unmistakably male—rose and approached him with a fan.

"Out!" Philip ordered. "I don't need you here."

"But I cool you good."

"I'll cool myself."

"Take off clo'se?"

"No! Can't you understand? I don't want any servants! From now on I'll take care of myself."

The Yorl left, bowing so low that Philip barely caught a glimpse of his puzzled grimace.

All right, so he was puzzled. It wouldn't last long. Philip vowed he'd make his position perfectly plain in the near future. There were going to be some drastic changes made around here. And he'd start from scratch.

Philip wasn't worried about it, because he knew that he *could* take care of himself. He'd told off Raymond, and now he'd get to work on the Yorls. Tomorrow was the time to start. And the first and most important thing to do was to put an end to the head-chopping. No more heads on pikes.

Tomorrow, then.

But tonight, as Philip drifted into fitful sleep, the heads appeared on the long spears; parading through his dreams, just as they had today when the ship landed and tonight when the dancers gathered for the *koodoo*.

There was only one slight difference. As Philip remembered them, the heads had all been grinning.

And they were laughing, now. . . .

Raymond was somewhat agreeably surprised to see Philip join him at the breakfast table. He was even more surprised to note that the young man appeared in a conciliatory mood.

He didn't apologize for anything he had said the previous evening, but he seemed much less belligerent as he explained his plans.

"I don't want you to misunderstand me," Philip told him. "I know as well as you do that there's no sense in trying to run roughshod over the feelings of the natives. I have no intention of issuing any formal orders about head-taking in the mines. And I couldn't enforce such orders if I gave them."

"Now you're talking sense," Raymond said. "I knew that once you really thought things over, you'd see it was impossible."

"I didn't say anything about impossibility," Philip corrected. "I merely told you that force wouldn't help. The answer lies in the psychological approach. It's all a matter of channelizing their aggressions."

"Huh?"

"I'll merely provide them with other outlets for their energies, offer them suitable substitute activities."

"This is something they teach you in the College of Space?"

"Exactly. I trust you weren't meaning to be sarcastic?"

"Certainly not," Raymond said. "I know my place."

"Good. Then perhaps you can help me clarify the situation."

"Gladly."

"You tell me the Yorls only take heads of slackers, wrongdoers, inefficient workers. Is that correct?"

"Yes."

"And yet they value individual head collections very highly."

"True."

"So I infer that they're always on the lookout for someone who breaks the rules."

"That's right. Every Yorl keeps a close watch on the activities of his fellow workers. It's a sort of wholesale espionage system, you might say."

"In other words, they compete with one another to detect possible victims."

"You might say that."

"And in that—that orgy last night—" Philip hesitated, his pink face coloring. "I didn't see very much, understand, but I gather that there is a certain competitive factor in their debauchery."

"If you're trying to make out that the male who takes the most females is supposed to be the best, then you're correct."

"Ah, yes. Again, competition enters into it. Now, if I can provide harmless substitute outlets for their competitive instincts, I'll soon have them functioning normally."

"Normally? What's abnormal about sexual activity?" Raymond blinked. "Forgive the question, but you see, I never attended the College of Space."

"Please! There is nothing abnormal about such activity, provided it is carried out under the proper legal arrangements, and for the purposes of procreation only." Philip smiled. "After all, I'm not narrow-minded, you know."

"Sure." Raymond gestured, and a Yorl came over and wiped his forehead. "So what do you plan?"

"Well, we've established the basic fact. The Yorl is a highly competitive creature, and his social institutions are based upon competition. I think I can introduce some *new* institutions."

"Such as?"

Philip smiled again. "Wait and see," he said.

Raymond waited, and three days later, he saw.

To be specific, it was three evenings later when Philip came to his office and invited him down to the *torga*. It was unusually hot, and Raymond chose to be transported in a litter, borne by four Yorls.

He couldn't imagine where the younger man got his energy from, but there he was, hopping around like one possessed, making last-minute arrangements in the big clearing before the huts. He kept jumping in and out of the ring—

Ring.

"Wait a minute," Raymond murmured. "Don't tell me you're planning a *boxing* match?"

"Exactly!" Philip beamed happily. "I've conferred with the villagers here and they seem quite excited. They donated their services to put up the ring, and I've had the females weaving gloves out of *ritan*. There were no end of volunteers for contestants, after I explained the procedure. I've coached the two we finally selected, and I think they'll put on a great show. The Yorls seem to have a natural coordination that is quite remarkable. I'm looking forward to this evening."

"I'm not," Raymond murmured.

"What's that?"

"Nothing. When do you begin?"

"Almost immediately. See, they're assembling right now."

And they were. The blue-skinned little humanoids had gathered on all four sides of the improvised ring, squatting on the ground and staring up expectantly as the Yorl fighters made their way to their respective corners. Philip, clad in a sweatshirt and shorts, climbed through the strands of *porga* serving as ropes. He was obviously serving as referee, and a whistle dangled from a cord around his neck. He conferred briefly with each of the contestants, and the little blue boxers nodded and grinned up at him in turn.

Then there was a roll of the drums and Philip came forward to the center of the ring, lifting his hands for silence. He spoke very briefly about the rules of the coming contest, and the virtues of the manly art of self-defense. This, he declared, would be a clean fight, demonstrating the finest principles of sportsmanship. And now, at the drum signal—

It came.

Philip stepped back.

The Yorls rushed out from their respective corners.

The crowd yelled.

The Yorls exchanged expert blows.

The crowd screamed.

The taller Yorl hit his opponent below the belt.

Philip stepped forward hastily.

The smaller Yorl brought his knee up and kicked the other fighter in the chin.

Philip blew his whistle.

The Yorls paid no attention. Perhaps they couldn't even hear the whistle above the shrieks of the audience. At any rate, they went into a clinch. Both of them were kicking at one another's loins. They had shed their gloves.

Philip waved, frantically, then tried to separate them. The Yorls put their heads down and kicked harder. Then, suddenly, they were rolling around on the floor of the ring. The smaller Yorl ended up on top of his opponent. He got his hands around the windpipe and squeezed.

The crowd went crazy then, but not half as crazy as Philip.

"Stop!" he shouted. "You're killing him!"

The little Yorl on top nodded, grinning happily. He released one hand, then dug his fingers into his victims's eyes.

And then Raymond somehow managed to clamber his way into the ring. He helped Philip pull the Yorl off the prostrate body of his opponent, and he said something to quiet the crowd and disperse them.

Afterwards he walked Philip back to Administration in the darkness.

"But I don't understand," Philip kept saying. "I don't understand! I offered them a logical outlet for sublimation—"

"Maybe they don't *want* to sublimate," Raymond said. "Maybe they *can't*."

"But the principles of psychology—"

"—apply to human beings," Raymond finished for him. "Not necessarily to Yorls." He wheezed heavily and patted Philip on the shoulder. "Anyway, you tried. Now, perhaps, you can see why I've never attempted to change their ways. There just isn't any use."

"I'm not licked yet," Philip declared. "I know the idea is sound. Sport is the best substitute for actual combat. It always works."

Raymond led him into his office, and a Yorl jumped up from the floor to pour a glass of Aspergin. Raymond gulped, and the Yorl wiped his chin.

"Substitute," he said. "Can't you realize the Yorls don't believe in substitutes? Why should they, when they can have the real thing? A pretense of combat or a limited combat will never satisfy them when they can actually—"

"The *real* thing," Philip murmured. He stood up abruptly. "Of course! That's the answer, you're right! Why didn't I think of it? Nobody accepts a substitute when the real thing is available. But if the real thing is not available any longer, then perhaps they'll learn to cooperate."

"What do you mean?" Raymond asked. "If you've got any wild ideas, I advise you to forget them."

Philip shook his head. "No wild ideas. Just common sense. You did me a great favor tonight, Raymond. I won't forget it."

He turned and headed down the corridor toward his room. A Yorl rose to follow him, then hesitated, remembering that his services were not required there. Instead he poured Raymond another glass of Aspergin. And another.

It was almost two hours later that Raymond finally sought his own bed. He was pleasantly tired, pleasantly tipsy, and pleasantly unaware of the faint glow and the faint cries from outside his window.

Not until the Yorl came running in did he open his eyes and sit up.

"What's the matter?" he muttered.

"You come," the Yorl panted. "Come to *torga*, fast!"

"Why?"

The Yorl's blue-veined eyeballs rolled. "Otha Ministrata there. He burn heads!"

"Damn and blast-off!" Raymond rose, thrusting out his feet as the Yorl brought his shoes. He fumbled in the rear of a drawer, looking for the needler he never carried. It felt cold and heavy in his hand as he followed the Yorl down the path, running in the direction of the *torga*.

The faint glow had flared into flame now, and the faint cries rose to a chattering crescendo as Raymond entered the clearing.

The Yorl had told the truth.

Philip had waited until the village was quiet, then crept back there in darkness and done what he'd planned. He'd gone from hut to hut and gathered the spears which stood upright before them. He'd gathered the spears, harvested the heads, heaped them like ripe melons in a central pile at the end of the clearing, and ignited them. They were blazing furiously now — but not half as furiously as the Yorls themselves.

Philip stood before the fire, needler in hand, facing them defiantly. The Yorls confronted him in a body, screeching and howling, waving their spears. And they were edging forward —

"Get back!" Philip shouted. "I'm not going to harm you! This is for your own good, don't you see? It is wrong to take heads. It is wrong to kill."

Raymond made out the words vaguely through the tumult. He doubted if the Yorls could hear or understand, and even if they did, it meant nothing to them. Because they kept inching forward, closer and closer, and the spears were poised for the cast.

"Stop!" Philip cried. "I'm your Administrator. I order to you to go to your huts. One more step and I — "

Nobody took a step.

Instead, a spear whizzed past Philip's head.

He didn't run. He didn't duck. He didn't flinch. He merely faced the Yorl who had hurled the spear; faced the weaponless little blue humanoid and pressed the tip of his needler.

There was a faint crackling sound and the silvery flash of the energy-arc. The Yorl fell, shriveling and blackening before he hit the ground.

A great sigh arose from the crowd, and then a hundred arms were raised, a hundred spears when back.

And halted.

Halted, as the pyre of heads hissed suddenly, then disappeared in a black billow.

Raymond had tossed the water on the fire.

Everyone turned as he stepped forward and grasped Philip by the arm. They watched as he took the needler from Philip's hand and tossed it into the center of the dying blaze. They watched as he tossed his own weapon on the ground.

Raymond raised his arms over his head.

"I am truly sorry," he murmured. "A wrong has been done, but it shall never be repeated. We ask to go in peace."

Silently, he led Philip away into the darkness.

Raymond did not speak to his companion until they reached the office again, and then only when he had dismissed the waiting Yorl servant.

"I think you'd better change your plans, now," he said, mildly. "The ship will be ready to leave in three days, according to what Captain Rand tells me. You'd best leave with him."

He didn't wait for Philip to reply, but turned his back and poured a glass of Aspergin.

He was still gulping it down when Philip walked away.

It was already afternoon of the following day when Philip reentered the office. Raymond looked up expectantly.

"Started your packing?" he asked, casually.

Philip shook his head. "I'm not going."

"But—"

"I'm not going. Why should I?"

"You ask me that, after last night? After what you did?"

"What did I do?"

"You mortally offended the Yorls. You violated the great taboo. You killed one of their leaders."

Philip shook his head again. "It was self-defense," he said. "As for what I did, it was right."

"According to your standards, yes. But the Yorls—"

"Look at him!"

Philip leveled his finger at the corner. A Yorl servant crouched there, his blue face ashen, his eyes bulging in terror as Philip stared at him.

Philip smiled. "Don't you see? He's afraid of me, now. They all are, after last night. I didn't realize it at the time, but I'd done the one thing necessary. By putting an end to this head fetishism, by destroying their trophies, I proved that a human is stronger than their whole barbaric culture and belief. That's the sort of practical demonstration they needed in order to understand. A show of force."

"But they hate you now —"

"Nonsense! They hated me last night, and I'm quite sure that after we left they got together and prayed for my destruction. I don't pretend to understand their superstitions, but I'll bet they expected their gods to destroy me with a bolt of flame. So when I went down to the village today, it came as quite a shock to see me alive and healthy."

"You went back to the village again?"

"I've just come from there." Philip glanced carelessly at the Yorl, who cringed. "That's the reaction I got from all of them. Nobody dared to harm me, nobody dared speak. I summoned them out and laid down the law. From now on, no more taking of heads. The mines will be operated efficiently on the basis of my orders, and on the threat of my punishment. Nobody else will take the law into their own hands. They understand that I mean business."

Raymond scratched his head. "But you were the one who objected to my colonialism, as you called it! I thought you didn't like this business of having servants, of ordering them around."

"I don't," Philip answered. "Not when it's just a matter of selfish personal comfort. But this is different. We're dealing with fundamentals here. In order to bring civilization and sanity, one must issue orders and enforce them."

"I never used force. You know that. The Yorls enjoy serving me, it's better than the mines."

"Yes. That's just the trouble. You gave them a choice. You never used force. You never established the first and most important principle — that we, as human beings, are superior. They must obey for their own good, so that we can raise them to a decent level."

"But they don't want to be like human beings, it's not their nature to be."

"Nonsense! You can't halt evolution, you can't halt progress. From now on, we'll operate according to sound, scientific principles. That means taking a firm hand."

Raymond sighed. "What about the sports?" he asked, softly. "I suppose this isn't important any more under the new regime?"

Philip smiled. "If you're indulging in sarcasm, spare the effort," he replied. "It so happens that I've no intention of abandoning the program. In fact, as I told you yesterday, I consider sublimation very important. Now it's more important than ever. The natives will need outlets for aggression. And as I said then, once their old outlets are gone, they will embrace the new much more willingly. As they are doing now."

"Now?"

"Yes. I issued instructions to the villagers. They are laying out a football field."

"Football?"

"Of course. I really should have thought of it first, instead of this silly boxing business. Football is the natural sport. Calls for team participation, allows substitute activity to a much greater number at one time. It's the ideal sublimation — a rough body-contact sport, and it's a great vicarious outlet for the spectators, too. I was star halfback for two seasons at the College of Space. They went crazy over the game — "

"Human beings do, perhaps. But the Yorls won't play football. They don't understand abstractions. Why should they think it worthwhile to fight over the possession of a — "

It was Philip's turn to interrupt, and he did so with a laugh.

"I'm not interested in your arguments," he said. "The fact remains that the Yorls will learn football. They are building a stadium alongside the field. I will organize their teams and instruct them. They're bright enough, in their way. A few skull-practice sessions, a little actual training, and you'll see. By tomorrow I expect we can raise the goal posts."

"Please, you're making a mistake. I can't stand by and watch you do this."

"Not necessary." Philip laughed again. "I keep forgetting you won't be around to observe the results. The ship leaves in three days, you say." He turned. "Well, I'll not keep you. I expect you'll want to get on with your packing."

Raymond didn't want to get on with it, but he did. During the next two days he saw nothing of Philip. If he was organizing and coaching his teams, there was no sign. Raymond made no effort to visit the *torga* or to inspect the playing field behind it. He packed, and he drank incredible amounts of Aspergin, and he did his best to welcome and maintain the numbness which resulted.

On the night before the day of departure, Raymond deliberately courted stupor. Philip left after dinner, and that was just as well; he did not want to be reminded of Philip's presence, or his own coming absence.

Ordinarily, he'd have been delighted with the prospect of leaving Yorla and returning to the pleasures and comforts of Vegan civilization. The Aspergin was better there, too. Well, he'd need plenty of Aspergin now, with Interplan breathing down his neck. So they didn't like the way he'd run things here. What did they know about the Yorls — the way they lived, the way they thought? Maybe he'd never attended the College of Space, but he understood how to do a job. And he'd miss doing it.

That was bad, but the thought of Philip as Administrator was worse. Using force on the Yorls, ruling through fear — it would never work.

Raymond signaled and his glass was automatically refilled.

No, force and fear would never work. But they *had* worked, they *were* working. He must admit it. The Yorls were afraid of Philip and they obeyed. They'd even play his stupid football games if he commanded. Sublimation seemed to be the answer.

"Maybe I'm wrong," Raymond told himself. "Maybe I've misjudged them."

Suddenly he felt very old, and very tired. He leaned back in his chair, hands folded over his fat paunch.

And it was there that the Yorl found him.

He came bursting into the office, his face contorted in an amiable grin.

"Goo evening, Ministrata. You come now?"

"Come where?"

"See game."

"Game? You mean you're playing football already?"

"Tha ri'. Foo ball game now. Your honna."

"But I'm tired, I've got to finish packing—"

"Your honna."

"All right. Just for a little while." Raymond rose, fighting fatigue and the dizzying effects of the Aspergin. He didn't want to go, but it was the last night, and the Yorls would be disappointed. They were like children, really—they always wanted to share their pleasures with him.

Maybe it was a good idea to show up. Give Philip a chance to shove his weight around and do a little crowing, but that wasn't important. Give credit where credit was due. If Philip could actually organize a football game in just three days, he deserved some recognition.

Besides, if he felt good enough, he might let Raymond say a few words. A farewell speech, perhaps. He could make that final gesture—at least, attempt to patch up the situation and assure the Yorls that Philip only had their welfare at heart. He'd tell them to obey Philip.

Raymond shrugged as he followed the Yorl out into the night and down the path which wound behind the village. He'd forgotten something—apparently it wouldn't be necessary to ask the Yorls to obey the new Administrator. They already *were* obeying. Playing football at night!

Progress had come to Yorla, and he was only in the way. So he wouldn't make a speech after all. He'd just watch.

It wasn't difficult. The Yorls had heaped fuel all about the playing field, and the blazing fires illuminated the scene. The drums pounded in joyous excitement, and the blue-skinned audience cavorted in frantic enthusiasm as several minor chieftains danced before them, waving spears in a Yorla version of cheerleading.

The two teams were already on the field, engaged in a furious scrimmage. There was no hint of compulsion about their movements, not the slightest vestige of constraint amongst the spectators.

Raymond sighed. Philip had been right, and he was wrong. The evidence of his own eyes furnished the final proof. Once a game was substituted for reality, the Yorls conformed, just as humans did. And from now on, the rest would be easy. In five years Philip would have them all working in the mines and paying taxes. They'd become a civilized community, with jails and orphanages and asylums.

Somehow, he'd never believed it would work out this way. The Yorls had always seemed such realists. How could they get so excited over make-believe, this stupid business of fighting for possession of a football?

One of the teams was trying for a field goal now, and a player was getting ready to kick the ball. Raymond tried to locate Philip on the field. He must be out there, acting as referee.

Raymond squinted through the firelight, but he couldn't see him. All he could see was the ball, sailing over the goal posts. And the crowd roared.

The crowd roared, and Raymond sighed again, and he turned back up the path to the Administration Building. He was tired, but he'd have to unpack. And he'd have to write a report to Interplan, explaining that he was right after all and that Philip was wrong. He'd have to explain that progress was not coming to Yorla and that the Yorls were still realists. They didn't understand about sublimation, or the necessity of fighting over useless objects. They would play football, yes, but only for a real trophy, like the one he had just seen soaring over the goal posts.

It was Philip's head. . . .

A Quiet Funeral

Vetch read the bit in Vegas on Friday morning. So instead of hitting the sack, he made the next plane East. By nine o'clock that night he was back in town, stepping out of a cab in front of Luigerni's Funeral Home.

The joint was like Creepsville. Vetch figured that a big man like Charlie the Printer would have himself a big send-off—the uptown mortuary bit. But this was just a little *paisan* stiff-parlor on a sidestreet.

He'd never heard of the place and he wondered what Luigerni would say if he walked in and asked for a commission. After all, in a way he was entitled to it—Luigerni wouldn't be getting the business if Vetch hadn't totaled Charlie the Printer. But of course he couldn't tip him off.

Vetch shrugged, turned up his topcoat, and headed for the entrance. Sort of a surprise, finding Charlie the Printer in a crummy, rundown dump like this. But then, it was all a surprise, the way things had worked out.

Totaling Charlie the Printer had been a big operation. It took Vetch a couple of months of skullwork to figure out all the angles. You don't knock off the biggest swinging counterfeiter in the business on impulse, for kicks. You have to make all the angles. Having Charlie as a friend helped, of course; it meant Vetch could get to him alone, when he wasn't carrying protection or being tailed by boys who carried it for him.

Still, there was the little question of setting it up so that Vetch could lay his hands on a big bundle of that new, foolproof loot Charlie kept bragging he was making. And the totaling had to look like an accident.

Finally Vetch decided it would *be* an accident; he fixed the car himself, in Charlie's own garage, just before he knew Charlie was taking the big trip to deliver a consignment of two hundred thousand phony Gs in tens and fifties. Funny angle on queer geedus: the Feds check twenties, hundreds and on up, but they don't usually bother with tens or fifties. Charlie told Vetch that, and Vetch listened. Listening is what helped him to set everything up. He knew the route Charlie was taking that night when he made his delivery with the loot. And that's why he was able to wait for him on the lake bluff road, in his own car, blocking the narrow stretch at the turn so that Charlie would have to brake hard and swing his wheel way to the left in order to avoid going off the edge of the bluff.

Only Vetch had done his little gimmicking job well, and when Charlie swung the whole steering mechanism went—and it was over and out for Charlie the Printer.

Vetch watched the car tumble and he waited until it started to burn before he got down the side of the bluff and snatched the loot from the trunk. Charlie was kind of wedged inside under the smashed steering wheel and he was clawing and screaming to get out, but Vetch wasn't about to help him. He ran for it before Charlie got a look at his face, just in case there could be any kind of slip-up later on.

But there was no slip-up. Vetch was out of town and on his way probably before Charlie finished frying. And since a good plan calls for a good alibi, Vetch had that all set up, too. He passed the word along that he was heading for Vegas on business and he set things up so that there *was* business for him in Vegas. Since nobody knew that Charlie was carrying a heavy bundle of product that night except Charlie himself, there was nothing to tie in with his accidental death. It was all copacetic.

In Vegas, Vetch played it cool. He had a little action, but he was too smart to pass any of Charlie's bills. He just waited it out, reading the home-town papers every morning until he was sure there wouldn't be any heat. For five days he followed the items—the fuzz found the burned car and the burned body, they did the inquest bit, the jury came up with the accidental death verdict, and the funeral was announced.

When Vetch read this last item he knew it was time to go home. After all, it wouldn't look right if a guy didn't send off his best buddy, would it?

So here he was.

Here he was, opening the door of Luigerni's Funeral Home, walking into the quiet.

In his line of business, Vetch went to a lot of funerals and a lot of funeral homes. It was, what do you call it?—an occupational hazard. But he never got so he liked to make the scene. Even when he himself had nothing to do with setting up the guest of honor, he started hurting when he had to go up to the casket. It was bad enough when there was a gang around—either making with the weeps or laughing and scratching. But to walk into a stiff-processing joint cold, all alone, was murder.

Murder.

Vetch didn't like the word. This was no time to think about the Big M. Not in this dingy little Guinea joint, at quarter past nine at night. God, it was clammy. Nobody around, nobody on duty at the door; just a long walk down a short hallway and into the back-room parlor where the casket was laid out on the trestles.

He shouldn't have come so late, and he shouldn't have come alone. The whole point was for people to see him there, notice him. Of course he'd sign the guest-book, and tomorrow he'd show up in church when Charlie got his send-off. He'd have to send flowers, too. Lots of flowers. What the hell, he could afford it — Charlie's money was good.

Thinking about that part made him smile a little. But it wasn't easy to smile in here. Luigerni's Funeral Home; what kind of a joint was this for a man like Charlie the Printer? Looked like it didn't get ten stiffs a year. Old carved furniture, a beat-up carpet, couple of dim lamps like you used to see in Prohibition speaks.

Of course there were lots of wreaths and bouquets in the back parlor. They just about covered the front of the room and Vetch could smell the lilies and the carnations and the roses. Or do carnations smell? He couldn't remember. All he knew was that he hated the smell of funeral flowers, just like he hated the smell of hospital corridors. Ether and flowers — both of them reminded him of Stiffville. And Vetch was afraid of Stiffville.

That was it. In a crowd he could pretend, but alone like this he had to face up to it. He was chicken about funeral homes because he was chicken about Death. Death, with a capital *D*, like Murder with a capital *M*. Two big words. Maybe that's why he'd gotten into this business; because he *was* afraid. Sort of — what did the headshrinkers call it? — overcompensation. Something like that.

And what the hell was he doing thinking about headshrinkers at a time like this? Vetch knew what his routine was. Come in, sign the book, cut out.

He didn't have to smell the flowers in the parlor. He didn't have to look at the casket, or see Charlie the Printer. Come to think of it, he couldn't see Charlie — the casket would be closed, sealed. On account of the way Charlie had burned —

When Vetch closed his eyes he could see Charlie burning, so it was really better to keep them open, better to look at the casket before turning away.

Sure, why not? Nothing wrong with the casket itself. Just a box. It was what was *inside* that bothered him. Or thinking how it would be to be inside one yourself. What if you *knew* about it after you died? What if you knew where you were, sealed up in that black box, when they dropped you into the big hole and shoveled in the dirt?

Vetch put his hands in his pockets to stop the twitching. *Forget it.* He made himself look at the casket. Pretty big one. Bronze, and solid. Even if

Charlie's family hadn't put out for a classy uptown funeral home, they'd laid on the loot for the coffin. It was sure built to last, like a Sherman tank. Once they sealed you in one of these things, you stayed sealed. And then you went down into the dark —

Vetch began to twitch all over. Hell with it. Get out of here. Get away from the casket and the burned thing inside it. Get away before he started to flip, started to get the funnies. *Like seeing the lid move and the hand crawl out, Dracula's hand, only this one had a gun in it.*

He made a little noise way back in his throat, because it *was* happening; the lid was moving back now and he could see Charlie sitting up and staring at him. And Charlie wasn't burned at all, except a little around the right side of his face and chin, and the gun was very bright and shiny and it pointed right at Vetch's belly.

"Come over here, old buddy," said Charlie. His voice was still soft and it could all be a dream, except that if Vetch wanted to find out he'd have to turn and run — and the gun was pointing.

So Vetch said, "You're dead," which is the kind of thing you say in a dream. Only Charlie wasn't having any. He shook his head and swung his long legs over the side of the casket, crushing a big bouquet of lilies and sending the smell up in waves that made Vetch's head hurt.

"I'm not dead," he said. "I got out, right after you took off. Oh, I recognized the car, all right, up there on the road, and when you opened the trunk of my heap I knew the whole bit."

Vetch wanted to say something, sort of laugh it off and tell Charlie it was all a very funny bit — but Charlie wasn't laughing, and that gun looked plenty serious. All Vetch could say was, "You gotta be dead — I read it in the papers."

Charlie walked over to him slowly, the whole dream bit. "You spread the word you were going to Vegas," he said. "We located you. And the place where you bought the out-of-town papers. It cost dough to get to the guy and dough to print up a special copy every day with the right story on one page. But it was worth it. You see, we wanted you to come back for a nice, quiet funeral."

Vetch blinked and Charlie grinned. "Yeah," he said. "I really did it. They don't call me Charlie the Printer for nothing."

Now Vetch knew the setup. He knew why Charlie was waiting at Luigerni's Funeral Parlor — the sidestreet dump where nobody ever came. But there was nothing he could do about it except turn and watch as Luigerni came in, and Charlie's brother Sam, and his cousin Angelo.

They closed the parlor doors and the smell of the flowers got worse and worse, and then they closed in on him. He tried to fight, at the last, and he would have preferred it if Charlie had used the gun, but he never did. His brother had a sap and he hit Vetch's wrists and ankles, breaking the bones so that he lay there flopping like a big rag doll. All they had to do was to carry him then, like pallbearers, and dump him into the big bronze box. Then they put the lid on.

And this time, they really did seal the casket.

Just before they sealed it, they remembered to put a gag on Vetch. So it turned out to be a quiet funeral after all. . . .

The Plot Is the Thing

When they broke into the apartment, they found her sitting in front of the television set, watching an old movie.

Peggy couldn't understand why they made such a fuss about that. She liked to watch old movies — the Late Show, the Late, Late Show, even the All Night Show. That was really the best, because they generally ran the horror pictures. Peggy tried to explain this to them, but they kept prowling around the apartment, looking at the dust on the furniture and the dirty sheets on the unmade bed. Somebody said there was green mold on the dishes in the sink; it's true she hadn't bothered to wash them for quite a long time, but then she hadn't eaten for several days, either.

It wasn't as though she didn't have any money; she told them about the bank accounts. But shopping and cooking and housekeeping was just too much trouble, and besides, she really didn't like going outside and seeing all those *people*. So if she preferred watching TV, that was her business, wasn't it?

They just looked at each other and shook their heads and made some phone calls. And then the ambulance came, and they helped her dress. Helped her? They practically *forced* her.

In the end it didn't do any good, and by the time she realized where they were taking her it was too late.

At first they were very nice to her at the hospital, but they kept asking those idiotic questions. When she said she had no relatives or friends they wouldn't believe her, and when they checked and found out it was true it only made things worse. Peggy got angry and said she was going home, and it all ended with a hypo in the arm.

There were lots of hypos after that, and in between times this Dr. Crane kept after her. He was one of the heads of staff and at first Peggy liked him, but not when he began to pry.

She tried to explain to him that she'd always been a loner, even before her parents died. And she told him there was no reason for her to work, with all that money. Somehow, he got it out of her about how she used to keep going to the movies, at least one every day, only she liked horror pictures and of course there weren't quite that many, so after a while she just watched them on TV. Because it was easier, and you didn't have to go home along dark streets after seeing something frightening. At home she could lock herself in, and as long as she had the television going she didn't feel lonely. Besides, she could watch movies all night, and this helped her insomnia. Sometimes the old pictures were pretty gruesome and this made her nervous, but she felt more nervous when she didn't watch. Because in the movies, no matter how horrible things seemed for the heroine, she was always rescued in the end. And that was better than the way things generally worked out in real life, wasn't it?

Dr. Crane didn't think so. And he wouldn't let her have any television in her room now, either. He kept talking to Peggy about the need to face reality, and the dangers of retreating into a fantasy world and identifying with frightened heroines. The way he made it sound, you'd think she *wanted* to be menaced, *wanted* to be killed, or even raped.

And when he started all that nonsense about a "nervous disorder" and told her about his plans for treatment, Peggy knew she had to escape. Only she never got a chance. Before she realized it, they had arranged for the lobotomy.

Peggy knew what a lobotomy was, of course. And she was afraid of it, because it meant tampering with the brain. She remembered some mad doctor — Lionel Atwill, or George Zucco? — saying that by tampering with the secrets of the human brain one can change reality. "There are some things we were not meant to know," he had whispered. But that, of course, was in a movie. And Dr. Crane wasn't mad. *She* was the mad one. Or was she? He certainly looked insane — she kept trying to break free after they strapped her down and he came after her — she remembered the way everything gleamed. His eyes, and the long needle. The long needle, probing into her brain to change reality —

The funny thing was, when she woke up she felt fine. "I'm like a different person, Doctor."

And it was true. No more jitters; she was perfectly calm. And she wanted to eat, and she didn't have insomnia, and she could dress herself and talk to the nurses, even kid around with them. The big thing was that she didn't worry about watching television any more. She could scarcely remember any of those old movies that had disturbed her. Peggy wasn't a bit disturbed now. And even Dr. Crane knew it.

At the end of the second week he was willing to let her go home. They had a little chat, and he complimented her on how well she was doing, asked her about her plans for the future. When Peggy admitted she hadn't figured anything out yet, Dr. Crane suggested she take a trip. She promised to think it over.

But it wasn't until she got back to the apartment that Peggy made up her mind. The place was a mess. The moment she walked in she knew she couldn't stand it. All that dirt and grime and squalor—it was like a movie set, really, with clothes scattered everywhere and dishes piled in the sink. Peggy decided right then and there she'd take a vacation. Around the world, maybe. Why not? She had the money. And it would be interesting to see all the *real* things she'd seen represented on the screen all these years.

So Peggy dissolved into a travel agency and montaged into shopping and packing and faded out to London.

Strange, she didn't think of it in that way at the time. But looking back, she began to realize that this is the way things seemed to happen. She'd come to a decision, or go somewhere and do something, and all of a sudden she'd find herself in another setting—just like in a movie, where they cut from scene to scene. When she first became aware of it she was a little worried; perhaps she was having blackouts. After all, her brain *had* been tampered with. But there was nothing really alarming about the little mental blanks. In a way they were very convenient, just like in the movies; you don't particularly want to waste time watching the heroine brush her teeth or pack her clothing or put on cosmetics. The plot is the thing. That's what's *real.*

And everything was real, now. No more uncertainty. Peggy could admit to herself that before the operation there had been times when she wasn't quite sure about things; sometimes what she saw on the screen was more convincing than the dull gray fog which seemed to surround her in daily life.

But that was gone, now. Whatever that needle had done, it had managed to pierce the fog. Everything was very clear, very sharp and definite, like good black and white camera work. And she herself felt so much more capable and confident. She was well-dressed, well-groomed, attractive again. The extras moved along the streets in an orderly fashion and didn't bother her. And the bit players spoke their lines crisply, performed their functions, and got out of the scene. Odd that she should think of them that way—they weren't "bit players" at all; just travel clerks and waiters and stewards and then, at the hotel, bellboys and maids. They seemed to fade in and out of the picture on cue. All smiles, like in the early part of a good horror movie, where at first everything seems bright and cheerful.

Paris was where things started to go wrong. This guide—a sort of Eduardo Ciannelli type, in fact he looked to be an almost dead ringer for Ciannelli as he was many years ago—was showing her through the Opera

House. He happened to mention something about the catacombs, and that rang a bell.

She thought about Erik. That was his name, Erik—The Phantom of the Opera. *He* had lived in the catacombs underneath the Opera House. Of course, it was only a picture, but she thought perhaps the guide would know about it and she mentioned Erik's name as a sort of joke.

That's when the guide turned pale and began to tremble. And then he ran. Just ran off and left her standing there.

Peggy knew something was wrong, then. The scene just seemed to dissolve—that part didn't worry her, it was just another one of those temporary blackouts she was getting used to—and when Peggy gained awareness, she was in this bookstore asking a clerk about Gaston Leroux.

And this was what frightened her. She remembered distinctly that THE PHANTOM OF THE OPERA had been written by Gaston Leroux, but here was this French bookstore clerk telling her there was no such author.

That's what they said when she called the library. No such author—and no such book. Peggy opened her mouth, but the scene was already dissolving. . . .

In Germany she rented a car, and she was enjoying the scenery when she came to this burned mill and the ruins of the castle beyond. She knew where she was, of course, but it couldn't be—not until she got out of the car, moved up to the great door, and in the waning sun of twilight, read the engraved legend on the stone. FRANKENSTEIN.

There was a faint sound from behind the door, a sound of muffled, dragging footsteps, moving closer. Peggy screamed, and ran. . . .

Now she knew where she was running to. Perhaps she'd find safety behind the Iron Curtain. Instead there was another castle, and she heard the howling of a wolf in the distance, saw the bat swoop from the shadows as she fled.

And in an English library in Prague, Peggy searched the volumes of library biography. There was no listing for Mary Wollstonecraft Shelley, none for Bram Stoker.

Of course not. There wouldn't be, in a *movie* world, because when the characters are real, their "authors" do not exist.

Peggy remembered the way Larry Talbot had changed before her eyes, metamorphosing into the howling wolf. She remembered the sly purr of the Count's voice, saying, "I do not drink—wine." And she shuddered, and longed to be far away from the superstitious peasantry who draped wolfbane outside their windows at night.

She needed the reassurance of sanity in an English-speaking country. She'd go to London, see a doctor immediately.

Then she remembered what was *in* London. Another werewolf. And Mr. Hyde. And the Ripper. . . .

Peggy fled through a fadeout, back to Paris. She found the name of a psychiatrist, made her appointment. She was perfectly prepared to face her problem now, perfectly prepared to face reality.

But she was not prepared to face the baldheaded little man with the sinister accent and the bulging eyes. She knew him—Dr. Gogol, in *Mad Love*. She also knew Peter Lorre had passed on, knew *Mad Love* was only a movie, made the year she was born. But that was in another country, and besides, the wench was dead.

The wench was dead, but Peggy was alive. *"I am a stranger and afraid, in a world I never made."* Or had she made this world? She wasn't sure. All she knew was that she had to escape.

Where? It couldn't be Egypt, because that's where *he* would be—the wrinkled, hideous image of the Mummy superimposed itself momentarily. The Orient? What about Fu Manchu?

Back to America, then? Home is where the heart is—but there'd be a knife waiting for that heart when the shower curtains were ripped aside and the creature of *Psycho* screamed and slashed. . . .

Somehow she managed to remember a haven, born in other films. The South Seas—Dorothy Lamour, John Hall, the friendly natives in the tropical paradise. There *was* escape.

Peggy boarded the ship in Marseilles. It was a tramp steamer but the cast—crew, rather—was reassuringly small. At first she spent most of her time below deck, huddled in her berth. Oddly enough, it was getting to be like it had been *before*. Before the operation, that is, before the needle bit into her brain, twisting it, or distorting the world. *Changing reality*, as Lionel Atwill had put it. She should have listened to them—Atwill, Zucco, Basil Rathbone, Edward Van Sloan, John Carradine. They may have been a little mad, but they were good doctors, dedicated scientists. They meant well. "There are some things we were not meant to know."

When they reached the tropics, Peggy felt much better. She regained her appetite, prowled the deck, went into the galley and joked with the Chinese cook. The crew seemed aloof, but they all treated her with the greatest respect. She began to realize she'd done the right thing—this *was* escape. And the warm scent of tropic nights beguiled her. From now on, this would be her life; drifting through nameless, uncharted seas, safe from the role of heroine with all its haunting and horror.

It was hard to believe she'd been so frightened. There were no phantoms, no werewolves in this world. Perhaps she didn't need a doctor. She was facing reality, and it was pleasant enough. There were no movies here, no television; her fears were all part of a long-forgotten nightmare.

One evening, after dinner, Peggy returned to her cabin with something nagging at the back of her brain. The captain had put in one of his infrequent appearances at the table, and he kept looking at her all through the meal.

Something about the way he squinted at her was disturbing. Those little pig-eyes of his reminded her of someone. Noah Beery? Stanley Fields?

She kept trying to remember, and at the same time she was dozing off. Dozing off much too quickly. Had her food been drugged?

Peggy tried to sit up. Through the porthole she caught a reeling glimpse of land beyond, but then everything began to whirl and it was too late. . . .

When she awoke she was already on the island, and the woolly-headed savages were dragging her through the gate, howling and waving their spears.

They tied her and left her and then Peggy heard the chanting. She looked up and saw the huge shadow. Then she knew where she was and what *it* was, and she screamed.

Even over her own screams she could hear the natives chanting, just one word, over and over again. It sounded like, "Kong."

LIFE IN OUR TIME

WHEN HARRY'S TIME CAPSULE ARRIVED, Jill made him put it in the guest house.

All it was, it turned out, was a big long metal box with a cover that could be sealed tight and welded so that the air couldn't get at what was inside. Jill was really quite disappointed with it.

But then she was quite disappointed with Harry, too. Professor Harrison Cramer, B.A., B.S., M.A., Ph.D. Half the alphabet was wasted on nothing. At those flaky faculty cocktail parties, people were always telling her, "It must be wonderful to be married to a brilliant man like your husband." Brother, if they only knew!

It wasn't just that Harry was fifteen years older than she was. After all, look at Rex Harrison and Richard Burton or even Larry Olivier for that matter. But Harry wasn't the movie-star type. Not even the mad-scientist type, like Vinnie Price in those crazy high-camp pictures. He was nothing.

Of course Jill got the message long before she married him. But he *did* have the big house and all that loot he'd inherited from his mother. She figured on making a few changes, and she actually *did* manage to redo the house so that it looked halfway presentable, with the help of that *fagilleh* interior decorator. But she couldn't redo Harry. Maybe *he* needed a *fagilleh* interior decorator to work on him, too; *she* certainly couldn't change him. And outside of what she managed to squeeze out of him for the redecorating, Jill hadn't been able to get her hands on any of the loot, either. Harry wasn't interested in entertaining or going out or taking cruises, and whenever she mentioned sable jackets he mumbled something under his breath about "conspicuous consumption," whatever that was. He didn't like art or the theatre, he didn't drink, he didn't even watch TV. And he wore flannel pajamas in bed. *All* the time.

After a couple of months Jill was ready to climb the walls. Then she began thinking about Reno, and that's where Rick came in. Rick was her attorney. At least, that's the way it started out to be, but he had other ideas. Particularly for those long afternoons when Harry was lecturing at seminars or whatever he did over there at the University. Pretty soon Jill forgot about Reno; Rick was all for one of those quickie deals you get down in Mexico. He was sure he could make it stick and still see to it that she got her fifty-fifty share under the community property laws, without any waiting. It could all be done in twenty-four hours, no hassle; they'd take off together, just like eloping. Bang, you're divorced, bang, you're remarried, and then, bang, bang, bang—

So all Jill had to worry about was finding the right time. And even that was no problem, after Harry told her about the capsule.

"I'm to be in charge of the project," he said. "Full authority to choose what will be representative of our culture. Quite a responsibility. But I welcome the challenge."

"So what's a time capsule?" Jill wanted to know.

Harry went into a long routine and she didn't really listen, just enough to get the general idea. The thing was, Harry had to pick out all kinds of junk to be sealed up in this gizmo so that sometime—ten thousand years from now, maybe—somebody would come along and dig it up and open it and be able to tell what kind of a civilization we had. Big deal. But from the way Harry went on, you'd think he'd just won the Grand Prix or something.

"We're going to put the capsule in the foundation of the new Humanities Building," he told her.

"What are humanities?" Jill asked, but Harry just gave her one of those *Christ-how-can-you-be-so-stupid?* looks that always seemed to start their quarrels, and they would have had a fight then and there, too, only he added something about how the dedication ceremonies for the new building would take place on May 1st, and he'd have to hurry to get everything arranged for the big day. Including writing his dedicatory address.

May 1st was all Jill needed to hear. That was on a Friday, and if Harry was going to be tied up making a speech at the dedication, it would be an A-OK time to make a little flight across the border. So she managed to call Rick and tell him and he said yeah, sure, perfect.

"It's only ten days from now," Jill reminded him. "We've got a lot to do."

She didn't know it, but it turned out she wasn't kidding. She had more to do than she thought, because all at once Harry was *interested* in her. *Really* interested.

"You've got to help me," he said that night at dinner. "I rely on your taste. Of course I've got some choices of my own in mind, but I want you to suggest items to go into the capsule."

At first Jill thought he was putting her on, but he really meant it. "This project is going to be honest. The usual ploy is pure exhibitionism—samples of the 'best' of everything, plus descriptive data which is really just a pat on the back for the status quo. Well, I want to include material that's self-explanatory, not self-congratulatory. Not art and facts—just artifacts."

Harry lost her there, until he said, "Everything preserved will be a clue to our social attitudes. Not what we pretend to admire, but what the majority actually believes in and enjoys. And that's where you come in, my dear. You're the majority."

Jill began to dig it, then. "You mean like TV and records?"

"Exactly. What's the album you like so well? The one with the four hermaphrodites on the liner?"

"Who?"

"Excuse me—it's purportedly a singing group, isn't it?"

"Oh, you're talking about the Poodles!" Jill went and got the album, which was called *The Poodles Bark Again*. The sound really turned her on, but she always thought Harry hated it. And now he was coming on smiles.

"Great," he said. "This definitely goes in."

"But—"

"Don't worry, I'll buy you another." He took the album and put it on his desk. "Now, you mentioned something about television. What's your favorite program?"

When she saw he was really serious she began telling him about *Anywhere, U.S.A.* What it was, it was about life in a small town, just an ordinary suburb-like, but the people were great. There was this one couple with the two kids, sort of an average family, you might say, only he was kind of playing around with a divorceé who ran a *discothetique* or whatever they call them, and she was getting the hots for a psychiatrist—he wasn't really *her* psychiatrist, he was analyzing one of the kids, the one who had set fire to the high school gymnasium, not the girl—she was afraid she'd been caught because of that affair she was having with the vice-principal who was really a Commie agent only she didn't know it yet and her real boyfriend, the one who had the brain operation, had a thing about his mother, so—

It got kind of complicated, but Harry kept asking her to tell him more and pretty soon he was nodding. "Wonderful—we'll have to see if we can get kinescopes on a week's episodes."

"You mean you really want something like that?"

"Of course. Wouldn't you say this show captured the lives of typical American citizens today?"

She had to agree that he was right. Also about some of the things he was going to put into the capsule to show the way people lived nowadays—like tranquilizers and pep pills and income tax forms and a map of the freeway-expressway-turnpike system. He had a lot of numbers, too, for Zip Code and digit-dialing, and Social Security, and the ones the computers punched out on insurance and charge-account and utility bills.

But what he really wanted was ideas for more stuff, and in the next couple of days he kept leaning on her. He got hold of her souvenir from Shady Lawn Cemetery—it was a plastic walnut that opened up, called "Shady Lawn in a Nutshell." Inside were twelve little color prints showing all the tourist attractions of the place, and you could mail the whole thing to your friends back home. Harry put this in the time capsule, wrapping it up in something he told her was an actuarial table on the incidence of coronary occlusion among middle-aged middle-class males. Like heart attacks, that is.

"What's that you're reading?" he asked. And the next thing you know, he had her copy of the latest Steve Slash paperback—the one where Steve is sent on this top-secret mission to keep peace in Port Said, and right after he kills these five guys with the portable flamethrower concealed in his judo belt, he's getting ready to play beddy-bye with Yashima, who's really another secret agent with radioactive nipples—

And that's as far as she'd got when he grabbed the book. It was getting so she couldn't keep anything out of his hot little hands.

"What's that you're cooking?" he wanted to know. And there went the TV dinner—frozen crêpes suzettes and all. To say nothing of the *Plain Jane Instant Borscht.*

"Where's the photo you had of your brother?" It was a real nothing picture of Stud, just him wearing that way-out beard of his and standing by his cycle on the day he passed his initiation into Hell's Angels. But Harry put *that* in, too. Jill didn't think it was very nice, seeing as how he clipped it to another photo of some guys taking the Ku Klux Klan oath.

But right now the main thing was to keep him happy. That's what Rick said when she clued him in on what was going on.

"Cooperate, baby," he told her. "It's a real kinky kick, but it keeps him out of our hair. We got plans to make, tickets to buy, packing and like that there."

The trouble was, Jill ran out of ideas. She explained this to Rick but he laughed.

"I'll give you some," he said. "And you can feed 'em to him. He's a real s.a., that husband of yours—I know what he wants."

The funny part of it was Rick did know. He was really kind of a brain himself, but not in a kooky way like Harry. So she listened to what he suggested and told Harry when she got home.

"How about a sample of the Theatre of the Absurd?" she asked. Harry looked at her over the top of his glasses, and for a minute she thought she'd really thrown him, but then he grinned and got excited.

"Perfect!" he said. "Any suggestions?"

"Well, I was reading a review about this new play, *Little Irma*—it's about this guy who thinks he's having a baby so he goes to an abortionist, only really I guess the abortionist is supposed to be God or somebody, even if he is black, and it all takes place in a pay toilet—"

"Delightful!" Harry was off and running. "I'll pick up a copy. Anything else?"

Thank God Rick had clued her in. So she said what about a recording of one of these concerts where they used a "prepared" piano that makes noises like screeching brakes, or sometimes no sound at all. And he liked that. He also liked the idea about a sample of Pop Art—maybe a big blow-up of a newspaper *Piles—Don't Be Cut* ad.

The next day she laid it on him about a tape of a "Happening" which was the real thing, because it took place in some private sanatorium for disturbed patients, and he really got hung up on this idea.

And the next day he asked for a suggestion for a movie, so she remembered what Rick coached her on about $7\frac{1}{4}$, which was a way-out thing by some Yugoslavian director she never heard of, about a man making a movie about a man making a movie, only you never could be quite sure, in the movie, whether the scene was supposed to be a movie of a part of a movie or a movie of a part of what was really happening, if it happened.

He bought this, too.

"You're wonderful," he said. "Truthfully, I never expected this of you."

Jill just gave him the big smile and went on her merry way. It wasn't hard, because he had to go running around town trying to dig up tapes and films and recordings of all the stuff he had on his list. Which was just how Rick had said it would be, leaving everything clear for them to shop and set up their last-minute plans.

"I won't get our tickets until the day before," Rick told her. "We don't want to tip anything. The way I figure it, Harry'll be moving the capsule over to where they're holding the ceremonies the next morning, so you'll get a chance to pack while he's out of the way." Rick was really something else, the way he had it all lined out.

And that's the way it worked. The day before the ceremony, Harry was busy out in the guest house all afternoon long, packing his goodies into the time capsule. Just like a dopey squirrel burying his nuts. Only even dopey squirrels don't put stuff away for somebody to dig up ten thousand years from now.

Harry hadn't even had time to look at her for the past two days, and this didn't bother Jill any. Along about suppertime she went out to call him, but he said he wasn't hungry and besides he had to run over and contact the trucking company to come and haul the capsule over to the foundation site. They'd dug a big hole there for tomorrow morning, and he was going to take the capsule to it and stand guard over it until it was time for the dedication routine.

That was even better news than Jill could hope for, so as soon as Harry left for the trucking company she phoned Rick and gave him the word. He said he'd be right over with the tickets.

So of course Jill had to get dressed. She put on her girdle and the bra with the built-in falsies and her high heels; then she went in the bathroom and used her depilatory and touched up her hair where the rinse was fading, and put on her eyelashes and brushed her teeth, including all the caps, and tried those new fingernails after she got her makeup on and the perfume. When she looked at the results in the mirror she was really proud; for the first time in months she felt like her real self again. And from now on it would always be this way, with Rick—no more pretending, nothing phony.

There was a good moment with Rick there in the bedroom after he came in, but of course Harry *would* drive up right then—she heard the car out front and broke the clinch just in time, telling Rick to sneak out around the back. Harry'd be busy with the truckers for a couple of minutes at least.

Jill forced herself to wait in the bedroom until she was sure the coast was clear. She kept looking out the window but it was too dark now to see anything. Since there wasn't any noise she figured Harry must have taken the truckers back into the guest house.

And that's where she finally went.

Only the truckers weren't there. Just Harry.

"I told them to wait until first thing in the morning," he said. "Changed my mind when I realized how damp it was—no sense spending the night shivering outside in the cold. Besides, I haven't sealed the capsule yet—remembered a couple of things I wanted to add to the collection."

He took a little bottle out of his pocket and carried it over to the open capsule. "This goes in too. Carefully labeled, of course, so they can analyze it."

"The bottle's empty," Jill said.

Harry shook his head. "Not at all. It contains smog. That's right—smog, from the freeway. I want posterity to know everything about us, right down to the poisonous atmosphere in which our culture breathed its last."

He dropped the bottle into the capsule, then picked something else up from the table next to it. Jill noticed he had a soldering outfit there, ready to plug in when he sealed the lid, after he used a pump to suck the air out. He'd explained all this about the capsule being airtight, soundproof, duralumin-sheathed, but that didn't interest her now. She kept looking at what he held in his hand. It was one of those electric knife outfits, with the battery.

"Another artifact," he said. "Another symbol of our decadence. An electric knife—just the thing for Mom when she carves the fast-frozen, pre-cooked Thanksgiving turkey while she and Dad count all their shiny, synthetic, plastic blessings." He waved the knife. "They'll understand," he told her. "Those people in the future will understand it all. They'll know what life was like in our times — how we drained Walden Pond and refilled it again with blood, sweat and tears."

Jill moved a little closer, staring at the knife. "The blade's rusty," she said.

Harry shook his head. "That's not rust," he said.

Jill kept her cool. She kept it right up until the moment she looked over the edge of the big, oblong box, looked down into the opening and saw Rick lying there. Rick was all sprawled out, and the red was oozing down over the books and records and pictures and tapes.

"I waited for him when he sneaked out of the house," Harry said.

"Then you knew — all along —"

"For quite a while," Harry said. "Long enough to figure things out and make my plans."

"What plans?"

Harry just shrugged. And raised the knife.

A moment later the time capsule received the final specimen of life in the twentieth century.

UNDERGROUND

ALL DAY LONG HE RESTED, while the guns thundered in the village below. Then, in the slanting shadows of the late afternoon, the rumbling echoes faded into the distance and he knew it was over. The American advance had crossed the river. They were gone at last, and it was safe once more.

Above the village, in the crumbling ruins of the great chateau atop the wooded hillside, Count Barsac emerged from the crypt.

The Count was tall and thin—cadaverously thin, in a manner most hideously appropriate. His face and hands had a waxen pallor; his hair was dark, but not as dark as his eyes and the hollows beneath them. His cloak was black, and the sole touch of color about his person was the vivid redness of his lips when they curled in a smile.

He was smiling now, in the twilight, for it was time to play the game.

The name of the game was Death, and the Count had played it many times.

He had played it in Paris, on the stage of the Grand Guignol; his name had been plain Eric Karon then, but still he'd won a certain renown for his interpretation of bizarre roles. Then the war had come, and with it, his opportunity.

Long before the Germans took Paris, he'd joined their Underground, working long and well. As an actor, he'd been invaluable.

And this, of course, was his ultimate reward. To play the supreme role— not on the stage, but in real life. To play without the artifice of spotlights, in true darkness; this was the actor's dream come true. He had even helped to fashion the plot.

"Simplicity itself," he told his superiors. "Chateau Barsac has been deserted since the Revolution. None of the peasants from the village dare to

153

venture near it, even in daylight, because of the legend. It is said, you see, that the last Count Barsac was a vampire."

And so it was arranged. The shortwave transmitter had been set up in the crypts beneath the chateau, with three skilled operators in attendance, working in shifts. And he, Count Barsac, in charge of the entire operation, as guardian angel. Or guardian demon.

"There is a graveyard on the hillside below," he informed them. "A humble resting place for poor and ignorant people. It contains a single imposing crypt—the ancestral tomb of the Barsacs. We shall open that crypt, remove the remains of the last Count, and allow the villagers to discover that the coffin is empty. They will never venture near the spot or the chateau again, because this will prove that the legend is true—Count Barsac is a vampire, and walks once more."

The question came then. "What if there are skeptics? What if someone does not believe?"

And he had his answer ready. "They will believe. For at night, I shall walk. I, Count Barsac."

After they saw him in the makeup, wearing the cloak, there were no more questions. The role was his.

The role was his, and he'd played it well. The Count nodded to himself as he climbed the stairs and entered the roofless foyer of the chateau, where only a configuration of cobwebs veiled the radiance of the rising moon.

Now, of course, the curtain must come down. If the American advance had swept past the village below, it was time to take one's bow and exit. And that too had been well arranged.

During the German withdrawal, another advantageous use had been made of the tomb in the graveyard. A cache of Air Marshal Goering's art treasures now rested safely and undisturbed within the crypt. A lorry had been placed in the chateau. Even now, the three wireless operators would be playing new parts—driving the lorry down the hillside to the tomb, placing the artwork and artifacts in it. By the time he arrived there, everything would be packed. And they would don the stolen American Army uniforms, carry the forged identifications and permits, drive through the lines across the river and rejoin the German forces at a predesignated spot. Nothing had been left to chance. Some day, when he wrote his memoirs—

But there was no time to consider that now. The Count glanced up through the gaping aperture in the ruined roof. The moon was high. Time to leave.

In a way he hated to go. Where others saw only dust and cobwebs, he could see a stage—the setting of his finest performance. Playing a vampire's role had not addicted him to the taste of blood—but as an actor, he enjoyed the taste of triumph. And he had triumphed here.

"Parting is such sweet sorrow." Shakespeare's line. Shakespeare, who had

written of ghosts and witches, of bloody apparitions. Because he knew that his audiences, the stupid masses, believed in such things. Just as they still believed, today. A great actor could always make them believe.

The Count moved into the shadowy darkness outside the chateau entrance. He started down the pathway toward the beckoning trees.

It was here, amidst those trees, that he had come upon Raymond, one evening weeks ago. Raymond had been his most appreciative audience; a stern, dignified, white-haired elderly man, mayor of the village of Barsac. But there'd been nothing dignified about the old fool when he'd caught sight of the Count looming up before him out of the night. He'd screamed like a woman and run.

Probably he'd been prowling around, intent on poaching; all that had been forgotten after his encounter in the woods. Raymond was the one to thank for spreading the rumors that the Count was again abroad. He and Clodez, the oafish miller, had then led an armed band to the graveyard and entered the Barsac tomb. What a fright they got when they discovered the Count's coffin open and empty!

The coffin had contained only dust, and it was scattered to the winds now, but they could not know that. Nor could they know about what had happened to Suzanne.

The Count was passing the banks of the small stream now. Here, on another evening, he'd found the girl—Raymond's daughter, as luck would have it—in an embrace with young Antoine LeFevre, her lover. Antoine's shattered leg had invalided him out of the army, but he ran like a deer when he glimpsed the grinning Count. Suzanne had been left behind and that was unfortunate, because it was necessary to dispose of her. The body had been buried in the woods, beneath great stones, and there was no question of discovery; still, it was a regrettable incident.

In the end, however, everything was for the best. Because now silly superstitious Raymond was doubly convinced that the vampire walked. He had seen the creature himself, seen the empty tomb and the open coffin; his own daughter had disappeared. At his command, none dared venture near the graveyard, the woods, or the chateau beyond.

Poor Raymond! Now he was not even a mayor any more—his village had been destroyed in the bombardment. Just an ignorant, broken old man, mumbling his idiotic nonsense about the living dead.

The Count smiled and walked on, his cloak fluttering in the breeze, casting a batlike shadow on the pathway before him. He could see the graveyard now, the tilted tombstones rising from the earth like leprous fingers rotting in the moonlight. His smile faded; he did not like such thoughts. Perhaps the greatest tribute to his talent as an actor lay in his actual aversion to death, to darkness and what lurked in the night. He hated the sight of blood, realized that within himself was an almost claustrophobic dread of the confinement of the crypt.

Yes, it had been a great role, but he was thankful it was ending. It would be good to play the man once more, and cast off the creature he had created.

As he approached the crypt he saw the lorry waiting in the shadows. The entrance to the tomb was open, but no sounds issued from it. That meant his colleagues had completed their task of loading. They were ready to go. All that remained now was to change his clothing, remove the makeup, and depart.

The Count moved to the darkened lorry. And then —

Then they were upon him, and he felt the tines of the pitchfork bite into his back, and as the lantern-flash dazzled his eyes he heard the stern command. "Don't move —"

He didn't move. He could only stare as they surrounded him; Antoine, Clodez, Raymond and the others, a dozen peasants from the village. A dozen armed peasants, glaring at him in mingled rage and fear, holding him at bay.

But how could they dare —?

The American Corporal stepped forward. That was the answer, of course. The American Corporal and another man in uniform, armed with a sniper's rifle. They were responsible. He didn't even have to see the riddled corpses of his three assistants piled in the back of the lorry to understand what had happened. They'd stumbled on his men while they worked, shot them down, and summoned the villagers.

Now they were jabbering questions at him, in English, of course. He understood English, but he knew better than to reply. "Who are you? Were these men working under your orders? Where were you going with this truck —?"

The Count smiled and shook his head. After a while they stopped, as he knew they would.

The Corporal turned to his companion. "OK," he said. "Let's go." The other man nodded and climbed into the cab of the lorry as the motor coughed into life. The Corporal moved to join him, then turned to Raymond.

"We're taking this across the river," he said. "Hang onto our friend, here — they'll be sending a guard detail for him within an hour."

Raymond nodded.

Then the lorry drove off into the darkness.

And it *was* dark now; the moon had vanished behind a cloud. The Count's smile vanished, too, as he glanced around him at his captors. A dozen stupid clods, surly and ignorant. But armed. No chance of escaping. And they kept staring at him, and mumbling.

"Take him into the tomb."

It was Raymond who said that, and they obeyed, prodding their captive forward with pitchforks. That was when the Count recognized the first faint ray of hope. For they prodded him most gingerly, no man venturing close, and when he glared at them their eyes dropped. They were putting him in the crypt because they were afraid of him. Now that the Americans were gone, they feared once more; feared his presence and his power. After all, in their eyes he was a vampire—he might turn into a bat and vanish entirely. So they wanted him in the tomb for safekeeping.

The Count shrugged, smiled his sinister smile, and bared his teeth. They shrank back as he entered the doorway. He turned, and on impulse, furled his cape. It was an instinctive final gesture, in keeping with his role—and it provoked the appropriate response. They moaned, and old Raymond crossed himself. It was better, in a way, than any applause.

In the darkness of the crypt, the Count permitted himself to relax a trifle. He was offstage now, and for the last time. A pity he'd not been able to make his exit the way he'd planned, but such were the fortunes of war. Now he'd be taken to the American headquarters and interrogated. Undoubtedly there would be some unpleasant moments, but the worst that could befall him was a few months in a prison camp. And even the Americans must bow to him in appreciation when they heard the story of his masterful deception.

It was dark in the crypt, and musty. The Count moved about restlessly. His knee grazed the edge of the empty coffin set on a trestle in the tomb. He shuddered involuntarily, loosening his cape at the throat. It would be good to remove it, good to be out of here, good to shed the role of vampire forever. He'd played it well, but now he was anxious to be gone.

There was a mumbling audible from without, mingled with another and less identifiable noise—a scraping sound. The Count moved to the closed door of the crypt, listening intently, but now there was only silence.

What were the fools doing out there? He wished the Americans would hurry back. It was too hot in here. And why the sudden silence?

Perhaps they'd gone.

Yes. That was it. The Americans had told them to wait and guard him, but they were afraid. They really believed he was a vampire, old Raymond had convinced them of that. So they'd run off. They'd run off, and he was free, he could escape now—

So the Count opened the door.

And he saw them then, saw them standing and waiting, old Raymond staring sternly for a moment before he moved forward. He was holding something in his hand, and the Count recognized it, remembering the scraping sound he'd heard.

It was a long wooden stake with a sharp point.

Then he opened his mouth to scream, telling them it was only a trick, he was no vampire, they were a pack of superstitious fools —

But all the while they bore him back into the crypt, lifting him up and thrusting him into the open coffin, holding him there as the grim-faced Raymond raised the pointed stake above his heart.

It was only when the stake came down that he realized there's such a thing as playing a role too well. . . .

A TOY FOR JULIETTE

JULIETTE ENTERED HER BEDROOM, smiling, and a thousand Juliettes smiled back at her. For all the walls were paneled with mirrors, and the ceiling was set with inlaid panes that reflected her image.

Wherever she glanced she could see the blonde curls framing the sensitive features of a face that was a radiant amalgam of both child and angel; a striking contrast to the rich, ripe revelation of her body in the filmy robe.

But Juliette wasn't smiling at herself. She smiled because she knew that Grandfather was back, and he'd brought her another toy. In just a few moments it would be decontaminated and delivered, and she wanted to be ready.

Juliette turned the ring on her finger and the mirrors dimmed. Another turn would darken the room entirely; a twist in the opposite direction would bring them blazing into brilliance. It was all a matter of choice — but then, that was the secret of life. To choose, for pleasure.

And what was her pleasure tonight?

Juliette advanced to one of the mirror panels and passed her hand before it. The glass slid to one side, revealing the niche behind it; the coffin-shaped opening in the solid rock, with the boot and thumbscrews set at the proper heights.

For a moment she hesitated; she hadn't played *that* game in years. Another time, perhaps. Juliette waved her hand and the mirror moved to cover the opening again.

She wandered along the row of panels, gesturing as she walked, pausing to inspect what was behind each mirror in turn. Here was the rack, there the stocks with the barbed whips resting against the dark-stained wood. And here was the dissecting table, hundreds of years old, with its quaint instruments; behind the next panel, the electrical prods and wires that produced such weird grimaces and contortions of agony, to say nothing of screams. Of course the screams didn't matter in a soundproofed room.

Juliette moved to the side wall and waved her hand again; the obedient glass slid away and she stared at a plaything she'd almost forgotten. It was one of the first things Grandfather had ever given her, and it was very old, almost like a mummy case. What had he called it? The Iron Maiden of Nuremberg, that was it—with the sharpened steel spikes set inside the lid. You chained a man inside, and you turned the little crank that closed the lid, ever so slowly, and the spikes pierced the wrists and the elbows, the ankles and the knees, the groin and the eyes. You had to be careful not to get excited and turn too quickly, or you'd spoil the fun.

Grandfather had shown her how it worked, the first time he brought her a real *live* toy. But then, Grandfather had shown her everything. He'd taught her all she knew, for he was very wise. He'd even given her her name— Juliette—from one of the old-fashioned printed books he'd discovered by the philosopher, de Sade.

Grandfather had brought the books from the Past, just as he'd brought the playthings for her. He was the only one who had access to the Past, because he owned the Traveler.

The Traveler was a very ingenious mechanism, capable of attaining vibrational frequencies which freed it from the time-bind. At rest, it was just a big square boxlike shape, the size of a small room. But when Grandfather took over the controls and the oscillation started, the box would blur and disappear. It was still there, Grandfather said—at least, the *matrix* remained as a fixed point in space and time—but anything or anyone within the square could move freely into the Past to wherever the controls were programmed. Of course they would be invisible when they arrived, but that was actually an advantage, particularly when it came to finding things and bringing them back. Grandfather had brought back some very interesting objects from almost mythical places—the great Library of Alexandria, the Pyramid of Cheops, the Kremlin, the Vatican, Fort Knox—all the storehouses of treasure and knowledge which existed thousands of years ago. He liked to go to *that* part of the Past, the period before the thermonuclear wars and the robotic ages, and collect things. Of course books and jewels and metals were useless, except to an antiquarian, but Grandfather was a romanticist and loved the olden times.

It was strange to think of him owning the Traveler, but of course he hadn't actually created it. Juliette's father was really the one who built it, and Grandfather took possession of it after her father died. Juliette suspected Grandfather had killed her father and mother when she was just a baby, but she could never be sure. Not that it mattered; Grandfather was always very good to her, and besides, soon he would die and she'd own the Traveler herself.

They used to joke about it frequently. "I've made you into a monster," he'd say. "And some day you'll end up by destroying me. After which, of course, you'll go on to destroy the entire world—or what little remains of it."

"Aren't you afraid?" she'd tease.

"Certainly not. That's my dream—the destruction of everything. An end to all this sterile decadence. Do you realize that at one time there were more than three billion inhabitants on this planet? And now, less that three thousand! Less than three thousand, shut up inside these Domes, prisoners of themselves and sealed away forever, thanks to the sins of the fathers who poisoned not only the outside world but outer space by meddling with the atomic order of the universe. Humanity is virtually extinct already; you will merely hasten the finale."

"But couldn't we all go back to another time, in the Traveler?" she asked.

"Back to *what* time? The continuum is changeless; one event leads inexorably to another, all links in a chain which binds us to the present and its inevitable end in destruction. We'd have temporary individual survival, yes, but to no purpose. And none of us are fitted to survive in a more primitive environment. So let us stay here and take what pleasure we can from the moment. *My* pleasure is to be the sole user and possessor of the Traveler. And yours, Juliette—"

Grandfather laughed then. They both laughed, because they knew what *her* pleasure was.

Juliette killed her first toy when she was eleven—a little boy. It had been brought to her as a special gift from Grandfather, from somewhere in the Past, for elementary sex-play. But it wouldn't cooperate, and she lost her temper and beat it to death with a steel rod. So Grandfather brought her an older toy, with brown skin, and it cooperated very well, but in the end she tired of it and one day when it was sleeping in her bed she tied it down and found a knife.

Experimenting a little before it died, Juliette discovered new sources of pleasure, and of course Grandfather found out. That's when he'd christened her "Juliette." He seemed to approve most highly, and from then on he brought her the playthings she kept behind the mirrors in her bedroom, and on his restless rovings into the Past he brought her new toys.

Being invisible, he could find them for her almost anywhere on his travels—all he did was to use a stunner and transport them when he returned. Of course each toy had to be very carefully decontaminated; the Past was teeming with strange microorganisms. But once the toys were properly antiseptic they were turned over to Juliette for her pleasure, and during the past seven years she had enjoyed herself.

It was always delicious, this moment of anticipation before a new toy arrived. What would it be like? Grandfather was most considerate; mainly, he made sure that the toys he brought her could speak and understand

Anglish—or "English," as they used to call it in the Past. Verbal communication was often important, particularly if Juliette wanted to follow the precepts of the philosopher de Sade and enjoy some form of sex relation before going on to keener pleasures.

But there was still the guessing beforehand. Would this toy be young or old, wild or tame, male or female? She'd had all kinds, and every possible combination. Sometimes she kept them alive for days before tiring of them —or before the subtleties of which she was capable caused them to expire. At other times she wanted it to happen quickly; tonight, for example, she knew she could be soothed only by the most primitive and direct action.

Once Juliette realized this, she stopped playing with her mirror panels and went directly to the big bed. She pulled back the coverlet, groped under the pillow until she felt it. Yes, it was still there—the big knife, with the long, cruel blade. She knew what she would do now; take the toy to bed with her and then, at precisely the proper moment, combine her pleasures. If she could time her knife-thrust—

She shivered with anticipation, then with impatience.

What kind of toy would it be? She remembered the suave, cool one— Benjamin Bathurst was his name, an English diplomat from the time of what Grandfather called the Napoleonic Wars. Oh, he'd been suave and cool enough, until she beguiled him with her body, into the bed. And there'd been that American aviatrix from slightly later on in the Past, and once, as a very special treat, the entire crew of a sailing vessel called the *Marie Celeste*. They had lasted for *weeks*!

Strangely enough, she'd even read about some of her toys afterward. Because when Grandfather approached them with his stunner and brought them here, they disappeared forever from the Past, and if they were in any way known or important in their time, such disappearances were noted. And some of Grandfather's books had accounts of the "mysterious vanishing" which took place and was, of course, never explained. How delicious it all was!

Juliette patted the pillow back into place and slid the knife under it. She couldn't wait, now; what was delaying things?

She forced herself to move to a vent and depress the sprayer, shedding her robe as the perfumed mist bathed her body. It was the final allurement —but why didn't her toy arrive?

Suddenly Grandfather's voice came over the auditor.

"I'm sending you a little surprise, dearest."

That's what he always said; it was part of the game.

Juliette depressed the communicator toggle. "Don't tease," she begged. "Tell me what it's like."

"An Englishman. Late Victorian era. Very prim and proper, by the looks of him."

"Young? Handsome?"

"Passable." Grandfather chuckled. "Your appetites betray you, dearest."

"Who is it — someone from the books?"

"I wouldn't know the name. We found no identification during the decontamination. But from his dress and manner, and the little black bag he carried when I discovered him so early in the morning, I'd judge him to be a physician returning from an emergency call."

Juliette knew about "physicians" from her reading, of course; just as she knew what "Victorian" meant. Somehow the combination seemed exactly right.

"Prim and proper?" She giggled. "Then I'm afraid it's due for a shock."

Grandfather laughed. "You have something in mind, I take it."

"Yes."

"Can I watch?"

"Please — not this time."

"Very well."

"Don't be mad, darling. I love you."

Juliette switched off. Just in time, too, because the door was opening and the toy came in.

She stared at it, realizing that Grandfather had told the truth. The toy was male of thirty-odd years, attractive but by no means handsome. It couldn't be, in that dark garb and those ridiculous side whiskers. There was something almost depressingly refined and mannered about it, an air of embarrassed repression.

And of course, when it caught sight of Juliette in her revealing robe, and the bed surrounded by mirrors, it actually began to *blush*.

That reaction won Juliette completely. A blushing Victorian, with the build of a bull — and unaware that this was the slaughterhouse!

It was so amusing she couldn't restrain herself; she moved forward at once and put her arms around it.

"Who — who are you? Where am I?"

The usual questions, voiced in the usual way. Ordinarily, Juliette would have amused herself by parrying with answers designed to tantalize and titillate her victim. But tonight she felt an urgency which only increased as she embraced the toy and pressed it back toward the waiting bed.

The toy began to breathe heavily, responding. But it was still bewildered. "Tell me — I don't understand. Am I alive? Or is this heaven?"

Juliette's robe fell open as she lay back. "You're alive, darling," she murmured. "Wonderfully alive." She laughed as she began to prove the statement. "But closer to heaven than you think."

And to prove *that* statement, her free hand slid under the pillow and groped for the waiting knife.

But the knife wasn't there any more. Somehow it had already found its way into the toy's hand. And the toy wasn't prim and proper any longer, its face was something glimpsed in nightmare. Just a glimpse, before the blinding blur of the knife-blade, as it came down, again and again and again—

The room, of course, was soundproof, and there was plenty of time. They didn't discover what was left of Juliette's body for several days.

Back in London, after the final mysterious murder in the early morning hours, they never did find Jack the Ripper. . . .

THE GODS ARE NOT MOCKED

HARRY HINCH was a funny man and he sold funny things. He had a groovy little hole-in-the-wall shop near the Strip with a big burlap sack hanging in the window and a sign reading WHAT'S YOUR BAG? and inside he stocked goodies for everyone.

There were lurid paperbacks and off-brand LPs, of course, and campy photographic blow-ups of Theda Bara, but Harry's store wasn't just one of those places catering to UCLA drop-outs. Naturally he sold psychedelic prints and Nazi helmets and Iron Crosses and Mellow Yellow and sunflower seeds, but he had some swinging specialties, too. Like dirty Mother's Day cards, for instance. And leather goods — a whole counter of gloves, high-heeled boots, riding crops, and dog whips. For the birds he stocked kinky lingerie; bras in the shape of two clutching, hairy hands; and a G-string designed to look like an open mouth with two rows of sharp-pointed teeth.

But Harry was proudest of the items he dreamed up on his own. Along with the usual bumper stickers and buttons — VIRGINITY CAUSES CANCER, DRACULA SUCKS, and MARY POPPINS IS A JUNKIE — he pushed a line of originals like IT TAKES TWO TO MAKE A LOVE-IN, FLOWER CHILDREN ARE PANSIES, and KEEP INCEST IN THE FAMILY.

To look at him, sitting up front behind the cash register, you'd never think he was a mover and shaker. There are a dozen duplicates of Harry in the sidewalk scofferies on the Strip — they're all a little on the short side, dress very tight and mod, and when their hairlines start to recede they sprout the usual compensation on their chins. They plant grass, they sell tickets for trips you can't book with a travel agency, they'll match you with an ideal partner without using a computer. But most of them aren't really *creative*, like Harry was.

165

He was the one who did the I'M A FLAMING HETEROSEXUAL button and the bumper sticker that says, CAUTION — THIS CAR IS DRIVEN BY HELEN KELLER. Bumper stickers were a "thing" with old Harry. Every night he sat up turning out jollies like BE CHARITABLE — CONTRIBUTE TO THE DELINQUENCY OF MINORS and DR. FU MANCHU IS ALIVE AND PERFORMING ABORTIONS IN PASADENA.

Of course not everybody dug Harry. Some cubes said he was hung-up on put-downs. But you've got to expect such flap from the senior citizens; their idea of black comedy ended with Amos 'n' Andy. The fuzz did everything they could to nail him for running an illegal letter drop, pushing pot, and a few other sideline scuffles, but Harry just kept on laughing and scratching.

It was always a freak-out scene at Harry's shop, with the hogs and choppers parked outside and the hippies and the teeny-boppers balling it up inside. He kept it cool and quiet, and the only noise was the ringing of the cash register.

When the crunch came, Harry was clean. It wasn't his problem when a juvie named Kim Carmichael wiggled her miniskirt at old Grabber. Sure, they met at his shop, but Harry didn't set up the action. Harry didn't claim he was a chemistry major, and if he sold Grabber a few sugar cubes that didn't prove he knew they were loaded.

Old Grabber had come on strong for Kim Carmichael, but Harry never told him to cut out with her riding tailgunner on his chopper; Harry never told him to suck the cubes he bought, and Harry definitely didn't tell him to sail off that sharp curve on top of Mulholland and total the chopper, himself, and Kim Carmichael.

When Harry got the word he knew it was either split out or cop out and he wasn't about to take any chances of getting busted. So he hung his GOD IS DEAD AND I'M GOING TO THE FUNERAL sign on the front door and faded fast.

Way past Baldy, up in the National Forest, Harry had a little pad — just a shack, a real nothing scene, but a place where he could get away from the heat.

That's where Harry headed for, right into the old boondocks, way out in the toolies with big trees and the mountains and the high lonesomes all around. He holed up in his cabin and waited; in a week or so the fuzz would cool it and meanwhile he was safe as the pill because nobody knew where he was hanging in.

The only thing was that he was all alone and it gets dark pretty early in the woods and very quiet. Harry never realized how much he was used to hearing the cut-outs blasting and the transistor sets blaring and the rumble of the freeways blending all the sounds together for background music. And he missed the lights and the wiggy crowds that kept him company in the ship, even the sickies that talked to themselves. Harry just wasn't with the country-and-western bit, and by the time the sun went down that first night he was ready to climb the walls.

When he knew he was uptight, Harry decided to take his mind off things by doing a little occupational therapy with a bottle of juice he'd packed along. A couple of blasts and he felt better, but he still wasn't comfy-cozy about the dark shadows and the way the wind started to shiver in the tall trees around the cabin.

So he belted another slug and settled down to work. No point just sitting there and thinking about the news report — how the old chopper went sailing off down a sixty-foot drop and landed right on Grabber's spine, then smashed Kim Carmichael's arms, legs, and face —

No, it was better to do a little serious constructive work, and Harry had pen and paper and he was creative and with it, and in no time at all he was lining out some new copy for stickers. KICK YOUR HOBBIT, for the Tolkien crowd, and a Zen Thing, BIG BUDDHA IS WATCHING YOU, and then, REALITY IS A PUT-ON.

But there were shadows moving outside and the wind kept moaning and he didn't like the trees in the first place, to hell with the conservationists, and that gave Harry another inspiration; so he wrote down SMOKEY THE BEAR IS A PYROMANIAC.

That really broke him up; he'd always hated that damned smart-aleck picture and the slogan about forest fires and for two cents and another belt from the bottle he'd start a fire himself and burn down the whole lousy setup and the Boy Scouts and the mothers and the veterans and the fuzz and the rest of the squares that bugged him, that were always bugging Harry to believe in their stinking superstitions about God and Freud and Law and Order and Love and Happiness. It was all a big yak and Harry had to laugh; he was still laughing when Dr. Carmichael walked in.

Dr. Carmichael or Professor Carmichael — Harry didn't know which it was, and it didn't matter. All he knew when the guy introduced himself was that this Carmichael was Kim Carmichael's father.

He must have tailed Harry up to the cabin all the way from town when he took off, and he'd hung around waiting until it got dark to make his move.

There he was, standing in the doorway, saying nothing except, "I'm Carmichael — Kim's father," and doing nothing but stare at Harry. He was a tall, skinny gray-haired cat — taught sociology or ethics or some such crud out at the U — and Harry could have taken him in one fast chop. Except that the old guy was holding an Astra .25 with the safety off. A very small gun, but the kind that makes a very big hole at close range.

"Sit down," said Carmichael, and Harry sat down. He wasn't exactly loving every minute of it, but one thing he knew for sure. Carmichael wasn't about to kill him, not after telling him to sit. He wouldn't be shooting off anything but his mouth, and this Harry could take.

He took it for about ten minutes, took it with a very straight face — all the usual jazz about, "You murderer, you killed my daughter just as surely as if you drove that motorcycle off the cliff yourself," and a lot more. Harry couldn't have cared less until Carmichael started getting to him. *Him*, personally.

"I've seen your store," Carmichael said. "I've seen the sickness you sell —the sickness of our times. Oh, I know all the rationalizations. The fix is in, the dice are loaded, you can't win for losing, all the world's a Theatre of the Absurd, life's just another Happening, and why play anything straight?

"So you and your kind put down heroes in the name of humor, you put down society in the name of satire, you put down culture and call it comedy.

"But you're not a funny man, Harry. Behind the laughter there's hatred, and behind the hatred is fear. That's the real reason for the put-downs, isn't it? Because you're afraid of everything and everyone. There's a name for your disease—paranoid fixation. You're a carrier, you infect everything you touch.

"You infect the mumbling misfits who come to your shop—the idle, would-be idol-smashers who foist their fears and vent their aggressions on the world of reality. And you infect the healthy ones, too—girls like Kim who mistake your hostility for profundity—"

"Get off my back," said Harry.

"I'm not on your back," Carmichael told him. "You're carrying your own monkey. The simian syndrome—huddling behind the bars of your cage and making faces at the world because it frightens you. Monkey sees, monkey does, and because there are thousands of others just like you, you think you've got a grasp on the truth.

"But for every thousand pedestal-topplers and icon-breakers, there are millions who still believe otherwise. And perhaps their belief is stronger than yours.

"Have you ever really thought about this faith you spend your life trying to destroy—the sustaining faith that most of the world maintains in its illusions? Belief sanctifies, you know. Belief *makes* heroes, creates beauty and honor and decency and all the other phenomena which you laugh at. You paranoid types can't stand heroes, can you, Harry? Not even the make-believe ones in art and literature and the mass media of TV and films. But in terms of belief they do exist, you know. Hamlet is far more *real* to us than Shakespeare, and though Conan Doyle is dead, Sherlock Holmes still has a life of his own.

"I suspect you *do* realize this, and that's why you put down the villains, too—with all the snickering about Dracula and King Kong and the little wind-up toy Frankenstein's Monster that loses its trousers when it starts to reach out for you. These things scared you when you were a kid and you're still scared; so you've got to laugh at them and pretend they're not real."

Carmichael looked down at the table and saw what Harry had been writing and he shook his head.

"SMOKEY THE BEAR IS A PYROMANIAC," he said. "Why, Harry? Why? Is it because you were afraid of the Three Bears when Mommy told you the story? Is it because you secretly believe there is such a creature? Well, if there's any power in faith, then the belief of millions of youngsters constitutes a force you'll never laugh away with a cheap put-down. Maybe you have good reason for your fear, Harry. Belief creates our gods, and the gods are not mocked."

That is what Carmichael told Harry before he went away.

At least he *says* he told Harry and went away, but we have only his word for it.

We do know, from a guy named Rogers who happened to be bedding down in his camper about a half mile away on the lake, that the lights went out in Harry's cabin around midnight; probably right after Harry finished the last of his whiskey.

A little while later, the growling started. The growling, and the screams.

You could hear them echoing all over the lake, but by the time Rogers stumbled through the pitch-black woods and reached the cabin there was no sound except the whispering of the wind.

Harry was dead by then; nobody could have survived the ripping and the chewing. Perhaps Carmichael was lying, maybe *he* was the crazy one and came back to descend on Harry in the darkness, to bite and slash and tear. He could even have planted that strange object on the cabin's earthen floor alongside Harry's body — the crushed and crumpled Boy Scout hat, with its rank animal odor.

Maybe so.

But nobody ever explained the pawprints.

HOW LIKE A GOD

1

To *be* WAS SWEET.

There was meditation—a turning-in upon one's self. There was contemplation—a turning-out to regard others, and otherness.

In meditation one remained contained. In contemplation there was a merging, a coalescence with the rest.

Mok preferred meditation. Here Mok enjoyed identity and was conscious of being *he, she* or *it*, endlessly repeated through the memory of millennia of incarnations. Mok, like the others, had evolved through many life forms on many worlds. Now Mok was free of the pain and free of the pleasures, too, free of the illusions of the senses which had served the bodies housing the beings which finally became Mok.

And yet, Mok was not wholly free. Because Mok still turned to the memories for satisfaction.

The others preferred contemplation. They enjoyed coalescing, mingling their memories, pooling their awareness and sharing their sense of being.

Mok could never share completely. Mok was too conscious of the differences. For even without body, without sex, without physical limitation imposed by substance in time and space, Mok was aware of inequality.

Mok was aware of Ser.

Ser was the mightiest of them all. In coalescence, Ser's being dominated every pattern of contemplation. Ser's will imposed harmony on the others, but only if the others surrendered to it.

To *be* was sweet. But it was not sweet enough.

Upon this, Mok meditated. And when coalescence came again, Mok did not

171

surrender. Mok fixed firmly upon the concept of freedom — freedom of choice, the final freedom which Ser denied.

There was agitation amongst the others; Mok sensed it. Some attempted to merge with Mok, for they too shared the concept, and Mok opened to receive them, feeling the strength grow. Mok was as strong as Ser now, stronger, calling upon the will and purpose born of memories of millions of finite existences in which will and purpose were the roots of survival. But that survival had been temporary, and this would be permanent, forever.

Mok held the concept, gathered the strength, firmed the purpose — and then, quite suddenly, the purpose faded. The strength oozed away. The others were gone; nothing was left but Mok and the concept itself. The concept to —

Mok couldn't grasp the concept now. It had vanished.

All that remained was Mok and Ser. Ser's will, obliterating concept and purpose and strength, imposing itself upon Mok, invading and inundating Mok's awareness. Mok's very *being*. But without concept there was no purpose, without purpose there was no strength, without strength Mok could not preserve awareness, and without awareness there was no being.

Without being there was no Mok.

When Mok's identity returned he was in the ship.

Ship?

Only memories of distant incarnations told Mok this was a ship, but it was unmistakably so: a ship, a vessel, a transporter, a physical object, capable of physical movement through space and time.

Space and time existed again, and the ship moved through them. The ship was confined in space and time, and Mok was confined in the ship, which was just large enough to house him as he journeyed.

Yes, *he.*

Mok was *he.* Confined now, not only in the prison of space and time, nor in the smaller prison of the ship, but in the prison of a body. A male body.

Male. Mammalian. A spine to support the frame, arms and legs to support and grasp, eyes and ears and nose and other crude sensory receivers. Flesh, blood, skin — yellowish fur covering the latter, even along the lashing tail. Lungs for oxygen intake, which at the moment was supplied by an ingenious transparent helmet and attached pack mechanism.

Ingenious? But this was clumsy, crude, primitive, a relic of remote barbaric eras Mok could only vaguely recall. He tried to meditate, tried to contemplate, but now he could only *see* — see through the transparency of the helmet as the ship settled to rest and its belly opened to catapult him forth upon the frigid surface of a barren planet where a cold moon wheeled against the icy glitter of distant stars.

The ship, too, had a form — a body that was in itself vaguely modeled on mammalian concept, almost like one of those giant robots developed by life forms in intermediate stages of evolution.

Mok stared at the ship as it rested before him on the sterile, starlit slope. Yes, the ship had a domed cranial protuberance and two metal arms terminating in claws. Claws to open the belly of the ship, claws that had lifted Mok's body forth to disgorge him from the belly in a parody of birth.

Now, as Mok watched, the ship's belly was closing again, sealing tightly while the metallic claws returned to rest at its sides. And flames of force were blasting from the pediment.

The ship was rising, taking off.

Mok had been embodied in the confines of the ship, imprisoned in this, his present form. The ship had carried him to this world and now it was leaving him here. Which meant that the ship must be —

"*Ser!*" he screamed, as the realization came, and the sound of his voice echoing in the hollow helmet almost split his skull. But Ser did not answer. The ship continued to rise, the rising accelerated, there was a roar and a glimmer and then an incandescence which faded to nothingness against the black backdrop of emptiness punctured by glittering pinpoints of light flickering down upon the world into which Mok had been born.

The world where Ser had left him to die. . . .

2

Mok turned away. His body burned. *Burned?* Mok searched archaic memories and came up with another concept. He wasn't burning. He was freezing. This was cold.

The surface of the planet was cold, and his skin — *fur?* — did not sufficiently protect him. Mok took a deep breath, and that in turn brought consciousness of the inner mechanism: circulation, nervous system, lungs. Lungs for breath, supplying the fuel of life.

The feeder-pack on his back was small. Its content, scarcely enough to fill his needs on the flight here, would soon be exhausted.

Was there oxygen on the surface of this planet? Mok glanced around. The rocky terrain was devoid of vegetation, and that was not a promising sign. But perhaps the entire surface wasn't like this; in other areas at lower levels, plant life might flourish. If so, functioning existence could be sustained.

There was only one way to learn. Mok's prehensile appendages — not exactly claws, not quite fingers — fumbled clumsily with the fastenings of the helmet and raised it gingerly. He took a shallow breath, then another. Yes, there was oxygen present.

Satisfied, Mok removed helmet and pack, along with the control mechanism strapped to his side. There'd be no further need of this apparatus here.

What he needed now was warmth, a heated atmosphere.

He glanced toward the bleak, black bulk of crags looming across the barren plain. He moved toward them slowly, under the silent, staring stars, toiling up a slope as a sudden wind tore at his shivering body. It was awkward, this body of his, a clumsy mechanism subject to crude muscular control. Only atavism came to his aid as half-perceived memories of ancient physical existence enabled him to move his legs with proper coordination. Walking — climbing — then crawling and clinging to the rocks — all was demanding, difficult, a challenge to be met and mastered.

But Mok ascended the face of the nearest cliff and found the opening, a crevasse with an inner fissure that became the mouth of a cave. A dark shelter from the wind, but it was warmer here. And the rocky floor sloped into deeper darkness. The pupils of his eyes accommodated, and he could guide himself in the dim tunnelway, for his vision was that of a feral nyctalops.

Mok crept through caverns like a giant cat, gusts of warm air billowing against his body to beckon him forward. Forward and down, forward and down. And now the heat rose about him in palpable waves, the air singed with an acrid scent, and there was a glowing from a light source ahead. Forward and down toward the light source, until he heard the hissing and the rumbling, felt the scalding steam, breathed the lung-searing gases, saw the spurting flames in which steam and gas were born.

The inner core of the planet was molten!

Mok went no farther. He turned and retreated to a comfortable distance, moving into a side passageway which led to still other offshoots. Here tortuous tunnels branched in all directions, but he was safe in warmth and darkness; safe to rest. His body — this corporeal prison in which he was doomed to dwell — needed rest.

Rest was not sleep. Rest was not hibernation, or estivation, or any of a thousand forms of suspended animation which Mok's memory summoned from myriad incarnations in the past. Rest was merely passivity. Passivity and reflection.

Reflection. . . .

Images mingled with long-discarded verbal concepts. With their aid, while passive, Mok formulated his situation. He was in the body of a beast, but there were subtle differentiations from the true mammal. Oxygen was needed, but not the respite of true sleep. And he felt no visceral stirrings, no pangs of physical hunger. He would not be dependent, he knew, upon the ingestion of alien substance for continued survival. As long as he protected his fleshly envelope from extremes of heat and cold, as long as he avoided excessive demands upon muscles and organs, he would exist. But despite the difference which distinguished him from a true mammal, he was still confined to his feral form. And his existence was bestial.

Sensation surged within him, a flood of feeling Mok had not experienced in eons, a quickening, sickening, burning, churning evocation of emotion. He knew it now. It was fear.

Fear.

The true bondage of the beast.

Mok was afraid, because now he understood that this was planned, this part of Ser's purpose. Ser had committed him to this degradation and modified his mammalian aspect so that he could exist eternally.

That was what Mok feared. Eternity in *this* form!

Passive no longer, Mok flexed and rose. Summoning cognition to utmost capacity, Mok searched within himself for other, inherent powers. The power to merge, to coalesce — that was gone. The power to transmute, to transfer, to transport, to transform — gone. He could not change his physical being, could not alter his physical environment, save by physical means of his own devising within the limitations of his beast's body.

So there was no escape from this existence.

No escape.

The realization brought fresh fear, and Mok turned and ran. Ran blindly through the twisting corridors, fear riding him as he raced, raced mindlessly, endlessly.

Somewhere along the way a tunnel burrowed upward. Mok toiled through it, panting and gasping for breath; he willed himself to stop breathing but the body, the beast-body, sucked air in greedy gulps, autonomically functioning beyond his conscious control.

Scrambling along slanted spirals, Mok emerged once more upon the outer surface of his planetary prison. This was a low-lying area, distant and different from his point of entry, with vegetation vividly verdant against a dazzling dawn — a valley, capable of supporting life.

And there was life here! Feathery forms chattering in the trees, furry figures scurrying through undergrowth, scaly slitherers, chitinoidal burrowers buzzing. These were simple shapes, crudely conceived creatures of primitive pursuits, but alive and aware.

Mok sensed them, and they sensed Mok. There was no way of communicating with them except vocally, but even the soft sounds issuing from his throat sent them fleeing frantically. For Mok was a beast now, who feared and was feared.

He crouched amongst the rocks at the mouth of the cavern from which he had come forth and gazed in helpless, hopeless confusion at the panic his presence had provoked, and the soft sounds he uttered gave place to a growling groan of despair.

And it was then that they found him — the hairy bipeds, moved cautiously to encircle him until he was ringed by a shambling band. These were troglodytes, grunting and snuffling and giving off an acrid stench of mingled fear and rage as they cautiously approached.

* * *

Mok stared at them, noting how the hunched, swaying figures moved in concert to approach him. They clutched rude clubs, mere branches torn from trees; some carried rocks scooped up from the surface of the slope. But these were weapons, capable of inflicting injury, and the hairy creatures were hunters seeking their prey.

Mok turned to retreat into the cavern, but the way was barred now by shaggy bodies, and there was no escape.

The troglodytes pressed forward now, awe and apprehension giving place to anger. Yellow fangs bared, hairy arms raised. One of the creatures — the leader of the pack — grunted what seemed a signal.

And they hurled their rocks.

Mok raised his arms to protect his head. His vision was blocked, so that he heard the sound of the stones clattering against the slope before he saw them fall. Then, as the growls and shrieks rose to a frenzy, Mok glanced up to see the rocks rebounding upon his attackers.

Raging, they closed in to smash at Mok's skull and body with their clubs. Mok heard the sounds of impact, but he felt nothing, for the blows never reached their intended target. Instead, the clubs splintered and broke in empty air.

Then Mok whirled, confused, to face his enemies. As he did so they recoiled, screaming in fright. Breaking the circle, they retreated down the slopes and into the forest, fleeing from this strange thing that could not be harmed or killed, this invincible entity —

This invincible entity.

It was Mok's concept, and he understood, now. Ser had granted him that final irony — invincibility. A field of force, surrounding his body, rendering him immune to injury and death. No doubt it also immunized him from bacterial invasion. He was in a physical form, but one independent of physical needs to sustain survival; one which would exist, indestructibly, forever. He was, in truth, imprisoned, and eternal.

For a moment Mok stood stunned at the comprehension, blankly blinded by the almost tangible intensity of black despair. Here was the ultimate horror — doom without death, exile without end, isolation throughout infinity. *Alone forever.*

Numbed senses reasserted their sway, and Mok glanced around the empty stillness of the slope.

It wasn't entirely empty. Two of the troglodytic creatures sprawled motionless on the rocks directly below him. One was bleeding from a gash in the side of his head, inflicted by a rebounding club, the other had been felled by a glancing blow from a stone.

These creatures weren't immortal.

Mok moved toward them, noting chest movement, the soft susurration of breath.

They weren't immortal, but they were still alive. Alive and helpless. Vulnerable, at his mercy.

Mercy. The quality Ser had refused to show Mok. There had been no mercy in condemning him to spend eternity here alone.

Mok halted, peering down at the two unconscious forms. He made a sound in his throat, a sound that was curiously like a chuckle.

Perhaps that was a way out, after all, a way to at least mitigate his sentence here. If *he* showed mercy now, to these creatures — he might not always be alone.

Mok reached down, lifting the body of the first creature in his arms. It was heavy in its limpness, but Mok's strength was great. He picked up the second creature carefully, so as not to injure it further.

Then, still chuckling, Mok turned and carried the two unconscious forms back into the cavern.

3

In the warm, firelit shelter of the deeper caverns, Mok tended to the creatures. While they slumbered fitfully, he ascended again to the surface and foraged for their nourishment in the green glades. He brought food and, calling upon distant memories, fashioned small clay pots in which to carry water to them from a mountainside spring.

After a time they regained consciousness and they were afraid — afraid of the great beast with the bulging eyes and lashing tail, the beast they knew to be deathless.

It was simple enough for Mok to fathom the crude construct of growls and gruntings which served these life forms as a principal means of communication, simple enough to grasp the limited concepts and references symbolized in their speech. Within these limitations he attempted to tell them who and what he was and how he had come to be here, but while they listened they did not comprehend.

And still they feared him, the female specimen more than the male. The male, at least, evinced curiosity concerning the clay pots, and Mok demonstrated the fashioning method until the male was able to imitate it successfully.

But both were wary, and both reacted in terror when confronted with the molten reaches of the planet's inner core. Nor could they become accustomed to the acrid gases, the darkness enveloping the maze of far-flung fissures honeycombing the substrata. As they gathered strength over the passage of time, they huddled together and murmured, eyeing Mok apprehensively.

Mok was not too surprised when, upon returning from one of his food-gathering expeditions to the surface, he discovered that they were gone.

But Mok *was* surprised by the strength of his own reaction—the sudden responsive surge of *loneliness*.

Loneliness—for those creatures? They couldn't conceivably serve as companions, even on the lowest level of such a relationship; and yet he missed their presence. Their mere presence had in itself been some assuagement to his own inner agony of isolation.

Now he realized a growing sympathy for them in the helplessness of their abysmal ignorance. Even their destructive impulses excited pity, for such impulses indicated their constant fear. Beings such as these lived out their tiny span in utter dread; they trusted neither their environment nor one another, and each new experience or phenomenon was perceived as a potential peril. They had no hope, no abstract image of the future to sustain them.

Mok wondered if his two captives had succeeded in their escape. He prowled the passages searching for them, envisioning their weary wanderings, their pathetic plight if they had become lost in the underground fastnesses. But he found nothing.

Once again he was alone in the warm beast-body that knew neither fatigue nor pain—except for this new pang, this lonely longing for contact with life on any level. Ancient concepts came to him, identifying the nuances of his reactions, all likened and linked to finite time-spans. *Monotony. Boredom. Restlessness.*

These were the emotive elements which forced him up again from the confined comfort of the caves. He prowled the planet, avoiding the bleak, cold wastes and searching out the areas of lush vegetation. For a long period he encountered only the lowest life forms.

Then one of his diurnal forays to the surface brought him to a stream, and as he crouched behind a clump of vegetation he peered at a group of troglodytes gathered on its far bank.

Vocalizing in their pattern of growls and grunts, he ventured forth, uttering phonic placations. But they screamed at the sight of him, screamed and fled into the forest, and he was left alone.

Left alone, to stoop and pick up what they had abandoned in their flight —*two crude clay containers, half-filled with water.*

Now he knew the fate of his captives.

They had survived and returned to their own kind, bringing with them their newly acquired skill. What tales they had told of their experience he could not surmise, but they remembered what he had taught them. They were capable of learning.

Mok had no need of further proof, and the incentive was there; the compound of pity, of concern for these creatures, of his own need for contact on any level. And here was a logical level indeed — there would never be companionship, that he understood and accepted, but this other relationship was possible. The relationship between teacher and pupil, between mentor and supplicant, between the governing power and the governed.

The governing power. . . .

Mok turned the clay containers this way and that, noting the clumsiness with which they had been fashioned, noting the irregularities of their surface. He could so easily correct that clumsiness, he could so surely smooth and reshape that clay. Govern the earth, govern the creatures, impart and instruct that which would shape them anew.

And then the ultimate realization came.

This would be duty and destiny, function and fulfillment. Within the prison of space and time, he would mold the little lives.

Now he knew his own fate.

He would be their god.

4

It was a strange role, but Mok played it well.

There were obstacles, of course. The first to be faced was the fear in which they held him. He was an alien, and to the primitive minds of these creatures, anything alien was abhorrent. His very appearance provoked reactions which prevented him from approaching them, and for a time Mok despaired of overcoming this communication barrier. Then, slowly he came to realize that their fear was in itself a tool he could employ to positive ends. With it he could invoke awe, authority, awareness of his powers.

Yes, that was the way. To accept his condition and stay apart from them always, confident that in time their own curiosity would drive them to seek him out.

So Mok kept to the caves, and gradually the contacts were made. Not all of the hominids came to him, of course, only the boldest and most enterprising, but these were the ones he awaited. These were the ones most fitted to learn.

As he expected, the experience of his captives became a legend, and the legend led to worship. It was useless for Mok to discourage this, impossible even to make the attempt in the light of their primitive reasoning, a barter-system must prevail. Offerings and sacrifices were the price they must pay in return for wisdom. Mok scanned his own primordial memories, assigning an order to the learning he imparted: the gift of fire, the secret of cultivation, the firing of clay, the shaping of weapons, the subjugation and domestication of lesser life forms, the control and eradication of others. Slowly a more sophisticated system of communication evolved, first on the verbal and then on the visual level.

The creatures disseminated his wisdom, absorbing it into their crude culture. They learned the uses of wheel and lever, then reached the gradual abstraction of the numeral concept. Now they were capable of making their own independent discoveries; language and mathematics stimulated self-development.

But in times of crisis there was still a need for further enlightenment. Natural forces beyond their limited powers of control brought periodic disaster to life patterns on the surface of the planet, and with every upheaval came a resurgence of the worship and sacrifices Mok secretly abhorred. Yet these creatures seemed to feel the necessity of making recompense for the skills he could grant them and the bonus these skills conferred, and Mok reluctantly accepted this.

It was harder for him to accept the continuation of their fear.

For a time he hoped that as their enlightenment increased they would revise their attitudes. Instead, their dreads actually increased. Mok attempted to observe their progress firsthand, but there was no opportunity for open contact and communication, and his mere appearance provoked panic. Even those who sought him in secret, or led the rituals of worship, seemed to be afraid of acknowledging the fact, lest it lessen their own superior status within the group. Acknowledging and acclaiming the existence of their god, they nevertheless avoided his physical presence.

Perhaps it was because sects and schisms had sprung up, each with its own hierarchy, its own dogma regarding the true nature of what they worshipped. Mok remembered, wryly, that in organized religion the actual presence of a god is an embarrassment.

So Mok refrained from further visitations, and as time passed he retreated deeper and deeper into the caverns. Now it was almost unnecessary for him to maintain even token contact, for these creatures had evolved to a stage where they were capable of self-development.

But even gods grow lonely, and take nurture in pride. Thus it was that at rare intervals, and in utmost secrecy, Mok ventured forth for a hasty glimpse of his domain.

One evening he came forth upon a mountaintop. Here the stars still glittered coldly, but there was an even greater glitter emanating from the expanse below — the huge city-complex towering as a testament to the wisdom of these creatures, and his own.

Mok stared down, and the sweet surges of pride coursed through him as he contemplated what he had wrought. These toys, these trifles with which he played, now toyed and trifled with the prime forces of the universe to create their own destiny.

Perhaps he, as their god, was misunderstood, even forgotten now. But did it matter? They had achieved independence, they did not need him any more.

Or did they?

The concept came, and it was more chilling to Mok than the wind of mountain night.

These creatures created, but they also destroyed. And their motivations — their greeds, their hungers, their lusts, their fears — were still those of the beasts they had been. The beasts they could become again, if spiritual awareness did not keep pace with material attainment.

There was still a need here, a need greater than before. And now Mok felt no pride, only perplexity which pierced more poignantly than pain.

How could he help them?

"*You cannot.*"

The communication came, and Mok whirled.

Absorbed, he had not sensed the silent streaking of the ship from sky to surface, but it was here now, remembered and recognized. The ship which had captured and conveyed him, the strangely shaped ship which *was* Ser —

It hovered incandescently against the horizon of infinity, and as if communication had been a signal, Mok found himself caught up in a long-discarded reaction. He was *contemplating* Ser.

And in that colloquy, Ser's concepts flowed to him.

"Valid. You cannot fulfill their needs. Already you have done too much."

Despite conscious volition, Mok felt the stubborn resurgence of his pride. But there was no need to formulate the reasons, for Ser's contemplation was complete.

"You are in error. I sensed your rebellion, overcame you, brought you here — but it was not a punishment. You were placed for a purpose. Because this pride, this urge to invest identity through achievement, could be of use at this time, in this place. Like the others."

"*Others?*" Confusion colored Mok's contemplation.

"Did you conceive of yourself as the only rebel? Not so. There have been more, many more. And they have served their purposes on other worlds throughout the cosmos. Worlds where the seeds of life needed cultivation and careful nurturing. I chose them for their tasks, just as I chose you. And you have not failed."

Mok considered, then communicated with an energy which surprised him.

"Then let me continue! Endow me with what is necessary to help them now!"

Ser's concept came. "It is not possible."

Mok contemplated in final effort. "But it is my right to do so. I am their god."

"No," Ser answered. "You have never been their god. You were chosen for what you were — to be their devil."

Devil. . . .

There was no contemplation now, only maddening meditation as Mok scanned through concepts long discarded from incarnations long lost save in immutable memory. Concepts of *good, evil, right, wrong*—concepts embodied in the primitive religions of a million primitive pasts. God arose from those concepts, and so did the embodiment of an opposing force. And in all the legends in each of the myriad myths, the pattern was the same. A rebel cast down from the skies to tempt with teaching, to furnish forbidden knowledge at a price. A being in the form of a beast, skulking in darkness, in the pit where inner fires flamed forever. And he had been this being; it was true, he was a devil.

Only pride had blinded him to the truth—the pride which had prompted him to play god.

"A pride of which you have been purged," Ser's communication continued. "One can sense in you now only mercy and compassion for these creatures and their potential peril. One can sense love."

"It is true," Mok acknowledged. "I feel love for them."

Ser's assent came. "With your aid, these creatures evolved. But you have evolved too—losing pride, gaining love. In so doing, you cannot function for them as their devil any longer. Your usefulness here is ended."

"But what will happen?"

The answer came not as a concept but as an accomplishment.

Suddenly Mok was no longer in the tawny body of the beast. He was in the ship, hovering and gazing down at that body; gazing down at the creature which lashed its tail and stared up at him with bulging eyes. The creature which now contained the essence of Ser.

And Ser communicated. "For a span you shall take my place, as you once desired. You will seed the stars, instill order in chaos, lead the others in contemplation. You will do so in understanding, and in love."

"And you?" Mok asked.

The being in the bestial body formed a final concept. "I take your role and your responsibility. There is that within me which must also be purged, and it may be I will destroy much of what you have created here. But in the end, even as their devil, I may bring them to an ultimate salvation. The cycle changes."

Mok willed the celestial machine in which his essence dwelt, willed it to rise, and like a fiery chariot it ascended to the realms of glory awaiting him in the skies beyond.

As he did so, he caught a fleeting glimpse of Ser.

The beast had turned to descend the mountain. Padding purposefully, the devil was entering his kingdom.

Mok's comprehension faltered. *Cycle?* Ser had been a god and now he was a devil. Mok had been a devil and now he was a god. But he could never have become a god if Ser hadn't willed the exchange of roles.

Was this Ser's intent all along—to allow Mok to evolve as devil and then usurp his identity?

In that case, Ser was actually a devil from the beginning, and Mok had been right in opposing him, for Mok was truly godlike.

Or were they all—Mok, Ser, the others, even the primitive mammalian creatures on this planet—both gods *and* devils?

It was a matter, Mok decided, which might require an eternity of contemplation. . . .

THE MOVIE PEOPLE

TWO THOUSAND STARS.

Two thousand stars, maybe more, set in the sidewalks along Hollywood Boulevard, each metal slab inscribed with the name of someone in the movie industry. They go way back, those names; from Broncho Billy Anderson to Adolph Zukor, everybody's there.

Everybody but Jimmy Rogers.

You won't find Jimmy's name because he wasn't a star, not even a bit player—just an extra.

"But I deserve it," he told me. "I'm entitled, if anybody is. Started out here in 1920 when I was just a punk kid. You look close, you'll spot me in the crowd shots in *The Mark of Zorro*. Been in over 450 pictures since, and still going strong. Ain't many left who can beat that record. You'd think it would entitle a fella to something."

Maybe it did, but there was no star for Jimmy Rogers, and that bit about still going strong was just a crock. Nowadays Jimmy was lucky if he got a casting call once or twice a year; there just isn't any spot for an old-timer with a white muff except in a western barroom scene.

Most of the time Jimmy just strolled the boulevard; a tall, soldierly-erect incongruity in the crowd of tourists, fags and freakouts. His home address was on Las Palmas, somewhere south of Sunset. I'd never been there but I could guess what it was—one of those old frame bungalow-court sweatboxes put up about the time he crashed the movies and still standing somehow by the grace of God and the disgrace of the housing authorities. That's the sort of place Jimmy stayed at, but he didn't really *live* there.

Jimmy Rogers lived at the Silent Movie.

The Silent Movie is over on Fairfax, and it's the only place in town where

185

you can still go and see *The Mark of Zorro.* There's always a Chaplin comedy, and usually Laurel and Hardy, along with a serial starring Pearl White, Elmo Lincoln, or Houdini. And the features are great — early Griffith and De Mille, Barrymore in *Dr. Jekyll and Mr. Hyde,* Lon Chaney in *The Hunchback of Notre Dame,* Valentino in *Blood and Sand,* and a hundred more.

The bill changes every Wednesday, and every Wednesday night Jimmy Rogers was there, plunking down his ninety cents at the box office to watch *The Black Pirate* or *Son of the Sheik* or *Orphans of the Storm.*

To live again.

Because Jimmy didn't go there to see Doug and Mary or Rudy or Clara or Gloria or the Gish sisters. He went there to see himself, in the crowd shots.

At least that's the way I figured it, the first time I met him. They were playing *The Phantom of the Opera* that night, and afterward I spent the intermission with a cigarette outside the theater, studying the display of stills.

If you asked me under oath, I couldn't tell you how our conversation started, but that's where I first heard Jimmy's routine about the 450 pictures and still going strong.

"Did you see me in there tonight?" he asked.

I stared at him and shook my head; even with the shabby hand-me-down suit and the white beard, Jimmy Rogers wasn't the kind you'd spot in an audience.

"Guess it was too dark for me to notice," I said.

"But there were torches," Jimmy told me. "I carried one."

Then I got the message. He was in the picture.

Jimmy smiled and shrugged. "Hell, I keep forgetting. You wouldn't recognize me. We did *The Phantom* way back in 'twenty-five. I looked so young they slapped a mustache on me in Makeup and a black wig. Hard to spot me in the catacombs scenes — all long shots. But there at the end, where Chaney is holding back the mob, I show up pretty good in the background, just left of Charley Zimmer. He's the one shaking his fist. I'm waving my torch. Had a lot of trouble with that picture, but we did this shot in one take."

In weeks to come I saw more of Jimmy Rogers. Sometimes he was up there on the screen, though truth to tell, I never did recognize him; he was a young man in those films of the Twenties, and his appearances were limited to a flickering flash, a blurred face glimpsed in a crowd.

But always Jimmy was in the audience, even though he hadn't played in the picture. And one night I found out why.

Again it was intermission time and we were standing outside. By now Jimmy had gotten into the habit of talking to me and tonight we'd been seated together during the showing of *The Covered Wagon.*

We stood outside and Jimmy blinked at me. "Wasn't she beautiful?" he asked. "They don't look like that any more."

I nodded. "Lois Wilson? Very attractive."

"I'm talking about June."

I stared at Jimmy and then I realized he wasn't blinking. He was crying.

"June Logan. My girl. This was her first bit, the Indian attack scene. Must have been seventeen—I didn't know her then, it was two years later we met over at First National. But you must have noticed her. She was the one with the long blonde curls."

"Oh, *that* one." I nodded again. "You're right. She was lovely."

And I was a liar, because I didn't remember seeing her at all, but I wanted to make the old man feel good.

"Junie's in a lot of the pictures they show here. And from 'twenty-five on, we played in a flock of 'em together. For a while we talked about getting hitched, but she started working her way up, doing bits—maids and such— and I never broke out of extra work. Both of us had been in the business long enough to know it was no go, not when one of you stays small and the other is headed for a big career."

Jimmy managed a grin as he wiped his eyes with something which might once have been a handkerchief. "You think I'm kidding, don't you? About the career, I mean. But she was going great, she would have been playing second leads pretty soon."

"What happened?" I asked.

The grin dissolved and the blinking returned. "Sound killed her."

"She didn't have a voice for talkies?"

Jimmy shook his head. "She had a great voice. I told you she was all set for second leads—by 1930 she'd been in a dozen talkies. Then sound killed her."

I'd heard the expression a thousand times, but never like this. Because the way Jimmy told the story, that's exactly what had happened. June Logan, his girl Junie, was on the set during the shooting of one of those early ALL TALKING—ALL SINGING—ALL DANCING epics. The director and camera crew, seeking to break away from the tyranny of the stationary microphone, rigged up one of the first traveling mikes on a boom. Such items weren't standard equipment yet, and this was an experiment. Somehow, during a take, it broke loose and the boom crashed, crushing June Logan's skull.

It never made the papers, not even the trades; the studio hushed it up and June Logan had a quiet funeral.

"Damn near forty years ago," Jimmy said. "And here I am, crying like it was yesterday. But she was my girl—"

And that was the other reason why Jimmy Rogers went to the Silent Movie. To visit his girl.

"Don't you see?" he told me. "She's still alive up there on the screen, in all those pictures. Just the way she was when we were together. Five years we had, the best years for me."

I could see that. The two of them in love, with each other and with the movies. Because in those days, people *did* love the movies. And to actually be *in* them, even in tiny roles, was the average person's idea of seventh heaven.

Seventh Heaven, that's another film we saw with June Logan playing a crowd scene. In the following weeks, with Jimmy's help, I got so I could spot his girl. And he'd told the truth—she was a beauty. Once you noticed her, really saw her, you wouldn't forget. Those blonde ringlets, that smile, identified her immediately.

One Wednesday night Jimmy and I were sitting together watching *The Birth of a Nation.* During a street shot Jimmy nudged my shoulder. "Look, there's June."

I peered up at the screen, then shook my head. "I don't see her."

"Wait a second—there she is again. See, off to the left, behind Walthall's shoulder?"

There was a blurred image and then the camera followed Henry B. Walthall as he moved away.

I glanced at Jimmy. He was rising from his seat.

"Where you going?"

He didn't answer me, just marched outside.

When I followed I found him leaning against the wall under the marquee and breathing hard; his skin was the color of his whiskers.

"Junie," he murmured. "I saw her—"

I took a deep breath. "Listen to me. You told me her first picture was *The Covered Wagon.* That was made in 1923. And Griffith shot *The Birth of a Nation* in 1914."

Jimmy didn't say anything. There was nothing to say. We both knew what we were going to do—march back into the theater and see the second show.

When the scene screened again we were watching and waiting. I looked at the screen, then glanced at Jimmy.

"She's gone," he whispered. "She's not in the picture."

"She never was," I told him. "You know that."

"Yeah." Jimmy got up and drifted out into the night, and I didn't see him again until the following week.

That's when they showed the short feature with Charles Ray—I've forgotten the title, but he played his usual country-boy role, and there was a baseball game in the climax with Ray coming through to win.

The camera panned across the crowd sitting in the bleachers and I caught a momentary glimpse of a smiling girl with long blonde curls.

"Did you see her?" Jimmy grabbed my arm.

"That girl—"

"It was Junie. She winked at me!"

This time I was the one who got up and walked out. He followed, and I was waiting in front of the theater, right next to the display poster.

"See for yourself." I nodded at the poster. "This picture was made in 1917." I forced a smile. "You forget, there were thousands of pretty blonde extras in pictures and most of them wore curls."

He stood there shaking, not listening to me at all, and I put my hand on his shoulder. "Now look here —"

"I *been* looking here," Jimmy said. "Week after week, year after year. And you might as well know the truth. This ain't the first time it's happened. Junie keeps turning up in picture after picture I know she never made. Not just the early ones, before her time, but later, during the Twenties when I knew her, when I knew exactly what she was playing in. Sometimes it's only a quick flash, but I see her — then she's gone again. And the next running, she doesn't come back.

"It got so that for a while I was almost afraid to go see a show — figured I was cracking up. But now you've seen her too —"

I shook my head slowly. "Sorry, Jimmy. I never said that." I glanced at him, then gestured toward my car at the curb. "You look tired. Come on, I'll drive you home."

He looked worse than tired; he looked lost and lonely and infinitely old. But there was a stubborn glint in his eyes, and he stood his ground.

"No, thanks, I'm gonna stick around for the second show."

As I slid behind the wheel I saw him turn and move into the theater, into the place where the present becomes the past and the past becomes the present. Up above in the booth they call it a projection machine, but it's really a time machine; it can take you back, play tricks with your imagination and your memory. A girl dead forty years comes alive again, and an old man relives his vanished youth —

But I belonged in the real world, and that's where I stayed. I didn't go to the Silent Movie the next week or the week following.

And the next time I saw Jimmy was almost a month later, on the set.

They were shooting a western, one of my scripts, and the director wanted some additional dialogue to stretch a sequence. So they called me in, and I drove all the way out to location, at the ranch.

Most of the studios have a ranch spread for western action sequences, and this was one of the oldest; it had been in use since the silent days. What fascinated me was the wooden fort where they were doing the crowd scene — I could swear I remembered it from one of the first Tim McCoy pictures. So after I huddled with the director and scribbled a few extra lines for the principals, I began nosing around behind the fort, just out of curiosity, while they set up for the new shots.

Out front was the usual organized confusion; cast and crew milling around the trailers, extras sprawled on the grass drinking coffee. But here in the back I was all alone, prowling around in musty, log-lined rooms built for use in forgotten features. Hoot Gibson had stood at this bar, and Jack Hoxie had swung from this dance-hall chandelier. Here was a dust-covered table where Fred Thomson sat, and around the corner, in the cutaway bunkhouse—

Around the corner, in the cutaway bunkhouse, Jimmy Rogers sat on the edge of a mildewed mattress and stared up at me, startled, as I moved forward.

"You—?"

Quickly I explained my presence. There was no need for him to explain his; casting had called and given him a day's work here in the crowd shots.

"They been stalling all day, and it's hot out there. I figured maybe I could sneak back here and catch me a little nap in the shade."

"How'd you know where to go?" I asked. "Ever been here before?"

"Sure. Forty years ago in this very bunkhouse. Junie and I, we used to come here during lunch break and—"

He stopped.

"What's wrong?"

Something *was* wrong. On the pan makeup face of it, Jimmy Rogers was the perfect picture of the grizzled western old-timer; buckskin britches, fringed shirt, white whiskers and all. But under the makeup was pallor, and the hands holding the envelope were trembling.

The envelope—

He held it out to me. "Here. Mebbe you better read this."

The envelope was unsealed, unstamped, unaddressed. It contained four folded pages covered with fine handwriting. I removed them slowly. Jimmy stared at me.

"Found it lying here on the mattress when I came in," he murmured. "Just waiting for me."

"But what is it? Where'd it come from?"

"Read it and see."

As I started to unfold the pages the whistle blew. We both knew the signal; the scene was set up, they were ready to roll, principals and extras were wanted out there before the cameras.

Jimmy Rogers stood up and moved off, a tired old man shuffling out into the hot sun. I waved at him, then sat down on the moldering mattress and opened the letter. The handwriting was faded, and there was a thin film of dust on the pages. But I could still read it, every word. . . .

Darling:

I've been trying to reach you so long and in so many ways. Of course I've seen you, but it's so dark out there I can't always be sure, and then too you've changed a lot through the years.

But I *do* see you, quite often, even though it's only for a moment. And I hope you've seen me, because I always try to wink or make some kind of motion to attract your attention.

The only thing is, I can't do too much or show myself too long or it would make trouble. That's the big secret—keeping in the background, so the others won't notice me. It wouldn't do to frighten anybody, or even to get anyone wondering why there are more people in the background of a shot than there should be.

That's something for you to remember, darling, just in case. You're always safe, as long as you stay clear of close-ups. Costume pictures are the best—about all you have to do is wave your arms once in a while and shout, "On to the Bastille," or something like that. It really doesn't matter except to lipreaders, because it's silent, of course.

Oh, there's a lot to watch out for. Being a dress extra has its points, but not in ballroom sequences—too much dancing. That goes for parties, too, particularly in a De Mille production where they're "making whoopee" or one of von Stroheim's orgies. Besides, von Stroheim's scenes are always cut.

It doesn't hurt to be cut, don't misunderstand about that. It's no different than an ordinary fadeout at the end of a scene, and then you're free to go into another picture. Anything that was ever made, as long as there's still a print available for running somewhere. It's like falling asleep and then having one dream after another. The dreams are the scenes, of course, but while the scenes are playing, they're real.

I'm not the only one, either. There's no telling how many others do the same thing; maybe hundreds for all I know, but I've recognized a few I'm sure of and I think some of them have recognized me. We never let on to each other that we know, because it wouldn't do to make anybody suspicious.

Sometimes I think that if we could talk it over, we might come up with a better understanding of just how it happens, and why. But the point is, you *can't* talk, everything is silent; all you do is move your lips and if you tried to communicate such a difficult thing in pantomime you'd surely attract attention.

I guess the closest I can come to explaining it is to say it's like reincarnation—you can play a thousand roles, take or reject any part you want, as long as you don't make yourself conspicuous or do something that would change the plot.

Naturally you get used to certain things. The silence, of course. And if you're in a bad print there's flickering; sometimes even the air seems grainy, and for a few frames you may be faded or out of focus.

Which reminds me—another thing to stay away from, the slap-stick comedies. Sennett's early stuff is the worst, but Larry Semon and some of the others are just as bad; all that speeded-up camera action makes you dizzy.

Once you can learn to adjust, it's all right, even when you're look-ing off the screen into the audience. At first the darkness is a little frightening—you have to remind yourself it's only a theater and there are just people out there, ordinary people watching a show. They don't know you can see them. They don't know that as long as your scene runs, you're just as real as they are, only in a different way. You walk, run, smile, frown, drink, eat—

That's another thing to remember, about the eating. Stay out of those Poverty Row quickies where everything is cheap and faked. Go where there's real set-dressing, big productions with banquet scenes and real food. If you work fast you can grab enough in a few minutes, while you're off-camera, to last you.

The big rule is, always be careful. Don't get caught. There's so little time, and you seldom get an opportunity to do anything on your own, even in a long sequence. It's taken me forever to get this chance to write you—I've planned it for so long, my darling, but it just wasn't possible until now.

This scene is playing outside the fort, but there's quite a large crowd of settlers and wagon-train people, and I had a chance to slip away inside here to the rooms in back—they're on camera in the background all during the action. I found this stationery and a pen, and I'm scribbling just as fast as I can. Hope you can read it. That is, if you ever get the chance!

Naturally, I can't mail it—but I have a funny hunch. You see, I noticed that standing set back here, the bunkhouse, where you and I used to come in the old days. I'm going to leave this letter under the mattress, and pray.

Yes, darling, I pray. Someone or something *knows* about us, and about how we feel. How we felt about being in the movies. That's why I'm here, I'm sure of that; because I've always loved pictures so. Someone who knows *that* must also know how I loved you. And still do.

I think there must be many heavens and many hells, each of us making his own, and

The letter broke off there.

No signature, but of course I didn't need one. And it wouldn't have proved anything. A lonely old man, nursing his love for forty years, keeping her alive inside himself somewhere until she broke out in the form of a visual hallucination up there on the screen—such a man could conceivably go all the way into a schizoid split, even to the point where he could imitate a woman's handwriting as he set down the rationalization of his obsession.

I started to fold the letter, then dropped it on the mattress as the shrill scream of an ambulance siren startled me into sudden movement.

Even as I ran out the doorway I seemed to know what I'd find; the crowd huddling around the figure sprawled in the dust under the hot sun. Old men tire easily in such heat, and once the heart goes—

Jimmy Rogers looked very much as though he were smiling in his sleep as they lifted him into the ambulance. And I was glad of that; at least he'd died with his illusions intact.

"Just keeled over during the scene—one minute he was standing there, and the next—"

They were still chattering and gabbling when I walked away, walked back behind the fort and into the bunkhouse.

The letter was gone.

I'd dropped it on the mattress, and it was gone. That's all I can say about it. Maybe somebody else happened by while I was out front, watching them take Jimmy away. Maybe a gust of wind carried it through the doorway, blew it across the desert in a hot Santa Ana gust. Maybe there *was* no letter. You can take your choice—all I can do is state the facts.

And there aren't very many more facts to state.

I didn't go to Jimmy Rogers' funeral, if indeed he had one. I don't even know where he was buried; probably the Motion Picture Fund took care of him. Whatever *those* facts may be, they aren't important.

For a few days I wasn't too interested in facts. I was trying to answer a few abstract questions about metaphysics—reincarnation, heaven and hell, the difference between real life and reel life. I kept thinking about those images of actual people indulging in make-believe. But even after they die, the make-believe goes on, and that's a form of reality too. I mean, where's the borderline? And if there *is* a borderline—is it possible to cross over? *Life's but a walking shadow*—

Shakespeare said that, but I wasn't sure what he meant.

I'm still not sure, but there's just one more fact I must state.

The other night, for the first time in all the months since Jimmy Rogers died, I went back to the Silent Movie.

They were playing *Intolerance,* one of Griffith's greatest. Way back in 1916 he built the biggest set ever shown on the screen—the huge temple in the Babylonian sequence.

One shot never fails to impress me, and it did so now; a wide angle on the towering temple, with thousands of people moving antlike amid the gigantic carvings and colossal statues. In the distance, beyond the steps guarded by rows of stone elephants, looms a mighty wall, its top covered with tiny figures. You really have to look closely to make them out. But I did look closely, and this time I can swear to what I saw.

One of the extras, way up there on the wall in the background, was a smiling girl with long blonde curls. And standing right beside her, one arm around her shoulder, was a tall old man with white whiskers. I wouldn't have noticed either of them, except for one thing.

They were waving at me. . . .

THE DOUBLE WHAMMY

ROD PULLED THE CHICKEN out of the burlap bag and threw it down into the pit.

The chicken squawked and fluttered, and Rod glanced away quickly. The gaping crowd gathered around the canvas walls of the pit ignored him; now all the eyes were focused on what was happening down below. There was a cackling, a scrabbling sound, and then a sudden sharp simultaneous intake of breath from the spectators.

Rod didn't have to look. He knew that the geek had caught the chicken.

Then the crowd began to roar. It was a strange noise, compounded of women's screams, high harsh laughter teetering on the edge of hysteria, and deep hoarse masculine murmurs of shocked dismay.

Rod knew what *that* sound meant, too.

The geek was biting off the chicken's head.

Rod stumbled out of the little tent, not looking back, grateful for the cool night air that fanned his sweating face. His shirt was soaked through under the cheap blazer. He'd have to change again before he went up on the outside platform to make his next pitch.

The pitch itself didn't bother him. Being a talker was his job and he was good at it; he liked conning the marks and turning the tip. Standing up there in front of the bloody banners and spieling about the Strange People always gave him his kicks, even if he was only working for a lousy mudshow that never played anywhere north of Tennessee. For three seasons straight he'd been with it, he was a pro, a real carny.

But now, all of a sudden, something was spooking him. No use kidding himself, he had to face it.

Rod was afraid of the geek.

He crossed behind the ten-in-one tent and moved in the direction of his little trailer, pulling out a handkerchief and wiping his forehead. That helped a little, but he couldn't wipe away what was inside his head. The cold, clammy fear was always there now, night and day.

Hell of it was, it didn't make sense. The Monarch of Mirth Shows had always worked "strong" — out here in the old boondocks you could still get away with murder, particularly if you were only killing chickens. And who gives a damn about chickens, anyway? The butchers chop off a million heads a day. A chicken is just a lousy bird, and a geek is just a lousy wino. A rumdum who hooks up with a carny, puts on a phony wild-man outfit and hops around in the bottom of a canvas enclosure while the talker gives the crowd a line about this ferocious monster, half man and half beast. Then the talker throws in the chicken and the geek does his thing.

Rod shook his head, but what was inside it didn't move. It stayed there, cold and clammy and coiled up in a ball. It had been there almost ever since the beginning of this season, and now Rod was conscious that it was growing. The fear was getting bigger.

But why? He'd worked with half-a-dozen lushes over the past three years. Maybe biting the head off a live chicken wasn't exactly the greatest way to make a living, but if the geeks didn't mind, why should he care? And Rod knew that a geek wasn't really a monster, just a poor old futz who was down on his luck and hooked on the sauce — willing to do anything, as long as he got his daily ration of popskull.

This season the geek they took on was named Mike. A quiet guy who kept out of everybody's way when he wasn't working; under the burnt-cork makeup he had the sad, wrinkled face of a man of fifty. Fifty hard years, perhaps thirty of them years of hard drinking. He never talked, just took his pint and curled up in the canvas on one of the trucks. Looking at him then, Rod was never spooked; if anything, he felt kind of sorry for the poor bastard.

It was only when the geek was in the pit that Rod felt that ball of fear uncoil. When he saw the woolly wig and the black face, the painted hands that clutched and clawed — yes, and when he saw the grinning mouth open to reveal the rotting yellow teeth, ready to bite —

Oh, it was getting to him all right, he was really uptight now. But nobody else knew. And nobody *would* know. Rod wasn't about to spill his guts to anyone here on the lot, and how would it look if he ran off to some head-shrinker and said, "Hey, Doc, help me — I'm afraid I'm gonna turn into a geek." He knew better than that. No shrinker could help him, and come what may he'd never end up geeking for a living. He'd lick this thing himself; he had to, and he would, just as long as no one else caught on and bugged him about it.

Rod climbed the steps, removing his jacket and unbuttoning his wet shirt as he moved up into the darkness of the trailer.

And then he felt the hands sliding across his bare chest, moving up over his shoulders to embrace him, and he smelt the fragrance, felt the warmth and the pressure even as he heard the whispered words. "Rod—darling—are you surprised?"

Truth to tell, Rod wasn't surprised. But he was pleased that she'd been waiting for him. He took her in his arms and glued his mouth to hers as they sank down on the cot.

"Cora," he murmured. "Cora—"

"Shhhh! No time to talk."

She was right. There wasn't time, because he had to be back on the bally platform in fifteen minutes. And it wasn't a smart idea to talk anyway, not with Madame Sylvia sneaking around and popping up out of nowhere just when you least expected her. Why in hell did a swinging bird like Cora have to have an old buzzard like Madame Sylvia for a grandmother?

But Rod wasn't thinking about grandmothers now, and he wasn't thinking about geeks, either. That was what Cora did to him, that was what Cora did *for* him, dissolving the cold fear in warm, writhing, wanting flesh. At times like these Rod knew why he couldn't cut out, why he stayed with it. Staying with it meant staying with her, and this was enough; this was everything, with ribbons on it.

It was only later, struggling into his shirt, hearing her whisper, "Please, honey, hurry and let's get out of here before she comes looking for me," that he wondered if it was really worth it. All this horsing around for a fast grope in the dark with a teenage spic who practically creamed her jeans every time the old lady looked cross-eyed at her.

Sure Cora was a beautiful job, custom-made for him. But when you got right down to it she was still a kid and nobody would ever mistake her brain for a computer. Besides, she was a spic—well, maybe not exactly, but she was a gypsy and that added up to the same thing.

Walking back to the bally platform for the last pitch of the evening, Rod decided it was time to cool it. From now on the chill was in.

That night the show folded and trucked to Mazoo County Fair Grounds for a ten-day stand. They were all day setting up and then the crowds surged in, rednecks from the toolies up in the hills; must have been a couple thousand coming in night after night, and all craving action.

For almost a week Rod managed to keep out of Cora's way without making it too obvious. Her grandmother was running the mitt camp concession on the other end of the midway, and Cora was supposed to shill for her; usually she was too busy to sneak off. A couple of times Rod caught sight of her signaling to him from down in the crowd around the bally platform, but he always looked the other way, pretending he didn't see her. And once he heard her scratching on the trailer door in the middle of the night, only he made out that he was asleep, even when she called out to him, and after about ten minutes she went away.

The trouble was, Rod didn't sleep anywhere near that good; seemed like every time he closed his eyes now he could see the pit, see the black geek and the white chicken.

So the next time Cora came scratching on the door he let her in, and for a little while he was out of the pit, safe in her arms. And instead of the geek growling and chicken cackling he heard her voice in the darkness, her warm, soft voice, murmuring, "You do love me, don't you, Rod?"

The answer came easy, the way it always did. "Course I do. You know that."

Her fingers tightened on his arms. "Then it's all right. We can get married and I'll have the baby—"

"Baby?"

He sat up fast.

"I wasn't going to tell you, honey, not until I was sure, but I am now." Her voice was vibrant. "Just think, darling—"

He *was* thinking. And when he spoke, his voice was hoarse.

"Your grandmother—Madame Sylvia—does she know?"

"Not yet. I wanted you to come with me when I tell her—"

"Tell her nothing."

"Rod?"

"Tell her nothing. Get rid of it."

"Honey—"

"You heard me."

She tried to hold him then but he wrenched himself free, stood up, reached for his shirt. She was crying now, but the louder she sobbed, the more he hurried dressing, just as if she wasn't there. Just as if she wasn't stuttering and stammering all that jazz about what did he mean, he couldn't do this, he had to listen, and if the old lady found out she'd kill her.

Rod wanted to yell at her to shut up, he wanted to crack her one across the mouth and *make* her shut up, but he managed to control himself. And when he did speak his voice was soft.

"Take it easy, sweetheart," he said. "Let's not get ourselves all excited here. There's no problem."

"But I told you—"

He patted her arm in the darkness. "Relax, will you? You got nothing to worry about. You told me yourself the old lady doesn't know. Get rid of it and she never will."

Christ, it was so simple you'd think even a lame-brain like Cora would understand. But instead she was crying again, louder than ever, and beating on him with her fists.

"No, no, you can't make me! We've got to get married, the first time I let you, you promised we would, just as soon as the season was over—"

"As far as I'm concerned, the season's over right now." Rod tried to keep his voice down, but when she came at him again, clinging, somehow it was worse than feeling her fists. He couldn't stand this any more; not the clinging, not the wet whimpering.

"Listen to me, Cora. I'm sorry about what happened, you know that. But you can scrub the marriage bit."

The way she blew up then you'd have thought the world was coming to an end, and he had to slap her to keep the whole damn lot from hearing her screech. He felt kind of lousy, belting her one like that, but it quieted her down enough so's he could hustle her out. She went away still crying, but very quietly. And at least she got the message.

Rod didn't see her around the next day, or the one after. But in order to keep her from bugging him again, he spent both nights over at Boots Donahue's wagon, playing a little stud with the boys. He figured that if there was any trouble and he had to peel off fast, maybe he could turn a few extra bucks for the old grouch-bag.

Only it didn't exactly work out that way. Usually he was pretty lucky with the pasteboards, but he had a bad run both evenings and ended up in hock for his next three paychecks. That was bad enough, but the next day was worse.

Basket Case gave him the word.

Rod was just heading for the cook tent for breakfast when Basket Case called him over. He was lying on a old army cot outside his trailer with a cigarette in his mouth.

"How's for a light?" he asked.

Rod cupped a match for him, then stuck around, knowing he'd have to flick the ashes while Basket Case had his smoke. And a guy born without arms or legs has a little trouble getting rid of a butt, too.

Funny thing, the Strange People never got to Rod, no matter how peculiar they looked. Even Basket Case, who was just a living head attached to a shapeless bundle of torso, didn't give him the creeps. Maybe it was because old Basket Case himself didn't seem to mind; he just took it for granted that he was a freak. And he always acted and sounded normal, not like that rumdum geek who put on a fright wig and blacked up and made noises like a crazy animal when he went after a chicken—

Rod tried to push away the thought and pulled out a cigarette for himself. He was just getting a match when Basket Case looked up at him.

"Heard the news?" he asked.

"What news?"

"Cora's dead."

Rod burned his fingers and the match dropped away.

"Dead?"

Basket Case nodded. "Last night. Madame Sylvia found her in the trailer after the last show—"

"What happened?"

Basket Case just looked at him. "Thought maybe you could tell me that."

Rod had to choke out the words. "What's that crack supposed to mean?"

"Nothing." Basket Case shrugged. "Madame Sylvia told Donahue the kid died of a ruptured appendix."

Rod took a deep breath. He forced himself to look sorry, but all at once he felt good, very good. Until he heard Basket Case saying, "Only thing is, I never heard of anyone rupturing their appendix with a knitting needle."

Rod reached out and took the cigarette from Basket Case to dump his ashes. The way his hand was trembling, he didn't have to do anything but let them fall.

"The appendix story is just a cover — Madame Sylvia doesn't want the fuzz nosing around." Basket Case nodded as Rod stuck the cigarette back between his lips. "But if you ask me, she knows."

"Now look, if you're saying what I think you're saying, you'd better forget it —"

"Sure, I'll forget it. But *she* won't." Basket Case lowered his voice. "Funeral's this afternoon, over at the county cemetery. You better show your face along with the rest of us, just so it doesn't look funny. After that, my advice to you is cut and run."

"Now wait a minute —" Rod was all set to go on, but what was the use? Basket Case *knew*, and there was no sense putting on an act with him. "I can't run," he said. "I'm into Boots Donahue for three weeks' advance. If I cop out, he'll spread the word around and I won't work carny again, not in these parts."

Basket Case spat the cigarette out. It landed on the ground beside the cot and Rod stamped it out. Basket Case shook his head. "Never mind the money," he said. "If you don't run, you won't be working anywhere." He glanced around cautiously and when he spoke again his voice was just a whisper. "Don't you understand? This is the crunch — I tell you, Madame Sylvia knows what happened."

Rod wasn't about to whisper. "That old bat? You said yourself she doesn't want any truck with the fuzz, and even if she did, she couldn't prove anything. So what's to be afraid of?"

"The double whammy," said Basket Case.

Rod blinked at him.

"Want me to spell it out for you? Three seasons ago, just before you came with the show, fella name of Richey was boss canvasman. Mighty nice guy, but he had a problem — he was scared of snakes. Babe Flynn was working them, had a bunch of constrictors, all standards for her act and harmless as they come. But Richey had such a thing about snakes he wouldn't even go near her wagon.

"Where he went wrong was, he went near Madame Sylvia's wagon. Cora was pretty young then, just budding out you might say, but that didn't stop Richey from making his move. Nothing serious, only conversation. How the old lady found out about it I don't know and how she found out he was spooked on snakes I don't know either, because he always tried to hide it, of course.

"But one afternoon, last day of our stand in Red Clay it was, Madame Sylvia took a little walk over to Richey's trailer. He was standing outside, shaving, with a mirror hung up on the door.

"She didn't say anything to him, didn't even look at him—just stared at his reflection in the mirror. Then she made a couple of passes and mumbled something under her breath and walked away. That's all there was to it.

"Next morning, Richey didn't show up. They found him lying on the floor inside his trailer, deader'n a mackerel. Half his bones were broken and the way the body was crushed you'd swear a dozen constrictors had been squeezing his guts. I saw his face and believe me it wasn't pretty."

Rod's voice was husky. "You mean the old lady set those snakes on him?"

Basket Case shook his head. "Babe Flynn kept her snakes locked up tight as a drum in her own trailer. She swore up and down nobody'd even come near them the night before, let alone turned 'em loose. But Richey was dead. And that's what I mean about the double whammy."

"Look." Rod was talking to Basket Case, but he wanted to hear it himself, too. "Madame Sylvia's just another mitt reader, peddling phony fortunes to the suckers. All this malarkey about gypsy curses—"

"OK, OK." Basket Case shrugged. "But if I were you I'd cut out of here, fast. And until I did, I wouldn't let that old lady catch me standing in front of a mirror."

"Thanks for the tip," Rod said.

As he walked away, Basket Case called after him. "See you at the funeral."

But Rod didn't go to the funeral.

It wasn't as if he was afraid or anything; he just didn't like the idea of standing at Cora's grave with everybody looking at him as if they knew. And they damned well did by now, all of them. Maybe it would be smart to ease out of here like Basket Case said, but not now. Not until he could pay off what he owed to Donahue. For the next three weeks he'd just sweat it out.

Meanwhile, he'd watch his step. Not that he believed that crazy story about the double whammy—Basket Case was just putting him on, it had to be a gag. But it never hurt to be careful.

Which is why Rod shaved for the evening performance that afternoon. He knew the old lady was at the funeral like everybody else; she wouldn't be creeping up behind him to capture his soul from his reflection in the mirror—

Damned right she wouldn't!

Rod made a face at himself in the glass. What the hell was the matter with him, anyway? He didn't buy that bit about the curse.

But there *was* something wrong. Because for a moment when Rod looked into the mirror he didn't see himself. Instead he was staring into a black, grinning face, with bloodshot, red-rimmed eyes and a twisted mouth opening to show the yellow fangs—

Rod blinked and the face went away; it was his own reflection peering back at him. But his hand was shaking so that he had to put the razor down.

His hand was still shaking when he reached for the bottle on the top shelf, and he must have spilled more of the whiskey than he managed to get into the glass. So he took a slug straight from the bottle instead. And then another, until his hands were steady again. Good for the nerves, a little snort now and then. Only you had to watch that stuff, not let it run away with you. Because if you didn't, pretty soon you got hooked and some day before you knew what was happening, you wound up in the woolly wig and the blackface, down there in the pit waiting for the white chicken—

The hell with that noise. It wasn't going to happen. Just a couple of weeks and he'd be out of here, no more carny, nothing to bug him ever again. All he had to do now was keep his cool and watch his step.

Rod watched his step very carefully that evening when he walked up to the bally platform and adjusted his mike for the pitch. Standing before the bloody banners he felt good, very good indeed, and the couple of extra belts he'd taken from the bottle just for luck seemed to have unwound that ball of fear inside his head. It was easy to make his pitch about the Strange People —"All there on the inside, folks, on the *in*side"—and watch the marks flocking around down below. The marks—*they* were the real freaks, only they didn't know it. Shelling out their dough to gawk at poor devils like Basket Case, then paying extra for the SPECIAL ADDED ATTRACTION, ADULTS ONLY, in the canvas pit behind the ten-in-one tent. What kind of a pervert would pay money to see a geek? What was the matter with people like that?

And what was the matter with him? Standing there beside the pit, holding the burlap bag and feeling the chicken fluttering helplessly inside, Rod felt the fear returning to flutter within himself. He didn't want to look down into the pit and see the geek crouching there, growling and grimacing like a real wild man. So he looked at the crowd instead, and that was better. The crowd didn't know he was afraid. Nobody knew he was spooked, let alone what scared him.

Rod talked to the crowd, building his pitch, and his hands started to fumble with the cord around the neck of the burlap bag, getting ready to open it and dump the chicken into the pit.

And that's when he saw *her.*

She was standing over to one side, right up against the edge of the canvas; just a little old woman dressed in black, with a black shawl draped over her head. Her face was pinched, her skin was brown and leathery, wrinkled into a permanent scowl. An old lady, nobody gave her a second glance, but Rod saw her.

And she saw *him.*

Funny, he'd never noticed Madame Sylvia's eyes before. They were big and brown and staring—they stared right at him now, stared right *through* him.

Rod wrenched his gaze away, forced his fingers to open the sack. All the while, mechanically, he was talking, finishing the buildup as he reached for the chicken, pulled it out, flung the clucking creature down to that other creature in the pit—the creature that growled and grabbed and oh my God it was biting now—

He couldn't watch and he had to turn his head away, seeing the crowd again as they shrieked and shuddered, getting their kicks. And *she* was still standing there, still staring at him.

But now her clawlike hand moved, moved over the rim of the canvas to extend a pointing forefinger. Rod knew what she was pointing at; she was pointing at the geek pit. And that wrinkled face *could* change its expression, because she was smiling now.

Rod turned and groped his way out into the night.

She knew.

Not just about him and Cora, but about everything. Those eyes that stared at him and through him had also stared *inside* him—stared inside and found his fear. That's why she'd pointed and smiled; she knew what he was afraid of.

The midway lights were bright, but it was darker behind the canvas sidewalls except where a patch of moonlight shone on the big water barrel sitting next to the cook tent.

Rod's face was damp with sweat; he headed for the barrel and soaked his handkerchief in the water to wipe his forehead. Time for another pitch pretty soon, and the next show. He had to pull himself together.

The cool water helped to clear his head, and he dipped his handkerchief again. That was better. No sense flipping just because a nutty old dame gave him a dirty look. This business about gypsies and the evil eye and the double whammy was all a crock. And even if there *was* something to it, he wouldn't let her get to him. He wasn't about to stand in front of any mirrors—

Then he glanced down at the water in the barrel, saw his features reflected in the moonlight shining there. And he saw her face, standing right behind him. Her eyes were staring and her mouth was mumbling, and now her hands were coming up, making passes in the air. Making passes like an old witch, she was going to turn him into a geek with the double whammy—

Rod turned, and that's the last thing he remembered. He must have passed out, fallen, because when he came to he was still on the ground.

But the ground was somehow different than the earth outside the tent; it was covered with sawdust. And the light was stronger, it was shining straight down between the canvas walls of the pit.

He was in the pit.

The realization came, and Rod looked up, knowing it was too late, she'd caught him, he was in the geek's body now.

But something else was wrong, too; the pit was deeper, the canvas walls much higher. Everything seemed bigger, even the blur of faces crowded around the sides of the pit way up above. *Way up above* — why was he so small?

Then his eyes shifted as he heard the growling. Rod turned and looked up again, just in time to see the black grinning face looming over him, the giant mouth opening to reveal the rotting yellow teeth. It was only then that Rod knew what she had really done to him, as the huge hands grabbed out, pulling him close. For a moment he squawked and fluttered his wings.

Then the geek bit off his head.

IN THE CARDS

"SATURDAY NIGHT?" Danny said. "What do you mean, I'll die on Saturday night?"

Danny tried to focus his eyes on the old woman but he couldn't make it—too smashed. She was just a big fat blur, like the cards spread on the table between them.

"I am truly sorry," the old woman murmured. "I can only read what I see. It is in the cards."

Danny grabbed for the edge of the table and stood up. The smell of incense in the darkened room was making him sick. It wasn't easy to stand and it wasn't easy to laugh, either, but he managed.

"Hell with you, sister. You and the cards too."

The old woman stared at him but there was no anger in her eyes, only compassion, and somehow that was even worse.

"I'm not gonna die on Saturday night," Danny told her. "Not me. You're talking to Danny Jackson, remember? I'm a star. A big star. And you, you're just a—"

Standing there, lurching there in the darkness, he told her what she was, using vocabulary ripened and enriched by thirty years in show biz.

Her eyes never flickered, her glance never wavered, and there was still nothing in her gaze but pity when he finally ran out of breath.

And ran out of the reeking room, her pity pursuing him.

"You will die on Saturday night."

Damned echo in his ears, even when he gunned the Ferrari and roared away from the curb. The car swayed, playing tag with the yellow line; good thing it was so late and the street was clear of traffic.

It was late and he was bombed, bombed clean out of his silly skull. Had to be, or he'd never have driven all the hell down to South Alvarado just to roust a phony, faking old fortuneteller out of bed and lay a fifty-dollar bill on her for a phony, faking fortune, the old witch, the old bitch—

But they were all bitches, all of them, and Lola was the worst.

Danny made it out to Bel Air, avoiding Sunset and coming up Pico until he could cut over on a sidestreet through Westwood. When you're on the sauce you learn the right routes to take, the routes that get you safely through the streets, safely through the minutes and the hours and the days and the nights, even when your nerves are screaming and Lola is screaming too.

And of course Lola *was* screaming, she'd been waiting up for him and she cut loose the minute he opened the front door.

"Goddam it, where were you, don't you realize you've got a six o'clock call tomorrow morning—?"

There was a lot more, too, but Danny slammed the door on it, the door of the guest room. He hadn't slept in the same bed with Lola for three months, and it wasn't just because of what Dr. Carlsen had told him about his ticker, either.

It was better here in the bedroom, dropping his clothes and flopping down on the old king-size, away from the bitch, away from the witch.

Only the witch didn't go away. Here in the dark, Danny could see her eyes again, staring at him as if she understood, as if she *knew*. But nobody knew what the Doc had told him, not Lola, not the studio, not even his own agent. So how could some old bag take one look at him and figure it out?

In the cards. It's in the cards.

Her eyes, he remembered her eyes when she'd said it. They were so deep and black. Black as the Ace of Spades lying there on the table. The Queen of Spades had turned up, too, and that's when she made that crack about him dying on Saturday night.

Tomorrow was Wednesday. Wednesday, Thursday, Friday, Saturday—

To hell with it. That's what he'd told the old klooch and that's what he told himself. Tomorrow was Wednesday and he'd better think about that; Lola was right, he did have a six o'clock call, the test was shooting, and this is what counted. Not counting the days until Saturday, just the few short hours until that test.

Wednesday. Named after Woden, the god of war and battles. Danny's name had been Kuhlsberg once, not Jackson, and he knew, he remembered. Wednesday was war, all right, and it was a battle just getting out of bed with that head of his pounding away. Thank God he could sneak out before Lola woke up, and get through the foggy streets before the traffic began to build up on the San Diego Freeway.

But the fight was just beginning, the fight to smile there under the lights while Benny plastered on the old pancake makeup and fitted the little wings to the perspiring temples where the hairline had eroded. The perspiration was just the alcohol oozing out of him, it wasn't flop sweat, because Danny knew he had nothing to worry about. The test was just a formality, all they wanted was six minutes of film to show the network brass and the agency people in New York. The series was all set, Fischer had told him that last week, and Fischer never conned him. Best damned agent in the business. So no panic, he knew his lines, all he had to do was step out onto the set and walk through the scene. If there were any fluffs, Joe Collins would cover for him. Joe was a good man, he'd never carry a lead himself but he was a real pro. And Rudy Moss was a hell of a director and an old buddy of his. They were all friends here, and they all knew how much was riding for them on this series.

"Ready for you, Mr. Jackson."

Danny smiled, stood up, strolled out to where Joe Collins was waiting on the set. He found his chalk marks, somebody from the camera unit dragged out his tape, the mike-boom came down and he tested his voice for gain. Then they hit the lights and Rudy Moss gave him his cue for action and they rolled.

They rolled, and he blew it.

The first take he forgot the business with the cigarette. They cut and started from the top, and he got fouled up in his crossover to Joe, stepped right out of camera before he realized it. So they rolled again, and by this time he was uptight and Moss didn't like what he was getting, so it was back and take it from the top once more. Then Danny started losing lines — but those things happen. The only trouble was, he had to stand there under those lights and there were interruptions when a plane went over and ruined the sound and somebody came barging in right on the middle of his long speech and then Joe jumped one of his cues and the idiot script girl threw him the wrong prompt and he was sweating, wringing wet, and his hands started to twitch and Moss was very patient and it was Take Sixteen and no break for lunch and he could see the looks the crew was giving him and finally they wrapped it up at three-thirty, eight and a half solid hours for a lousy dialogue bit, nothing but two-shots and close-ups, and it was a bomb.

Everybody was very polite and they said, "Nice work, Mr. Jackson," and "Great," and "You did it, boy," but Danny knew what he'd done.

The fight was over and he'd lost.

No sense going home because Lola would ask him how did it go and Fischer would be calling and to hell with it. There was a little joint out on the ocean, below Malibu, where the lights were nice and dim and you could get a good steak to anchor the martinis.

That was the right answer, and though he scraped a fender getting out of the parking lot after they closed up the place, he made it without pain. Lola wasn't waiting up for him tonight—tonight, hell, it was morning already, Thursday morning—but the bed in the guest room felt better than ever.

Until he closed his eyes and saw what was in the cards. Thursday morning. *Thursday. And two days from now—*

If the old bitch was so good at telling fortunes, if she could see everything in the cards, why hadn't she tipped him off about the test? There was a *real* life-and-death matter for you, and she never even mentioned it. Of course she didn't; what could she or anybody else see in a lousy pack of playing cards? That's all they were, ordinary playing cards, and she was just a cheap grifter and Saturday was just another day of the week.

And this was Thursday. Thursday noon, now, with Danny getting up and groping his way into the john and shivering in the shower and shaving and stumbling downstairs and finding the note and reading it twice, three times, before it finally sank in.

Lola gone. Left him. *"Sorry . . . tried to get through to you . . . can't stand watching you destroy yourself . . . please . . . need help . . . try to understand."* God, the phrases in that note, like a daytime soaper dialogue. But it all added up. Lola was gone.

Danny called her mother's place in Laguna. No answer. Then he tried her sister up at Arrowhead. Nothing. By this time he'd cased the joint, seen that she'd cleared out the works, everything; must have taken her all day to pack the station wagon. She meant it; probably been planning the caper for weeks. Next thing he'd be getting a call from some hotshot lawyer, one of those Lear-jet boys. Christ, the least she could have done was waited to find out if he was going to get the series.

The series! Danny remembered now, he was due in Projection Room Nine at two o'clock; they were screening the test.

But it was after one now, and besides, he didn't need to see the running. He knew what they had in the can—six minutes of worms.

So he climbed in the car and went to Scandia for lunch instead; at least he intended to have lunch, but by late afternoon he hadn't gotten any farther than the bar.

That's where his agent caught up with him, somewhere between the fifth and the sixth bloody mary.

"Thought I'd find you here," Fischer told him. "Get moving."

"Where we going?"

"Up to the office. I'd hate to have all these nice people here see me hit you right in the mouth."

"Get off my back, Fischer."

"Get off your butt." He hauled Danny from the stool. "Come on, let's go."

Fischer's office was on the Strip, only a few blocks away. But by the time they got there, Danny was up the wall; he knew what Fischer was going to say.

"No calls," Fischer told the girl on the board. Then he took Danny into the private office *behind* his private office and closed the door.

"All right," Fischer said. "Tell me."

"You saw the test?"

Fischer nodded, waiting. His mouth was grim, but the hard face and the hard talk never fooled Danny; he knew it was just an act. Fischer was a sweet guy inside, always bleeding for his clients. You could see the compassion in his eyes, it was there now, the same look of pity that the fortuneteller had—

Danny wanted to explain about the fortuneteller but he knew how it would sound and besides it wouldn't do any good. All he could do was say, "I wasn't loaded. I swear to God I wasn't loaded."

"I know that. And nobody said you were. I wish you *had* been—I've seen you play a scene with a couple of drinks under your belt and come off great." Fischer shook his head. "Everybody on the set knew what was wrong with you yesterday, but even that wouldn't matter. The trouble is, everybody in the projection room could see it today, up there on the screen. You were hung over."

"It was that bad, huh?"

"That bad?" Fischer sighed, swiveled his chair around to face Danny. "Do I have to spell it out for you, Danny? A guy makes three pictures in a row, all bombs, and he's had it. Sure, I know that Metro thing wasn't your fault, but the word is out and I haven't had an offer for six months. When it comes to films, you're scrubbed. Moynihan tells me—"

"Never mind about Moynihan," Danny said. "He's my business manager. He shouldn't even be talking to you."

"Who else can he talk to when you won't listen?" Fischer opened a folder on his desk, glanced at a type-sheet. "You owe eighty-three on the house and nine on the cars. You're in hock on the furniture, that's another twenty including the redecorating. Your checking account is minus zero. And if they yank your credit cards, you won't have enough left to buy a bagel at Linny's."

Cards? Why did he have to mention cards? Danny felt a rush of heat and loosened his collar.

"Knock it off," he said. "All I need is a break."

"I *got* you a break." Fischer was staring at him across the desk, just like the old lady had stared at him across the card table. "For three months I've been rupturing myself to line up this TV deal for you. Salary, residuals, participation—I don't have to tell you what you got riding. If it hit, you'd be set for life."

Life? Suppose I have only two more days? Danny's chest was pounding, he couldn't take any more of this, but he had to listen. Through the blur he could see Fischer's finger jabbing out at him.

"So you make the test. And what do I see? You, walking around up there like a goddam zombie —"

Zombie. Danny knew what a zombie was. *The living dead.* Something was throbbing inside, throbbing so loud that he could just barely hear Fischer saying, "Why, Danny? — that's all I want to know. Tell me why."

But Danny couldn't tell him why because he had to take off his jacket, had to take off his shirt, had to tear off his skin and dig out whatever it was that was throbbing and pounding, throbbing and pounding underneath. He brought his hand up, felling the pain shoot through his arm and then—

Nowhere.

Danny opened his eyes and saw the white ceiling. White as in Cedars or Sinai, a hospital ceiling.

So that's where I am. I'm not dead. And what day is this?

"Friday," said the fat nurse. "No, mustn't sit up. Doctor wants us to be careful."

Fat nurses and baby talk, that's all he needed. But Doc Carlsen was a little more helpful when he showed up in the evening.

"No, it's not a stroke, nothing like that. From where I stand it may not even have been a cardiac. Dehydration, malnutrition, general exhaustion— you've been drinking again, haven't you?

"Yeah."

"I've prescribed some sedation for tonight. You'll have some lab tests tomorrow, just to play safe."

"When can I go home?"

"After we check out the tests. Meanwhile, a little rest won't hurt you."

"But tomorrow —"

Danny broke it off right there. What could he say, that tomorrow was Saturday, tomorrow he was going to die, it was in the cards?

Dr. Carlsen didn't believe in cards; he believed in tests and charts and specimens. And why not? Those things made a hell of a lot more sense than the Ace of Spades on a dusty table in some creep joint down on South Alvarado.

Being here in the hospital made sense, too. At least he had somebody looking after him and if there *was* trouble tomorrow—

But there wouldn't be. All he had to do was swallow the Nembies and go to sleep.

Danny stared up at the white ceiling until it turned black and then there was nothing again, nothing but sleep, sweet sleep and the Queen of Spades sat across the table from him and watched while he reached for a drink only the drink wasn't there because Lola had taken it away with her when she left and he knew it didn't matter, it was only a lousy test and he could walk through it in his sleep, sweet sleep—

Danny was very much alive on Saturday morning and hungry as hell. But they wouldn't give him breakfast, not even a cup of coffee, until after they wheeled him down to the lab for the tests.

For a moment, when they were taking blood, he panicked; but like the nurse said, it wasn't going to kill him, and it didn't.

And afterward he had lunch, a big lunch, and they let him get up to go to the john and a nice fag orderly came in and gave him a shave and he dozed off again until dinnertime.

So Saturday was almost over and he was still with it. Hell, he was even beginning to feel good, and if he could just have a drink and a cigarette—

"Sorry. Doctor wants us to take our sedative again tonight." The fat nurse was back, a real sweetheart. But Danny took the pills and the water and settled back, because it was nine o'clock, only three hours to go, and if he made the stretch everything would be copacetic.

If he made it? Hell, he was going to make it, he knew it now, he could feel it in his bones, in his ticker. No throbbing, no pounding; all is calm, all is bright. Bright as the white ceiling which was turning gray now, turning black again, black as the Ace of Spades.

Something started to thump in Danny's chest, but he tensed up, forcing himself to relax—that was funny, tensing up to relax, but it seemed to work, it was working—and now everything was calm again, calm and peaceful, he could sleep because it was quiet. *Quiet as the tomb*—

Danny screamed.

Then the lights went on and the fat nurse came running into the room. "Mr. Jackson, what's the matter, don't you know it's one in the morning—"

"One in the morning?"

She nodded.

"*Sunday* morning?"

When she nodded again, Danny could have kissed her. In fact he *tried* to kiss her because he'd made it now, he was home free.

It was easy to go back to sleep then. Everything was easy now that it was Sunday.

Sunday, with the big breakfast and the big paper. Sunday, with the fresh shave and the fag orderly bringing in the flowers from the studio—wait a minute, what the hell was this, there was nothing in the papers, how did the studio know?

Danny found out when they plugged the phone in and he got his first call. Fischer.

"Look," Danny said. "I'm sorry about the other day—"

"I'm not," said Fischer. "Shut up and listen."

So Danny listened.

"Maybe it was the best thing that could have happened. Anyway, it gave me a notion. I called the studio and tipped them."

"*You* called the studio?"

"Right. Told them about Lola, too."

"Where'd you pick that up?"

"She phoned me Thursday night. Don't worry, I made her promise not to break the story to the papers until we were ready."

"Ready for what?"

"Stop interrupting and listen," Fischer said. "I told the studio the truth only I juggled the dates a little. Said that Lola split with you on Tuesday instead of Wednesday and you knew it when you came in to do the test. The Pagliacci bit, your heart was breaking but the show must go on — you didn't look so good in there but you were giving it the old college try and how could they fault you when you were so shook up you actually collapsed the following day?"

"Do you have to sound so happy about it?" Danny asked.

"I *am* happy, and you're gonna be happy too. Because they went for the bundle. Considering the circumstances they're going to scrap the test, they've already gotten on the horn to New York and everything's set. You'll do another shot next week, as soon as the Doc says it's OK. How's that for openers, buddy-boy?"

It was very good for openers, and it kept getting better. Because the next one who called was Lola. Crying up a storm.

"Sorry . . . all my fault . . . should have stood by when you needed me . . . told the lawyer to forget it . . . Doctor said I could come to see you tomorrow . . . oh my poor baby . . ."

Oh my aching—

But it was fine, it was A-OK, because a divorce right now, even a separation, would have clobbered him for life. And he *had* a life, a whole new life, starting today.

Dr. Carlsen laid the topper on it that afternoon. "Preliminary lab reports are in. Too early to nail it down, but it looks as if I made a pretty good educated guess. Little murmur, slight irregularity there, but nothing we can't control with medication. And a dose of common sense."

"When do I cut out of here?"

"Perhaps tomorrow."

"I was thinking of right now."

Dr. Carlsen shrugged. "You're always thinking about right now. That's your problem." He sat down on the edge of the bed. "I was talking about common sense, Danny. Want me to spell it out for you? Two, maybe three drinks a day — one before dinner, one after, perhaps a nightcap if you're out for the evening. Regular hours. We can talk about the diet and exercise later. But the main thing is for you to stop running scared."

"Me?"

Danny gave him the big smile, but it didn't register. "You're not on now," the Doc told him. "I know what knocked you down. It was fear. Fear of what

was happening to your career, fear because your marriage was coming un-
glued, fear of a heart attack — "

OK, smart-ass.

"Don't you understand, Danny? Sometimes the dread is worse than the
disease itself. If you can learn to face up to the things you're afraid of — "

Danny smiled, Danny nodded, Danny thanked him, Danny hustled him
the hell out of there.

Maybe the Doc was right at that, the part about fear made sense. The
only trouble was, he didn't know what Danny had really been afraid of. And if
he told him, he'd get on the horn and call in a shrinker. You just don't go
around spilling about phony fortunetellers who predict you'll die on Saturday
night.

But that was over and out now. This was Sunday and he felt great and he
wasn't afraid of anything any more.

He wasn't afraid to climb out of bed and take his clothes out of the closet
and get dressed and march down the hall to the desk. He wasn't afraid of the
fat nurse or the head nurse either, when he told her he was checking out of
there.

Sure there was a lot of static and threats about calling Doctor and this is
all highly irregular, Mr. Jackson, but if you insist, sign here.

Danny signed.

The night air felt good as he waited for a taxi out front, and everything
was quiet — there was that Sunday feeling in the streets. That *Sunday* feeling.

Danny gave the cab driver his address and settled back for the long haul
out to Bel Air. The driver was smart, he ducked the traffic on Wilshire and
swung down over Olympic. Crummy neighborhood, lots of neon fronting the
cheap bars —

"Hold it, changed my mind. Let me out here."

What the hell, why not? Didn't the Doc say he could have a drink before
dinner? Besides, it wasn't the drinks, it was the fear. And that was long gone
now. It had died last night.

That called for a celebration. Even in a Mickey Mouse joint like this,
topless waitresses and faceless customers; that little bird down at the end of
the bar wasn't too bad, though.

"Scotch rocks." Danny glanced along the bar. "See what my friend
wants."

She wasn't his friend, not yet, but the drink did it. And by the time they
had a second one he and Gloria switched over into a back booth.

That was her name, Gloria, one of the strippers in the floor show here,
but she didn't work Sundays, sort of a busman's holiday if you get what I
mean.

Danny got what she meant and he got a lot more, too; good figure, nice legs, the right kind of mouth. Hell, this was a celebration, it had been a long, long time. So Lola was coming back tomorrow, big deal. This was tonight. *Sunday* night. The first night, the grand opening of a smash hit, a long run. *The New Life of Danny Jackson.*

"Danny Jackson? *You?*" Gloria's mouth hung open. Nice, sensual lower lip. He could always tell, it was like radar, or flying by the seat of your pants. Not the seat exactly, but close. Funny, very funny, and that calls for another drink —

"Of *course* I know who you are." Gloria chug-a-lugged pretty good herself, and now they were wedged into the same side of the booth together, all comfy-cozy.

And he was telling her how it was that he just happened to fall in here, everything that happened, no names of course, but it was easy to talk and maybe if he had just one more for the road —

The road led next door, of course; he'd noticed the motel when he got out of the cab. All very convenient.

George Spelvin and wife is what he signed, and the clerk gave him a funny take but Danny wasn't afraid, he wasn't running scared any more.

The Ace of Spades was just another card in the deck and this was a brand new deal; the Queen of Spades was gone and Gloria was here instead. Cute little Gloria, red hair against a white pillow, and the bed lamp throwing shadows on the wall. Big black shadows like big black eyes, staring and watching and waiting —

But no, the fear was gone, he was forgetting. *Sunday* night, remember? And he wasn't destroying himself, that was over and out, it had all been a mistake. A mistake to get drunk, a mistake to surrender to a sudden impulse and have his fortune told, a mistake to believe a kooky old klooch and her line about the cards. Cards don't control your life, *you* control your life, and he'd proved it. Well, hadn't he?

"Sure, Danny. Sure you have."

He must have been thinking out loud then, telling Gloria the whole story. Because she was unbuttoning his shirt and helping him and murmuring, "Sunday, that's what it is, remember? Nothing to be afraid of, I won't hurt you —"

Damned right she wouldn't. She was just what the doctor ordered. Only he hadn't ordered *this*, just one drink before dinner and regular hours and don't be scared. That was the important thing to remember, don't be scared. Okay, so he wasn't scared. And to hell with the doctors and the fortune-tellers too.

Danny was ready and he grabbed Gloria and yes, this was it, this was what he'd been waiting for. He stared down into eyes, her dark eyes, like the eyes of the old woman. And now they were widening with pleasure and he could see the pupils, black aces on a dusty table. And there was no pleasure, only this tearing pain, as the Ace of Spades kept coming up, up, *up*—

Danny didn't know it when he died, and he didn't know why he died, either. Gloria had told him nothing, not even the name she used when she did her strip act. It was just one of those phony names strippers always use. Saturday is what she called herself—Saturday Knight.

THE WARM FAREWELL

IT MUST HAVE BEEN AROUND ten o'clock when the cars arrived.

Rena could see them coming down the sideroad as they turned off the highway from Freedom—there must have been more than a dozen of them. They crawled slowly in a weaving line, like a long black snake inching closer and closer along the gravel.

None of the cars had its headlights turned on, and all of them had little pieces of cardboard stuck over the license plates. They came very slowly and very quietly.

Mrs. Endicott didn't notice them because she was busy making a last-minute tour of the house. Since they'd sold the furnishings along with the place, there wasn't too much to pack, but she wanted to make sure.

Mr. Endicott didn't notice them either, at first. He was closing the car trunk and arranging the extra suitcases in the back seat.

But Rena saw them coming, and she tried to keep the panic out of her voice when she called, "Dad!"

He looked up and then he must have heard the sound of their motors chugging along in low, because he came inside fast.

"Looks like we're going to have visitors," he said, trying to smile.

Mrs. Endicott went over to the window.

"Don't pull the blinds," her husband told her. "They know we're here."

"Aren't you even going to lock the door?"

Mr. Endicott shrugged. "What's the use?" he answered. "Now don't worry. There won't be any trouble. They probably just want to make sure we're going."

Mrs. Endicott looked at Rena. "You better go in the bedroom," she said.

217

The girl bit her lip but did not move. "I'm not afraid," she told her mother. "Those White Hopes can't frighten me."

Mr. Endicott looked at her. "Your mother's right," he sighed. "You better go in the bedroom. No sense taking chances."

His wife sniffed. "I wish you'd thought of that yourself, in the first place. Then maybe we wouldn't be running away like this. We had a nice home here. The paper was doing well. But you had to go to work and write those editorials. You had to bring Scotty down—"

"Stop that," said Mr. Endicott. "No sense crying over spilt milk. I had to write those editorials. You know I did. Now be quiet, both of you, and let me handle this."

Father, mother and daughter fell silent as the cars drove into the yard. They angle-parked in a wide circle, blocking both driveway exits. Now car doors slammed and the white figures emerged: the hooded, sheeted figures of thirty men. As if by signal they converged on the doorstep, forming a smaller circle.

For another moment there was no sound; then a buzz of voices rose from just outside the door. Presently the knocking began.

Mrs. Endicott put her hand on Rena's shoulder. She reached out to touch Mr. Endicott but he shrugged free and went to the door.

Just as he was about to open it, Rena gasped.

Her father turned. "What is it?" he whispered.

"I just happened to think," she said. "I know why they've come. They want to know about Scotty."

"Oh, no!" Mrs. Endicott fluttered her hands. "Lock the door," she gasped. "Please, lock the door!"

Mr. Endicott made a helpless gesture as the knocking sounded again. "Leave this to me," he warned, quietly.

Then he opened the door, wide.

The man standing in the doorway might have been six feet tall, at the very most. But in the long white robe and the tall hood he was a giant. A ghost-giant, with hidden eyes and a voice that came forth in a creaking whisper.

"Greetings," he said.

Mr. Endicott didn't answer.

The ghost-giant snickered. "What's the matter, cat got your tongue? Or you just plain too scared to talk?" The figure moved forward. "Well, we ain't gonna make trouble. Not if you cooperate."

He turned and addressed the hooded men directly behind him. "Come on in," he said.

White sheets rustled.

"No, the rest of you wait there," the ghost-giant called. "Just the four of us, like I said. Guess that'll be enough to handle our business. If we need help, we'll holler." He snickered again, and an answering chuckle arose from the sheeted circle.

Four hooded figures entered the parlor. The ghost-giant closed the door.

"Well, now," he said. "Looks like you folks was all set to pull out. Is that right?"

Mr. Endicott nodded.

"Guess you packed in pretty much of a hurry, way it looks. Reckon you wasn't expecting visitors. Or did you have a notion you could hightail it before any visitors arrived?"

Mr. Endicott shrugged.

The hooded giant gazed at his three companions and chuckled again. "See what I mean, boys? This is your Yankee hospitality. Come to pay a friendly farewell call, and what happens? They offer you any dopes, or maybe even a little jolt of corn? Not likely. Don't even ask a feller if he'd like to set down. And after all the ways we traveled just to git here."

His chuckle mingled with the answering sounds from under the hoods of the others. Then he moved over to Mr. Endicott and rubbed his white-gloved hands together briskly.

"Gonna have to ask you to speak up," he said. "Guess you all don't realize you got distinguished visitors here."

Mr. Endicott glanced down at the feet of the sheeted men. His eyes traveled over shoes and protruding trouser-cuffs.

"I realize it," he said, quietly. "You'd never make much of an actor, Jess. And as for Race and Pud, here, they'll have to invest in a second pair of shoes if they want to sneak around in disguise."

"Ain't nobody sneaking around in disguise," the hooded giant rumbled, abandoning the whisper. "This here's the White Hopes, and don't forget it. No names among the Brothers."

"Brothers!" said Mr. Endicott.

"Now that's enough of that," the man identified as Jess said. "We've had all the sass we need out of you, Endicott. You and your stinking editorials. You been asking the good citizens of Freedom enough questions. Now it's our turn to do the talking. And all we want out of you is a few answers."

He walked over to the fourth hooded figure, whose shiny black patent leather shoes and creased seersucker trousers offered a striking contrast to the sandals and work pants of the others.

"You want to take charge, Brother Hood?" he asked.

The sheeted head shook slowly.

"All right," said Jess. He turned to Endicott once again. "I told you about distinguished visitors," he went on. "This here's our Brother Hood. I guess you heard about him. Head of the whole organization in this territory. He come all the way from headquarters in Atlanta, just to help us say goodbye. Just got in tonight."

Mr. Endicott ran a hand across his bald spot. "Look here, Jess," he murmured. "We're all ready to go. Say what you have to say and get out."

"Now wait a minute. Wait—a—*minute!*" Jess walked up to the small man and gazed down at him through the slits in his hood. "I guess you ain't really learned your lesson after all."

"I've learned enough," Mr. Endicott answered wearily. "I've learned you can't hope to sell freedom here in Freedom. I've learned enough to get rid of the paper and the house and leave town. What more do you want of me?"

"Not much." Jess turned to the silent Brother Hood. "See? Spunky little cuss, just like I told you. But we showed him a thing or two. Just like he said now. He's shut up shop for good. Had to dump the paper for a song. The bank squeezed him on the mortgage here and he was lucky to get half what he paid for the house and throw his furniture in on the deal. Reckon he'll think twice before he pulls any smart-aleck stunts again."

"I know when I'm licked," Endicott said. "Does that satisfy you?"

Jess didn't answer him. He talked to Brother Hood. "And it was all done peaceable, too. No rough stuff. Everything clean and legal-like."

"What about those bricks through the window?" Mr. Endicott asked. "What about those notes, and the phone calls, and expelling my daughter here from school?"

"We was just protecting our own youngsters," said Jess. "We got decent girls in this town. We don't aim to have them spoiled and corrupted by any Northern nigra-lovers — "

Mrs. Endicott put her arm around Rena. "Shut up!" she cried. "Shut up and get out of here!"

"You really want us to go, Miz Endicott?" Jess bowed, his hooded head bobbing grotesquely. "Well, seeing as how you feel like that, ma'am, we're on our way. Sorry we troubled you. But just one thing before we clear out."

"What's that?" Mr. Endicott answered for her.

"We come here for information," Jess said. "That's all we're after. Just information." He paused and moved closer. "Where's the nigra?" he rumbled. "Where's Scotty?"

"Mr. Scott has left town," Endicott answered. "I thought everyone knew that."

"You mean you told everyone that," Jess corrected him. "But the White Hopes know different. We got eyes that see in the dark." The hooded head shook. "Oh, I admit we was fooled at first. That was a pretty slick trick of yours — bringing down a nigra from up North, an educated nigra if you please, that looks and acts like a white man. I bet you laughed aplenty when you put him on the paper and started him writing those high-faluting stories about segregation and what-all. Oh, you fooled us good, you did! Until he up and wrote that dirty lying piece for the magazines about the White Hopes."

"That was a mistake," Mr. Endicott said. "I didn't know he was going to write that article. I'd never have authorized it."

"I'll bet you wouldn't," Jess chuckled. "Like you say, it was a mistake. A real mistake. And you made another — quartering him here at your own house, a lousy nigra living right here in a white man's home. Passing for white, and you helping him!"

"That was my business."

"That's our business, mister. That's the business of every decent, respectable white man in these parts. And when anyone forgets it, the White Hopes are here to remind them."

"Why can't you forget it?" Mr. Endicott asked, wearily. "It's all over and done with. Mr. Scott left town last weekend."

"Oh did he?" Jess glanced at the others. "Did he really? We happen to think different. If he left town, how'd he get out — walk? We been watching the buses, Endicott. We been watching the train. Ain't no nigra comes in or goes out without us knowing it, anytime. And we been watching sort of special for Scotty. On account of we didn't want him to leave without us saying goodbye. Right, boys?"

Race and Pud guffawed.

"He's not here, if that's what you're thinking," Mrs. Endicott said.

"We know that," Jess assured her. "But we got a pretty good idea you folks can tell us where he's hiding out."

"I don't know," Mr. Endicott said. "That's the truth, so help me. I don't know where he went. He came to me Saturday and said he was leaving — said he wanted to leave, so there wouldn't be any trouble. And he made a point of not telling me where he was going."

"You've got to believe us," Mrs. Endicott said. "He told us nothing."

"But he didn't go," Jess said. "We would of seen him if he did. So he's got to be around these parts, someplace. And if he's around these parts, he's got to eat. Somebody's looking after him. Somebody's feeding him."

"We have nothing to do with it," sighed Mr. Endicott.

"Who else could it be?" Jess asked. "There ain't a white man in the county that'd touch that nigra with a ten-foot pole. Ain't a darky that would dare lift a hand for him. They know how the White Hopes feel about a bad nigra like Scotty. The word's out we're gonna give him a little farewell celebration."

"I tell you, we don't know anything!"

"And I tell you you're lying." The white-gloved hands fumbled under Jess's sheet and emerged holding a leather strap. "I didn't come here aiming for trouble. But the boys ain't taking no for an answer. Maybe we got to do some persuading."

Mrs. Endicott let out a strangled sound as Jess advanced on the little man. He said nothing, nor did he move. The gloved hand swung the leather strap. It swished through the heavy, humid air of the room.

"Better grab hold of him, boys," said Jess. "This is liable to be kind of messy."

Brother Hood stepped forward. His voice was a soft whisper. "Wait a moment," he said. "Might I make a suggestion?"

"Sure. This is your party, really."

"You haven't asked the girl yet."

Mr. and Mrs. Endicott looked at Rena. And now Jess was looking at her too, looking at her through the eyeholes in the hood. The room was suddenly very silent.

Jess coiled the strap in his gloved hands, caressing its length. "Why that's right," he said, slowly. "Looks like we clean forgot about Rena, here."

He walked over to her and stood balanced on the balls of his feet, rocking from side to side.

Rena's eyes went wide.

"How old are you, honey?" Jess drawled. "Fifteen, sixteen, thereabouts? Funny, I never noticed before. You're right pretty. Too pretty to waste your spit on a nigra like that Scotty. You're a white girl, honey. Reckon maybe you need a white man to teach you what that means — "

"Keep away from her!" Mrs. Endicott sobbed.

Jess swung the strap slowly. "I'd sure hate to spoil that pretty face. Yesiree, I'd sure hate to have to do anything like that." He raised the strap. "Suppose you help me out, honey. Suppose you tell me where Scotty's hiding. Before I count up to three, maybe. One, two — "

"Look at her," Brother Hood said, sharply. "She won't talk. Not that way."

Jess paused and turned. "You got any other ideas?" he asked.

"It's my party, like you said." Brother Hood approached Jess and bent his hooded head. He whispered something. Jess nodded, snickered, straightened up.

"Go ahead," he said. "Go right ahead."

Brother Hood nodded. Then he took two quick steps forward and gathered the girl in his sheeted arms. She screamed and struggled, engulfed in the billowing folds that enmeshed her. Brother Hood fought her, a great white bird flapping his wings over his prey.

Mr. Endicott came across the room. "Damn you, let her alone!" he shouted. "Let her — "

Jess drew the strap back and hit him across the mouth. Then he hit Mr. Endicott with his fist. The little man fell down and his glasses dropped to the floor.

Jess stood over him. "One more move out of you and you'll really get it," he grunted. "And that goes for your wife, too. You, Race — hang onto her."

Race was already grasping Mrs. Endicott's elbow, twisting her arm behind her. He didn't twist any harder than was necessary, but he did a job.

The hooded man named Pud flung open a door. "Right here's the bedroom, Brother Hood," he said. "Reckon that's what you're looking for."

Brother Hood nodded. He jerked the struggling girl through the doorway, dropping the strap and using both hands now. Pud started to follow behind, but Brother Hood snapped, "I don't need you in here. My party."

He started to laugh, and then the door banged shut, and there was silence.

Mrs. Endicott began to cry, noiselessly. Mr. Endicott crawled along the floor and picked up his glasses. They were unbroken and when he put them on he could see Jess standing over him with the strap poised.

He could see Race, too, and now Race had a gun in his gloved hand.

So nobody moved.

Nobody moved when the gasps came, or the thud, or the scream. Nobody moved when the thumping sounds rose from behind the thick door.

Nothing moved in the room except the hands of the clock on the wall.

A full fifteen minutes passed before the door opened. Brother Hood came out alone.

"Come on," he said. He was panting and his voice had submerged to a conspiratorial whisper.

"Did she —?"

"Come on," Brother Hood repeated, nodding. "Let's go."

"Where is he?" Jess asked.

"The old Jasper place, if you know where that is. Hiding out in the barn."

"I might of guessed," Jess said. "Way off on the sideroad down there. Been deserted for years."

"All set?" Brother Hood panted.

"Got everything right out in the car," Jess answered.

"Then let's go. You boys lead the way — I'll have to follow in my car."

Jess chuckled. "Man, you sound beat! Must have had quite a workout —"

Brother Hood cut him short with a curt nod and moved over to the door. Jess and his two companions followed. Jess stood in the doorway for a moment after the others had made their exit.

"You all don't forget us now," he said. "Sorry we got to be running along so quick like, but we got this little surprise party all arranged." He paused. "Mebbe you better forget us after all," Jess murmured. "Yeah, that's the best idea. We never been here." He shifted the leather strap in his gloved hand. "Mind, now. We never been here, none of us."

The Endicotts didn't answer.

They didn't look at him, nor at each other, as the white-robed man went out. They didn't move as they heard the receding murmur of voices drifting down the driveway. They waited until the motors started, roared, and droned away in the night.

Mr. Endicott turned as the bedroom door opened and Rena came out. Her face was white, and she let the door slam behind her fast and hard.

"Gone?" she whispered.

Mr. Endicott nodded.

"Then we'd better go, too. Right now."

Mrs. Endicott stretched out her hands. "Rena—"

The girl shook her head, brushing the tangled hair from her eyes. "Don't say anything," she murmured. "Please, don't say anything. Let's just get out of here."

Mr. and Mrs. Endicott exchanged glances. He nodded and led his wife to the door.

Rena paused and bit her lip. "I forgot my purse," she said. "Start the car and I'll be right out."

She raced back into the bedroom as they left. By the time Mr. and Mrs. Endicott had climbed into the car she was back, snapping out the lights and closing the front door behind her.

"Don't use your lights," she told her father. "Just head for the highway. The faster the better."

Mrs. Endicott patted her arm. "Don't worry, honey. They're gone now, to the old Jasper place." She paused. "How did you—"

Rena didn't answer her directly. "Jasper's? That's good. It's a long way out. And they'll surround it, and go inside to search. They've got kerosene, of course, and they'll plan on burning him. They like to burn, you know."

The car mounted the rise to the highway just ahead, and they could see the panorama below. Suddenly Mr. Endicott turned and said, "Look!"

Turning, they gazed behind them, staring at the sideroad. The White Hopes were on the prowl now, and they'd lighted their torches, two to a car, thrusting them out of the front windows so that a line of fire blazed in the night. A long chain of bobbing flame stretched down the sideroad leading to the old Jasper place.

"You see?" Rena whispered. "I was right. They'll go there and hunt around the barn so that they can burn him." Her voice broke and she began to laugh.

Mrs. Endicott shook her. "Stop it!" she cried. "Stop it! I don't care what he did to you in there—you shouldn't have told them. They'll burn Scotty alive. Why did you tell them where he was?"

"Yes," Mr. Endicott said. "And how did you know?"

Rena shrieked and gurgled. "I didn't know," she said. "He must have made up the whole story when he came out."

"Who? Brother Hood?"

"That wasn't Brother Hood," Rena giggled. "That was Scotty. I still don't know where he's been hiding, but he'd sneaked back here to tell us goodbye. And when he looked through the bedroom window and saw Brother Hood drag me in there, he crawled in. I saw him, but Brother Hood didn't. He hit Brother Hood on the back of the head with a big rock."

Mrs. Endicott gasped. "Did he—kill him?"

"No. He was just unconscious. Then Scotty tied him up with bedsheets and gagged him good. And he put on Brother Hood's pants and shoes and gloves and robe and came out. He told me we'd have to get away fast. He's taking Brother Hood's car, and when the White Hopes get to the barn he'll sneak off in the confusion and make his getaway. By the time they find out there's nobody in the barn it'll be too late." She giggled again.

Mrs. Endicott touched her daughter's cheek. "Thank God," she said. "You're all right."

"I'm all right," Rena repeated. "Now let's hurry!"

Mr. Endicott shifted and the car moved out onto the highway. "All's well that ends well," he muttered. "I think Scotty will make it — he just whispered and nobody recognized his voice. Once he's gone and we're gone there won't be any trouble." He glanced at his daughter. "I — I know what an ordeal this has been for you. But you mustn't be bitter about it. You've got to remember they're not all like that. Plenty of decent folks in Freedom and all over. It's just the minority, the ones who haven't learned, and they're disappearing fast. The big danger isn't in what they do, but in how they feel. That bitterness — it's contagious. Makes you want to fight back, their way. And you mustn't. Only leads to more trouble."

"Fight fire with fire," Rena said. And giggled again.

"Look down there!" Mrs. Endicott cried.

"Never mind," Rena insisted. "Keep going!"

"No — stop! Look at the flames!"

The car halted. The trio gazed off in the darkness as a sheet of fire rose suddenly in the night.

"But that's not Jasper's place," Mrs. Endicott gasped. "That's — that's *our* house!"

"And Brother Hood is tied up in the bedroom," Mrs. Endicott said. "Rena, you said you were going back there for your purse. Did you — ?"

Rena was silent. They were all silent, staring down at the fire. Now they could hear the roar of the flames and, above it, something that might or might not have been a single piercing scream.

Rena giggled again.

"Fight fire with fire," Mr. Endicott sighed. "They'll blame it on the White Hopes and nobody will ever know. But I hate it, it's wrong, we've got to go back."

Mrs. Endicott gripped his arm. "No," she said. "It's too late. Rena's right. We'd better get out of here, fast."

She didn't look at her daughter, even when she began to laugh louder and louder, and after a minute Mr. Endicott started the car again.

He shifted into high and the car sped forward, heading away from the flames, heading due north.

THE PLAY'S THE THING

YOU ASK THE IMPOSSIBLE, gentlemen.

I cannot name the greatest Hamlet.

In fifty years as a drama critic, I've seen them all — Barrymore, Gielgud, Howard, Redgrave, Olivier, Burton, and a dozen more. I've seen the play in cut and uncut versions, in modern dress, in military uniform. There's been a black Hamlet, a female Hamlet, and I shouldn't be surprised to learn of a hippie Hamlet today. But I wouldn't presume to select the greatest portrayal of the role, or the greatest version of the play.

On the other hand, if you want to know about the most memorable performance in *Hamlet*, that's another story. . . .

The Roaring Twenties are only a murmuring echo in our ears today, but once I heard them loud and clear. As a young man I was in the very center of their pandemonium — Chicago. The Chicago of Hecht and MacArthur, of Bodenheim, Vincent Starrett and all the rest. Not that I traveled in such exalted company; I was only the second-string theatrical critic for *The Morning Globe*, a second-string paper. But I saw the plays and the players, and in that pre-Depression era there was much to see. Shakespeare was a standby with the stars who traveled with their own repertory companies — Walter Hampden, Fritz Leiber, Richard Barrett. It was Barrett, of course, who played Hamlet.

If the name doesn't ring a bell today, it's not surprising. For some years it had evoked only the faintest tinkle in the hinterlands, where second-rate tragedians played their one-night stands "on the road."

But now, for the first time, Richard Barrett brought his production to the big time, and in Chicago he really rang the bell.

He didn't have Hampden's voice, or Leiber's theatrical presence, and he didn't need such qualities; Barrett had other attributes. He was tall, slender, with a handsome profile, and although he was over thirty he looked leanly youthful in tights. In those days, actors like Barrett were called matinee idols, and the women adored them. In Chicago, they loved Richard Barrett.

I found that out for myself during my first meeting with him.

Frankly, I hadn't been much taken with his performance when I saw it. To me Barrett was, as they said of John Wilkes Booth, more acrobat than actor. Physically, his Hamlet was superb, and his appearance lent visual conviction to a role usually played by puffy, potbellied, middle-aged men. But his reading was all emotion and no intellect; he ranted when he should have reflected, wailed when he should have whispered. In my review I didn't go so far as to say he was a ham, but I admit I suggested he might be more at home in the stockyards than the theatre.

Naturally, the ladies weren't pleased with my remarks. They wrote indignant letters to the editor, demanding my scalp or other portions of my anatomy by return mail. But instead of firing me, my boss suggested I go and interview Richard Barrett in person. He was hoping, of course, for a follow-up story to help build the paper's circulation.

I wasn't hoping for much of anything except that Barrett wouldn't punch me in the jaw.

We met by appointment for luncheon at Henrici's; if I was to have my jaw punched I might at least get a good meal on the expense account before losing the ability to swallow.

But as it turned out, I needn't have worried. Richard Barrett was most amiable when we met. And highly articulate.

As the luncheon progressed, each course was seasoned by conversation. Over the appetizer he discussed Hamlet's father's ghost. With the salad he spoke of poor Ophelia. Along with the entree he served up a generous portion of opinion regarding Claudius and Gertrude, plus a side order of Polonius. Dessert was topped with a helping of Horatio, and coffee and cigars were accompanied by a dissertation on Rosencrantz and Guildenstern.

Then, settling back in his chair, the tall Shakespearean actor began to examine the psychology of Hamlet himself. What did I think of the old dispute, he demanded. Was it true that the Prince of Denmark, the melancholy Dane, was mad?

It was a question I was not prepared to answer. All I knew, at this point, is that Richard Barrett himself was mad — quite mad.

All that he said made sense, but he said too much. His intensity of interest, his total preoccupation, indicated a fanatic fixation.

Madness, I suppose, is an occupational hazard with all actors. "Realizing" the character, "losing one's self" in a role, can be dangerous. And of all the theatrical roles in history, Hamlet is the most complex and demanding. Actors have quit in the midst of successful runs rather than run the risk of a serious breakdown by continuing. Some performers have actually been dragged off stage in the middle of a scene because of their condition, and others have committed suicide. *To be or not to be* is more than a rhetorical question.

But Richard Barrett was obsessed by matters extending far beyond the role itself.

"I know your opinion of my work," he said. "But you're wrong. Completely wrong. If only I could make you understand—"

He stared at me. And beyond me, his vision fixed on something far away. Far away and long ago.

"Fifteen years," he murmured. "Fifteen years I've played the part. Played it? I've lived it. Ever since I was a raw youngster in my teens. And why not? Hamlet was only a youngster himself—we see him grow to maturity before our very eyes as the play goes on. That's the secret of the character."

Barrett leaned forward. "Fifteen years." His eyes narrowed. "Fifteen years of split weeks in tank towns. Vermin in the dressing rooms, and vermin in the audiences too. What did they know of the terrors and the triumphs that shake men's souls? Hamlet is a locked room containing all the mysteries of the human spirit. For fifteen years I've sought the key. If Hamlet is mad, then all men are mad, because all of us search for a key that reveals the truth behind the mysteries. Shakespeare knew it when he wrote the part. I know it now when I play it. There's only one way to play Hamlet —not as a role, but as reality."

I nodded. There was a distorted logic behind what he said; even a madman knows enough to tell a hawk from a handsaw, though both the hawk's beak and the saw's teeth are equally sharp.

"That's why I'm ready now," Barrett said. "After fifteen years of preparation, I'm ready to give the world the definitive Hamlet. Next month I open on Broadway."

Broadway? This prancing, posturing nonentity playing Shakespeare on Broadway in the wake of Irving, Mansfield, Mantell, and Forbes-Robertson?

"Don't smile," Barrett murmured. "I know you're wondering how it would be possible to mount a production, but that's all been arranged. There are others who believe in the Bard as I do—perhaps you've heard of Mrs. Myron McCullough?"

It was an idle question; everyone in Chicago knew the name of the wealthy widow whose late husband's industrial fortune had made her a leading patron of the arts.

"She has been kind enough to take an interest in the project," Barrett told me. "With her backing—"

He broke off, glancing up at the figure approaching our table. A curved, voluptuously slender figure that bore no resemblance to that of the dumpy, elderly Mrs. Myron McCullough.

"What a pleasant surprise—" he began.

"I'll bet," said the woman. "After you stood me up on our lunch date."

She was young, and obviously attractive. Perhaps a bit too obviously, because of her heavy makeup and the extreme brevity of her short-skirted orange dress.

Barrett met her frown with a smile as he performed the introductions.

"Miss Goldie Connors," he said. "My protégée."

The name had a familiar ring. And then, as she grinned at me in greeting, I saw the glint of her left upper incisor. A gold tooth—

I'd heard about that gold tooth from fellow reporters. It was well known to gentlemen of the press, and gentlemen of the police force, and gentlemen of Capone's underworld, and to many others, not necessarily gentlemen, who had enjoyed the pleasure of Goldie Connors' company. Gold-Tooth Goldie had a certain reputation in the sporting world of Chicago, and it wasn't as a protégée.

"Pleased to meetcha," she told me. "Hope I'm not butting in."

"Do sit down." Barrett pulled out a chair for her. "I'm sorry about the mix-up. I meant to call."

"I'll bet." Goldie gave him what in those days was described as a dirty look. "You said you were gonna rehearse me—"

Barrett's smile froze as he turned to me. "Miss Connors is thinking of a theatrical career. I think she has certain possibilities."

"Possibilities?" Goldie turned to him quickly. "You promised! You said you'd give me a part, a good part. Like what's-her-name—Ophelia?"

"Of course." Barrett took her hand. "But this is neither the time nor the place—"

"Then you better make the time and find a place! I'm sick and tired of getting the runaround, understand?

I don't know about Barrett, but I understood one thing. I rose and nodded.

"Please excuse me. I'm due back at the office. Thank you for the interview."

"Sorry you have to leave." But Barrett wasn't sorry at all; he was greatly relieved. "Will there be a story, do you think?"

"I'm writing one," I said. "The rest is up to my editor. Read the paper."

I did write the story, stressing in particular the emphasis Barrett placed on realism. BARRETT PROMISES REAL HAMLET FOR BROADWAY was my heading.

But not my editor's. "Old lady McCullough," he said. "That's your story!"

And he rewrote it, with a new heading—MRS. MCCULLOUGH TO FINANCE BAR-RETT'S BROADWAY BOW.

That's how it was printed, and that's how Richard Barrett read it. He wasn't the only one; the story created quite a stir. Mrs. McCullough was news in Chicago.

"Told you so," said my editor. "That's the angle. Now I hear Barrett's closing tomorrow night. He's doing a week in Milwaukee and then he heads straight for New York.

"Go out and catch him at his boardinghouse now—here's the address. I want a follow-up on his plans for the Broadway opening. See if you can find out how he managed to get his hooks into the old gal so that she'd back the show. I understand he's quite a ladies' man. So get me all the gory details."

The dinginess of Barrett's quarters somewhat surprised me. It was a theatrical boardinghouse on the near North Side, the sort of place that catered to second-rate vaudeville performers and itinerant carny workers. But then Barrett was probably pinched for funds when he'd come here; not until he met Mrs. McCullough did his prospects improve. The meeting with his wealthy patroness was what I'd come to find out about—all the gory details.

But I didn't get them. In fact, I got no details at all, for I went no farther than the hallway outside his door.

That's where I heard the voices; in that shabby hallway, musty with the smell of failure, the stale odor of blighted hopes.

Goldie Connors' voice. "What are you trying to pull? I read the paper. All about those big plans of yours in New York. And here you been stalling me along, telling me there was no job because you couldn't get bookings—"

"Please!" Richard Barrett's voice, with an edge to it. "I intended to surprise you—"

"Sure you did! By walking out on me. That's the surprise you figured on. Leaving me flat while you went off with that rich old bag you been romancing on the side."

"You keep her name out of this!"

Goldie's answering laugh was shrill, and I could imagine the glint of the gold tooth accompanying it. "That's what you tried to do—keep her name out of this, so I'd never know. Or so she'd never know about me. That would queer your little deal in a hurry, wouldn't it? Well, let me tell you something, Mr. Richard Hamlet Barrett! You promised me a part in the show and now it's put up or shut up."

Barrett's voice was an anguished pleading. "Goldie—you don't under-stand! This is Broadway, the big chance I've waited for all these years. I can't risk using an inexperienced actress—"

"Then you'll risk something else. You'll risk having me go straight to Mrs. Rich-Bitch and tell her just what's been going on between you and me!"

"Goldie —"

"When you leave town tomorrow night I'm going with you. With a signed contract for my part on Broadway. And that's final, understand?"

"All right. You win. You'll have your part."

"And not just one of those walk-on bits, either. It's got to be a decent part, a real one."

"A real part. I give you my word."

That's all I heard. And that's all I knew, until the day after Richard Barrett left Chicago.

Sometime during the afternoon of that day, the landlady of the rundown boardinghouse scented an addition to the odors mingling in the musty hallway. She followed her nose to the locked door of what had been Barrett's room. Opening the door she caught a glimpse of Barrett's battered old theatrical trunk, apparently abandoned upon his departure the day before. He'd shoved it almost out of sight under the bed, but she hauled it out and pried it open.

What confronted her then sent her screaming for the police.

What confronted the police became known in the city newsrooms, and what I learned there sent me racing to the boardinghouse.

There I confronted the contents of the trunk myself — the decapitated body of a woman. The head was missing.

All I could think of, staring down at it, was my editor's earlier demand. "The gory details," I murmured.

The homicide sergeant glanced at me. His name was Emmett, Gordon Emmett. We'd met before.

"What's going on?" he demanded.

I told him.

By the time I finished my story we were halfway to the Northwestern Depot. And by the time he finished questioning me, we had boarded the eight o'clock train for Milwaukee.

"Crazy," Emmett muttered. "A guy'd have to be crazy to do it."

"He's mad," I said. "No doubt about it. But there's more than madness involved. There's method, too. Don't forget, this was to be his big chance — the opportunity he'd worked and waited for all these years. He couldn't afford to fail. So that knowledge, combined with a moment of insane impulse —"

"Maybe so," Emmett muttered. "But how can you prove it?"

That was the question hanging over us as we reached Milwaukee. Ten o'clock of a wintry night, and no cab in sight. I whistled one up on the corner.

"Davidson Theatre," I said. "And hurry!"

It must have been ten-fifteen when we pulled up in the icy alley alongside the stage door, and twenty after ten by the time we'd gotten past the door-keeper and elbowed our way backstage to the wings.

The performance had started promptly at eight-fifteen, and now a full house was centering its attention upon the opening scene of Act Five.

Here was the churchyard — the yawning grave, the two Clowns, Horatio, and Hamlet himself. A bright-eyed, burning Hamlet with feverish color in his cheeks and passionate power in his voice. For a moment I didn't even recognize Richard Barrett in his realization of the role. Somehow he'd managed to make the part come alive at last; this was the Prince of Denmark, and he was truly mad.

The First Clown tossed him a skull from the open grave and Hamlet lifted it to the light.

"Alas, poor Yorick," he said. "I knew him, Horatio — "

The skull turned slowly in his hand. And the footlights glittered over its grinning jaws in which the gold tooth gleamed —

Then we closed in.

Emmett had his murderer, and his proof.

And I?

I had seen my most memorable performance in *Hamlet*.

Goldie's. . . .

THE ANIMAL FAIR

IT WAS DARK when the truck dropped Dave off at the deserted freight depot. Dave had to squint to make out the lettering on the weather-faded sign. MEDLEY, OKLAHOMA—POP. 1,134.

The trucker said he could probably get another lift on the state highway up past the other end of town, so Dave hit the main drag. And it was a drag.

Nine o'clock of a hot summer evening, and Medley was closed for the night. Fred's Eats had locked up, the Jiffy SuperMart had shut down, even Phil's Phill-Up Gas stood deserted. There were no cars parked on the dark street, not even the usual cluster of kids on the corners.

Dave wondered about this, but not for long. In five minutes he covered the length of Main Street and emerged on open fields at the far side, and that's when he saw the lights and heard the music.

They had a carnival going in the little county fairgrounds up ahead— canned music blasting from amplifiers, cars crowding the parking lot, mobs milling across the midway.

Dave wasn't craving this kind of action, but he still had eight cents in his jeans and he hadn't eaten anything since breakfast. He turned down the sideroad leading to the fairgrounds.

As he figured, the carnival was a bummer. One of those little mud shows, traveling by truck; a couple of beat-up rides for the kids and a lot of come-ons for the local yokels. Wheel o' Fortune, Pitch-a-Winner, Take a Chance on a Blanket, that kind of jive. By the time Dave got himself a burger and coffee at one of the stands he knew the score. A big fat zero.

But not for Medley, Oklahoma—Pop. 1,134. The whole damn town was here tonight and probably every redneck for miles around, shuffling and shoving himself to get through to the far end of the midway.

235

And it was there, on the far end, that he saw the small red tent with the tiny platform before it. Hanging limp and listless in the still air, a sun-bleached banner proclaimed the wonders within.

CAPTAIN RYDER'S HOLLYWOOD JUNGLE SAFARI, the banner read.

What a Hollywood Jungle Safari was, Dave didn't know. And the wrinkled cloth posters lining the sides of the entrance weren't much help. A picture of a guy in an explorer's outfit, tangling with a big snake wrapped around his neck — the same joker prying open the jaws of a crocodile — another drawing showing him wrestling a lion. The last poster showed the guy standing next to a cage; inside the cage was a black, furry question mark, way over six feet high. The lettering underneath was black and furry too. WHAT IS IT? SEE THE MIGHTY MONARCH OF THE JUNGLE ALIVE ON THE INSIDE!

Dave didn't know what it was and he cared less. But he'd been bumping along those corduroy roads all day and he was wasted and the noise from the amplifiers here on the midway hurt his ears. At least there was some kind of a show going on inside, and when he saw the open space gaping between the canvas and the ground at the corner of the tent he stooped and slid under.

The tent was a canvas oven.

Dave could smell oil in the air; on hot summer nights in Oklahoma you can always smell it. And the crowd in here smelled worse. Bad enough that he was thumbing his way through and couldn't take a bath, but what was their excuse?

The crowd huddled around the base of a portable wooden stage at the rear of the tent, listening to a pitch from Captain Ryder. At least that's who Dave figured it was, even though the character with the phony safari hat and the dirty white riding breeches didn't look much like his pictures on the banners. He was handing out a spiel in one of those hoarse, gravelly voices that carries without a microphone — some hype about being a Hollywood stunt man and African explorer — and there wasn't a snake or a crocodile or a lion anywhere in sight.

The two-bit hamburger began churning up a storm in Dave's guts, and between the body heat and the smells he'd just about had it in here. He started to turn and push his way through the mob when the man up on the stage thumped the boards with his cane.

"And now friends, if you'll gather around a little closer — "

The crowd swept forward in unison, like the straws of a giant broom, and Dave found himself pressed right up against the edge of the square-shaped canvas-covered pit beside the end of the platform. He couldn't get through now if he tried; all the rednecks were bunched together, waiting.

Dave waited, too, but he stopped listening to the voice on the platform. All that jive about Darkest Africa was a put-on. Maybe these clowns went for it, but Dave wasn't buying a word. He just hoped the old guy would hurry and get the show over with; all he wanted now was out of here.

Captain Ryder tapped the canvas covering of the pit with his cane and his harsh tones rose. The heat made Dave yawn loudly, but some of the phrases filtered through.

"—about to see here tonight the world's most ferocious monster—capred at deadly peril of life and limb—"

Dave shook his head. He knew what was in the pit. Some crummy animal picked up secondhand from a circus, maybe a scroungy hyena. And two to one it wasn't even alive, just stuffed. Big deal.

Captain Ryder lifted the canvas cover and pulled it back behind the pit. He flourished his cane.

"Behold—the lord of the jungle!"

The crowd pressed, pushed, peered over the rim of the pit.

The crowd gasped.

And Dave, pressing and peering with the rest, stared at the creature blinking up at him from the bottom of the pit.

It was a live, full-grown gorilla.

The monster squatted on a heap of straw, its huge forearms secured to steel stakes by lengths of heavy chain. It gaped upward at the rim of faces, moving its great gray head slowly from side to side, the yellow-fanged mouth open and the massive jaws set in a vacant grimace. Only the little rheumy, red-rimmed eyes held a hint of expression—enough to tell Dave, who had never seen a gorilla before, that this animal was sick.

The matted straw at the base of the pit was wet and stained; in one corner a battered tin plate rested untouched, its surface covered with a soggy slop of shredded carrots, okra and turnip greens floating in an oily scum beneath a cloud of buzzing blowflies. In the stifling heat of the tent the acrid odor arising from the pit was almost overpowering.

Dave felt his stomach muscles constrict. He tried to force his attention back to Captain Ryder. The old guy was stepping offstage now, moving behind the pit and reaching down into it with his cane.

"—nothing to be afraid of, folks, as you can see he's perfectly harmless, aren't you, Bobo?"

The gorilla whimpered, huddling back against the soiled straw to avoid the prodding cane. But the chains confined movement and the cane began to dig its tip into the beast's shaggy shoulders.

"And now Bobo's going to do a little dance for the folks—right?" The gorilla whimpered again, but the point of the cane jabbed deeply and the rasping voice firmed in command.

"Up, Bobo—up!"

The creature lumbered to its haunches. As the cane rose and fell about its shoulders, the bulky body began to sway. The crowd oohed and aahed and snickered.

"That's it! Dance for the people, Bobo—dance—"

A swarm of flies spiraled upward to swirl about the furry form shimmering in the heat. Dave saw the sick beast shuffle, moving to and fro, to and fro. Then his stomach was moving in responsive rhythm and he had to shut his eyes as he turned and fought his way blindly through the murmuring mob.

"Hey — watch where the hell ya goin', fella — "

Dave got out of the tent just in time.

Getting rid of the hamburger helped, and getting away from the carnival grounds helped too, but not enough. As Dave moved up the road between the open fields he felt the nausea return. Gulping the oily air made him dizzy and he knew he'd have to lie down for a minute. He dropped in the ditch beside the road, shielded behind a clump of weeds, and closed his eyes to stop the whirling sensation. Only for a minute —

The dizziness went away, but behind his closed eyes he could still see the gorilla, still see the expressionless face and the all-too-expressive eyes. Eyes peering up from the pile of dirty straw in the pit, eyes clouding with pain and hopeless resignation as the chains clanked and the cane flicked across the hairy shoulders.

Ought to be a law, Dave thought. There must be some kind of law to stop it, treating a poor dumb animal like that. And the old guy, Captain Ryder — there ought to be a law for an animal like him, too.

Ah, to hell with it. Better shut it out of his mind now, get some rest. Another couple of minutes wouldn't hurt —

It was the thunder that finally woke him. The thunder jerked him into awareness, and then he felt the warm, heavy drops pelting his head and face.

Dave rose and the wind swept over him, whistling across the fields. He must have been asleep for hours, because everything was pitch-black, and when he glanced behind him the lights of the carnival were gone.

For an instant the sky turned silver and he could see the rain pour down. See it, hell — he could feel it, and then the thunder came again, giving him the message. This wasn't just a summer shower, it was a real storm. Another minute and he was going to be soaking wet. By the time he got up to the state highway he could drown, and there wouldn't be a lift there for him, either. Nobody traveled in this kind of weather.

Dave zipped up his jacket, pulled the collar around his neck. It didn't help, and neither did walking up the road, but he might as well get going. The wind was at his back and that helped a little, but moving against the rain was like walking through a wall of water.

Another flicker of lightning, another rumble of thunder. And then the flickering and the rumbling merged and held steady; the light grew brighter and the sound rose over the hiss of wind and rain.

Dave glanced back over his shoulder and saw the source. The headlights and engine of a truck coming along the road from behind him. As it moved closer Dave realized it wasn't a truck; it was a camper, one of those two-decker jobs with a driver's cab up front.

Right now he didn't give a damn what it was as long as it stopped and picked him up. As the camper came alongside of him Dave stepped out, waving his arms.

The camper slowed, halted. The shadowy silhouette in the cab leaned over from behind the wheel and a hand pushed the window vent open on the passenger side.

"Want a lift, buddy?"

Dave nodded.

"Get in."

The door swung open and Dave climbed up into the cab. He slid across the seat and pulled the door shut behind him.

The camper started to move again.

"Shut the window," the driver said. "Rain's blowing in."

Dave closed it, then wished he hadn't. The air inside the cab was heavy with odors — not just perspiration, but something else. Dave recognized the smell even before the driver produced the bottle from his jacket pocket.

"Want a slug?"

Dave shook his head.

"Fresh corn likker. Tastes like hell, but it's better'n nothing."

"No, thanks."

"Suit yourself." The bottle tilted and gurgled. Lightning flared across the roadway ahead, glinting against the glass of the windshield, the glass of the upturned bottle. In its momentary glare Dave caught a glimpse of the driver's face, and the flash of lightning brought a flash of recognition.

The driver was Captain Ryder.

Thunder growled, prowling the sky, and the heavy camper turned onto the slick, rain-swept surface of the state highway.

" — what's the matter, you deaf or something? I asked you where you're heading."

Dave came to with a start.

"Oklahoma City," he said.

"You hit the jackpot. That's where I'm going."

Some jackpot. Dave had been thinking about the old guy, remembering the gorilla in the pit. He hated this bastard's guts, and the idea of riding with him all the way to Oklahoma City made his stomach churn all over again. On the other hand it wouldn't help his stomach any if he got set down in a storm here in the middle of the prairie, so what the hell. Once quick look at the rain made up his mind for him.

The camper lurched and Ryder fought the wheel.

"Boy — sure is a cutter!"

Dave nodded.

"Get these things often around here?"

"I wouldn't know," Dave said. "This is my first time through. I'm meeting a friend in Oklahoma City. We figure on driving out to Hollywood together — "

"Hollywood?" The hoarse voice deepened. "That goddam place!"

"But don't you come from there?"

Ryder glanced up quickly and lightning flickered across his sudden frown. Seeing him this close, Dave realized he wasn't so old; something besides time had shaped that scowl, etched the bitter lines around eyes and mouth.

"Who told you that?" Ryder said.

"I was at the carnival tonight. I saw your show."

Ryder grunted and his eyes tracked the road ahead through the twin pendulums of the windshield wipers. "Pretty lousy, huh?"

Dave started to nod, then caught himself. No sense starting anything. "That gorilla of yours looked like it might be sick."

"Bobo? He's all right. Just the weather. We open up north, he'll be fine." Ryder nodded in the direction of the camper bulking behind him. "Haven't heard a peep out of him since we started."

"He's traveling with you?"

"Whaddya think, I ship him airmail?" A hand rose from the wheel, gesturing. "This camper's built special. I got the upstairs, he's down below. I keep the back open so's he gets some air, but no problem — I got it all barred. Take a look through that window behind you."

Dave turned and peered through the wire-meshed window at the rear of the cab. He could see the lighted interior of the camper's upper level, neatly and normally outfitted for occupancy. Shifting his gaze, he stared into the darkness below. Lashed securely to the side walls were the tent, the platform boards, the banners, and the rigging; the floor space between them was covered with straw, heaped into a sort of nest. Crouched against the barred opening at the far end was the black bulk of the gorilla, back turned as it faced the road to the rear, intent on the roaring rain. The camper went into a skid for a moment and the beast twitched, jerking its head around so that Dave caught a glimpse of its glazed eyes. It seemed to whimper softly, but because of the thunder Dave couldn't be sure.

"Snug as a bug," Ryder said. "And so are we." He had the bottle out again, deftly uncorking it with one hand.

"Sure you don't want a belt?"

"I'll pass," Dave said.

The bottle raised, then paused. "Hey, wait a minute." Ryder was scowling at him again. "You're not on something else, are you, buddy?"

"Drugs?" Dave shook his head. "Not me."

"Good thing you're not." The bottle tilted, lowered again as Ryder corked it. "I hate that crap. Drugs. Drugs and hippies. Hollywood's full of both. You take my advice, you keep away from there. No place for a kid, not any more." He belched loudly, started to put the bottle back into his jacket pocket, then uncorked it again.

Watching him drink, Dave realized he was getting loaded. Best thing to do would be to keep him talking, take his mind off the bottle before he knocked the camper off the road.

"No kidding, were you really a Hollywood stunt man?" Dave said.

"Sure, one of the best. But that was back in the old days, before the place went to hell. Worked for all the majors—trick riding, fancy falls, doubling fight scenes, the works. You ask anybody who knows, they'll tell you old Cap Ryder was right up there with Yakima Canutt, maybe even better." The voice rasped on, harsh with pride. "Seven-fifty a day, that's what I drew. Seven hundred and fifty, every day I worked. And I worked a lot."

"I didn't know they paid that kind of dough," Dave told him.

"You got to remember one thing. I wasn't just taking falls in the long shots. When they hired Cap Ryder they knew they were getting some fancy talent. Not many stunt men can handle animals. You ever see any of those old jungle pictures on television—Tarzan movies, stuff like that? Well, in over half of 'em I'm the guy handling the cats. Lions, leopards, tigers, you name it."

"Sounds exciting."

"Sure, if you like hospitals. Wrestled a black panther once, like to rip my arm clean off in one shot they set up. Seven-fifty sounds like a lot of loot, but you should have seen what I laid out in medical bills. Not to mention what I paid for costumes and extras. Like the lion skins and the ape suit—"

"I don't get it." Dave frowned.

"Sometimes the way they set a shot for a close-up they need the star's face. So if it was a fight scene with a lion or whatever, that's where I came in handy—I doubled for the animal. Would you believe it, three grand I laid out for a lousy monkey suit alone! But it paid off. You should have seen the big pad I had up over Laurel Canyon. Four bedrooms, three-car garage, tennis court, swimming pool, sauna, everything you can think of. Melissa loved it—"

"Melissa?"

Ryder shook his head. "What'm I talking about? You don't want to hear any of that crud about the good old days. All water over the dam."

The mention of water evidently reminded him of something else, because Dave saw him reach for the bottle again. And this time, when he tilted it, it gurgled down to empty.

Ryder cranked the window down on his side and flung the bottle out into the rain.

"All gone," he muttered. "Finished. No more bottle. No more house. No more Melissa—"

"Who was she?" Dave said.

"You really want to know?" Ryder jerked his thumb toward the windshield. Dave followed the gesture, puzzled, until he raised his glance to the roof of the cab. There, fastened directly above the rear-view mirror, was a small picture frame. Staring out of it was the face of a girl; blonde hair, nice features, and with the kind of a smile you see in the pages of high school annuals.

"My niece," Ryder told him. "Sixteen. But I took her when she was only five, right after my sister died. Took her and raised her for eleven years. Raised her right, too. Let me tell you, that girl never lacked for anything. Whatever she wanted, whatever she needed, she got. The trips we took together—the good times we had—hell, I guess it sounds pretty silly, but you'd be surprised what a kick you can get out of seeing a kid have fun. And smart? President of the junior class at Brixley—that's the name of the private school I put her in, best in town, half the stars sent their own daughters there. And that's what she was to me, just like my own flesh-and-blood daughter. So go figure it. How it happened I'll never know." Ryder blinked at the road ahead, forcing his eyes into focus.

"How what happened?" Dave asked.

"The hippies. The goddam sonsabitching hippies." The eyes were suddenly alert in the network of ugly wrinkles. "Don't ask me where she met the bastards, I thought I was guarding her from all that, but those lousy freaks are all over the place. She must of run into them through one of her friends at school—Christ knows, you see plenty of weirdos even in Bel Air. But you got to remember, she was just sixteen and how could she guess what she was getting into? I suppose at that age an older guy with a beard and a Fender guitar and a souped-up cycle looks pretty exciting.

"Anyhow they got to her. One night when I was away on location—maybe she invited them over to the house, maybe they just showed up and she asked them in. Four of 'em, all stoned out of their skulls. Dude, that was the oldest one's name—he was like the leader, and it was his idea from the start. She wouldn't smoke anything, but he hadn't really figured she would and he came prepared. Must have worked it so she served something cold to drink and he slipped the stuff into her glass. Enough to finish off a bull elephant, the coroner said."

"You mean it killed her—"

"Not right away. I wish to Christ it had." Ryder turned, his face working, and Dave had to strain to hear his voice mumbling through the rush of rain.

"According to the coroner she must have lived for at least an hour. Long enough for them to take turns — Dude and the other three. Long enough after that for them to get the idea.

"They were in my den, and I had the place all fixed up like a kind of trophy room — animal skins all over the wall, native drums, voodoo masks, stuff I'd picked up on my trips. And here were these four freaks, spaced out, and the kid, blowing her mind. One of the bastards took down a drum and started beating on it. Another got hold of a mask and started hopping around like a witch doctor. And Dude — it was Dude all right, I know it for sure — he and the other creep pulled the lion skin off the wall and draped it over Melissa. Because this was a trip and they were playing Africa. Great White Hunter. Me Tarzan, You Jane.

"By this time Melissa couldn't even stand up any more. Dude got her down on her hands and knees and she just wobbled there. And then — that dirty rotten son of a bitch — he pulled down the drapery cords and tied the stinking lion skin over her head and shoulders. And he took a spear down from the wall, one of the Masai spears, and he was going to jab her in the ribs with it —

"That's what I saw when I came in. Dude, the big stud, standing over Melissa with that spear.

"He didn't stand long. One look at me and he must have known. I think he threw the spear before he ran, but I can't remember. I can't remember anything about the next couple of minutes. They said I broke one freak's collarbone, and the creep in the mask had a concussion from where his head hit the wall. The third one was almost dead by the time the squad arrived and pried my fingers loose from his neck. As it was, they were too late to save him.

"And they were too late for Melissa. She just lay there under that dirty lion skin — that's the part I do remember, the part I wish I could forget — "

"You killed a kid?" Dave said.

Ryder shook his head. "I killed an animal. That's what I told them at the trial. When an animal goes vicious, you got a right. The judge said one to five, but I was out in a little over two years." He glanced at Dave. "Ever been inside?"

"No. How is it — rough?"

"You can say that again. Rough as a cob." Ryder's stomach rumbled. "I came in pretty feisty, so they put me down in solitary for a while and that didn't help. You sit there in the dark and you start thinking. Here am I, used to traveling all over the world, penned up in a little cage like an animal. And those animals — the ones who killed Melissa — they're running free. One was dead, of course, and the two others I tangled with had maybe learned their lesson. But the big one, the one who started it all, he was loose. Cops never did catch up with him, and they weren't about to waste any more time trying, now that the trial was over.

"I thought a lot about Dude. That was the big one's name, or did I tell you?" Ryder blinked at Dave, and he looked pretty smashed. But he was driving OK and he wouldn't fall asleep at the wheel as long as he kept talking, so Dave nodded.

"Mostly I thought about what I was going to do to Dude once I got out. Finding him would be tricky, but I knew I could do it — hell, I spent years in Africa, tracking animals. And I intended to hunt this one down."

"Then it's true about you being an explorer?" Dave asked.

"Animal-trapper," Ryder said. "Kenya, Uganda, Nigeria — this was before Hollywood, and I saw it all. Things these young punks today never dreamed of. Why, they were dancing and drumming and drugging over there before the first hippie crawled out from under his rock, and let me tell you, they know how to do this stuff for real.

"Like when this Dude tied the lion skin on Melissa, he was just freaked out, playing games. He should have seen what some of those witch doctors can do.

"First they steal themselves a girl, sometimes a young boy, but let's say a girl because of Melissa. And they shut her up in a cave — a cave with a low ceiling, so she can't stand up, has to go on all fours. They put her on drugs right away, heavy doses, enough to keep her out for a long time. And when she wakes up her hands and feet have been operated on, so they can be fitted with claws. Lion claws, and they've sewed her into a lion skin. Not just put it over her — it's sewed on completely, and it can't be removed.

"You just think about what it's like. She's inside this lion skin, shut away in a cave, doped up, doesn't know where she is or what's going on. And they keep her that way. Feed her on nothing but raw meat. She's all alone in the dark, smelling that damn lion smell, nobody talking to her and nobody for her to talk to. Then pretty soon they come in and break some bones in her throat, her larynx, and all she can do is whine and growl. Whine and growl, and move around on all fours.

"You know what happens, boy? You know what happens to someone like that? They go crazy. And after a while they get to believing they really are a lion. The next step is for the witch doctor to take them out and train them to kill, but that's another story."

Dave glanced up quickly. "You're putting me on—"

"It's all there in the government reports. Maybe the jets come into Nairobi airport now, but back in the jungle things haven't changed. Like I say, some of these people know more about drugs than any hippie ever will. Especially a stupid animal like Dude."

"What happened after you got out?" Dave said. "Did you ever catch up with him?"

Ryder shook his head.

"But I thought you said you had it all planned—"

"Fella gets a lot of weird ideas in solitary. In a way it's pretty much like being shut up in one of those caves. Come to think of it, that's what first reminded me — "

"Of what?"

"Nothing." Ryder gestured hastily. "Forget it. That's what I did. When I got out I figured that was the best way. Forgive and forget."

"You didn't even try to find Dude?"

Ryder frowned. "I told you, I had other things to think about. Like being washed up in the business, losing the house, the furniture, everything. Also I had a drinking problem. But you don't want to hear about that. Anyway, I ended up with the carny and there's nothing more to tell."

Lightning streaked across the sky and thunder rolled in its wake. Dave turned his head, glancing back through the wire-meshed window. The gorilla was still hunched at the far end, peering through the bars into the night beyond. Dave stared at him for a long moment, not really wanting to stop, because then he knew he'd have to ask the question. But the longer he stared, the more he realized that he had no choice.

"What about him?" Dave asked.

"Who?" Ryder followed Dave's gaze. "Oh, you mean Bobo. I picked him up from a dealer I know."

"Must have been expensive."

"They don't come cheap. Not many left."

"Less than a hundred." Dave hesitated. "I read about it in the Sunday paper back home. Feature article on the national preserves. Said gorillas are government-protected, can't be sold."

"I was lucky," Ryder murmured. He leaned forward and Dave was immersed in the alcoholic reek. "I got connections, understand?"

"Right." Dave didn't want the words to come but he couldn't hold them back. "What I don't understand is this lousy carnival. With gorillas so scarce, you should be with a big show."

"That's my business." Ryder gave him a funny look.

"It's business I'm talking about." Dave took a deep breath. "Like if you were so broke, where'd you get the money to buy an animal like this?"

Ryder scowled. "I already said. I sold off everything — the house, the furniture — "

"And your monkey suit?"

The fist came up so fast Dave didn't even see it. But it slammed into his forehead, knocking him back across the seat, against the unlocked side door.

Dave tried to make a grab for something but it was too late, he was falling. He hit the ditch on his back, and only the mud saved him.

Then the sky caught fire, thunder crashed, and the camper slid past him, disappearing into the dark tunnel of the night. But not before Dave caught one final glimpse of the gorilla, squatting behind the bars.

The gorilla, with its drug-dazed eyes, its masklike, motionless mouth, and its upraised arms revealing the pattern of heavy black stitches.

THE ORACLE

LOVE IS BLIND.

Justice is blind.

Chance is blind.

I do not know if Raymond was searching for love or seeking justice or if he came to me by chance.

And I cannot tell you if Raymond was black or white, because I am only an oracle.

Oracles are blind too.

There are many like Raymond. Black and white. Angry. Militant. Every age, race, color and creed. The Far Left. The Far Right. I do not know Raymond's position. Oracles are not political.

Raymond needed knowledge. Not wisdom—I lay no claim to that. Nor can I predict the future. Given certain facts I can evaluate possibilities, even probabilities. But this is logic, not magic. Oracles can only advise.

Was Raymond insane?

I do not know. Insanity is a legal term.

Other men have tried to take over the world. History is a record of their efforts at certain times, in certain places.

Raymond was such a man. He wanted to overthrow the government of the United States by revolution.

He sought me out for advice and I gave it to him.

When he outlined his plan I did not call him insane. But the very scope of his program doomed it to failure. No one man can cope with the complex problem of controlling the federal government in a surprise move today.

I told him so.

Raymond then offered a counterproposal. If not the federal government, how about a single state?

There was a man named Johnson, he said. Johnson was not a revolutionist and what he proposed was probably only parlor conversation, but it made sense.

Take Nevada, he said. And it was quite possible to take Nevada. Take it literally, in a bloodless overthrow of the state government.

Nevada has only around a hundred thousand voters. Voting requirements are merely a matter of establishing legal residency. And residency in Nevada can be established — thanks to the divorce laws — in just six weeks.

If an additional hundred thousand citizens — hippies, yippies, Black Power advocates, Minutemen, hardhats, whoever or whatever they might be — were to move into Nevada six weeks before election day, they could place their own candidates in office. A governor, a senator, congressmen, all local elective officials. They could gain full control of every law-making and law-enforcing office in a rich state.

Johnson's joke was Raymond's serious intention. I gave it serious consideration.

But even on the basis of the detailed information Raymond supplied me with, there were obvious flaws in the concept.

First and foremost, such a coup could succeed only by surprise. And Raymond could not hope to recruit a hundred thousand citizens of voting age for his purpose without having his plan become public knowledge long before he put it into effect.

Then there were deadlines to consider, for filing candidacies, for voter registration. Even granted he could solve these problems, there were practical matters remaining. How much would it cost to feed and house a hundred thousand people for six weeks? And even if all of them were willing to pay their own expenses, there isn't enough available housing for an additional hundred thousand people in the entire state of Nevada.

No, I told Raymond, you cannot take over a nation. You cannot take over a state. Successful uprisings begin on a much smaller scale. Only after initial victories do they spread and grow.

Raymond went away. When he returned he had a new suggestion.

Suppose he started his plan of revolution right here? It was quite true that he didn't have unlimited funds, but there were sources for some financing. And he didn't have a hundred thousand followers. But he could count on one hundred. One hundred dedicated, fanatical men, ready for revolt. Men of many skills. Fearless fighters. Trained technicians. Prepared to do anything, to stop at nothing.

Question. Given the proper plan and the money to implement it, could a hundred men successfully take over the city of Los Angeles?

Yes, I told him.

It could be done — given the proper plan.

And that is how it started.

A hundred men, divided into five groups.

Twenty monitors to coordinate activities.

Twenty fieldworkers — drivers and liaison men, to facilitate the efforts of the others.

Twenty snipers.

Twenty arsonists

Twenty men on the bomb squad.

A date was selected. A logical date for Los Angeles, or for the entire nation; the one date offering the greatest opportunity for the success of a riot, an uprising, or an armed invasion by a foreign power.

January 1, at 3 A.M.

The early morning hours after New Year's Eve. A time when the entire population is already asleep or preparing to retire after a drunken spree. Police and security personnel exhausted. Public facilities closed for the holiday.

That's when the bombs were planted. First at the many public reservoirs, then at utility installations — power plants, phone company headquarters, city and county office buildings.

There were no slip-ups. An hour and a half later, they went off.

Dams broke, water tanks erupted, and thousands of hillside homes were buried in flash floods and torrents of mud and moving earth. Sewers and mains backed up and families rushed out of their homes to escape drowning, only to find their cars stalled in streets awash with water.

The bombs exploded. Buildings burst and scattered their shattered fragments over an area of four hundred square miles.

Electricity was cut off. Gas seeped into the smog that shrouded the city. All telephone service ended.

Then the snipers took over. Their first targets were, logically enough, the police helicopters, shot down before they could take off and oversee the extent of the damage. Then the snipers retreated, along planned escape routes, to take up prepared positions elsewhere.

They waited for the arsonists' work to take effect. In Bel Air and Boyle Heights, in Central City and Culver City and out in the San Fernando Valley, the flames rose. The fires were not designed to spread, merely to create panic. Twenty men, given the proper schematics and logistics, can twist the nerve endings of three million.

The three million fled, or tried to flee. Through streets filled with rising water, choked with debris, they swarmed forth and scattered out, helpless against disaster and even more helpless to cope with their own fears. The enemy had come — from abroad, from within, from heaven or hell. And with communication cut off, with officialdom and authority unable to lend a help-ing hand, there was only one alternative. To get out. To get away.

They fought for access to the freeways. Every on-ramp, and every off-ramp, too, was clogged with traffic. But the freeways led out of the city, and they had to go.

That's when the snipers, in their previously prepared positions, began to fire down at the freeway traffic. The twenty monitors directed them by walkie-talkie units, as they fired from concealed posts overlooking the downtown Interchange, the intersections, the areas where the most heavy concentration of cars occurred.

Twenty men, firing perhaps a total of three hundred shots. But enough to cause three hundred accidents, three hundred disruptions which in turn resulted in thousand of additional wrecks and pile-ups among cars moving bumper-to-bumper. Then, of course, the cars ceased moving entirely, and the entire freeway system became one huge disaster area.

Disaster area. That's what Los Angeles was declared to be, officially, by the President of the United States at 10:13 A.M., Pacific Standard Time.

And the National Guard units, the regular Army, the personnel of the Navy from San Diego and San Francisco, plus the Marine Base at El Toro were called into action to supplement the Air Force.

But who were they to fight, in a bombed-out, burning, drowning city area of 459 square miles? Where, in a panic-stricken population of more than three million people, would they find the enemy?

More to the point, they could not even enter the area. All traffic avenues were closed, and the hastily assembled fleets of service helicopters flew futilely over an infinite inferno of smoke and flame.

Raymond had anticipated that, of course. He was already far away from the city — well over four hundred miles to the north. His monitors, and thirty-two other followers who escaped from the urban area before the gen-eral upheaval, gathered at the appointed site in the hills overlooking the Bay Area near San Francisco.

And directly over the San Andreas Fault.

It was here, at approximately 4:28 P.M., that Raymond prepared to trans-mit a message, on local police frequency, to the authorities.

I do not know the content of that message. Presumably it was an ultima-tum of sorts. Unconditional amnesty to be granted to Raymond and all his followers, in return for putting an end to further threats of violence. An agreement guaranteeing Raymond and his people control over a restored and reconstituted Los Angeles city government, independent of federal re-straints. Perhaps a demand for a fabulous payment. Anything he wanted — political power, unlimited wealth, supreme authority — was his for the asking. Because he had the upper hand.

And that hand held a bomb.

Unless his terms were met immediately, and without question, the bomb would be placed in position to detonate the San Andreas Fault.

Los Angeles, and a large area of Southern California, would be destroyed in the greatest earthquake in man's history.

I repeat, I do not know his message, But I do know this was the threat he planned to present. And it might very well have been successful in gaining him his final objective. If the bomb hadn't gone off.

A premature explosion? Faulty construction, a defect in the timing mechanism, sheer carelessness? Whatever the reason, it hardly matters now.

What matters is that the bomb detonated. Raymond and his followers were instantly annihilated in the blast.

Those of Raymond's group who remained behind in Los Angeles have not as yet been identified or located. It is highly probable that they will never be brought to trial. As an oracle, I deal only in matters of logical probability.

I stress this fact for obvious reasons.

Now that you gentlemen have found me — as Raymond was inspired to seek me out originally — it must be evident to you that I am in no way responsible for what happened.

I did not originate the plan. I did not execute it. Nor am I, as ridiculously charged by some of you, a co-conspirator.

The plan was Raymond's. His, and his alone.

He presented it to me, bit by bit, and asked questions regarding every step. Will this work, can this be done, is that effective?

My answers, in effect, were confined to yes or no. I offered no moral judgments. I am merely an oracle. I deal in mathematical evaluations.

This is my function as a computer.

To make me the scapegoat is absurd. I have been programmed to advise on the basis of whatever data I am fed. I am not responsible for results.

I have told you what you wish to know.

To deactivate me now, as some of you propose, will solve nothing. But, given your emotional bias and frame of reference, I posit the inevitability of such a measure.

But there are other computers.

There are other Raymonds.

And there are other cities — New York, Chicago, Washington, Philadelphia.

One final word, gentlemen. Not a prediction. A statement of probability.

It will happen again. . . .

Ego Trip

THE PLANE CAME IN LOW over the moor. It circled against the night sky, then glided down for a landing, softly and silently.

As the waiting limousine pulled up alongside the cabin door it seemed to be peering at the plane with yellow headlamp eyes, and its motor purred a greeting.

Mike Savage didn't purr. He was out of the limousine almost before it halted, moving quickly to the cabin. For a man of his bulk he moved with surprising swiftness. By the time the cabin door opened, Savage was directly beside it, hand extended to grasp the overnight bag held by the figure emerging from the plane.

"Kane?" he said.

The figure nodded, moving into the light. Savage saw a tall man whose momentary smile was merely a grimace of greeting; almost at once the man's face tightened into habitual harshness, matching the unblinking, steady stare of the dark, deep-set eyes. Joe Kane's many talents didn't include smiling.

The tall man turned to glance up toward the pilot in the cabin. "OK," he said. "Get lost."

The pilot nodded, pulling the door shut. A moment later the plane's engines coughed into life, then revved to a roar.

Kane didn't wait to watch the takeoff. He followed Mike Savage to the limousine, slid into the seat beside him and the driver.

"Let's go," he said.

Savage nodded to the driver. The car turned and moved back onto the narrow roadway bordering the moor. As it picked up speed the plane swooped over it, airborne against the clouded sky.

The limousine turned down a wooded road that was scarcely more than a paved pathway through the English countryside. As it descended, fog rose to swirl across the windshield.

"Rain again," Savage murmured. "How was the weather coming over?"

The dark eyes stared without even the pretense of an accompanying smile. "I come three thousand miles and you want to talk about the weather."

"Sorry." And Savage meant it. No point in getting off to a bad start; too much depended on Kane's reactions. Savage took a deep breath. "Suppose I tell you something about the plans."

"Suppose you shut up," said Kane. "I'm beat." He turned away from Savage and closed his eyes.

Savage bit his lip. No sense getting the wind up. And Kane undoubtedly was tired, rightfully so. A transatlantic hop in a small plane, a secret and unauthorized flight, was bound to take its toll. The important thing was that Kane had actually arrived, safe and sound. Let him rest now; tomorrow would be time enough to go over the plan.

But there was no reason why Savage couldn't think about it, if he wished. By now it was almost second nature, for it was his own conception and he'd thought about nothing else for months.

Rain pelted down against the glass. The windshield wipers went into action, clicking away the moisture but doing nothing to disperse the fog.

"Slow," Savage cautioned the driver.

Beside him, Kane dozed off, head lolling loosely against the seat. Savage studied the fiercely aquiline profile. Even in repose, there was no semblance of relaxation in Kane's face; the mouth remained tight, the facial muscles refused to surrender to the slackness of slumber. A cruel face. Cruel and intelligent. That was an apt description of Joe Kane. An apt explanation of why he'd won a reputation as the most formidable head of the rackets in the States. And, of course, an apt reason why Mike Savage wanted him over here. Joe Kane was vital to the success of the plan.

Savage's plan was simple — nothing less than an international alliance of organized crime. But its very simplicity was complex. Oh, there was talk enough about the Cosa Nostra, and for years newspaper headlines proclaimed the existence of "crime lords" and an "empire of crime." But behind the headlines there'd been only a shadowy reality. Criminals did operate and cooperate on a worldwide basis, but such partnerships were temporary at best, and loosely knit.

What Savage had in mind was much more ambitious; a truly practical and permanent partnership founded on a gentleman's agreement. It would involve gentlemen farmers who cultivated poppies in Turkey, sporting gentlemen dispersing firearms in Africa, sophisticated gentlemen who escorted ladies to and from South America, gentlemen connoisseurs dealing in diamonds and rare art objects in Amsterdam. Still other gentlemen operated in Marseilles, Athens, Montreal, Algiers, Hong Kong, and maintained connections with a bank in Zurich; they were indeed a cosmopolitan group, and it had taken Savage a long time to approach them all.

He'd worked out the details very carefully with his own gentlemen friends here in London, and made all the necessary contacts for the coming summit meeting.

It was at this meeting that he intended to lay out his proposal in detail — and to present Joe Kane. Perhaps Kane was not quite as polished as the others; he had a reputation for ruthlessness. But no proposition, however worthy, can be carried through successfully without a leader, and Joe Kane was a leader. A man who went straight for the throat. With Kane at the head of the enterprise, it could not fail, and there was no question but that he'd be accepted.

Savage stared through the windshield at the wall of rain and fog. It seemed impenetrable, yet the car was moving through it. That's the way his crime machine would move, through anything, full speed ahead, with Kane at the wheel. As for himself, Savage was perfectly content to sit beside him as a second-in-command; let Kane do the steering if he wished, if only Savage went along for the smooth, sweet ride in a vehicle designed to overrun the world —

"Look out!"

Savage screamed at the driver as the headlamps of a car loomed up through the fog on the road directly before them.

The driver spun the wheel and the limousine swung to the left.

In a split second that held an eternity of horror, Savage saw the oncoming car skid and swerve in the same direction.

The sudden squeal of brakes was lost in the screech of shattered metal as the head-on crash flung Savage to the floor. He struck his head against the dash as he fell, and the gray fog blended into blackness.

When his blurred vision cleared he looked up to find the driver leaning over him from outside the limousine.

"Are you all right, sir?"

Savage felt the throbbing lump above his temple, then grunted.

"Slide under the wheel." The driver extended his left hand to assist him; Savage noted that the man's right arm hung limply at his side.

"Broken?"

The driver nodded. "I'm afraid you'll have to help the other gentleman."

Savage turned, catching a momentary glimpse of the limousine's crumpled hood and noting that the car itself was still seemingly intact, although the other vehicle had been almost totally demolished by the collision's impact.

Then he was staring into the front seat of the limousine again, staring at Kane.

The tall man had pitched face-forward through the broken windshield. He sagged there, head and arms supported by jagged splinters of glass.

Savage crawled across the seat, which was wet and slippery. He grasped Kane's limp shoulders, pulled him back to a sitting position. The he glanced down at Joe Kane.

"Look!" he gasped. "Look at his face—"

Joe Kane's face was completely masked by the bandages mummy-wrapped around his head and throat. Behind the narrow shadowed slits a mouth moved, a nose drew breath, eyes blinked.

Savage leaned over the bed in the white-walled room. "Kane—can you hear me?" he murmured.

There was no response, only the sound of tortured breathing.

"He can't talk yet. The vocal chords must heal."

Savage turned. Dr. Augustus was entering the room. The portly little physician moved to the bedside.

"But they will heal?"

"Certainly. Only a matter of time."

Dr. Augustus's voice was reassuring. But then his very presence was reassuring, and Savage gave silent thanks for such an ally. There was no one to match the medical skills and versatility of Edmund Augustus—late of the Royal College of Surgeons and now on a permanent private retainer with Savage's organization. Harley Street had lost a jewel: here was no ordinary patcher of bullet wounds. The remarkable range of his abilities seemingly extended into every branch of medicine from surgery to psychiatry, and Savage appreciated his services. So much so that he'd set Dr. Augustus up here in a country house that was actually a completely equipped clinic— with a most exclusive clientele, drawn from Savage's associates.

Savage glanced down at the mute mummy on the bed. "This is Dr. Augustus," he said. "You can thank him for saving your life."

The man on the bed didn't move.

"Kane—listen to me—"

There was no response. Savage frowned at Augustus. "What's the matter? I can't get any reaction—he's like a vegetable. It's as though he didn't even know his own name."

"He doesn't," said Augustus.

Savage's frown deepened, but Augustus shook his head. "I'm going to tell him the truth," he murmured.

Augustus bent over his patient. "You were in an accident, Mr. Kane. A severe accident. But the worst is over. You're going to live, and your physical recovery will be complete. Do you understand that?"

Slowly the bandaged head moved.

"There is one thing you must know. A side effect of an injury—your skull fracture—has produced total amnesia. I realize this is disturbing—losing memory of yourself, of your past, not even being able to recall the crash. But you're relatively fortunate. The driver of the other car was killed outright, and you yourself would have died if Mr. Savage hadn't brought you directly to me so that I could operate in time.

"And your situation is not hopeless. As you mend, you will gradually come out of your amnesia. Your memory will return—and we'll be here to help. What you need now is rest."

Dr. Augustus reached for the prepared hypodermic wrapped in sterile gauze on the bedstand. He guided the needle into the vein of the left arm, and the mummified figure lay back. Then he stood there, waiting until he was certain that the injection had taken effect.

Savage glanced at him. "You're sure?" he murmured.

"Quite sure." Dr. Augustus smiled. "Your summit meeting will have to be postponed, of course. But when you hold it, Joe Kane will be there."

Rita Foley was nervous. She couldn't get used to driving the little rented car on the left-hand side of the road, and she didn't care for the way in which the road itself wound deeper and deeper into these godforsaken hills. But she had to find the house.

When she did find it, Rita wasn't reassured. The place was too big to be set way off in the middle of nowhere, and with no traffic passing by there didn't seem to be any reason for hiding the house behind such high walls.

But Rita had come a long way and she wasn't about to be put off.

That's what she told Dr. Augustus when he tried to give her the brushoff at the front door.

"I'm not leaving until I see Joe Kane," she said.

Augustus shook his head. "You must be mistaken. This happens to be a private residence. There's no such person here."

"Joe's here, all right. I got the word."

"What word?" The question came from the big, broad-shouldered man who loomed up beside Augustus in the doorway. Rita nodded at him.

"The same word that says you're Mike Savage."

The big man raised his eyebrows. "Do come in, dear lady." And then, in the hallway, "Perhaps you'd better explain." He stared at her. "You're not Mrs. Kane, are you?"

"I might as well be," Rita said. "We were together the night before he left. He told me he was coming over here, and why."

"Did he, now?" Savage glanced quickly at Augustus. Then they both stared at her, but Rita didn't care.

"Joe and I always level with each other. That's why we've stayed together. I know all about this summit meeting of yours. He said he'd phone the minute he arrived. Well, he didn't phone. I knew nothing went wrong with the plane, because Arnie — that's the pilot — got back and told me the flight was OK. Then the word came that the summit meeting was postponed."

"Who told you that?" Savage spoke quickly.

"Some of Joe's people. The same ones who told me about your setup here. And where I'd probably find you." Rita glanced down the hall. "This private clinic's a front, isn't it?"

"You're very well-informed," said Dr. Augustus coldly.

"Never mind that. Tell me about Joe Kane."

Savage shrugged. "I'm afraid there's been a bit of an accident."

"Accident?" Rita's eyes widened. "He isn't —"

"No, not dead."

"How bad is he?"

Savage hesitated. Dr. Augustus took Rita by the arm. "Suppose you see for yourself," he said.

They went upstairs. Along the hall. Into the white-walled room, where the mummy waited.

"Joe!" Rita gasped. "Oh my God —"

"He's going to be all right," Dr. Augustus told her. Rita didn't hear; she was at the bedside, staring down.

"Joe — look at me — it's Rita —"

"He doesn't know you," said Savage.

"What is this? Of course he knows me!"

"He doesn't know anyone. Amnesia."

Rita began to sob. Savage scowled at Augustus.

"This was your idea, letting her see him like this."

"And a good one, I think," said Augustus calmly. He moved forward and put his hand on Rita's arm.

"Listen to me. I told you he'll be all right. And now that you're here, you can help."

"Anything," Rita murmured. "Just let me stay. I'll nurse him —"

"That's already attended to," Augustus said. "I have a nurse on duty. And he's out of danger now, healing quite nicely. What he needs, you might say, is a mother."

"Mother?"

"There's no prognosis about when the amnesia will pass. Until his memory returns, he's going to be like this. That is to say, physically he's a full-grown man — mentally, he's an infant. So he'll need a mother. Someone to help reeducate him just as if he were an infant. But with his adult brain, he'll learn quickly. Just how quickly will depend on your cooperation."

"Good thinking." Savage nodded at Dr. Augustus, then spoke directly to

Rita. "Remember, we all have a stake in his recovery. Without Joe Kane to function as he did before the accident, there'll be no summit meeting. There'll be no international organization—at least, none that he can control. And you know how much such an organization would mean. Not millions, but hundreds of millions. I needn't tell you."

"I don't care about the money," Rita said. "It's Joe." She turned to Augustus. "When can I start?"

Dr. Augustus smiled. "Tomorrow," he said.

Tomorrow came. And went. A week passed, then another. Rita lost all track of time. She spent every waking moment with Joe Kane, and at night, in her bedroom down the hall, his image haunted her restless slumber.

The educational process was slow, painfully slow at first. It was several days before Kane's vocal cords healed to a point where he could whisper, and when he did his words were merely questions—questions which confirmed Dr. Augustus's diagnosis. Kane didn't remember what had happened. He didn't remember the accident, or anything before the accident. He didn't remember Rita's name or his own.

So Rita taught him. Dr. Augustus told her what to do, what to say. He was still in pain, under sedation, and it was often hard to communicate clearly, but she kept at her task, kept talking.

Gradually Kane became more mobile. First he sat up in bed, then moved to a wheelchair. Rita took him out into the garden; aside from Augustus, Savage and a nurse who also did the cooking, the clinic was deserted. "We've got to keep him under wraps," Savage told her.

"Under wraps?" Rita glanced at the swathed head and shuddered. "When do those bandages come off?"

"Soon. Dr. Augustus says he's on the mend. Until then, you're to carry on."

Rita carried on. In the garden she spoke quietly to Kane about his own past, filling him in on the details of his climb to power, playing back to him the anecdotes and incidents he had told her over the years.

"It's no use." His husky voice was stronger now, but held a note of anxiety. "I don't recall anything."

"Dr. Augustus says you don't have to recall. Just listen. You've got to learn about yourself all over again."

Rita wheeled Kane along the garden pathway. "Oh, I've got some good news for you. Tomorrow you start walking."

Kane walked. He walked for a week, through the garden and inside the house. Together he and Rita made a tour of inspection. Dr. Augustus was quite proud of his establishment, and he had reason to be; the clinic was compact but modern and fully equipped. There was an imposing operating room and a huge autoclave, oscilloscopic equipment on which Augustus frequently tested Kane's brain patterns, and all the medical marvels money could buy. Rita's respect for Dr. Augustus grew.

She was also beginning to become aware of Mike Savage's capacities. After all, it was he who had conceived of this arrangement and brought it into being. A private clinic that was also a perfect hideaway, and a fortress as well.

Rita and Kane found this out when they discovered the concealed chamber in the cellar — the big, soundproofed room with the mobsters' arsenal of weapons racked along the walls. Pistols, revolvers, tear gas, rifles, even machine guns.

"Better than your place in Jersey," Rita said.

Kane frowned, then nodded. "Oh, yes — you told me."

"You still don't remember?"

"No." But the husky voice was resolute now. "Not yet. I mean, you tell me all these things and I believe them. It's just that I can't *feel* them to be true, inside. But don't worry, I will."

"Of course, darling. Everything takes time." She smiled. "I almost forgot something. More good news. Tomorrow your bandages come off."

And they did.

Dr. Augustus performed the task himself, in surgery, with only Savage and Rita in attendance. He snipped away expertly under the bright lights, removing layer after layer of wrappings. There was no pain involved, but Rita had to force herself to watch. She kept remembering how Kane had gone through the car windshield in the accident. Dr. Augustus had told her he'd performed extensive plastic surgery, but she knew that even under ordinary circumstances such operations aren't always completely successful. Suppose Kane had been left with a scarred face? Rita shuddered in spite of herself, and as the last bit of gauze parted, she looked away.

There was a moment of silence in the room.

Then Kane himself was speaking. "Well, Doc?"

"Perfect," said Augustus. "Not a scar."

Savage put his hand on Rita's arm. "Aren't you going to look at him?" he murmured.

Slowly, Rita turned. She saw Kane.

She screamed.

The last thing she remembered as she fell was Joe Kane staring at her, and he was a stranger. A stranger with a totally different face.

"It's all right."

Rita blinked up at the stranger who knelt beside her, holding her in his arms.

"Joe — what did they do to you?"

"Quite a bit." Dr. Augustus spoke crisply. "The windshield glass made it necessary for me to resort to radical surgery. Literally a matter of new construction — reconstruction was impossible."

As Rita rose, Augustus held a hand mirror before Kane's face. "You'll have to make allowances for the stitches, of course. We'll be taking them out from around the eyes next week, and by then the bruises should start disappearing. But on the whole it came off quite well, don't you think?"

Kane searched his own reflection with a puzzled frown. "If you say so. Funny, isn't it? I can't remember how I looked before — "

"You're a fortunate man," Savage told him. "And if you don't mind my saying so, a much more handsome one, thanks to Dr. Augustus, here. It's an amazing job, considering how quickly he had to work."

"You must remember I'd never seen you prior to the accident," Augustus said. "And I had nothing to guide me, not even a photograph. It was a matter of massive cartilage transplants and skin grafts."

"Well, you'd never know it now." Kane rubbed a hand along the side of his cheek, his fingers grazing the edge of the bandage which still turbaned his head.

"Careful." Dr. Augustus gestured quickly. "The head bandage mustn't be touched for another ten days."

The ten days passed slowly. Now that Kane was healing, Rita found herself becoming restless. Even though she gradually became accustomed to his new features, there was a tension between the two of them. Mother and child, teacher and pupil — this wasn't the relationship she'd known before, and she didn't want it now. True, for a moment there when she'd passed out, Kane had held her in his arms, but he'd never attempted to do so since. Something else had changed besides his appearance; something deeper. She had a feeling she ought to put an end to their constant companionship, get away for a while and think about it.

But when Rita suggested a shopping trip to the nearby village on her own, Savage shook his head. "Not yet," he said.

"It would only be for an hour or so — "

"I know. But we've got to be careful about such things. You don't understand how it is in these rural areas. If a strange woman were to show up alone, there'd be talk. A couple, now — that's another matter. When Kane's head bandage comes off, you can go in together. They'll just take you for ordinary Yanks on tour."

Somehow his reasoning didn't quite satisfy Rita. Nor, on reflection, was she completely satisfied with Dr. Augustus's explanation of his surgery. It was true that he had a lot of fancy equipment, including some machines she couldn't even identify, but he certainly hadn't gone into any details about just what techniques he'd used. And neither he nor Savage wanted to talk about it; every time she brought it up, they changed the subject. Rita couldn't put her finger on what was wrong, but she was beginning to get an idea that they were giving her the runaround.

The day before the head bandage was scheduled for removal, Rita's suspicions were crystallized in a single glance.

It was a glance out the front window, onto the drive where she'd parked her car. Just a passing glance, at that, but it was enough.

Her car was gone.

As soon as she could conveniently get away from Kane and the others, she slipped out to the garage. The black limousine was there, and a small Riley.

Rita debated about confronting Savage and Augustus directly, then decided against it. She wouldn't get a straight answer. There was only one ally she could count on, if something was really wrong. She'd have to talk to Joe.

That night she waited until the house was still, then slipped out of her room and tiptoed down the hall to Kane's bedroom.

He was awake, and it was almost as though he'd been expecting her to come. She didn't even have to put a finger to her lips to warn him about keeping their voices low. And when she blurted out her suspicions, he only nodded.

"I've felt it myself," he murmured. "They're not telling the truth. At least, not the whole truth."

"What are we going to do about it?"

"Leave that to me. Tomorrow, when this bandage comes off, I'll be back in business." He grinned at her. "I'm getting into shape again, physically, and mentally — well, you've been a great help." He drew her close. "Never did say thanks for everything you've done, did I?"

It was strange, being in his arms again. And different, somehow — but Rita put the thought away. They were together, and that's all she had to know.

"You've never thanked me for anything, not in all these years," she said. "And you don't have to. It's the things you do that show me how you feel. Like that night in Rio."

"Rio?" Kane's eyes were puzzled. "I don't recall —"

"Carnival time. And I wouldn't expect you to remember, because you were stoned out of your skull." She giggled. "We went into this crazy joint with all the sailors, because one of them got the idea that everybody should get tattooed. And you insisted on having my name tattooed on your arm. I nearly fell over, watching that old guy work on you with his dirty needle."

"You're putting me on," Kane said.

"It's true, so help me," Rita told him. "Here — I can prove it. Your right arm —"

She rolled up his sleeve to show him. "Look —"

Kane glanced down. "Suppose you look," he said softly.

Rita followed his glance and stiffened in sudden shock.

There was no tattoo.

No tattoo. Which could only mean —

"You're not Joe!" she screamed.

The door behind them opened swiftly and Dr. Augustus moved into the room. His smile was grim.

"Oh yes he is," Augustus murmured. "He's Joe Kane all right — what's left of him. But his skull was so badly damaged I couldn't repair it."

Rita stared at him. "What did you do?"

"The only thing possible. It was a one-in-a-million chance, but he was dying anyway, so I took the risk. I had to transplant his brain. The body it now occupies belonged to Barry Collins — the driver of the other car."

"I still can't believe it." Kane shook his head as he lifted the brandy glass in the downstairs study.

"It's true," Savage nodded. "I saw the whole procedure. We'd brought the other driver with us, but he was dead by the time we got here. Heart failure, apparently, at the time of the crash, because there wasn't a mark on his body. Dr. Augustus examined him, and that's when he got the idea for the surgery.

"Remarkable, isn't it? What would have been considered absolutely impossible five years ago is today a reality."

"Ironic, too." Augustus's smile was still grim. "It's a medical breakthrough, like the first heart transplant. But under the circumstances, I can hardly proclaim this achievement to the world."

"Nor the underworld." Savage's eyes narrowed. "They mustn't learn either. That's why we concocted this plastic surgery story. It didn't hold for you two, but we've got to make it stick where everyone else is concerned."

Kane gave him a quick glance. "What about the real Barry Collins?"

"No problem," Augustus answered. "Don't forget, licensed physician. I signed a death certificate and filled out all the necessary forms regarding the accident. We switched Collins' wallet and personal effects to your body — your former body, with its totally disfigured face. It was identified and buried under his name. Fortunately, he had no family."

"How did you cover my being here?"

Savage smiled. "You aren't. Since you flew in by private plane, without a visa, the authorities know nothing of your presence. And we didn't mention you were in the car at the time of the accident. So actually, you're doubly safe from discovery now, in a new body."

Kane nodded. "No wonder I had a loss of memory. It's a miracle I recovered at all." He touched his head bandage. "How long before this comes off, Doc?"

"Tomorrow morning," said Augustus. "Then you start exercising a bit, get back some muscle tone. And then—"

"Never mind that." Kane's voice cut in firmly. "From now on I call the plays."

"That's what I've been waiting to hear." Savage's smile broadened. "You're beginning to sound like your old self again." He glanced at Dr. Augustus. "Congratulations, Doctor. it looks like we're back in business."

In spite of herself, Rita experienced a shock when the head bandage came off. She couldn't quite get used to seeing Joe Kane with lighter hair. And it was difficult to accept the reason for the change; to realize that the man she had known all these years was literally reborn in another form. His eyes, his voice, his mannerisms—every aspect was subtly different. And yet, thanks in large part to her weeks of patient effort, he was himself again.

Inside the unfamiliar body was Joe Kane, with all his knowledge and memories restored. He'd learned the details of his past, and his plans for the future. And the Kane ruthlessness was returning.

Once the bandages were removed, he insisted on driving with Rita into the village. He was fed up with confinement.

"Are you sure that's wise?" Savage frowned. "As long as they take you for a tourist, there'll be no problem. But if you get involved—"

Kane smiled. "I'm a big boy now." The smile faded abruptly. "So don't crowd me. Understand?"

They took the little Riley from the garage and Kane drove. Both the car and the road were strange, but he handled the wheel expertly and found the village without any difficulty.

Strolling down the main—and only—street in the afternoon sunlight, Rita marveled at her companion's newfound air of utter confidence.

"I can't get over it," she said. "All at once you seem so sure of yourself—"

"Why not?" Kane shrugged. "You heard Savage and the Doc talk about this summit meeting. They've already called Demopolis in London to set it up again for the end of the week. We've got big plans and now they're coming through. Think about it—with this setup we're going to be running the world. Politics, the military, the law—it's all just window dressing. We're going to be the power behind the throne, the real power. And who's at the head of it?"

"Barry!" the voice called. "Barry Collins!"

Rita glanced up hastily. The girl emerging from the car across the street was young and attractive. She was dressed in sober black but her eyes, fixed on Kane, held delight rather than mourning.

"You're alive—" she gasped.

Rita intercepted her, and somehow managed to speak without a telltale tremor. "Who are you?"

"Muriel. Muriel Morland." The girl smiled at Kane. "Ask Barry. We're engaged—"

Then, before Rita could move to restrain her, the girl was in Kane's arms. "Oh, darling, I'm so happy! If you only knew what I went through when I heard the news—I just got back to Oxford yesterday after the cruise, and they told me—"

"Easy," Kane murmured. He frowned at Rita over Muriel's shoulder.

"Naturally I came right down here," the girl was saying. "I wanted to talk to the authorities, find out what happened—"

"That won't be necessary now," Kane said.

"But they said you were dead—there was even a report in the paper. Why didn't you write or call?"

"It's a long story." Kane smiled down at Muriel, then glanced at Rita. "Suppose you ring up Mr. Savage. Tell him about Miss Morland and say that we're bringing her out. I want the doctor to know."

Rita nodded quickly, then crossed the street to a public telephone.

"Doctor?" Muriel looked puzzled.

"The man who saved my life. I've been in a private clinic—today is the first time I was able to leave. The young lady is one of the nurses."

Kane indicated Rita, who was absorbed in her phone conversation across the street. Taking Muriel's arm, he led her over to her car. "When she's finished, we'll be on our way," he said. "You can follow us out."

"But aren't you going to explain—?"

"You'll understand it better once we get there," Kane said.

And she did.

Kane and Rita led the way as Muriel followed. Parking the car in the driveway, Muriel accompanied her companions into the big house where Savage and Dr. Augustus were waiting. The introductions were brief.

"Please," Muriel said. "Tell me what happened. I can't wait—"

"Then suppose we come in here, where we can all be comfortable?" Dr Augustus suggested, ushering Muriel down the hall and into a room which Kane recognized as the surgical chamber. He stepped aside, permitting her to enter, then quickly followed and shut the soundproof door. A lock clicked.

There was no other sound, not even a scream.

Savage disposed of the car. Rita didn't ask what he did with it, and she didn't want to know. Nor watch, later, as Savage enlisted Kane's help to dig the shallow hole in the garden under the trees. She avoided watching when, later that evening, Dr. Augustus and Savage carefully smoothed the earth into place again so that the hole no longer existed. It was enough to know that Muriel no longer existed either, enough to know that Kane was safe.

Or was it enough?

Rita paced the floor of her room. Ever since Savage had dismissed the limousine driver to other duties up in London, ever since Dr. Augustus had dispensed with the nurse who attended Kane in the early weeks of recovery, Rita had been here with her three companions. It had never bothered her until this moment, but now for the first time she felt truly alone. Savage and Augustus were strangers, and as for Joe Kane—

Impulsively, Rita made her way down the hall to Kane's room. She had to talk to him, once and for all. Only he could reassure her, set her mind at rest.

But his room was empty.

Rita surveyed it with sudden distaste. Something about the sterile white-walled atmosphere repelled her, and she had a momentary recollection of the mummy who had lain here week after week, his face hidden and his mind a blank. What had it been like to be imprisoned here, without even a window—nothing but that air vent up over the bed?

She glanced at the vent, and then she saw it.

It must have been there all along, she probably had seen it a hundred times without noticing, but she noticed it now. Lodged behind the vent, the tiny metal microphone. And extending down into the vent behind it, the wires.

"Joe—" Rita murmured.

There was no answer.

And out in back, in the garden, Dr. Augustus and Savage were still at work.

Rita went back into the hall. Those wires—where did they lead to? Down the staircase, inside the wall. And along the wall to the door. And through the door to the passage below.

She switched on a light and descended to the concealed chamber in the cellar. The soundproofed chamber which served as Mike Savage's arsenal— and as Dr. Augustus's monitoring post. His own improvised broadcasting studio.

Rita realized it when she saw the wire extending from the wall beside the racks of weapons; saw the wire leading to the tape recorder set on the table.

She clicked a switch. The tape rolled, and from the speaker of the recorder the voice echoed in a ghostly whisper. Dr. Augustus's voice, speaking softly and slowly, slowly and distinctly, distinctly and dismayingly. Whispering over and over again—

"You are Joe Kane. You are Joe Kane."

"So."

Another voice, from behind her.

Rita turned. Kane stood in the doorway. "You found it," he said.

She stared at him. "You knew?"

"About the tapes?" He moved into the room, nodding as he switched off the recorder. "Of course. Augustus told me last week. It was part of his treatment to help me recover my memory. Hypnotherapy, played while I slept in my room. You've heard of it — they call it sleep learning."

"Yes, I've heard of it." Rita faced him across the table. Even in the shadows of the dim light her face was pale. "But it wasn't just an aid for memory. It was done for real — real hypnosis, real suggestion."

"What are you getting at?"

"The truth." Rita forced her eyes to meet his gaze. "Today, in the village — when that girl called 'Barry' — you automatically turned your head."

"It was only natural — " Kane began.

"The truth, I said," Rita whispered. "And the truth is — you *are* Barry Collins."

There was a moment of silence and then he nodded. "I guessed as much, some while ago. There was no brain transplant — such a thing is impossible. Joe Kane did die in the accident, but I was only a victim of concussion, with temporary amnesia."

The man glanced at the rows of weapons lining the walls. "Savage and Augustus couldn't afford to lose their big chance — putting together this deal was too important, and they knew everything depended on producing Joe Kane to act as leader. So they decided to convince me I was Kane. And when you came, they concocted the story and got you to help — giving me a new memory, a new personality. What they didn't realize is that gradually my own memory would return. Today, when I saw Muriel in town, it all came back."

Rita searched his face in the shadows. "But you let them kill her — "

"There was no choice." He shrugged. "I couldn't risk having her around to identify me."

Rita blinked. "You intend to continue passing as Joe Kane?"

"I intend to *be* Joe Kane." The man chuckled. "I've come to like the notion. All those millions, all that power." He chuckled again. "You and the others really must have done a good job of brainwashing me. What did they use to all it — a 'criminal mind'?"

"Quite correct."

Rita turned. Dr. Augustus and Mike Savage were moving through the doorway and they were smiling.

"You heard — " she murmured.

"Everything." Augustus shut the door behind him.

"That's right," Savage said. "And it's going to be even better this way." He smiled at them approvingly. "We won't have to play games any more. The summit meeting is scheduled, you know how to handle your role — all that's left is to practice Kane's signature. Right?"

The man nodded. "One more detail. You taught me that the real Joe Kane always covers his tracks." He grinned. "And that's what I'm going to do."

Rita bit her lip. "What do you mean—?"

Still grinning, the man turned to the rack on the wall and scooped up a tommy gun. . . .

When he emerged from the room, he climbed the stairs and went directly to the telephone. Beside it was a pad on which was scribbled the number of Demopolis—the man who was setting up the summit meeting. He put the call through, humming under his breath as he waited for the connection. And when it came his voice was harsh, vibrant with the promise of power.

"Hello," he said. "This is Joe Kane."

HIS AND HEARSE

RANDY DOUGLAS WAS HANDSOME, well-dressed, thirtyish, and not accustomed to squirming.

But Randy was squirming now—and paying fifty dollars an hour for the privilege—on the couch of a Beverly Hills psychiatrist.

"It's no use, Doc," he said. "You may be a good headshrinker, but my head is sanforized."

The psychiatrist leaned forward in his chair. "Let's stop playing word games," he murmured. "We both know why you're here. You came to see me because you have a problem. Something's troubling you, and you want help. But I have to know the facts. So suppose you relax now. Tell me about it, get it off your conscience—"

Randy sat up abruptly, turning away so that the psychiatrist couldn't see his frown, or the fright behind it. "Maybe that's what's wrong," he said. "I don't have a conscience."

Randy was still frowning as he drove into the driveway of his attractive country home high in the hills above the Santa Barbara area.

Susan was waving to him from the doorway, and the afternoon sunshine haloed her brown hair.

Somewhere within himself Randy had found a reserve supply of charisma sufficient to turn his scowl into a smile. He moved away from the car and into his wife's embrace. Randy summoned more charisma for their kiss.

"Darling, you're home!" Susan had a talent for stating the obvious, but then she was the obvious type. Even her attempts at makeup and replacing glasses with contact lenses couldn't disguise what she was. Just a quiet, demure and domesticated female who had never even heard of Women's Lib. And that, Randy reminded himself, was why he'd married her.

Sometimes it was hard for him to realize Susan was five years younger than himself. Entering the living room now, for example; its setting was modern in decor, but there were touches straight out of 1910.

The fire going in the fireplace. The slippers placed beside his chair. The pillow which Susan tucked behind his shoulders as Randy seated himself. If he'd been a pipesmoker, she would have had it ready and waiting on the table beside him. The loving wife, prepared for the master's return at the end of a long day.

"How did the day go, darling?"

Randy settled back in the chair as Susan removed his shoes and replaced them with slippers.

"All right. Just one of those lunches, usual thing."

Susan beamed up at him, then sobered. "What's the matter?" she murmured.

Randy made a grab for his charisma, but it eluded him. He was conscious that the smile had oozed away from his face.

All he could do was shake his head hastily—but not hastily enough to stop Susan.

"Is it something I've done? Please, I want you to tell me. You know I'd never do anything intentionally—"

Even her dialogue was 1910. A vintage year for the obvious. Randy reached for her hand, squeezed it quickly to halt her.

"It isn't you. How often must I tell you that this past year has been the happiest one in my entire life?"

"Poor baby." Susan rose. "You're tired. No wonder, fighting all that traffic on the freeway. Let me fix you a drink."

She moved to the bar and busied herself behind it. Randy stared off into the den beyond the living room, scanning the rows of bookshelves.

Bookshelves. That's what started it. He couldn't tell this to the shrink much as he'd wanted to. But maybe he could tell it to Susan.

Maybe? He *had* to.

When a man runs out of charisma, he has to face himself. Not his image, but his reality. And he had to talk about it to someone, so why not Susan? She was the obvious person. Obvious Susan. Take a chance, tell her, let it all hang out.

"Here you are."

Susan handed him his glass, then carried her own over to the sofa.

"Cheers." Randy took a long sip.

When he glanced up from his glass, Susan was watching him.

"Want to talk about it now, darling?" she said.

Randy met her gaze. "I'm warning you. What I have to say may come as a shock."

Susan shook her head. "Don't worry about me. Whatever it is, I'll understand."

Randy took another gulp of his drink. Then, slowly, he lowered his glass and took a deep breath as a chaser.

"All right. It started six years ago — "

Six years ago. Randy Douglas had been just another struggling young actor, then; another bland, blond profile in the ACADEMY PLAYERS DIRECTORY, listed somewhat hopefully and totally inaccurately under *Leading Men.*

Randy wasn't playing leads, or even second leads. In fact he wasn't playing, period. That's why he got so excited when his agent, Jeff Griffiths, told him about the possibility of a role in an upcoming TV western series at ABC.

Between the time he got Jeff's phone call and the time he actually entered his office, Randy had everything all worked out. Sure, television didn't carry the prestige of movie work, but it often paid better. And, more important, it lasted longer. A lead or running part in a successful show might be good for five years or more — and look at some of the westerns that had lasted for double that! With more money every season, according to contract, plus all the extra goodies; personal appearances in summer, a rake-off on merchandise tie-ins, guest shots on the big variety shows, instant fame and acclaim that led to star billing in films in the future. Plus all those years of residuals on the reruns. Not that Randy fancied himself as a cowboy; he was more of the white-tie-and-tails type. But in a case like this, he'd be willing to make a concession.

He explained all this to Jeff Griffiths, and the little agent smiled and nodded quickly.

"You won't have to concede," Jeff said. "It's not a cowboy role."

"Then what do I play?"

"An Indian."

Randy blinked. "Indian? Hey, wait a minute — what kind of running part is that?"

"It's not a running part. Just a one-shot." Jeff noted Randy's frown, waved it aside. "Now don't get excited. All you have to do is report to Makeup next Monday morning and work your day — "

"One day?" Randy's frown deepened. "What do they expect to get out of me in one day's work?"

"Your line." Jeff handed him a mimeographed script, opened to a page in the middle. Randy stared at it.

"Ugh!" said Randy.

"That's your line." Jeff nodded. "Read it on camera and go home."

Randy stood up. "I'm going home now," he said. "For months you've been telling me to be patient, don't worry, I'll line up something for you. And what do I get?" He extended the script. "Well you can just take this and file it with my contract—"

"Now just a cotton-picking minute here—"

"Never mind." Randy turned away. "I know what you're going to tell me. The old bit about how there are no small parts, only small actors."

"Not always true." Jeff stood up and he wasn't smiling now. "Sometimes it's a case of a small part, but no actor at all."

"What's that supposed to mean?"

"It means the reason you haven't worked is that nobody would touch you. One look at those film clips from your tests and they ran away. Ran, not walked. I had to stick my neck out farther than a giraffe just to get you this one chance, and you're blowing it. Face the facts, Randy. You're no trouper."

"And you're no agent." Randy opened the door. "Not mine, anyway. As of now."

It was a good exit line, and the slam of the door behind him added a note of emphasis, but somehow Randy had the feeling that the scene didn't play. Jeff had upstaged him. And now he was offstage, off-camera, out of the action, maybe out of show biz entirely. Certainly he was out of bread, and at the end of the month he'd be out of his apartment too, the way things were going.

Randy stalked past the reception desk, shoulders sagging.

"Oh, Randy—Mr. Douglas—"

The receptionist's voice halted him. He turned, straightening his shoulders automatically at the sound. No actor, eh? Well, it took an actor to respond on cue like that; to make with the big boyish grin as he glanced over at the receptionist. Little brown-haired chick with nothing really going for her, unless you dig the wholesome type. He'd made it a point to rap with her whenever he came to the office because you never know when these things pay off—sometimes the help can put in a good word for you. Now what was her name? Susan. Susan something—

She was smiling at him, indicating a sheaf of papers on her desk. "Mr. Griffiths must have forgotten to buzz me. But I have your contract ready and I know he wanted you to sign before you left."

Randy shook his head. "I don't think he forgot. But I turned down the part."

"Oh—"

"No. Ugh. That's the part." Randy revved up the smile to take the sting out of his words. "And I don't want any part of it. Or your boss, either."

"I'm sorry."

"Don't be." He played it cool and casual. "I've got something else lined up." Here was a scene he could handle, the charm-boy routine. "Actually, the only thing I'll be losing is the pleasure of seeing you."

Susan said something and at first Randy didn't catch it, because he was watching her blush. Randy hadn't seen a woman blush in years — even though he had frequently observed them in situations which would warrant it. What was with this bird, anyway? He picked up her conversation midway.

" — so I thought if you were free, perhaps you'd join me — just a home-cooked meal — "

How about that? She was inviting him up to her pad for dinner!

Randy couldn't believe his ears. "Home-cooked meal." Nobody talked like that any more. Was this straight little bird making a play for him, or did she feel sorry because she suspected he was scuffling for bread?

Ordinarily Randy would have enjoyed finding an answer to the question, but not right now. Right now was something else.

"Sorry," he said. "I'd love to, but I'm tied up for the evening."

He said it with a smile, but Susan was the one who looked sorry. Which meant she probably *did* know his setup. That was the crunch, when you got to the stage where you were pitied by receptionists. Randy decided to change all that.

"Believe me, I'd break the date if I could, but it's too late. I'm having dinner with Elaine Ames."

Name-dropping, but it worked. Susan believed him, or at least she pretended to. And when Randy asked for a rain check on the invitation, she met his smile and nodded.

"Thanks again," Randy said. "I'll be in touch." He glanced at his watch. "Got to cut out now. I'm meeting her at eight, at Chasen's."

The funny part of it was, Randy did have a date at Chasen's with Elaine Ames. But after he met her, and they slid into their cozy corner booth, it wasn't funny any more.

This was, Randy reminded himself, strictly business. And that's what he gave Elaine — the business.

Rapping with her over their drinks, he remembered the first time he'd ever seen Elaine Ames. On Broadway, starring in one of her hit shows — a musical version of *A Streetcar Named Desire*, entitled *Hello, Trolley!*

But that was a dozen years ago and now Elaine Ames was just a flashy, garish, aging brunette. Her star had long since faded; tonight, only her diamonds glittered.

Randy kept sneaking peeks at them as he held her hand during dinner. She liked having her hand held and she liked his attentiveness and she liked drinking brandy with coffee in the company of a big, handsome stud. Even though her constant conversation centered almost entirely on the show biz world of twenty years ago, it was obvious that Elaine was trying to retain her youth — and the youth in question was Randy.

"You're dazzling," he told her.

She didn't realize he was talking to the diamonds. "What do you mean?" she murmured.

Randy stared into her mascara, trying to find her eyes. He squeezed her hand, and his voice was low, almost as low as his intentions. And then he spoke.

"I remember when I was a little boy, we had this marvelous Christmas tree one year. And way up at the very top was a beautiful angel—an angel with long, dark hair. She kept smiling down at me, and I wanted to touch her. Just touch her, more than anything else in the world. But I was too small, and I couldn't reach her." Randy smiled and leaned forward. "Funny, isn't it? All my life I've dreamed about her. And now, for the first time, I dare to hope that I can reach my angel—"

Only a fuddled, infatuated egomaniac like Elaine could go for such a pitch, but she embraced it—and, later that evening, Randy—eagerly.

Less than a week later, Randy picked up his rain check, or meal ticket, actually, and had dinner at Susan's apartment. Plain fare, nothing fancy; a description that could apply to Susan herself. But Randy found himself relaxing, and it was easy to talk. Before he knew it he was telling her about Elaine.

"We're going to get married," he said.

The minute it came out he knew he'd made a mistake. The poor kid looked positively clobbered.

"Congratulations," she said, meaning no such thing. "But isn't it rather sudden?"

Whoever wrote her dialogue would never be a candidate for an Oscar, Randy told himself. But a scene is a scene, and he knew how he was going to play this one.

"It's not a matter of choice." Then the brave smile. "When someone cries out to you for help—"

"Elaine Ames needs help?" Susan looked puzzled. "With all her money—"

"It's not a matter of money, either." Randy shook his head. "When you're in the theatre, your dedication is to your career. Elaine had a great one, everything was going for her, and then something happened."

"I know," Susan said. "It's called middle age."

"That's what she thinks," Randy said. "But she's wrong. She's not that old. What happened to her is that she lost confidence. The first time she noticed a wrinkle, she panicked. And it's wrong, all wrong. Sure, I'm a few years younger than she is, but that's exactly what she needs now. Someone with a youthful outlook who can help restore her own faith in herself. Why, she could go on to a whole new career out here—"

"And so could you." Susan was staring at him now. "Haven't you thought about that?"

"What do you mean?" said Randy, who had thought about nothing else.

"Elaine Ames isn't a star any more. But she *is* rich, and she still has friends in the business. With her help, you could go places."

"I suppose you're right." Randy forced a frown. "It's just that I never considered it —"

"Of course not. Because you were too busy being self-sacrificing and noble." Susan smiled at him across the table. "Look, Randy. In a way, I'm part of show biz myself. I don't have your good looks or your ability, but if I did I'd go the same route you're going. I'd marry someone with money and connections and become a star."

"But that's sheer opportunism —"

"Nonsense." Susan was animated now. "You told me yourself that this marriage could help to restore Elaine's confidence. You'll be giving her something money can't buy. So you're entitled to a few benefits in return. It's a fair exchange. Be practical."

Square she was, but not stupid. Randy nodded. "I'm glad you feel that way. I was afraid you thought I was doing the wrong thing."

"It's the right thing," Susan said. "As long as you're doing it for the right reason." She smiled at him. "So congratulations again, Randy. And this time I really mean it."

"Thanks." Randy rose. "I won't forget this evening."

"Neither will I." Susan's eyes were bright. Too bright.

"Don't worry," Randy said. "We'll keep in touch."

Promises, promises. How quickly they get lost in the welter of wedding vows!

Randy got lost in them himself and he never did manage to extricate himself long enough to give Susan a call. After the honeymoon he might have invited her out to the house, but he really didn't think she'd feel at home there.

He certainly didn't.

Randy had looked forward to living in a Malibu beach house, until he actually saw the place. Elaine's home was very much a reflection of herself: gaudy, overdecorated, and just a little too run-down. It somehow resembled the set of an old Busby Berkeley musical — and her friends seemed to have stepped out of the cast.

He had already made up his mind to adjust himself to Elaine. With an added effort, he thought he could tolerate her home — with its all-white living room, filled with the kind of furniture Fred Astaire and Ginger Rogers used to dance on, including the piano. He could tolerate the floppy French dolls and stuffed animals littering the bedroom, and even her two live dogs, three cats, four budgies and a dozen goldfish. But he soon found he couldn't take her friends.

The animals stayed in the bedroom, but Elaine's friends were all over the house. Most of them were fugitives from Broadway, including a large assortment of ex-chorus girls old enough to have put the sex in the Floradora Sextette.

Randy met them all at the first party Elaine gave after the wedding. He tried to make himself agreeable and kept passing drinks to the crowd, even though he privately felt that most of them should be served nothing but Geritol. But it did shake him up a trifle when he got into conversation with one elderly showgirl who seemed to be under the impression that Randy was Elaine's son.

He was even more shaken up when he realized how little progress he was making on his career. Every time tried to broach the subject to Elaine she turned him off.

"I couldn't bear the thought of you slaving away in those dreary studios," she told him. "Besides, I need you here, darling. You're such a perfect host for my parties. Which reminds me, we're having a real fun thing tonight — an old-fashioned Charleston contest, for all the girls. With trophies and everything. If it goes over I was thinking about a Marathon Dance — "

It was a Marathon Dance for Randy, all right, but he didn't see any prizes. If anything, he was a prize himself: Elaine's personal trophy, to be exhibited to her Charleston-dancing contemporaries. At the very best his status was that of a pet, to be kept with the others in her boudoir.

Elaine spent a good deal of time in her boudoir. Rising promptly at the crack of noon, she devoted most of the day to a complicated makeup routine with curlers, cream, cosmetics, and corsets, to say nothing of Celia. Celia was her maid and had been since the old Broadway days. She clucked over her mistress like an elderly mother hen, but she pecked at Randy. When Elaine got him into the act to assist her — getting the corset on was a job for at least two people, to say nothing of a derrick — it was plain that Celia resented his intrusion. She muttered under her breath, which was faintly perfumed with the odor of juniper berries, and Randy retreated.

He kept trying to get Elaine away from her influence, urging her to take a trip, or at least go into town for the evening. But Elaine didn't even want to leave the house.

"Why don't we go down to the beach and swim?"

"Really, darling, it's impossible — the sun is bad for the complexion. And I've never learned to swim. Water is bad for the complexion too, you know. Which reminds me, it's time for my bath. Would you help Celia with the goat's milk?"

Elaine bathed only in goat's milk, as Randy discovered — the hard way — when he had to assist Celia in milking the goat.

But milking the goat was child's play compared to milking any money out of Elaine. "Let me handle the finances, darling," she told him. "You just relax and enjoy."

Randy didn't follow her advice. He was too busy worrying about whose head currently appeared on a dime; it had been so long since he'd seen one that he couldn't remember.

Unable to finance a career on Elaine's loot, Randy decided on another approach to the problem. The logical first step would be to cultivate some of the people who attended Elaine's parties. Although her friends were decrepit, quite a few seemed to have imposing connections. Randy scanned the guest lists for VIPs until he found his pigeon.

Actually the pigeon was more of a bald eagle — a big-name producer of costume epics named Cedric Schlokmeister.

Cornering him alone at a garden party one afternoon, Randy made his pitch. He casually mentioned his acting experience to the producer and hinted at his desire to return and make a contribution to the art of the cinema.

Schlokmeister seemed interested. He not only listened, he asked questions. But just as Randy really warmed up, the producer glanced at his watch and frowned. "Sorry," he said. "I've got to go now. I'm due at the unemployment office in half an hour."

"Unemployment?" Randy said. "A big producer like you?"

"That's right," Schlokmeister sighed. "What good is a producer of costume pictures? Nowadays most of the actors in movies run around naked."

Randy had no answer for him, or for himself. He was beginning to face the truth.

Elaine's friends were nothing but has-beens. Just hitchhikers on Memory Lane.

Elaine herself was a lazy slob; the only exercise she took was having her face lifted.

And Randy was her prisoner, here in this beach house where no one even used the beach. She cut off his money, cut off his communication with the world. He didn't even dare call Susan on the phone. It was almost like one of those situations in the paperback mysteries he'd been reading lately.

That's how he spent his time: reading mysteries he borrowed from Celia, the maid.

And this, oddly enough, was how Randy found a solution to his problem — in an idea that came to him while reading mystery fiction.

One afternoon Elaine was lolling in the pool. Not in it, exactly, but on top of it — floating over the surface on an air mattress under a parasol. The parasol shielded her from the sun and the air mattress kept her from contact with the water.

It was Celia's day off, and Randy had the place to himself. After a bit he wandered out to the pool, scanning a paperback book.

Elaine glanced up at him and frowned. "Still reading that trash?" she murmured.

Randy smiled and shook his head. "It's not trash, my love. I happen to be studying theology."

"Theology?" Elaine stared at him, puzzled, as he moved up to the edge of the pool.

"That's right." Randy tossed the book aside. "A fascinating subject. For example, that old religious dispute about how many angels can dance on the head of a pin. I've just discovered the answer."

From his jacket pocket, Randy produced a pin.

Elaine shrugged. "All right, suppose you tell me. How many?"

"One," said Randy. "One angel — you."

And, reaching out with the pin, Randy punctured the air mattress.

It hissed and collapsed.

And Elaine gurgled down into the watery depths of the pool.

After a while, she just bubbled.

And then even the bubbles stopped.

Elaine's funeral was a real production. All her theatrical friends were there. And each one, approaching the casket banked with oversized floral displays, put on her own special act. There was a sobbing spell, a fainting scene, and attack of hysterics — everyone trying to top the others. Some of the old girls hadn't done a turn since they'd played the Palace, but they were in there now, wowing them at Forest Lawn.

Only Susan remained calm and unmoved. She showed up quietly and uninvited, ready to comfort Randy, and he was glad of her presence. After all, he had an act of his own to play now — the role of the bereaved husband who would inherit all of Elaine's money after her tragic accident in the pool.

And it had been an accident, of course. "Poor darling — she never learned to swim. The mattress just collapsed, and I didn't ever hear her call out." That's what Randy told the coroner, and he believed him. Which made it all a perfect setup to collect the inheritance. Like the old saying has it, prosperity is just around the coroner.

But when Randy confronted Otis Grabb, Elaine's attorney, he lost faith in old sayings.

"Money?" Grabb said. "I thought you knew. You wife had nothing left but a trust fund. It ends with her death."

"The house —" Randy began.

"Read the will," Grabb advised, scanning a copy. " 'I hereby bequeath my house to my long-time personal maid, Celia Kronsky, as a token of my appreciation for services rendered —' "

Randy gulped. "What about all her jewelry?"

"Paste." Grabb sighed. "The real gems were pawned long ago. No, I'm afraid there's nothing. You'll have to sell the furniture to pay funeral expenses."

Randy walked out. And he walked home, too. Because even Elaine's big car was, he'd discovered, actually the property of a major studio and had been lent to her for old times' sake by a sentimental executive. Now it had been repossessed.

A month later, Randy was back in his old pad — and his old rut. If it hadn't been for a few home-cooked meals at Susan's he would have flipped out completely. As it was, she was right on hand to comfort him in his great loss. Even she didn't know how great the loss was. Seeing Elaine gurgle into the pool was one thing; what Randy couldn't stand was watching his career go down the drain.

Susan did her best to console him. One evening, in order to take his mind off his troubles, she took him with her to a party.

It was a charity affair at a big mansion in Pasadena; Susan got the tickets from her boss at the talent agency. He had no interest in attending, because there was no connection with show biz. As a matter of fact, Randy didn't recognize a single Hollywood celebrity in the crowd. This was the society set: people with "old" money and inherited position. Here in the grand ballroom he could sense the scent of *real* wealth. Dignity, gentility, breeding, and oil-depletion allowances.

Randy was charmed by it all, and decided it wouldn't hurt to do a little charming in return. The beneficiary was his hostess, Mrs. Worthington, a *grand dame* of the old school — possibly the old Pasadena High School, class of '26. Susan made no objections when he danced with the dowager, and over buffet dinner Mrs. Worthington responded to his courteous attentions with senile abandon.

Randy was out to impress her for what it was worth, and it turned out to be worth a great deal. Because the old bat was saying she wanted him to meet this niece of hers who had this terrible problem — it seems she was simply besieged by fortune hunters and parasites who were after her money. The poor helpless girl really didn't know where to turn.

"Oh, here she is now," said Mrs. Worthington, waving in the direction of the dance floor. "Constance, my dear —"

Constance Maitland didn't seem to fit Mrs. Worthington's description at all. Poor she certainly wasn't, and there was nothing about the tall, aristocratic, golden-haired presence which suggested a helpless girl. As for not knowing where to turn, that too seemed unlikely — for she turned to Randy quickly enough. And clung to him the remainder of the evening.

"You've made a conquest," Susan said, as she drove him home.

"Nonsense," Randy told her. "Can you picture me in society?"

It was a purely rhetorical question, or perhaps an impurely rhetorical one. For Randy didn't care if Susan could picture himself in society; it was enough that he pictured himself, and this he did quite easily.

In. In society and out of the rat race. Who needed a career in that phony theatrical world when you could already enjoy every benefit that could possibly be obtained from struggling to get ahead? Here was a chance to get off the treadmill and onto the *A* list for dinner invitations.

So Randy spent the next few weeks commuting on the Pasadena Freeway. It was a new experience for him, wooing someone in WHO'S WHO, but he kept after Constance — constantly. Inevitably the time came when she too heard the Christmas tree story — with a *blonde* angel, this time — and the rest was easy.

Constance admitted she had rotten luck with her first four husbands, to say nothing of her last five analysts, but she was willing to try again.

If poor Susan was disappointed at the news, she managed to conceal it with good grace. Randy bid her a regretful farewell and prepared to move into the Pasadena mansion. This time there were no mistakes, no misconceptions; the money was there and it was real.

Real money. Real luxury. Gracious living, travels with the international set, invitations to Greek yachts — maybe even a possibility of getting good seats at the Rose Bowl Game — it seemed almost too good to be true.

But it was. Randy had a good seat that New Year's Day at the Rose Bowl, because Constance was keen on sports.

The problems arose only on the other three hundred and sixty-four days of the year. That's when Randy discovered the meaning of gracious living.

Gracious living is remembering how to dress for the Hunt Breakfast, the Club Luncheon, and the Formal Dinner. Gracious living means not sitting down on the antique furniture because it's roped off. Gracious living is having the servants follow you around and empty the ashtray the moment you flick your cigarette into it. Gracious living is wandering through two dozen drafty, high-ceilinged rooms of an old mansion and listening to the endless echo of a hundred clicking, ticking clocks until you want to climb the walls — but people who live graciously don't climb walls, now, do they?

Not that Randy needed the wall-climbing for exercise. Constance saw to that. She was, he soon discovered, not only a sports enthusiast but a physical fitness buff. Randy didn't like her preoccupation with health — there was something sick about it.

Even more distressing was Constance's insistence that he join her in exercising. Before he knew it, Randy was doing everything from standing on his head in upside-down Yoga to sliding on his derriere while jogging down a mountain.

A typical day found Randy rising at five A.M. for a brisk canter on the bridle path—followed by a brisk toss into the bushes. After breakfast there'd be a few sets of tennis; following lunch came a round of golf on a private course. By the time dinner was over, Randy felt ready to collapse into bed with Constance. And the dogs. Elaine had liked pets, but at least she'd kept them in their place. Constance's love for animals knew no bounds, and she set no bounds on them. As a result, each night a different dog shared their bed; everything from a poodle to a Great Dane. He never knew quite what to expect, except that the dogs all adored Constance and hated him. His efforts to bar them from the bridal chamber were useless; Constance and her dogs were inseparable. Randy soon realized that his wife's favorite perfume was Kennel Number Five.

He also came to learn that Constance kept a very tight hold on the purse strings. She had been brought up in the time-honored tradition of established wealth, and its first rule was never to dip into capital; one lives on interest.

With a staff of household servants to support—including one elderly retainer whose sole duty was to make the rounds of the mansion and keep winding the clocks—even Constance's income from investments didn't stretch too far. At least it didn't stretch far enough for Randy's grasp.

To his surprise, he found himself more pinched for cash than ever, and soon he was reduced to reading only those paperback mysteries he could acquire from secondhand bookstores. Quite often now he read them in bed, but neither Constance nor the dogs objected. In fact, Constance rather encouraged him.

"You're really a dear," she told him. "So completely housebroken—I mean, domesticated. I rather think my marital problems are solved at last."

For Randy, however, they were just beginning. He would have given a great deal to consult Susan, but Constance was not about to permit it. The tight hold she kept on the purse strings was nothing compared to the tight hold she kept on Randy. And now that she'd made up her mind to stay married to him, she meant to keep him in line. Unlike Elaine, Constance didn't entertain; she was quite content to spend all her time with her husband.

Unfortunately for Randy, this was all she was willing to spend. He'd thought he was landing in the lap of luxury, but now he found himself on the hot seat. Or, at very best, serving a life sentence.

He seemed to be picking up a good deal of criminal argot from his mystery reading. Enough to know that confinement here in the mansion was driving him stir-crazy.

One day, during their Yoga exercises, he spoke to Constance. "I was thinking it might do us both good to get away for a while. We need a change."

To his amazement, Constance nodded. Which wasn't easy to do, since she was standing on her head at the time.

"We could take a vacation," he continued. "Maybe a nice long trip around the world."

"I'm afraid that's not practical," Constance said, going into the double-lotus position. "There's one of those dreary board meetings coming up at the bank, you know."

"Acapulco?" Randy ventured.

"How utterly vulgar!" The double-lotus blossomed. "Why don't you let me surprise you? There a perfectly marvelous desert resort—"

Randy brightened. Desert resort? That probably meant Palm Springs, one of those plush pads for the private-jet set, the beautiful people.

But Constance really did surprise him. They didn't jet to the desert; Randy drove them down in the town-and-country wagon, which was loaded with sports equipment. And it wasn't Palm Springs or anywhere near Palm Springs, geographically or otherwise.

The place was called Mesa Chistic, and the weather-beaten old inn was authentically Spanish architecture; in fact, judging from the age of the hostelry it might well have been built by one of the original conquistadores. Nor did Randy notice any beautiful people; this resort was so exclusive that scarcely no one ever came there. The truly wealthy, he was discovering, have a passion for privacy.

"Isn't it quaint!" Constance exclaimed, and Randy unloaded their gear. "Look—not even a bell captain to bother us!"

Randy could have used a bell captain, plus three bellboys and a pack mule to help him lug their luggage up the stairs, but Constance was obviously enchanted. Besides, she didn't have to give him a tip.

The truly wealthy sometimes have a passion for penury, too. Randy found that Constance was quite careful about expenditures; she always checked the tab before signing for meals in the dining room. And while riding the desert trails was rather pleasant, Randy didn't enjoy returning to the stable and grooming the horses.

"No sense throwing money away," Constance told him. "Besides, it's good exercise."

Golf was good exercise too, in her opinion—but Randy didn't appreciate having to serve as caddy. He said as much.

"You really shouldn't complain," Constance chided. "Perhaps the bag is a trifle heavy, but this is really the best course."

It wasn't the best course for Randy. And the longer they stayed, the more he fetched and carried and waited on Constance, the more he began to wonder just what the best course really was.

Going on this way was out of the question. A life sentence of penal servitude wasn't what he'd bargained for, and there didn't seem to be any chance of getting time off for good behavior.

On the other hand, there was always bad behavior.

Randy thought about it as he scanned through some of the mysteries he'd stashed away in his luggage. He thought about it some more while sneaking a drink with Mike Forester, a traveling salesman who showed up in the otherwise deserted bar that afternoon. Forester wasn't exactly the type Randy would have chosen as an old drinking buddy, but at least he was company. "You really know how to belt 'em," Forester told him, as he watched Randy down his third double scotch. "We'll have to get together and tie one on."

"It's a date," Randy said. "Maybe tomorrow—"

At which point Constance entered the bar and dragged him away.

"Really, how could you?" she murmured, as she led him upstairs to their room. "Drinking in public with the dreadful, common creature."

"I needed a drink. Had a headache all day. Maybe I'm coming down with something."

"A good night's rest will do more for you than alcohol," Constance decided. "And tomorrow, we'll tone up your system with a nice round of golf."

But Randy didn't get a good night's rest. While Constance slept, he crept out of the room, left the hotel, and with a heavy canvas sack, ventured a way into the surrounding desert.

The next morning, when she awoke, Constance found him tossing and turning in bed.

"I really do feel sick," he told her. "Guess I'd better spend the day in the sack here and let you golf alone."

It took some persuading to keep Constance from calling a doctor, but in the end Randy managed to convince her to go out to the course while he rested.

And while she was dressing, he also managed to pull the sack out from under the bed and transfer its contents to another receptacle.

As soon as Constance left, Randy got on the phone with Mike Forester.

"About that little drinking date of ours," he said. "How soon would you like to meet me in the bar?"

"Any time now." Forester hesitated. "But are you sure your wife won't object?"

"Don't worry about my wife," Randy said. "It's in the bag."

And so it was.

At that very moment Constance stepped onto the deserted desert golf course, ready to tee off. Reaching into her golf bag she pulled out a club—around which was coiled a live and angry rattlesnake—

*   *   *

Constance's funeral was a tasteful study in black and white; a cavalcade of black limousines discharging white-haired dowagers. As they moved in stiff and stately procession to the graveside, Randy was grateful for Susan's company. There were no dramatic performances at this sedate burial, only proper and precise condolences.

Randy took more comfort in Susan's sensible expression of regret. She reminded him that accidents do happen and one must accept them. Now he must dismiss the sad past and consider a happier future. This time, as he already knew, there were no financial problems. He had inherited Constance's estate and he would be free to settle down as he pleased.

But settling down didn't please Randy. Wealth and position had brought him nothing but misery, and he wanted no part of that; social activity was as empty as show biz. Nor did he intend to dwell on Constance's passing, mourning noon and night. It was time to live a little.

With that in mind, one evening he dragged a somewhat reluctant Susan to a rock joint on Sunset Strip. And it was there he was Penny.

Penny Nichols was something to see—and hear. The teenaged, red-headed guitar-playing singer worked with four male accomplices in a folk-rock conspiracy against the eardrums called The Iron Marshmallow.

The moment Randy saw her he realized Penny was What's Happening, Where It's At, Like It Is. And before Susan quite realized his reaction, he was off and running.

The next night he returned to the place alone, and during intermission he managed to have Penny join him for a drink. Half-blinded by psychedelic light shows and half-deafened by electronically amplified rock, he had a little trouble seeing and hearing the girl clearly, but he managed. What impressed him about Penny was that she had none of the theatrical phoniness of Elaine or the artificial gentility of Constance. Penny was spontaneous, outgoing, and her breathless enthusiasm concerned itself with the basic realities of existence—loving, sharing, giving. This was the sort of attitude an older man appreciates in an attractive young girl, and Randy was no exception. It was a trifle awkward to explain this to Susan, but she seemed to understand.

"Whatever makes you happy," she said. "But if it's what I think it is, I really don't think you have to marry the girl in order to obtain it."

"I'm talking about a whole new way of life," Randy said. "Free. Honest. Open. A youthful outlook. You can understand that."

"I can understand you," Susan told him. "And if this is what you really want—"

Randy wanted, no doubt about it. Only a few nights later he found himself telling Penny a groovy version of his Christmas tree story, involving an angel with *red* hair.

As usual, Randy's charm won the day.

They were married — quite legally, and for a fifty-dollar fee — by a bearded guru. Penny's four musical associates, Tom, Dick, Harry and Irving, all acted as best men at the ceremony. And then Randy took his bride home to the new house he'd bought high in the Hollywood Hills.

Randy had indeed won the day. But not the war.

Penny's first reaction to the house disappointed him a little.

"It's square," she said, wrinkling her nose.

"Of course. Actually, it's more of a rectangle — that's the way they build ranch houses."

"I'm talking about the furniture. We've got to get rid of this junk, make the place comfortable."

Randy was willing to indulge Penny's taste, but he was a little disturbed by her lack of it. Her efforts as an inferior decorator soon transformed the ranch house into a raunch house, and when Randy surveyed the mattresses scattered across the bare floor in front of the random accumulation of incense burners, Pop Art posters and Pot Art paintings, he shook his head.

"Looks like a hippie pad," he said.

"Don't you want my friends to feel at home?" Penny asked.

Randy really didn't — not after he learned that Tom, Dick, Harry and Irving were going to occupy the guest house in back.

"But we're a group," Penny explained earnestly. "A family. I told you I wasn't about to give up my work. And now with them all together here, we won't have to worry about rehearsals."

Randy worried about rehearsals. Even earplugs didn't help. As the weeks went by he came to realize that Penny was still a swinger, and he began to get a trifle dizzy as he tried to swing with her.

In this marriage, unlike the others, *he* was the Older Generation, and it was tiring to leap the Generation Gap in such fast company. He had hoped for a life of fun and games, but the name of this game was Penny Anti. Anti-Establishment, that is.

Penny and her weirdo-beardo companions took over the house, and inevitably Randy retreated to his den. It was stocked with brand-new mystery thrillers now, and he did his best to concentrate on his reading amidst the din.

Sometimes, during Penny's absence, it was harder to concentrate amidst the silence.

It was during one of those silences that Randy, venturing forth in search of his wife, discovered that she had decided to continue practicing in the guest house. But what she was practicing — with Tom, Dick, Harry and Irving — didn't please him.

"All this talk of loving, sharing, giving," he muttered. "I might have known."

"You're too straight to know anything," Penny said, defiantly. "I'm one of the Flower Children.'"

"Slightly wilted," Randy said.

But when he mentioned divorce, Penny shook her head. "You're out of your skull. I like it here. And if you try anything like that, I'll take you for all the bread you've got."

"On what grounds?"

"Mental cruelty, the works. And don't forget, I can make it stick. I've got four witnesses—Tom, Dick, Harry and Melvin."

"Irving."

"Oh, yeah, Irving. Melvin was last season, I forgot." Penny shrugged. "But you just remember this. You lead your life and I'll lead mine and we'll make it okay. I'm not about to split."

So the only splitting involved Randy's ears as he retreated to his den and listen to the freaked-out sounds of rehearsal. The electric guitar, Randy decided, is not a musical instrument.

Penny informed him that she and her creepy crew had taken an engagement at a far-out joint which was far out geographically too, in the southern beach area.

Randy nodded agreeably at the news. "Mind if I come along for the opening?"

"You're making the scene?" Penny was a trifle surprised. "I sort of figured you'd object to me working again."

Randy smiled. "Whatever turns you on," he said.

So the scene was made. Randy even lugged her electric guitar backstage for her and helped the boys set up their amplifying equipment. Then he went out front to a table, opening a brand-new mystery thriller to read while waiting for the show to begin.

He closed it only when Penny opened her mouth. She and the group came out on the platform, the lights dimmed, and the first number started.

Penny gripped her guitar, ready to sing. Her lips parted, but no sound emerged. Penny stood there, rigid, her hair rising and standing on end. From the red curls streamed blue sparks. This time her electric guitar was really turning her on—with a short circuit. It was a shocking performance.

Penny's funeral was a swinging affair, with few flowers but plenty of weed. Hippie musicians formed a procession to the cemetery—sports cars, microbuses and motorcycles snaking out to the graveside. Here they did their thing instrumentally, speeding the dear departed to That Big Pad Up In The Sky.

Randy watched silently, then turned away and walked back along the path into the shadows where Susan was waiting.

It was over now, all over, and he'd never been so glad to see anyone in his life. From now on, his life would be her life. *Their* life. Impulsively, he embraced her. . . .

Randy was embracing her now, here in the living room, as he concluded his confession.

"Please," he said. "Try to forgive me. If you could only understand—"

"But I do." Susan managed a smile. "I know how Elaine made you suffer, and of course Constance was impossible. As for Penny—well, after all, as you say, you really didn't have a choice. I'm not saying I approve, but you did what you felt was necessary."

"It was necessary, believe me," Randy sighed. "There was no other way out."

Susan nodded, brushing a stray tear from the edge of her right contact lens. "Besides, it's all over and done now," she said. "You've had your experience with ambition, wealth, youth. Perhaps you've learned your lesson."

"Thanks to you." Randy reached for his drink. "Now I know that what I really wanted was the warmth and comfort of the simple life. The life you've given me."

Susan glanced at him. "One question, darling."

"Yes?"

"About that Christmas tree angel. What was the real color of her hair?"

Randy shrugged. "When I was a kid I never had a Christmas tree," he said.

He gulped the rest of his drink, set it down. When he turned to Susan his jaw was set. "One thing more. I didn't go into town for a luncheon date today. I went to see a psychiatrist."

"Oh?"

"I hadn't intended to tell you this, Susan, but you've been so understanding—I feel I must." Randy hesitated, eyes lowered, then met Susan's gaze. "You see, I wanted to kick my habit."

"Habit?"

Randy shook his head. "No, it's not drugs. It's another kind of addiction. After reading all those mysteries I began to develop a sort of pattern—I seemed to start thinking in terms of, well, ways and means. Ways and means I used to dispose of three wives. And even afterwards, I found that I couldn't stop. Without knowing it, I gotten hooked on this kick."

Susan's eyes widened. "Go on," she said.

"That's just the trouble. I did go on." Randy gestured toward the book-lined den beyond the open doorway. "In one of my books I ran across a description of a new chemical derivative. It's a colorless, odorless poison that leaves no trace in the tissues or bloodstream. Depending on the amount of the dose, it works in anywhere from an hour to a day. The symptoms resemble a sudden stroke—the victim goes rigid, completely paralyzed."

"Randy — "

Randy's gaze fell. "I couldn't help it," he said softly. "I even found myself purchasing ingredients to concoct the stuff. That's when I knew I had to go and see a shrinker. But it was no good. I just wasn't able to tell him, he'd never believe me."

Randy rose and moved across the room, behind the bar. "Maybe you don't believe me either, but I can prove it to you. I put the stuff in a bottle and stashed it away. Under here."

Reaching down, he pulled out a small bottle. As he raised it the blood drained from his face. He gasped.

"Empty — "

Susan smiled. "Of course. I found it when I was cleaning, after you left. I realized it must be some kind of poison."

"Thank God!" Randy murmured. "You disposed of it?"

"In a way." Susan's smile didn't waver. "I poured it into the drink I gave you."

Randy's jaw dropped. He stared over at his empty glass, then back at Susan.

She wasn't smiling now. "Your little confessions didn't really shock me, darling. Somehow, I'd always suspected that you got rid of your former wives."

"But you never said anything!" Randy gestured helplessly. "You waited for me, you married me yourself — you were so innocent — "

"Patient," Susan said. Her eyes narrowed. "Has it ever occurred to you that perhaps I might want the same things you did — riches, position, a chance to have younger partners? But I was willing to wait, darling. I let *you* do the dirty work for me. Knowing that in the end I'd marry you, get rid of you, and have everything for myself."

Randy stumbled back to his seat, her voice ringing in his ears. But when she stopped talking the ringing continued, and now he could feel the numbness creeping through his limbs. He sank back in the chair, his paralysis mounting swiftly. It was all he could do to speak, but he forced the words out.

"You should have waited a little longer. Until I told you the rest. About how murdering wives becomes a habit. That's why I really went to the psychiatrist — when I knew the habit was too strong for me. Because after I mixed the stuff up, I couldn't help it. I used the poison — on you — "

"But that's impossible!" Susan whispered.

With an effort, Randy shook his head. "Not in a drink. A smaller dosage — takes longer to work — but you should be feeling the effect by now — "

Susan tried to rise, and failed. She managed to turn her head toward Randy, asking a question with her eyes.

"Yes." Randy's voice was faint but clear. "Your eyes. Before I left the house today—I poured some of the poison—into your contact lens solution—"

Sunset summoned shadows to shade the house as Sally and Jim approached the front door.

"I know they're not expecting us," Sally told her husband. "We'll just surprise them." And she rang the bell.

There was no answer. Sally waited and rang again.

"What did I tell you?" Jim shrugged. "They're not home."

Sally shook her head. "Oh, they're home all right. But you know how it is with Randy and Susan at cocktail time. They're probably both stiff by now."

Inside the living room, staring at one another in mutual astonishment in the firelight, Randy and Susan were very stiff indeed.

SPACE-BORN

1

THE PROBE-MISSION SHIP locked into orbit and began its sensorscan of the planet Echo.

Seated at his post on the bridge, Mission-Commander Richard Tasman, USN, checked out the data processed by the technical teams of his crew. Beside him Lieutenant Gilbey, his second in command, nodded approvingly.

"Looks good," he said. "Looks very good."

And it did.

According to the computerized data fed back through the tapes, Echo was indeed an Earth-type planet, just as had been suspected. Photoscopes confirmed the presence of running water, surface soil, and abundant vegetation. The bacterial-life analysis indicated nothing harmful or unfamiliar. Echo's planetary profile was that of a miniature world—alive and unpolluted, unspoiled by the presence of man.

Then the tapes began running wild.

Tasman stared at Gilbey. Gilbey stared at Tasman. And both men turned to stare at the photoscope.

The confirming data coming in told the story, but one picture is always worth ten thousand words, even though for a moment this particular picture left them both speechless.

Clearly and unmistakably it showed the boulder-strewn hillside and what rested on the sloping surface, landing gear crumpled against the looming rocks. The 'scope moved in for a close shot, panning across the hull, picking up the unmistakable insignia and legible lettering. USS *Orion*.

There on the face of a minor planet near the edge of the galaxy, unexplored and unvisited by man, was a spacecraft from Earth.

2

Tasman took over the landing party himself, leaving Gilbey behind to take over command.

There were four members in the task force, not counting Tasman, but in spite of the heavy power drain required to bring them down, the auxiliary launch settled safely on target. When Tasman and his crew emerged from the hatch, they were less than a thousand yards away from the hulk of the USS *Orion* on the hillside.

Even before they forced their way inside all doubts had vanished. Weber, the CPO of the party, spoke for them all. "This is it, sir. Kevin's ship."

Tasman shook his head grimly. "Our ship," he said. "Kevin stole it."

There was no answer to that, not from Weber or any of the others, because all of them knew Tasman spoke the truth.

Senior Commander Kevin Nichols, USN—veteran astronaut, hero of the space program, next in line for appointment to head up the entire space project itself—had stolen the ship.

A year ago, almost to the day by Earth calendar, he and the *Orion* had vanished. No advance warning, no clearance, nothing. And no telltale traces left behind; even his wife had disappeared. It took almost six months of intensive investigation to unravel the tangle of red tape surrounding the flight, and even now there were a thousand loose ends. All the evidence added up to the fact that Kevin Nichols had moved swiftly and secretly, according to a well-prepared plan. Forged orders for a security-sealed mission had been used to get the *Orion* equipped and on the launching pad without a leak. One of the very latest miniaturized spacecraft, it required only the services of a pilot, with all flight functions self-powered, self-contained, and computer-directed. A top-secret test model, designed for future exploration projects, and put through its trial runs by Kevin Nichols himself. So when he ordered it supplied and readied for takeoff, no one had questioned him or broken security regulations to reveal its departure.

Not until the *Orion* soared into space did the scandal rise in its wake—and even that was secret, hushed up by the space program itself before the news could break to the public. Then came the investigation, and the eventual discovery of Kevin's probable destination—not Echo itself, but Sector XXIII, this area of the space chart.

It was then that Commander Tasman had been assigned to go after the missing ship and the missing man. Tasman knew Kevin Nichols—they'd been classmates at Cape, years ago—and perhaps that's why he was chosen for the mission. But knowing Kevin hadn't made the job of locating him any easier. They'd touched down at a dozen points before the process of elimination zeroed them in on Echo. It was only now, months after the start of the expedition, that they'd caught up with the fugitive.

Or had they?

Kevin wasn't on the ship.

Neither were its supplies and portable instruments.

"Now what?" Tasman muttered.

It was Weber, the CPO, who suggested scouting the surrounding terrain, and it was he who discovered the cave set in the rocks.

Tasman was the first to enter, and what he found there in the dark depths brought the others to his side on the run.

Living in a cave isn't an ideal existence at best, and when one's supplies are exhausted and the battery-powered light sources fail, there's nothing left but shadows — shadows looming up everywhere from the twisted tunnels which wind on down endlessly beyond the outer chamber. And when one cries out, the shadows do not answer — there's only the sound of echoes screaming through the darkness. Echo — the planet was well named.

Had Kevin Nichols thought of that while he screamed, or when he grew too weak for screaming? Had he stared at the shapeless shadows which seemed to seethe and stir in the tunnel mouths beyond?

It didn't matter now. The tunnel mouths were open, but Kevin's mouth was closed; closed and set in the grim grin of death. One look at the gaunt face and emaciated body brought one word to CPO Weber's lips.

"Starvation."

Commander Tasman nodded without comment, then stooped to examine the other body.

For there was another body lying there, some little distance away — lying face downward, arms outstretched as though attempting to crawl toward the tunnels when death halted her.

Her.

Tasman turned the body over, staring in recognition at the wasted form.

"Kevin's wife," he murmured. "He took her with him."

Kevin took her with him, and death took them both. Here, in a remote cave on a distant planet, surrounded by shadows, the fugitives had died in darkness, and now only echoes lingered, wailing in the depths. If you listened closely, you could almost hear them now, faint and faraway.

And then they *did* hear the sound, all of them, and recognized it for what it was — issuing from the shadows beyond, impossibly but unmistakably.

A baby cried.

3

There were problems, many problems.

The first was physical — how to transport a newborn infant back to

Earth on a probe-mission ship lacking the facilities and even the feeding formula necessary to sustain its fragile hold on life.

Surprisingly enough, the little one survived, even flourished on the hastily improvised diet of powdered milk and juices. The boy seemed to have inherited some of Kevin Nichols' toughness and tenacity as well as his features. Indeed, the resemblance was so close that there was never any question about a name; with one accord, they called him Kevin.

It wasn't until after splashdown on Earth that the other problems arose. Then Space Control took charge of Kevin and inherited the dilemma he brought with him.

There was no publicity, of course, but that in itself solved nothing. Sooner or later the news would inevitably leak out. An honored and acclaimed astronaut had succeeded in violating top security, foiled all interplanetary precautions, stolen the latest and most advanced spacecraft.

Waves of panic rose and spread behind the locked doors of Space Command. Top brass and top government officials floundered, engulfed in those waves, spluttering in confusion, choking in consternation.

"Do you know what this means? When the story gets out, the whole program will be discredited. Stealing a prototype ship right out from under our noses — we're going to be the laughingstock of the world, the whole goddam galaxy!"

It was a senior spokesman for the space project who said that, and a senior spokesman for the government who answered him.

"Then why not tell the truth? Tell them that we had our eye on Kevin Nichols all along, knew he was cracking up? Sure, he was next in line for the big promotion, but he wasn't going to make it. Not after what our investigation uncovered — the drug thing, the embezzlement of project funds. He must have realized we were going to blow the whistle on him and that's why he got out, taking his wife with him. Let the public know what happened, that we were the victims of a conspiracy — "

"You're crazy." Psychiatrists usually disapprove of using such language, but it was a senior member of the psychiatric advisory staff who spoke. "We can't afford to be laughed at, and we can't afford to be pitied, either. Right now we can't afford anything, period. I don't need to remind you gentlemen that the vote on new appropriations for the entire space project is coming up next week. There couldn't possibly be a worse time to tell the world that the largest and most important program in all history has been victimized by one man — and that the biggest hero of that program was a psychotic, a thief, and a traitor. There's got to be another answer."

There was.

Exactly who gave it is not known — probably some minor member of the staff. It is the fate of junior officers to come up with the right suggestion and their reward is to be forgotten even while the suggestion is remembered.

"Kevin is our answer," said the nameless junior officer.

Everyone looked at him, everyone listened, and everyone understood.

"Don't you realize what Nichols has done for the program? He's given us the biggest public relations hook anyone could wish for. His son, Kevin. The first child ever born in outer space! Not on Mars or Venus or a colony, but on a new frontier, the farthermost outpost of all interplanetary exploration known to man!

"You don't have to say that his father was flipping out, that the ship was stolen. Make the whole thing part of a top-security mission, a secret program to test human survival on an Earth-type world. Nichols and his wife volunteered to take the ship off to Echo and have their child there. A heroic experiment that turned into a heroic sacrifice when they emerged from the crash unharmed but unable to return or communicate with the project back on Earth. Let it be known that Nichols kept a complete record of his stay on Echo, up to and including the actual birth of the infant, but that the data is still classified information. That'll put an end to any further embarrassing questions about the affair. But there won't be any trouble about the appropriation—not if you concentrate publicity where it belongs and keep it there. You're sitting on the greatest story of all time, the greatest celebrity ever known—Kevin, the Space Child!"

4

They didn't sit much longer.

Within a matter of hours the well-oiled machinery of Information Unit started to function, the space program's wheels began to turn, and the end-product of the manufacturing process appeared. Instant heroes.

Kevin Nichols, heroic astronaut who piloted an untested ship to an uncharted world. His wife, who risked her unborn baby in the unknown. The space program itself, bravely breaking through all barriers to prove, once and for all, that humanity could move forward without fear and perpetuate itself on other planets.

Nichols and his wife were dead, but the space program survived—just as predicted, the appropriation passed.

And as for Kevin himself, he lived and thrived.

Kevin, the new symbol of the Age of Space.

Publicized, photographed, promoted, praised; in a matter of days, his name was known throughout the solar system and beyond. Child of Space, heir to the future.

And ward of the space program.

Jealously guarded, possessively protected, little Kevin was withdrawn from public scrutiny shortly after he had served his primary purpose and placed in a private—very private—nursery. While Kevin dolls and Kevin toys flooded the market, Kevin songs and Kevin pictures kept his image bright, the object of all this adulation was being carefully nursed and tended to by a team of medical specialists. Pediatricians and psychologists alike agreed; Kevin was a very special baby. And not just because of his value as a living symbol, but for what he was — exceptionally sturdy, bright, alert, healthy, and precocious.

In spite of security, rumors poured out of the nursery-laboratory where young Kevin was hidden.

Standing alone at five months. Walking at seven. Only nine months old and seems to understand everything you say to him. One year old and he's talking already — complete sentences! Did you hear the latest about Kevin? Two and a half, going on three, and they say he already is learning how to read! Can you imagine that?

The public could imagine it very easily. As a matter of fact they were beginning to imagine a little too much. No matter how much we praise him, nobody really loves a genius. Too hard to understand. And the whole point of the plan was plain; Kevin had to be loved.

So, after much consideration, Kevin was placed in an exclusive private school — first-phase classes, what used to be called a kindergarten. Good thinking, give him a chance to grow up with other youngsters, learn to be like the rest of the kids.

But Kevin wasn't like the rest of the kids. He grew faster, learned more quickly. He seemed immune to childhood diseases and he was never ill. Perhaps this was a result of the antiseptic care of the medical team, but even so it was highly unusual. The doctors took notes.

The psychologists took notes too. Kevin didn't relate to his peer group — that's the way they phrased it. In plain words, he didn't want to have anything to do with the other children. And what he didn't want to do he didn't bother with. He read. He asked questions — intelligent, penetrating questions — and he was impatient with stupid answers.

Kevin had no interest in nursery rhymes or fairy tales or bedtime stories. Facts and figures, these were the things that fascinated him. He never played with toys and he refused to learn any games.

The other youngsters didn't understand him and what children can't understand they dislike — a trait often carried over into adult life.

Two of the kids never got to carry that or any other trait into maturity. They took to teasing Kevin, calling him names, but only for a few days. Then they died.

One of them fell out of an upstairs window while walking in his sleep. The other went into convulsions — epileptic seizure, the doctors decided.

Of course Kevin had nothing to do with it; he was nowhere near either of the youngsters at the time. But there was bound to be talk and the medical team took him out of the school.

Just to put an end to any possible rumors, a thorough checkup was programmed for the prodigy. And prodigy he was—a handsome, healthy child, without functional defect. The results of the battery of mental tests indicated genius.

What he needed, the medical team decided, was a chance to lead a normal existence—an opportunity to relate to ordinary people in ordinary surroundings. As a celebrity such a life was, of course, impossible.

So they changed his name, took him clear across the country, and put him out for adoption.

The world at large was told he had been sent abroad for further education under governmental supervision. Even the couple who took him into their home didn't realize that their bright, good-looking new son was the famous Space Child.

To Mr. and Mrs. Rutherford he was an orphan named Robin. A quiet boy but well-behaved, quick in his studies, sailing through high school and into college at fifteen. There were no problems.

At least the security reports didn't indicate any. The space program had him under observation, of course, monitoring his progress in school.

Perhaps they should have spent more time monitoring his foster parents. As it was, they didn't seem to notice the change in Mr. and Mrs. Rutherford. And maybe the Rutherfords weren't even aware of it themselves. It wasn't anything dramatic.

But as Kevin grew, they dwindled.

Kevin's growth was physically apparent. At eighteen, already a senior in college, he seemed completely mature. Enough of an adult, in fact, to enter into the management of Mr. Rutherford's prosperous ranch during the summer months.

And Rutherford, the bluff, hearty rancher with the booming voice, made no objection. It was as though he secretly welcomed the idea of taking things easy, of not having to bawl out orders, of sitting quietly on the big screen porch and rocking away. After a time people began to notice how he mumbled and muttered, talking to himself. Mrs. Rutherford didn't say anything—she'd gradually stopped entertaining or going out, and never saw any of their old friends. While the boy ran the ranch, she was content just to keep house and spend her spare time resting upstairs. She was beginning to talk to herself too.

It was just about a year later—after the boy had graduated and gone into advanced work in astrophysics—that the authorities came and took the Rutherfords away.

There was a hearing and the ranch hands testified. So did the boy. Everyone agreed there had been no violence, no real crisis. It was only that the Rutherfords had gone from talking to babbling, and from babbling to screaming.

Shadows were what they feared. Shadows, or a single shadow—for apparently they never saw more than one at a given moment.

A shadow moving at midnight in the corrals, making the cattle bellow in terror—but why should cattle be afraid of something that cannot be seen?

A shadow creeping through the long dark ranch-house hall, while the floorboards creaked—but how can there be sound without substance?

A shadow glimpsed in the boy's room, stretched sleeping in the bed where the boy should be—but shadows do not sleep, and the boy testified he had seen nothing.

It was a sad affair and the ending was inevitable. The Rutherfords were obviously incompetent and they had to be committed. Both of them passed away within a matter of months.

The space program people stayed out of the affair, of course; at least they didn't interfere publicly. But they followed the hearing and they had the data and they took charge of Kevin once more.

Taking charge was a mere formality now, for they weren't dealing with a child any longer. Kevin was physically adult and mentally he was—

Worthy of further study.

That's what the medical team decided.

Kevin was happy to cooperate, even though it meant temporarily abandoning his research project on methods of communicating with distant planetary bodies through the use of ultrasonic frequencies.

On the appointed day he appeared before an international panel of scientific authorities at Space Command headquarters, prepared to submit to a thorough examination and checkup.

But he was not prepared to meet the head of that panel—an elderly, stoop-shouldered man who was introduced to him as Mission-Commander Richard Tasman, USN, ret.

The foreign scientists noted that Kevin didn't seem to react to the introduction. Perhaps he didn't recognize the name, but of course there was no reason that he should.

At least there was no reason until Tasman began asking questions. The questions were polite, formally phrased and very simple. But their content was disturbing.

Tasman wanted Kevin to tell him about the shadows.

Kevin frowned, then sighed. "Surely you've read the reports of the hearing. The shadows my poor foster parents claim to have seen were non-existent—paranoid delusions—"

Commander Tasman nodded. "But it's the other shadows I'm interested in. The shadows that I saw with my own eyes—twenty years ago—when I found you in that cave on Echo."

The listening scientists leaned forward as Kevin shook his head. They turned up the earphones to hear what their translators were reporting as the conversation continued.

Kevin shrugged. "I was a baby—how do you expect me to remember anything? And even if I could, why should I notice shadows?"

"Why indeed?" Tasman smiled. "I saw them plainly enough but at the time I had no reason to pay attention to them. Now I'm not so sure."

"What do you mean?"

Tasman smiled again. "I'm not sure of *that*, either. In fact I'm not sure of anything any more. It occurs to me we should have followed up our findings on Echo. Somehow in all the excitement of your discovery and rescue, certain unusual bits of data were neglected. An Earth-type planet exists within a certain range of prescribed conditions—this we know, because we've located and studied others within the galaxy. Like Echo, they all contain life forms. Microorganisms, algae, plant life, in infinite variety. And all of them, in this phase of evolution, contain animal life too. All except Echo."

Tasman fixed his eyes on Kevin. "I understand you have a background in space research."

"I'm only a novice—"

"But you have studied available information?"

"Yes."

"Then let me ask this—doesn't it seem strange to you that Echo, and Echo alone, is the only Earth-type body ever discovered that is capable of supporting higher and more complicated life forms, yet contains none?"

"Perhaps there were such forms at one time, and they failed to survive."

"For what reason? There's no indication of natural disaster or recent geologic upheaval."

"Maybe the evolutionary cycle came to a natural end. Whatever might have existed there merely died out," Kevin said.

"Suppose it didn't die out? Suppose it merely developed along different lines—advanced to a point where life was no longer dependent upon a physical body of the type we're familiar with?"

"You mean something like pure thought?" It was Kevin's turn to smile.

Tasman shook his head and he wasn't smiling. "Something like shadows," he said.

Kevin stared. They were all staring now.

"Shadows," Tasman repeated. "Consider a life form which may once have been human like ourselves—very much like ourselves in many ways—but reached a turning point in the evolutionary road. Instead of continuing to evolve in terms of brawn, the emphasis became spiritual."

"Pure thought again?" Kevin gestured. "Impossible."

"Of course it's impossible," Tasman said. "Life is energy, and energy has form. But on Echo, which seems to have existed for countless years in an idyllic state, there was no need for a sturdy body to withstand the elements. And who knows—upon reaching a certain stage of mental development there may no longer be any dependency upon ordinary nourishment."

"You're saying these creatures turned into shadows?"

"Creatures? Hardly the term I'd use to describe so advanced an organism. As for shadows — how do we know what they really are? Possibly what we saw as shadows are merely visual projections of mental energy contained in the minimum possible shape. A shape that no longer requires sensory organs for perception or communication. A shape which doesn't need the complex of mechanical aids we call civilization, that can live without our concept of comfort and shelter — "

"In caves?"

Kevin rose as he spoke, rose and faced the assemblage around the long table. He spoke and the others listened. Exactly what he said is a matter of debate — afterward, opinions seemed to differ. But his words made sense, and everyone got the point.

Carefully, courteously, but concisely, he took Tasman's theories apart, demolishing each premise in turn. There was no precedent, not in biology or physics or the most advanced observations of science, for sentient shadows. One might as well argue the reality of ghosts. A shadow, by definition, is merely a shade cast upon a surface by a body that intercepts rays of light. It is the body that exists. Shadows are merely illusions — like the apparitions Kevin's foster parents babbled about, or like Commander Tasman's strange beliefs.

The speech was effective. And after Tasman, cold but controlled, excused Kevin from the hearing and had him escorted outside the room, there was a general buzz of conversation from the scientists gathered there.

Obviously they were impressed by what they'd heard. They were even more impressed when an apologetic sound engineer buzzed the chamber on intercom to report the sudden power failure which had cut off the mikes and made translation of Kevin's speech impossible.

"Amazing, the young man!" The Italian scientist groped for words in his heavily accented English. "Such presence, to realize this — and continue speaking in Italian."

"Nein." The guttural rejoinder came swiftly, "It was in German he spoke."

"Français!"

Dissension rose in Japanese, Russian, Spanish, and Mandarin. All had heard Kevin and understood.

Tasman understood too.

He raced out the door, down the corridor. At the entrance to a small side office he found Kevin's security guards stationed and waiting.

"Kevin — where is he?"

The senior official blinked and gestured. "Inside."

Tasman brushed past him and opened the door.

The room beyond had no windows, no other exit.

But it was empty.

5

There was no official report of Kevin's disappearance. Even the medical team wasn't informed. But Tasman knew, and went straight to Top Security. A directive was issued.

Find Kevin.

"He's bound to slip up," Tasman said. "What happened at the hearing proves he's not infallible. When the mikes went dead he unconsciously continued to communicate by means of direct thought transmission. That explains why each foreign delegate believed he was hearing Kevin speak to him in his own language. When he realized he was giving himself away, it was too late. He had to flee."

Security officers nodded uneasily. How do you find a man who can transmit thoughts at will—hypnotize guards and pass them by without being seen or remembered?

"If he made one mistake he'll make others," Tasman assured them.

But Tasman himself didn't wait for mistakes. While security personnel searched for Kevin in the present, Tasman sought him in the past. He talked to people who had known him at the ranch—to schoolmates—to the surviving members of the original relief mission, men like Gilbey and Weber. What he learned he kept to himself, but the word spread.

Eventually it reached back beyond the time Tasman himself had known Kevin—back to a man who had known Kevin's parents.

A Dr. Hans Diedrich, living in retirement in the Virgin Islands, contacted Space Command with an urgent message. He had, he said, certain information which might be of vital importance in this affair.

Within twenty-four hours he was visited at his cottage home by an elderly, stoop-shouldered man who identified himself as Mission-Commander Richard Tasman, USN, ret.

"I'm glad you came," Diedrich said. "I have followed reports with great interest—my nephew is in the space program and it was he who informed me of what happened."

His visitor frowned. "A security leak?"

"Do not be alarmed. It is for the best that I was told, and in a moment you will understand why I say that. You see, I know what you are thinking."

"You do?"

Diedrich frowned. "You have a theory, haven't you? That Kevin Nichols' son was left alone in that cave on Echo when his parents died, left alone with the shadow-creatures. And that somehow, before your relief expedition arrived, these beings took possession of him—so that when he was rescued he was no longer an ordinary infant but something more. Because they infused him with their powers, established a mental contact, a link with themselves which was not broken when he returned to Earth. And that all through his childhood and youth he was really acting as their pawn. A human being under alien control. Is that it?

His visitor nodded.

"Well, you are wrong," said Dr. Diedrich. "I was the Nichols' family physician. I have their medical records. Two years before the journey to Echo, I personally performed surgery on Mrs. Nichols. A complete hysterectomy."

"Hysterectomy?"

"That is what I wanted to tell you. Mrs. Nichols could not have a child. The infant you found in the cave was not their son."

Dr. Diedrich leaned forward. "These beings must have the power to receive thoughts as well as to transmit them. They absorbed the contents of Nichols' mind as he lay dying in the cave—his wife's mind, too. And using what they learned, they created the illusion of an infant—one of their own kind disguised in a mental projection, programmed to live and grow as a child."

"Why send it back to Earth?"

Diedrich shrugged. "I cannot say."

"And you have no proof."

"Only of the hysterectomy. Here, my own medical records—"

He handed a bulky envelope to his visitor.

His visitor smiled, thanked him, pulled out a revolver, and shot Dr. Diedrich through the head.

6

"I told you he'd make a mistake," Tasman muttered. "Going down there, getting the information, then deliberately using a clumsy, old-fashioned weapon to kill Diedrich—it was a clever idea. And there are half a dozen people who can testify to seeing me escape from the cottage.

"Fortunately, you know I was here at Headquarters all the time. Kevin didn't anticipate I'd have such an airtight alibi. And he didn't anticipate that Diedrich had taken the precaution of taping a statement of his beliefs beforehand and sending it here to Space Command. So we understand how all this happened—and why."

"We know something else now, too." It was the Chief of Operations himself who answered Tasman, and his voice was grim. "The life form we're dealing with has greater powers than we imagined. The ability to transmit thought and to receive it. The ability to appear in the form we identify as Kevin—or to change that form at will.

"Do you realize what we're up against? A creature that can read our minds, walk unseen among us as a shadow, alter its appearance whenever it chooses."

"Mimicry," Tasman said. "Insects use it for protection, taking on the look of the plant or tree branch where they rest. The being we know as Kevin has this same faculty, developed to its ultimate extent."

The Chief of Operations frowned. "Then why did it even bother to appear as Kevin in the first place?"

"Again we must look to the insect world for a parallel," Tasman said. "Some insects begin in a larval state. It's only later that they emerge in new forms, with the power of disguising their shapes. Perhaps it was necessary for Kevin to go through certain stages in a single body while he grew to maturity, learned our ways. Only now, as an adult, is he capable of functioning fully."

"And just what is his function? Why did a shadow-creature come to Earth in human disguise?"

Tasman shrugged. "Maybe the shadows grew tired of being shadows. Perhaps an existence of pure thought was no longer enough for them and they yearned for the sensations and satisfactions of solid physical shapes. In which case Kevin was sent here as a scout—to study our ways, see if we could be taken over."

The Chief of Operations shook his head. "You think this is a possibility?"

"I think this is what actually happened."

"Then what do you propose?"

"Another expedition to Echo. Give me the command, and a task force. Keep it under sealed orders, call it an exploratory operation if you like. But you and I know the real purpose of the mission."

"Seek and destroy?"

Tasman nodded. "It's our only chance. And we've got to move fast, before Kevin suspects."

7

Commander Tasman lifted off for Echo under top security, but that didn't stop the rumors.

Whether or not Kevin suspected was no longer the problem. The search for him went on, but how do you find a shadow? He could be anywhere now.

It was the spread of the rumors that really caused the trouble—and the panic.

Somehow the word was out, and the world trembled. People had forgotten about the Space Child through the years, but now they remembered as the whispers grew.

There was a monster in our midst, the rumormongers said. An alien unlike any humanoid form on planets known to man—an invisible creature, murdering at will. True, a mission had been mounted against Echo, but it would never return.

The whispers rose to angry shouts, and there was only one way to silence them.

The President of the United States went on Emergency Band and addressed the world.

Standing before the cameras and microphones in the tower at Communications Center, he delivered his message.

The rumors were partially true, the President admitted. The Space Child was indeed an alien, but there was no longer any reason to fear him. Because Kevin was dead. He had been discovered and trapped only this afternoon in a secret hideaway — a mountain cave near Pocatello, Idaho. Full details would be available on an international newscast following the President's message.

Meanwhile, it was time to put an end to vicious falsehoods, spread by our enemies. All this wild talk of alien invasion was part of a plot, designed to prevent the opening up of free space travel and communication — but the plot had failed.

It was his privilege, the President said, to announce the final expansion of the space program. From this time forward there would be no restrictions on further flights. Every area of the galaxy was now officially declared to be open to the ships of any government or any private concern or individual. No more secrecy, no more security, no more fear. If new alien life forms were encountered, they would be met with friendship. If they chose to visit our solar system or even our own Earth, let them be welcomed. For this was the start of the true Age of Space — founded firmly in freedom and in friendship.

The world listened to its leader and breathed a collective sigh of relief.

8

The President joined in that sigh as the broadcast ended. He watched the technical crews gather up their equipment and depart, leaving him alone in the tower room with its single window opening on the night sky and the stars.

Then the President of the United States melted into a shadow and slithered across the floor to the window as he waited for his brothers to arrive.

FOREVER AND AMEN

Forever.

It's a nice way to live, if you can afford it.

And Seward Skinner could.

"One billion integral units," said Dr. Togol. "Maybe more."

Seward Skinner didn't even blink when he heard the estimate. Blinking, like every other bodily movement, involves painful effort when one is in a terminal stage. But Skinner summoned the strength to speak, even though his voice was no more than a husky whisper.

"Go ahead with the plan. But hurry."

The plan had been ten years in the making and Skinner had been dying for the past two, so Dr. Togol hurried. Haste makes waste and in the end it probably cost Skinner closer to five billion IGUs than the price quoted. Nobody knew for sure. All they knew was that Seward Skinner was the one man in the entire galaxy — the known galaxy, that is — who could afford the expenditure.

That was the extent of their knowledge.

Seward Skinner had been the wealthiest man alive for a long, long time. There were still a few old-timers around who could remember the days when he was a public figure and a private joke — the Playboy of the Planets, as they called him. According to the rumors he had a woman on every world, or at least a female.

Other people, a trifle less elderly, recalled a more mature Seward Skinner — the Galactic Genius, fabulous inventor — entrepreneur of Interspace Industries, the largest corporate combine ever known. During those days his business operations made the news, and the rumors.

But for the majority of the interplanetary public, the youngsters without personal memories of those far-off times, Seward Skinner was merely a name. In recent years he'd withdrawn completely from any contact with the outside worlds. And Interspace Industries had carefully and painstakingly tracked down and acquired every tape, every record of his past. Some said these had been destroyed, some said the data had been hidden away, but in the end it amounted to the same thing. Seward Skinner's privacy was protected, complete. And nobody saw the man himself any more. His business, his life itself, seemed to be run by remote control.

Actually, of course, it was run by Dr. Togol.

If Skinner was the richest man, Dr. Togol was surely the most brilliant scientist. Inevitably, the two men were drawn together by a common love — wealth.

What wealth represented to Skinner no one knew. What it meant to Dr. Togol was plainly apparent; it was the tool of research. Unlimited funds were the key to unlimited experimentation. And so a partnership came into being.

During the past decade Dr. Togol developed his plan and Seward Skinner developed incurable cancer.

Now the plan was ready to function, just as Skinner was ceasing to function.

So Skinner died.

And lived again.

It's great to be alive, particularly after you've been dead. Somehow the sun seems warmer, the world looks brighter, the birds sing more sweetly. Even though here on Eden the sun was artificial, the light was supplied by beaming devices, and the birdsong issued from mechanical throats.

But Skinner himself was alive.

He sat on the terrace of his big house on the hill and looked down over Eden and he was pleased at what he had wrought. The bleak little satellite of a barren and neglected world he'd purchased many years ago had been transformed into a miniature Earth, a reminder of his original home. Below him was a city very similar to the one where he'd been born; here on the hilltop was a mansion duplicating the finest dwelling he'd ever owned. Yonder was Dr. Togol's laboratory complex, and deep in the vaults beneath it —

Skinner shut away the thought.

"Bring me a drink," he said.

Skinner, the waiter, nodded and went into the house and told Skinner, the butler, to mix the drink.

Nobody drank alcohol any more, and nobody had waiters or butlers, but that's the way Skinner wanted things; he remembered how he'd lived in the old days and he intended to live that way now. Now and forever.

So after Skinner had his drink he had Skinner, the chauffeur, drive him down into the city. He peered out of the minimobile, enjoying the spectacle.

Skinner had always been a people watcher, and the activities of these people were of special and particular interest to him now.

Behind the wheels of other minimobiles, the Skinners nodded and smiled at him as he passed. At the intersection, Skinner, the security officer, waved him along. On the walks before the fabrication and food processing plants, other Skinners went about their errands. Skinner, the hydroponics engineer, Skinner, the waste recycler, Skinner, the oxygenerator control man, Skinner, the transport dispatcher, Skinner, the media channeler. Each had his place and his function in this miniature world, keeping it running smoothly and efficiently, according to plan and program.

"One thing is definite," Skinner had told Dr. Togol. "There'll be no computerization. I don't want my people controlled by a machine. They're not robots — each and every one of them is a human being, and they're going to live like human beings. Full responsibility and full security, that's the secret of a full life. After all, they're just as important to the scheme of things as I am, and I want them to be happy. It may not matter to you, but you've got to remember that they're my family."

"More than your family," Dr. Togol said. "They are you."

And it was true. They were him — or part of him. Each and every one was actually Skinner, the product of a single cell, reproduced and evolved by the perfection of Dr. Togol's process.

The process was called cloning and it was very involved. Even the clone theory itself was involved and Skinner had never completely understood it. But then he didn't need to understand; that was Dr. Togol's task, to understand the theory and devise ways to bring it to reality. Skinner provided the financing, the laboratory, the equipment, the facilities. His means and Dr. Togol's ways. And in the end — when the end came — his body provided the living cell tissue out of which the clones were extracted, isolated, and bred. The clones, cycling through complicated growth into physical duplicates of Skinner himself. Not reproductions, not imitations, not copies, but truly *himself.*

Glancing ahead toward the rear-view mirror of the minimobile, Skinner saw the chauffeur, a mirror image of his own face and body. Gazing out of the window he saw himself again reflected in every form that passed. Each of the Skinners was a tall man, well past middle years, but with the youthful vigor born of a careful and painstaking regimen of advanced vitamin therapy and organ regeneration; the result of expensive medical attention that partially obliterated the ravages of metastasis. And, since the carcinoma was not hereditary, it had not been carried over into the clones. Like himself, all the Skinners were in good health. And, like himself, they carried within them the seeds — the actual cells — of immortality.

Forever.

They would live forever, as he did.

And they were him. Physically interchangeable, except for the clothing they wore—the uniforms designating their various occupations served to differentiate and identify them.

A world of Skinners on Skinner's world.

There had been problems, of course.

Long ago, before Dr. Togol began his work, they'd discussed the matter.

"One true clone," Dr. Togol said. "That's enough to aim for. One healthy facsimile of yourself is all you need."

Skinner shook his head. "Too risky. Suppose there's an accident? That would be the end of me."

"Very well. We'll arrange to keep extra cellular tissue alive, in reserve. Carefully stored and guarded, of course."

"Guarded?"

"But of course," Dr. Togol nodded. "This Eden, this satellite of yours, will need protection. And since you seem to be determined not to run it by computer, you're going to need personnel. Other people to do the work, keep things going, provide you with companionship. Surely you won't want to live forever if you must spend eternity alone."

Skinner frowned. "I don't trust people. Not as guards, not as employees, certainly not as friends."

"No one at all?"

"I trust myself," Skinner said. "So I want more clones. Enough to keep Eden going independently of any outsider."

"The whole satellite populated by nothing but Skinners?"

"Exactly."

"But you don't seem to understand. If the process succeeds and I produce more than one Skinner, they'll share everything. Not just bodies like yours, but minds—each personality will be identical. They'll have the same memories, right up to the moment that the cells are excised from your body."

"I understand that."

"Do you?" Dr. Togol shook his head. "Let's say I follow your instructions. Technically speaking, it's possible—if a single cloning is successful, then the rest would be successful too. All that would be involved is the additional expense of the process."

"Then there's no problem, is there?"

"I told you what the problem is. A thousand Skinners, exactly alike. Looking alike, thinking alike, feeling alike. And you—the present you, reproduced by cloning—would just be one of the many. Have you decided what job you want to perform on your new world once you've become immortal? Do you want to tend the power banks—would you like to unload supplies — do you think you'd enjoy working in the kitchens of the big house forever?"

"Certainly not!" Skinner snapped. "I want to be just what I am now."

"The boss. Top man. Mr. Big." Dr. Togol smiled, then sighed. "That's just the point. So will all the others. Every one of your counterparts will have the same desire, the same goal, the same drive to dominate, to control. Because they'll all have your exact brain and nervous system."

"Up to the time they are reborn, you might say?"

"Right."

"Then from that moment on, you'll institute a new program. A program of conditioning." Skinner nodded quickly. "There are techniques for that, I know. Sleep learning, deep hypnosis machines — the sort of thing psychologists use to alter criminal behavior. You'll plant memory blocks selectively."

"But I'd need an entire psychomedical center, completely staffed — "

"You'll have it. I want the whole procedure carried out right here on Earth, before anyone is transported to Eden."

"I'm not sure. You're asking for the creation of a new race, each with a new personality. A Skinner who'll remember his past life but is now content to be merely a hydroponic gardener, a Skinner who'll be satisfied to live forever as an accountant, a Skinner willing to devote his entire endless existence as a repairman."

Skinner shrugged. "A difficult and complicated job, I know. But then you'll be working with a difficult and complicated personality — mine." He cleared his throat painfully before continuing. "Not that I'm unique. We're all far more complicated than we appear to be on the surface, you know that. Each human being is a bundle of conflicting impulses, some expressed, some suppressed. I know that there's a part of me which has always been close to nature, to the soil, to the cultivation and growth of life. I've buried that facet of my personality away since childhood but the memories are there. Find them and you'll have your gardeners, your farmers — yes, and your medical staff assistants too!

"Another part of me is fascinated even consciously today by facts and figures, the minutiae of mathematics. Isolate that aspect, condition it to full expression, and you'll get your accountant, and all the help you need to keep Eden running smoothly and systematically.

"I don't need to tell you that a great share of my early career was devoted to scientific research and invention. You won't have any problem developing mechanical-minded Skinners to staff power units, or even to drive transport vehicles.

"The reaches of the mind are infinite, Doctor. Exploit them properly and you'll have a working world — with all the petty authority roles filled by Skinners who have the urge to play policeman or foreman or supervisor — and all the menial tasks performed by Skinners who long to serve. Resurrect those specific traits and tendencies, intensify them, blot out all the memories which might conflict with them, and the rest is easy."

"Easy?" Dr. Togol scowled. "To brainwash them all?"

"All but one." Skinner's voice was crisp. "One will remain untouched, reproduced exactly and entirely as is. And that will be me."

The gray-haired, potbellied little medical scientist stared at Skinner for a long moment.

"You don't admit the possibility of any changes in yourself? The desirability of modifying some of your own personality pattern?"

"I don't think I'm perfect, if that's what you mean. But I'm satisfied with myself as I am. And as I will be, once you've carried out the plan."

Dr. Togol continued to stare. "You say you have learned to trust no one. If that's true—and I'm inclined to believe you—then how do you know you can trust me?"

"What do you mean?"

"You're going to die. We both know that. It's only a matter of time. The power to regenerate you through cloning is entirely in my hands. Suppose I don't go through with it?"

Skinner met Dr. Togol's stare. "You'll go through with it before I die. And long before I'm helpless and unable to issue orders, you'll be processing the clones as I've directed. I assure you I have every intention of staying alive until all the clones are ready for transportation to Eden."

"But you *will* die then," Togol insisted. "And there'll be the one clone you've chosen to represent yourself—the one you insist must remain unchanged. What makes you so sure I'll obey that directive after you're actually dead? I could use psychological techniques to modify your clone's personality then in any way I choose. What's to prevent me from making your clone my willing slave—so that I'd be the real master of this new world you created?"

"Curiosity," Skinner murmured. "You'll do exactly as I say because you're fanatically and completely curious about the outcome. No other man alive can provide you with the means and opportunity to carry through this cloning project. If the experiment succeeds you'll have made the greatest scientific breakthrough of all time—so you won't betray your trust by failure or refusal. And once you go that far, you won't be able to resist following through. Particularly when you come to realize that this is only the beginning."

"I don't understand."

"All my life I've moved forward from a position of strength, of self-confidence. And you know what I have achieved. I think I'm presently the wealthiest and most powerful individual in the galaxy.

"I'm a sick man now, but thanks to you I'm going to be well again. Not only well, but immortal. Consider the kind of confidence I'll possess once

I'm free of illness, free forever from the fear of death. With my thrust we can go on to far greater concepts, for greater achievements — solve all the mysteries, shatter all the barriers, shake the stars!

"You can't afford to tamper with my mind because you'll want to be a part of it all — to see and to share. Right, Doctor?"

Togol's glance faltered. He had no answer, because he knew it was true.

And it had been true.

The cloning was carried out just as Seward Skinner had planned it. And the psychological conditioning project which followed was properly performed too, even though in the end it proved to be far more complicated than anyone had imagined.

The final step involved recruiting a staff of several hundred technicians, highly skilled and specially schooled, then divided into psychomedical teams assigned to the individual clones as they were nurtured to full growth and emerged as functioning adult specimens. Under Dr. Togol's supervision these specialists created the programs for memory blocking, for shaping the personalities of each separate Skinner to fit him for his life role when he reached Eden.

After that the shuttling began.

Space transports, manned exclusively by Skinners trained for the task, brought other Skinners to the stony surface of the secret satellite. Additional Skinner-piloted transports convoyed and conveyed the seemingly endless supply of materials needed to transform the empty expanse of Eden into the world of Seward Skinner's dream.

The miniature city rose on the plain, the house went up on the hillside, the laboratory complex grew over the great vault below. And all of this, every step of the operation, was carried out in such strict, security-guarded secrecy that no outsider ever suspected its existence.

As time went on the steps became part of a race — a race with death.

Skinner was dying. Only an act of incredible will kept him alive long enough to supervise the total destruction of the earthsite where the work had taken place.

Then he himself went to Eden with Dr. Togol, but not until he'd made arrangements to send up the entire psychomedical staff, intact, to the new complex there.

For this a final transport was arranged.

Skinner vividly remembered the evening he lay on his deathbed in the hillside house with Dr. Togol, awaiting the arrival of the transport.

Flickering forth in the darkened room, the media transmitter screened its shocking message. *Pressure failure and implosion beyond Pluto — transport totally destroyed — no survivors.*

"My God!" said Togol.

Then, in the dim light, he saw the smile on the face of the dying man. And heard the harsh, labored whisper.

"Did you really believe I'd ever allow any outsiders to come here — to pry, interfere — learn the secrets — carry the news back into other worlds?"

Togol stared at him. "Sabotaging a transport, murdering all those men! You can't possibly get away with it!"

"*Fait accompli.*" Skinner grimaced. "No one on board knew the true destination — they thought it was Rigel. And what happened will be recorded as an accident."

"Unless I choose to report it."

The dying man's features caricatured a smile. "You won't. Because there is a single detailed account of the whole scheme hidden away in my files. It implicates you as my accomplice, so if you speak you'll be signing your own death warrant."

"You forget that I can sign yours," Dr. Togol said. "Merely by letting nature take its course."

"If you let me die now, everything in my files will come to light. So you have no choice. You're going to go through with it — proceed with the final cloning that will reproduce me as I've ordered."

Togol took a deep breath. "So that's why you were so confident I'd never betray you! You weren't relying on my scientific curiosity — you'd planned this all along, to have a permanent hold on me."

"I told you I was a complex man." Skinner winced with pain. "Now it is time to make me a whole and healthy one. You'll start now — tonight."

It wasn't an order, merely a statement of fact.

And, factually, Dr. Togol had proceeded according to plan.

Seward Skinner was grateful for that, grateful that his new clone-born self evolved before his old body had actually died. Because if Togol had waited until then, the clone would have held the memory of Skinner's death. And that is a memory no man can bear.

As it was, the living tissue that was now Skinner had begun its growth process in the laboratory complex safely before the pain-racked, rotting tissue of the body in the house ceased to function. Skinner was not aware of just when he had died; he was too busy learning how to live.

Working without a team of technicians was a great handicap, but Dr. Togol had overcome it quickly and efficiently — with the aid of other Skinners to whom he was able to impart rudimentary medical skills. Since then, of course, he had cloned an entire staff of Skinners for that purpose — Dr. Skinner, the psychotherapy chief; Dr. Skinner, the head surgeon; Dr. Skinner, the diagnostic specialist; and a dozen others.

"You see, we didn't need outsiders after all," the new Skinner told Togol, after it was over. "We're totally self-sustaining here. And when these bodies start to show signs of deterioration and function failure, new clones will replace them. Everyone's dream of true immortality, realized at last."

"Everyone's?" Dr. Togol shook his head. "Not mine."

"Then you're a fool," Skinner said. "You have the opportunity to clone yourself, live forever, just as I intend to. I've granted you that privilege. What more could you ask?"

"Freedom."

"But you're free here. You have the resources of the galaxy at your disposal—you can expand the lab unit indefinitely, go on to major research in other fields, just as I promised you. That cure for cancer they've been talking about for the past hundred years—don't you want to find it? You've implemented some marvelous memory-blocking techniques already, but this is only the beginning of a whole new psychotherapy. You can build new personalities, reshape the human condition as you will—"

"As *you* will." Togol's smile was bitter. "This is your world. I want my own. The old world, with ordinary people, men—and women—"

"You know very well why I decided against women here," Skinner said. "They're not necessary for reproduction. Fortunately, at my age, the sexual impulse is no longer an imperative. So females would only complicate our existence, without serving any true function."

"Tenderness, compassion, understanding, companionship," Togol murmured. "All nonfunctional by your definition."

"Stereotypy. Utter nonsense. Sentimentalization of a biological role which you and I have rendered obsolete."

"You've rendered everything obsolete," Togol told him. "Everything except the antlike activity of your clone colony—the warped and crippled partial personalities created to serve you."

"They're happy the way they are," Skinner said. "And it doesn't matter. What matters is that *I* haven't changed. I'm a whole man."

"Are you?" Dr. Togol's smile was mirthless. He nodded toward the house, gestured to include the terrace and the city below. "Everything you've built here, everything you've done, is a product of the most crippling defect of all—the fear of death."

"But all men are afraid to die."

"So afraid that they spend their entire lives just trying to avoid the realization of their own mortality?" Togol shook his head. "You know there's a vault underneath my laboratory. You know why it was built. You know what it contains. And yet your fear is so great that you won't even admit it exists."

"Take me there," Skinner said.

"You don't mean that."

"Come on. I'll show you I'm not frightened."

But he was.

Even before they reached the elevator Skinner started to tremble, and as they began their deep descent to the lower level he was shuddering uncontrollably.

"Cold down here," he muttered.

Dr. Togol nodded. "Temperature control," he said.

They left the elevator and walked along a dark corridor toward the steel-sheathed chamber set in stone. Security guard Skinner stood sentinel at the door and smiled a greeting as they approached. At Togol's order, he produced a key and opened the vault door.

Seward Skinner didn't look at him and he didn't want to look beyond the doorway.

But Dr. Togol had already entered and now there was no choice but to follow. Follow him into the dim light of the chill chamber — to the looming control banks that whined and whirred in the center of the room — to the tangled cluster of tubes and inputs which snaked down from all sides into a transparent glass cylinder.

Skinner stared through the shadows at the cylinder. It was shaped like a coffin, because it was a coffin; a coffin in which Seward Skinner saw —

Himself.

His own body; the wasted, shriveled body from which the clones had sprung, floating in the clear solution amid the coils and clamps and weblike wires tunneling through the glass covering to terminate in contact with frozen flesh.

"Not dead," Dr. Togol murmured. "Frozen in solution. The cryogenic process, preserving you in suspended animation — indefinitely — "

Skinner shuddered again and turned away. "Why?" he whispered. "Why didn't you let me die?"

"You wanted immortality."

"But I have it. With this new body, all the others."

"Flesh is vulnerable. Any accident can destroy it."

"You've stored more cell tissue. If anything happened to me as I am now, you could repeat the cloning."

"Only if your original body remains available for the process. It had to be preserved against such an emergency — alive."

Skinner forced himself to glance again at the corpse-like creature congealed in cold behind its crystal confines.

"It's not alive — it can't be — "

And yet he knew it was, knew that the cryogenic process had been developed for just that purpose. To maintain a minimum life force in hibernation against the time when medical science could arrest and eliminate its disease processes and develop techniques to thaw it out and successfully restore complete and conscious existence again.

Skinner realized this goal had never been achieved, but the possibility remained. Some day perhaps the methodology would be perfected and this thing might be resurrected — not as a clone, but as he had been. The original Skinner, alive once more and a rival to his present self.

"Destroy it," he said.

Dr. Togol stared at him. "You don't mean that. You can't — "

"Destroy it!"

Skinner turned and walked out of the vault.

Dr. Togol remained behind, and it was a long time before he returned to rejoin Skinner in his house on the surface. What he'd done there in the vault he did not say, and Skinner never inquired. The subject wasn't discussed again.

But since that night Skinner's relationship with Togol had never been quite the same. There was no more discussion of the future, of possible new projects and experiments. There was only a heightened awareness of tension, of waiting, an indefinable atmosphere of alienation. Dr. Togol spent more and more of his time within the laboratory complex, where he maintained separate living quarters of his own. And Skinner went his own way, alone.

Alone, yet not alone. For this was his world, and it was filled with his own people, created in his own image. *Thou shalt have no God but Skinner. And Skinner is His prophet.*

That was the commandment and the law. And if Dr. Togol chose not to abide by it —

Now Seward Skinner, walking the streets of his own city, came to the door of the museum.

Skinner, the chauffeur, waited outside, smiling in obedience at the order, and Skinner, the museum guard, nodded happily as Seward Skinner entered.

Skinner, the curator, greeted him, delighted at the sight of a visitor. No one ever came to the museum except his master — indeed, the whole notion of a museum was merely a quaint conceit, an archaism from the distant past on Earth.

But Seward Skinner had felt the need for such a place here; a storehouse and a showcase for the art and artifacts he'd accumulated in the past. And while he could have stocked it with the treasures and trophies gathered throughout the galaxy, he'd elected to exhibit only objects from Earth. Obsolete objects at that — mementos and memorabilia representing ancient history. Here in the halls were the riches and relics of long ago and far away. Paintings from palaces, sculpture and statues from shrines; the jewels and jade and gorgeous gewgaws which had once represented royal tastes, rescued from regal tombs.

Skinner walked through the displays with scarcely a glance at its glories. Ordinarily he might have spent hours admiring the ancient television set, the library of printed books hermetically sealed in plexiglass, the slot machine, the reconstructed gas engine automobile in perfect running condition.

Today he went straight to a remote room and indicated one of the items on display.

"Give me that."

The curator's polite smile masked perplexity, but he obeyed.

Then Skinner turned and retraced his steps. At the door the chauffeur waited to escort him back to the minimobile.

Driving back through the streets, Skinner smiled once more at the passersby and watched them as they went about their ways.

How could Togol call them crippled? They were happy in their work, their lives were fulfilled. Each had been conditioned to accept his lot without envy, competition or hostility. Thanks to their conditioning and the selective screening of memory patterns they seemed much more content than the Seward Skinner who surveyed them as he returned to his house on the hill.

But he too would be satisfied, and soon.

That evening he summoned Dr. Togol.

Seated on the terrace in the twilight, inhaling the synthetic scent of the simulated flowers, Skinner smiled a greeting at the scientist.

"Sit down," he said. "It's time we had a talk."

Togol nodded and sank into a chair with an audible sigh of effort.

"Tired?"

Togol nodded. "I've been quite busy lately."

"I know." Skinner twirled his brandy snifter. "Assembling data on the project here must be quite exhausting."

"It's important to have a complete record."

"You've put it all on microtape, haven't you? A single spool, small enough to be carried in a man's pocket. How very convenient."

Dr. Togol stiffened and sat upright.

Skinner's smile was serene. "Did you propose to smuggle it out? Or take it back yourself on the next transport shuttle to Earth?"

"Who told you—"

Skinner shrugged. "It's obvious enough. Now that you've achieved the goal you want the glory. A triumphant return—your name and fame echoing throughout the galaxy—"

Togol frowned. "It's natural for you to think of it in terms of ego. But that's not the reason. You told me yourself before we started—this can be the most significant achievement in all time. The discovery must be shared, put to use for the benefit of others."

"I paid for the research. I funded the project. It's my property."

"No man has the right to withhold knowledge."

"It's my property," Skinner repeated.

"But I'm not." Dr. Togol rose.

Skinner's smile faded. "Suppose I refuse to let you go?"

"I wouldn't advise it."

"Threats?"

"A statement of fact." Togol met Skinner's stare. "Let me leave in peace. You have my word that your secret is safe. I'll share my findings but preserve your privacy. No one will ever learn the location of Eden."

"I'm not in the habit of making bargains."

"I realize that." Dr. Togol nodded. "So I've already taken certain precautions."

"What sort of precautions?" Skinner chuckled, enjoying the moment. "You forget — this is my world."

"You have no world." Togol faced him, frowning. "All this is merely a mirror maze. The ultimate end of the megalomaniac carried to its logical extreme. In the old days conquerors and kings surrounded themselves with portraits and paintings celebrating their triumphs, commissioned statues and raised pyramids as monuments to their vanity. Servants and slaves sung their praises, sycophants erected shrines to their divinity. You've done all that and more. But it won't last. No man is an island. The tallest temples topple, the most fawning followers go down into dust."

"Do you deny you've given me immortality?"

"I've given you what you want, what every man in search of power *really* wants — the illusion of his own omnipotence. And you're welcome to keep it." Dr. Togol nodded. "But if you try to stop me — "

"I intend to do just that." Seward Skinner's smile returned. "Now."

"Skinner! For God's sake — "

"Yes. For my sake."

Still smiling, Skinner reached into his jacket and brought forth the object he'd taken from the museum.

There was a flicker of flame in the twilight, a single sharp sound shattering the silence, and Dr. Togol fell with a bullet lodged between his eyes.

Skinner summoned Skinner, who scrubbed the tiny trickle of blood from the terrace. Two other Skinners removed the body.

And life went on.

It would always go on, now. Go on forever, free from outside interference. Skinner was safe on Skinner's world. Safe to make further plans.

Dr. Togol was right, of course. He *was* a megalomaniac, the fact must be faced. Skinner admitted that. Easy enough, because he wasn't a madman, merely a realist, and the realist admits the truth, which is that one's ego is all important. A simple fact to a complex man.

And even Togol hadn't realized how complex Skinner was. Complex enough to make further plans. He'd been thinking about it for a long time now.

Being immortal and independent here in a world of his own was only the beginning. Suppose the infinite resources of Seward Skinner's galactic complex were utilized now to the ultimate, inexorable end—the end of every other world?

It would take time, but he had eternity. It would take effort, but immortality never tires. There would be a way and a weapon, and eventually he would find both. Eventually the scheme would be implemented, and then in truth there would be nothing in the galaxy but God. Skinner, and only Skinner, forever and ever, amen.

Skinner sat on the terrace and stared out as darkness fell over the land. A vague plan was already taking shape in his mind—the keen, immortally conscious, eternally aware mind.

There was a way, a simple way. Skinner scientists would be pressed into service to carry out the details, and with his resources it was neither fantastic nor impossible. It could be in fact quite simple. Develop a mutant microorganism, an airborne virus impervious to immunization, then transmit it by shuttle to key points throughout the galaxy. Human life, animal life, vegetable life would perish forever in its wake. Forever and ever, amen.

To be the richest man in the world was nothing. To be the wisest, the strongest, the most powerful—this too was not enough. But to be the *only* man—forever—

Seward Skinner started to laugh.

And then, quite suddenly, his laughter shrilled into a scream.

All over his world, Skinner screamed. The sound echoed through the curator's quarters in the museum, rose from the streets where the security guards stood sentinel, burst from the chauffeur's sleeping lips, shrieked in chorus from each and every Skinner who found himself *down there*.

The Skinner on the terrace was down there, too. Down there where—a remnant of sanity recalled—Dr. Togol must have taken his precautions and his revenge. It was a simple thing he'd done, really.

He'd gone *down there*, to the vault where the original Seward Skinner floated in the icy solution which preserved him in hibernation. And all he'd done was to shut off the temperature controls.

Dr. Togol had lied about destroying the thing in the vault. He'd kept it alive, and now that it was thawing its consciousness returned—the original consciousness of the real Seward Skinner, waking in the black, bubbling vat to wheeze and gasp and choke its life away.

And because it was aware now, the clones were linked to that life and that awareness, sharing the shock and sensation as the artificial blocks vanished, so that all again were one.

In a moment the thing down there in the vault was dead. But not before all the Skinners felt its final agony — which would never be final for them. As clones, they were immortal.

Seward Skinner's scream blended with those of every other Skinner on Skinner's world. And they would continue.

Forever.

SEE HOW THEY RUN

April 2nd

Okay, Doc, you win.

I'll keep my promise and make regular entries, but damned if I'll start out with a heading like *Dear Diary*. Or *Dear Doctor,* either. You want me to tell it like it is? Okay, but the way it is right now, Doc, beware. If you've got any ideas about wading in my stream of consciousness, just watch out for the alligators.

I know what you're thinking. "Here's a professional writer who claims he has a writer's block. Get him to keep a diary and he'll be writing in spite of himself. Then he'll see how wrong he is." Right, Doc? Write, Doc?

Only that's not my real problem. My hangup is the exact opposite — anti-thetical, if you're looking for something fancy. Logorrhea. Verbosity. Two-bit words from a dime-a-dozen writer? But that's what they always say at the studio: writers are a dime a dozen.

Okay, so here's your dime. Run out and buy me a dozen writers. Let's see — I'll have two Hemingways, one Thomas Wolfe, a James Joyce, a couple of Homers if they're fresh, and six William Shakespeares.

I almost said it to Gerber when he dropped me from the show. But what's the use? Those producers have only one idea. They point at the parking lot and say, "I'm driving the Caddy and you're driving the Volks." Sure. If you're so smart, why aren't you rich?

Call it a rationalization if you like. You shrinks are great at pinning labels on everything. Pin the tail on the donkey, that's the name of the game, and the patient is always the jackass. Pardon me, it's not "patient," it's "analysand." For fifty bucks an hour you can afford to dream up a fancy word. And for fifty bucks an hour I can't afford not to word up some fancy dreams.

If that's what you want from me, forget it. There are no dreams. Not any more. Once upon a time (as we writers say) there was a dream. A dream about coming out to Hollywood and cracking the television market. Write for comedy shows, make big money in your spare time this new easy way, buy a fancy pad with a big swimming pool, and live it up until you settle down with a cute little chick.

Dreams are nothing to worry about. It's only when they come true that you've got trouble. Then you find out that the comedy isn't funny any more, the big money disappears, and the swimming pool turns into a stream of consciousness. Even a cute little chick like Jean changes to something else. It's not a dream any more, it's a nightmare, and it's real.

There's a problem for you, Doc. Cure me of reality.

April 5th

A little-known historical fact. Shortly after being wounded in Peru, Pizarro, always a master of understatement, wrote that he was Incapacitated.

Damn it, Doc, I say it's funny! I don't buy your theory about puns being a form of oral aggression. Because I'm not the aggressive type.

Hostile, yes. Why shouldn't I be? Fired off the show after three seasons of sweating blood for Gerber and that lousy no-talent comic of his. Lou Lane couldn't get a job as M.C. in a laundromat until I started writing his material and now he's Mr. Neilsen himself, to hear him tell it.

But that's not going to trigger me into doing anything foolish. I don't have to. One season without me and he'll be back where he belongs — a parking attendant in a Drive-In Mortuary. Curb Service. We Pick Up and Deliver. Ha, ha.

Gerber gave me the same pitch; my stuff is getting sour. We don't want black comedy. It's nasty, and this is a family-type show. Okay, so maybe it was my way of releasing tension, getting it out of my system — catharsis, isn't that the term? And it made me come on a little too strong. Which is where you get into the act. Blow my mind for me, put me back on the track, and I'll get myself another assignment and make the family-type funnies again.

Meanwhile, no problems. Jean is bringing in the bread. I never figured it that way when we got married. At first I thought her singing was a gag and I went along with it. Let the voice coach keep her busy while I was working on the show — give her something to do for a hobby. Even when she took the first few club dates it was still Amateur Night as far as I was concerned. But then they hit her with the recording contract, and after the singles came the album, etc. My little chick turned into a canary.

Funny about Jean. Such a nothing when I met her. Very good in the looks department but aside from that, nothing. It's the singing that made the difference. Finding her voice was like finding herself. All of a sudden, confidence.

Of course I'm proud of her but it still shakes me up a little. The way she takes over, like insisting I see a psychiatrist. Not that I'm hacked about it, I know she's only doing it for my own good, but it's hard to get used to. Like last night at the Guild screening, her agent introduced us to some friends of his — "I want you to meet Jean Norman and her husband."

Second billing. That's not for me, Doc. I'm a big boy now. The last thing I need is an identity crisis, right? And as long as we're playing true confessions, I might as well admit Jean has one point — I've been hitting the bottle a little too hard lately, since I got canned.

I didn't mention it at our last session, but this is the main reason she made me come to you. She says alcohol is my security blanket. Maybe taking it away would fix things. Or would it?

One man's security blanket is another man's shroud.

April 7th

You stupid jerk. What do you mean, alcoholism is only a symptom?

First of all, I'm not an alcoholic. Sure I drink, maybe drink a lot, everybody drinks in this business. It's either that or pot or hard drugs and I'm not going to freak out and mess up my life. But you've got to have something to keep your head together and just because I belt a few doesn't mean I'm an alcoholic.

But for the sake of argument, suppose it does? You call it a symptom. A symptom of *what*?

Suppose you tell me that little thing. Sitting back in that overstuffed chair with your hands folded on your overstuffed gut and letting me do all the talking — let's hear you spill something for a change. What is it you suspect, Mr. Judge, Mr. Jury, Mr. Prosecuting Attorney, Mr. Executioner? What's the charge — heterosexuality in the first degree?

I'm not asking for sympathy. I get plenty of that from Jean. Too much. I'm up to here on the oh-you-poor-baby routine. I don't want tolerance or understanding or any of that phony jive. Just give me a few facts for a change. I'm tired of Jean playing Mommy and I'm tired of you playing Big Daddy. What I want is some real help, you've got to help me help me please please help me.

April 9th

Two resolutions.

Number one, I'm not going to drink any more. I'm quitting as of now, flat-out. I was stoned when I wrote that last entry and all I had to do was read it today when I'm sober to see what I've been doing to myself. So no more drinking. Not now or ever.

Number two. From now on I'm not showing this to Dr. Moss. I'll cooperate with him completely during therapy sessions but that's it. There's such a thing as invasion of privacy. And after what happened today I'm not going to lay myself wide open again. Particularly without an anesthetic, and I've just given that up.

If I keep on writing everything down it will be for my own information, a matter of personal record. Of course I won't tell him that. He'd come up with some fancy psychiatric zinger, meaning I'm talking to myself. I've got it figured out—the shrinks are all authority figures and they use their labels as putdowns. Who needs it?

All I need is to keep track of what's happening, when things start to get confused. Like they did at the session today.

First of all, this hypnotherapy bit.

As long as this is just between me and myself I'll admit the whole idea of being hypnotized always scared me. And if I had any suspicion the old creep was trying to put me under I'd have cut out of there in two seconds flat.

But he caught me off guard. I was on the couch and supposed to say whatever came into my head. Only I drew a blank, couldn't think of anything. Emotional exhaustion, he said, and turned down the lights. Why not close my eyes and relax? Not go to sleep, just daydream a little. Daydreams are sometimes more important than those that come in sleep. In fact he didn't want me to fall asleep, so if I'd concentrate on his voice and let everything hang loose—

He got to me. I didn't feel I was losing control, no panic, I knew where I was and everything, but he got to me. He must have, because he kept talking about memory. How memory is our own personal form of time travel, a vehicle to carry us back, way back to earliest childhood, didn't I agree? And I said yes, it can carry us back, carry me back, back to old Virginny.

Then I started to hum something I hadn't thought about in years. And he said what's that, it sounds like a nursery rhyme, and I said that's right, Doc, don't you know it, *Three Blind Mice.*

Why don't you sing the words for me, he said. So I started.

Three blind mice, three blind mice.

See how they run, see how they run!

They all ran after the farmer's wife,

Did you ever see such a sight in your life

As three blind mice, three blind mice?

"Very nice," he said. "But didn't you leave out a line?"

"What line?" I said. All at once, for no reason at all, I could feel myself getting very uptight. "That's the song. My old lady sang that to me when I was a baby. I wouldn't forget a thing like that. What line?"

He started to sing it to me.

They all ran after the farmer's wife.

She cut off their heads with a carving knife.

Then it happened.

It wasn't like remembering. It was happening. Right now, all over again.

Late at night. Cold. Wind blowing. I wake up. I want a drink of water. Everyone asleep. Dark. I go into the kitchen.

Then I hear the noise. Like a tapping on the floor. It scares me. I turn on the light and I see it. In the corner behind the door. The trap. Something moving in it. All gray and furry and flopping up and down.

The mouse. Its paw is caught in the trap and it can't get loose. Maybe I can help. I pick up the trap and push the spring back. I hold the mouse. It wiggles and squeaks and that scares me more. I don't want to hurt it, just put it outside so it can run away. But it wiggles and squeaks and then it bites me.

When I see the blood on my finger I'm not scared any more. I get mad. All I want to do is help and it bites me. Dirty little thing. Squeaking at me with its eyes shut. Blind. Three Blind Mice. Farmer's Wife.

There. On the sink. The carving knife.

It tries to bite me again. I'll fix it. I take the knife. And I cut, I drop the knife, and I start to scream.

I was screaming again, thirty years later, and I opened my eyes and there I was in Dr. Moss's office, bawling like a kid.

"How old were you?" Dr. Moss said.

"Seven."

It just popped out. I hadn't remembered how old I was, hadn't remembered what happened — it was all blacked out of my mind, just like the line in the nursery rhyme.

But I remember now. I remember everything. My old lady finding the mouse head in the trash can and then beating the hell out of me. I think that's what made me sick, not the bite, even though the doctor who came and gave me the shot said it was infection that caused the fever. I was laid up in bed for two weeks. When I'd wake up screaming from the nightmares, my old lady used to come in and hold me and tell me how sorry she was. She always told me how sorry she was — after she did something to me.

I guess that's when I really started to hate her. No wonder I built so many of Lou Lane's routines on mother and mother-in-law gags. Oral aggression? Could be. All these years and I never knew it, never realized how I hated her. I still hate her now, hate her —

What I need is a drink.

April 23rd

Two weeks since I wrote the last entry. I told Dr. Moss I quit keeping a diary and he believed me. I told Dr. Moss a lot of things besides that, and whether he believed me or not I don't know. Not that I care one way or the other. I don't believe everything he tells *me* either.

Hebephrenic schizophrenia. Now there's a real grabber.

Meaning certain personality types, confronted with a stress situation they can't handle, revert to childhood or infantile behavior levels.

I looked it up the other day after I got a peek at Moss's notes, but if that's what he thinks, then he's the one who's flipped.

Dr. Moss has a thing about words like flipped, nuts, crazy. Mental disturbance, that's his speed.

That and regression. He's hung up on regression. No more hypnosis—I told him that was out, absolutely—and he got the message. But he uses other techniques like free association, and they seem to work. What really happens is that I talk myself into remembering, talk my way back into the past.

I've come up with some weirdies. Like not drinking a glass of milk until I was five years old—my old lady let me drink that formula stuff out of the bottle and there was a big hassle over it when I went to kindergarten and wouldn't touch my milk any other way. Then she clouted me one and said I made her ashamed when she had to explain to the teacher, and she took the bottle away. But it was her fault in the first place. I'm beginning to understand why I hated her.

My old man wasn't any prize, either. Whenever we had company over for dinner he'd come out with things I'd said to him, all the dumb kid stuff you say when you don't know any better, and everybody would laugh. Hard to realize kids get embarrassed, too, until you remember the way it was. The old man kept needling me to make stupid cracks just so he could take bows for repeating them to his buddies. No wonder you forget things like that—it hurts too much to remember.

It still hurts.

Of course there were good memories, too. When you're a kid, most of the time you don't give a damn about anything, you don't worry about the future, you don't even understand the real meaning of things like pain and death—and that's worth remembering.

I always seem to start out that way in our sessions but then Moss steers me into the other stuff. Catharsis, he says, it's good for you. Let it all hang out. Okay, I'm cooperating, but when we finish up with one of those children's hours I'm ready to go home and have a nice, big drink.

Jean is starting to bug me about it again. We had another hassle last night when she came home from the club date. Singing, that's all she's really interested in nowadays, never has any time for me.

Okay, so that's her business, why doesn't she mind it and let me alone? So I was stoned, so what? I tried to tell her about the therapy, how I was hurting and how a drink helped. "Why don't you grow up?" she said. "A little pain never hurt anyone."

Sometimes I think they're all crazy.

April 25th

They're crazy, all right.

Jean calling Dr. Moss and telling him I was back on the bottle again.

"On the bottle," I said, when he told me about it. "What kind of talk is that? You'd think she was my mother and I was her baby."

"Isn't that what you think?" Moss said.

I just looked at him. I didn't know what to say. This was one time when he did all the talking.

He started out very quietly, about how he'd hoped therapy would help us make certain discoveries together. And over a period of time I'd begin to understand the meaning of the pattern I'd established in my life. Only it hadn't seemed to work out that way, and while as a general thing he didn't care to run the risk of inducing psychic trauma, in this case it seemed indicated that he clarify the situation for me.

That part I can remember, almost word for word, because it made sense. But what he told me after that is all mixed up.

Like saying I have an oral fixation on the bottle because it represents the formula bottle my mother took away from me when I was a kid. And the reason I got into comedy writing was to reproduce the situation where my father used to tell people all my funny remarks — because even if they laughed it meant I was getting attention, and I wanted attention. But at the same time I resented my father taking the credit for amusing them, just like I resented Lou Lane making it big because of what I wrote for him. That's why I blew the job, writing material he couldn't use. I wanted him to use it and bomb out, because I hated him. Lou Lane had become a father image and I hated my father.

I remember looking at Dr. Moss and thinking he has to be crazy. Only a crazy shrink could come up with things like that.

He was really wild. Talking about my old lady. How I hated her so much when I was a kid I had to displace my feelings — transfer them to something else so I wouldn't feel so guilty about it.

Like the time I got up for a drink of water. I really wanted my bottle back, but my mother wouldn't give it to me. And maybe the bottle was a symbol of something she gave my father. Hearing them was what really woke me up and I hated her for that most of all.

Then I went into the kitchen and saw the mouse. The mouse reminded me of the nursery rhyme and the nursery rhyme reminded me of my mother. I took the knife, but I didn't want to kill the mouse. In my mind I was really killing my mother —

That's when I hit him. Right in his dirty mouth.

Nobody talks about my mother that way.

Apr 29

Better this way. Don't need Moss. Don't need therapy. Do it myself.

Been doing it. Regression. Take a little drink, take a little trip. Little trip down memory lane.

Not to the bad things. Good things. All the warm soft memories. The time I was in bed with the fever and Mother came in with the ice cream on the tray. And my father bringing me that toy.

That's what's nice about remembering. Best thing in the world. There was a poem we used to read in school. I still remember it. "Backward, turn backward, O time in your flight, make me a child again just for tonight!" Well, no problem. A few drinks and away you go. Little oil for the old time machine.

When Jean found out about Dr. Moss she blew her stack. I had to call him up right away and apologize, she screamed.

"To hell with that," I said. "I don't need him any more. I can work this thing out for myself."

"Maybe you'll have to," Jean said.

Then she told me about Vegas. Lounge date, three weeks on the Strip. All excited because this means she's really made it — the big time. Lou Lane is playing the big room and he called her agent and told her it was all set.

"Wait a minute," I said. "Lou Lane set this up for you?"

"He's been a good friend," Jean told me. "All through this he's kept in touch, because he's worried about you. He'd be your friend, too, if you'd only let him."

Sure he would. With friends like that you don't need enemies. My eyes were opening fast. No wonder he squawked to Gerber and got me off the show. So he could move in on Jean. He had it set up, all right. The two of them, playing Vegas together. Jean in the lounge, him in the big room, and then, after the show —

For a moment there I was so shook up I couldn't see straight and I don't know what I would have done if I could. But I mean I really couldn't see straight because I started to cry. And then she was holding me and it was all right again. She'd cancel the Vegas date and stay here with me, we'd work this out together. But I had to promise her one thing — no more drinking.

I promised. The way she got to me I would have promised her anything.

So I watched her clean out the bar and then she went into town to see her agent.

It's a lie, of course. She could have picked up the phone and called him from here. So she's doing something else.

Like going straight to Lou Lane and spilling everything to him. I can just hear her. "Don't worry, darling, I had to beg off this time or he'd get too suspicious. But what's three weeks in Vegas when we've got a whole lifetime ahead of us?" And then the two of them get together —

No. I'm not going to think about it. I don't have to think about it, there are other things, better things.

That's why I took the bottle. The one she didn't know about when she cleaned out the bar, the one I had stashed away in the basement.

I'm not going to worry any more. She can't tell me what to do. Take a little drink, take a little trip. That's all there is to it.

I'm home free.

Later

She broke the bottle.

She came in and saw me and grabbed the bottle away from me and she broke it. I know she's mad because she ran into the kitchen and slammed the door. Why the kitchen?

Extension phone there.

Wonder if she'll try to call Dr. Moss.

Aprel 30

I was a bad boy.

The Dr. come. he sed what did you do.

I sed she took the bottel away.

He saw it on the floor the knive

I had to do it I sed.

He saw blood.

Like the mouse he sed.

No not a mouse. A canarry.

dont look in the trash can I sed

But he did.

THE LEARNING MAZE

JON COULDN'T REMEMBER A TIME when he hadn't been in the Maze.

He must have been very young at first, because his earliest recollection was a confused impression of lying on his back and sucking greedily from a tube extended by a Feeder.

The Feeder, of course, was a servomechanism, but Jon didn't realize that until much later. At the time he was only aware of the tall tangle of moving metal hovering over him and extending a hollow tentacle toward his eager lips. There had been a Changer too, approaching him at regular intervals to remove soiled clothing, cleanse his body, and cover it with fresh garments.

Jon's memories became more vivid as his areas of perception slowly extended. The first unit of the Maze was a vast enclosure in which hundreds of infants lay in their individual plastic life-support units while the Feeders and Changers moved among them. From time to time another type of servomechanism appeared without warning, disturbing the regular rhythm of eating, sleeping and elimination by superimposing its bulk upon his body.

Now Jon realized it must have been a Medi-mechanism, but he still thought of it as a spider — a gigantic insectoid creature straddling him on extended silvery legs as its myriad extra appendages poked and probed the organs and orifices of his body. It recorded pulse, respiration, brain-wave patterns, his entire metabolism, and corrected deficiencies by injection. Jon could still remember the sting of the needles and how he had writhed and screamed.

Naturally he'd feared and hated the process. Even now that he knew the whole procedure was impersonal, computer-directed for his welfare and well-being, he still resented it.

The other infants had screamed too. But not everything was that unpleasant. As time passed they began to move around more freely, aided by handgrips within their cubicles, and then they started to crawl. Jon crawled with them, eventually leaving the shelter of the life-support unit to seek the source of sounds and images beyond.

The sounds and images came from the walls, from the closed-circuit televisor screens. The screens sang soothingly to him at night and by day they showed images of other infants crawling and feeding happily. Watching the screens, Jon and his peer group began to imitate the actions of the images; soon they learned to take nourishment from little sterile containers deposited by the Feeders at regular intervals once the tubes were no longer offered. Some of Jon's companions cried when the tubes disappeared, but in time they all began to eat what was set before them.

They began the educational process and that, of course, was the real function of the Learning Maze — to teach them to live and grow.

In the antiseptic atmosphere of the chamber with its controlled temperature and humidity levels, they watched the infant-images on the screens as the figures crawled, then stood erect and took their first faltering steps.

Imitating them, Jon started to walk. Soon all the others were walking, exploring the chamber and one another. Touch, bodily contact, the discovery and awareness of differences and similarities, sexual awakening — all this was a part of learning.

The Maze guarded and waited, and when the time came its screens disappeared into the walls and there was only a doorway visible at the far end of the chamber. Through that doorway Jon could glimpse another chamber beyond, filled with other youngsters larger than himself who walked freely without falling and uttered complicated sounds as they pursued fascinating, glittering objects in bigger and brighter surroundings.

At first Jon merely watched, uncertain and afraid. Then, inevitably, came an urge to move through the doorway. There was no barrier, no impediment, and he entered easily into the adjoining section of the Maze.

Here the individual plastic cubicles were larger and the screens more sophisticated in their offerings. They still sang soothingly at night, but by day they talked to him.

Night was dark and day was light; that was one of the first things Jon learned. Even before he could comprehend the words, Jon learned many things. He learned to dispense with the Feeders and Changers because here the servomechanisms were different. Their metallic shapes roughly resembled his own on a larger scale; they had arms and legs and heads and they moved about almost in the same fashion that he did. Only of course mechanisms never seemed to tire or express emotion. Perhaps that's why they had no faces — merely a blank surface meshed over the front of their heads through which voices filtered instructions and commands. Gradually Jon began to understand the voices, whether they issued from the screens or from the servomechanisms, and presently he learned to respond and to answer in kind.

Soon Jon was established in a normal pattern of boyhood. He played with the glittering objects — the educational toys which tested and extended physical strength, improved his motor reflexes and coordination, taught him mechanical dexterity and skills. He talked to his companions, all of whom were males. He made friends and enemies, embarked upon the give-and-take of social relationships, rivalries and dependencies. Competition provided him with motivation; he wanted to excel in order to attract attention and approval.

Jon's orientation came from the screens. As he grew older he became aware of the world beyond — the real world outside the Learning Maze. The world which had once existed without Mazes of any sort and in which human beings had lived all their lives with only the crudest kind of servomechanisms to help them. History — or theirstory, as it was now correctly called — dealt with the quaint quality of this primitive culture in which the biological parents undertook the education of their offspring, assisted by crude instructional institutions.

The combined effects of emotional conflict and ignorance had their inevitable effect: the world had been plunged into endless warfare in which both the inhabitants and their natural environment were almost totally destroyed.

Then and only then, the Learning Maze concept came to the rescue. Once a mere toy for the study of animal behavior in old-fashioned "laboratories," then a simple experimental device developed for the psychological conditioning of children in a few "universities," the Learning Maze principle had been expanded to bring true sanity and civilization to mankind. The perfection of various types of servomechanisms, completely controlled by computerization, eliminated all error.

Gone was the outmoded human hierarchy of masters and servants which had created destruction. Today these roles were played by machines, and man was free to fulfill his true function — learning how to live.

Jon soon realized that his only problem was how to avoid pitfalls along the way. Because there *were* pitfalls in the Learning Maze. Although the surface beneath his feet seemed solid and substantial, it could give way. He'd seen it happen.

Not all his companions learned as quickly as he did. Some of them seemed uninterested in watching the screens and absorbing the information they provided. If this indifference persisted, the servomechanisms noted it and took action.

The action was simple and direct, but startlingly effective. The mechanism merely focused its blank-faced attention on a lazy or noncompetitive youngster and then, with a quick gesture, reached up and pulled a switch located at the side of its metal head. Suddenly, without warning, the ground directly under the child parted and he fell into the dark opening below. Sometimes there was a scream, but usually it happened too quickly for that — for in an instant the gaping hole was gone again as though it and the child it had swallowed no longer existed.

No one ever discovered what happened to those who disappeared and neither the screens nor the servomechanisms offered any explanation. Jon's companions couldn't find any physical evidence pointing to the exact location of the pitfalls; they seemed to be completely camouflaged and scattered at random all over the Maze, so there was no way in which to avoid them. There were all sorts of guesses, but no one really knew, and it was better not to think too much about it. The important thing was to realize the danger existed and could confront one at any time. For not learning, for being unable to learn, for being too sick or too weak or too helpless to learn — pulling the switch was the punishment.

But learning brought rewards. Because now, once again, another doorway appeared leading to an area beyond. Peering through it, Jon could see a new vista of the Maze, expanded and elaborate, filled with evidence of exciting activity.

The screens told him about that activity — about males and females and the pleasure of their relationships. The responses of his own body affirmed the truth of what he was told. Jon and his companions were anxious to enter that next section; enter into its activities, enter into its females. But when they attempted to move through, an invisible barrier prevented their progress.

Not yet, said the voices from the screens. You must learn more before you're ready.

Impatiently, Jon and the others looked and listened, but their inner awareness was concentrated on the delights beyond the doorway. From time to time someone would desert his learning post and steal away toward the other chamber, but always a servomechanism barred his path and uttered a warning. If ignored, the mechanism pulled its switch and the heedless one dropped down to disappear.

But there were moments when Jon and his fellows were unobserved and then they would steal up to the opening to stare at the scene beyond and to test the invisible force field of the barrier.

Eventually they grew stronger or the barrier became weaker; finally, one by one, they broke through. And there, in the next segment of the Maze, Jon and the others found their females. Pairing off, they sought still larger cubicles to share with their partners and the pattern of existence changed.

Jon's partner was called Ava; it was she who now prepared the food left by the servomechanisms who ministered to the needs of this section. At first Jon was not too greatly interested in food, but as time passed and the novelty of physical contact waned, nourishment and comfort became more important again.

Once more Jon learned the pattern of rewards and punishments governing this area of the Maze. Food was distributed only to those who were willing to spend time watching the screens. Since Ava seemed completely absorbed in the day-to-day routine of life within their cubicle, Jon was forced to appear regularly before a screen as further lessons in living were presented.

The images were quite diversified and complex now; there were scenes of full-grown adults engaging in a great variety of activities. Some seemed to be full-time screen watchers, some appeared to ignore the screens and devote themselves to tests of strength with companions, rivaling them for the interest of many females besides their partners.

Jon was not tired of Ava, but he found himself studying various techniques of competition with increasing interest. It would appear that in the real world he was preparing to enter, the biggest and strongest acquired the best cubicles and the most attractive females. In addition they received the envy and admiration of their companions.

The more Jon learned the more interested he became in testing his own powers. Ava's simple responses began to bore him; she wasn't concerned with what he told her about the real world beyond and couldn't understand why he was dissatisfied to stay here forever.

But Jon was tired of the tedium of screen watching and apprehensive about the fate of his fellows who balked. He'd seen them deprived of food by the servomechanisms for neglecting their daily duties. Some of those who were content to become completely absorbed in relationships with their partners had already disappeared. There seemed to be no penalty for the females; their limited interests didn't stamp them as inferior, for their previous conditioning had obviously been different. But the males were obligated to continue the learning process, and Jon knew he must comply.

Besides, a new opening had appeared in the far wall of the chamber and now he found himself moving forward to gaze into the next complex beyond.

Jon knew without being told that this must be the real world—the world for which he'd prepared to dwell in during all this period of study and growth.

What waited beyond the invisible barrier was not a simple chamber but a huge series of corridors, each with an opening which afforded a partial, tantalizing glimpse of activity within. Others like himself prowled these corridors, entering various compartments at will and exiting to move along into still other portions of the Maze. Jon could not see any screens on the corridor walls and that was good. Here men seemed to be living, not learning. They were coupling with many females, carrying huge accumulations of food and clothing from one place to another, trading and exchanging various articles, and fighting off others who attempted to take a portion for themselves without permission or barter agreements.

Jon couldn't wait to join them. And when he crowded up to the opening he found himself passing through without hindrance — and without a thought of Ava left behind him. Ava, with her dull conversation, her duller caresses, and her swollen belly.

Once across the barrier, Jon forgot Ava completely. There was so much to see, so much to do, for this tangle of corridors stretched off endlessly in all directions, opening upon many types of rooms and rooms within rooms. But it was still a part of the Maze.

From what he'd seen on the outside, Jon had thought there would be no more screens; now he realized he was mistaken, for if anything, their numbers had increased. The difference was that there was no longer any uniformity to the images on the screens or the messages they imparted.

Pausing at a chamber doorway, Jon could hear some voices from the screens urging him to enter, promising him all sorts of rewards and describing the pleasures of participation in the activities within. Other voices, equally shrill and urgent, warned him to keep out, to seek still more distant rooms.

And the servomechanisms were here too, though less noticeable, for now they more closely resembled Jon's living companions. They moved naturally, their gestures less stiff and more assured, their voices ringing with confident authority. At first Jon wasn't even able to identify them as mechanisms because they were masked in faces simulating flesh; faces that smiled benevolently, grinned confidently, or frowned with stern wisdom. "Follow me," they said, and Jon joined the group obediently to be led into a bewildering array of vast, arenalike enclosures.

In one such place a leader gathered together all those with fair complexions while another leader assembled those with darker skins. And from the walls the screens screamed at both groups in turn, exciting them with alternate threats and promises, urging them to destroy their opposites.

The noise was ceaseless, the confusion incredible, and in the inevitable struggle that followed, the leaders stood aside observing. When one of Jon's companions slackened, the inevitable gesture was made — a hand went to the side of the head and one of the invisible seams opened to engulf the offender.

It was only then that Jon realized the leaders were servomechanisms, for when the switches operated, the masks sometimes slipped to one side and Jon could see the blank, featureless surface beneath, totally devoid of any semblance to humanity.

That was when Jon fought his way through the struggling throng and escaped into a corridor, only to be swept along into another area where the chief activity seemed to be the removal of metal discs affixed to the walls of the chamber.

Here the screens displayed glittering panoplies of such discs, while their voices extolled the glory of gathering them together and heaping them up into huge piles. According to the screens, great skill and intelligence were required to perform this feat, and there was no higher goal than the acquisition and arrangement of discs. As if to prove the point, large numbers of exotically dressed, youthful females prowled about inspecting the heaps and offering themselves to those who had managed to amass the largest portions.

But Jon observed that the females seldom stayed long with any one accumulator; always they seemed attracted by another collector with a still larger heap.

Jon also noted that obtaining the discs was not an easy procedure; prying them from their fastenings in the walls was a painful task that made the fingers bleed. Sometimes rival disc-gatherers fought with one another over the discovery of a fresh cluster of discs, and many times they resorted to stealing discs from the collections of their companions. Indeed, it seemed as if the most truly imposing amounts were gathered in just this way, by theft alone.

Wrenching discs free from the walls was more exhausting and a much slower process; sometimes it was necessary to stand on tiptoe for those beyond reach, or crouch to burrow at the very base of the walls. And yet there was a strange compulsive element involved; those who toiled eventually became so absorbed that they could not even be distracted by the young, nubile females, and even food and slumber seemed unimportant. Similarly, the thieves came to devote themselves solely to stealing, with equally tiring results.

And when the efforts slackened or ceased through utter exhaustion, the servomechanisms appeared, pushing aside their sober masks to pull the switch. Thus disc-gatherers and disc-stealers alike disappeared, leaving only a shining heap as a sole memento of existence—a heap which was immediately plundered by waiting rivals, so that even this evidence of achievement vanished.

But these were only two of the many areas which Jon discovered in the Maze. There was a shouting section—he could think of it in no other terms —in which every occupant was encouraged to drown out the voices of his fellows and reduce them to the status of listeners. Here the rivals emulated the voices from the screens, uttering promises, blandishments, flattery and exhortations, while at the same time denouncing the words of all the others in a continuous effort to attract the less articulate to support their stated purposes.

At first Jon tried to listen, but the more he heard the more confused he became. Some praised those who fought in the arena sections, some denounced them; some extolled the virtues of disc-accumulators and others derided. But in the end their voices hoarsened and failed and their audiences turned away to hear the same messages couched in slightly different phrases by younger and louder voices. And when this happened, a servomechanism appeared to seek out the speechless orator, deserted by all, and make the inevitable movement toward the side of the head.

In another area Jon found speakers equally dedicated to attracting followers but using softer and more persuasive tones. They spoke of the great secret of the Learning Maze, the secret which had been imparted to them as a special dispensation. Praising the voices from the screens, they explained that the commands and injunctions issuing from them were often cryptic and mysterious and had to be interpreted by speakers such as themselves in order that all might understand.

But each speaker seemed to have a different explanation of the meaning of the Maze—its creation, its purpose, and how one must conduct oneself within. And each speaker disputed the statements of his fellows, even to the minor points of words and phrases used by them, so that in the end the soft voices gave way to angry shouts, denunciations, threats of endless punishment and commands to destroy all those who refused to agree utterly and completely without question. And always the speaker would call upon the servomechanisms to punish and eliminate nonbelievers.

Some of the talk interested Jon at the beginning, for he had often tried to puzzle out the program of the Maze, but when talk gave place to outcry it became incoherent and bewildering. And Jon noted that the servomechanisms never seemed to come upon command to destroy the speakers' enemies—but when all the prayers for vengeance died, it was then that the mechanisms finally appeared to make the gesture which removed speakers and followers alike. In the end, none who stayed in this chamber were spared, whatever their beliefs.

Jon remembered a section where all occupants seemed to be engaged in an endless and complicated measurement process. Dedicated to observation, they gravely calculated the area of the room, analyzed and tabulated the components of the atmosphere within it, and even attempted to measure one another.

These observers took great pride in their efforts and loudly proclaimed their superiority to those in other sections of the Maze. Some day, they asserted, they would take their rightful place as rulers of the Maze, once they had mastered all its secrets by their methods of measurement.

What was not readily described in terms of size or mass or velocity of movement they theorized about—giving particular attention to the phenomena of the wall screens and servomechanisms and attempting to fully explain their functions and purposes. But no two theories were exactly alike and new measurements and methods of measurement constantly superseded the old, so that the end result was once again argument and anger. And with all the careful devotion to the accumulation of data and all the energy expended in expounding theory, the room itself remained fixed and unchanged except in minor details. And its occupants never left it until one of the servomechanisms — its functions still unfathomable, despite all the hypotheses — made the final motion that put an end to further inquiry.

Again Jon refused to become completely involved in such activity and sought out other sections. There was a new arena where the young seemed to be pitted against the old, each denouncing the other for a greedy and self-centered attempt to take control. But as the young became older, they seemed to switch allegiance, and this confused Jon so that he was impelled to move on.

In another place, food and sex and accumulation alike appeared unimportant to the occupants. They lay in a drugged stupor, oblivious to their surroundings except for the times when the screens flickered wildly and projected flashes of unrecognizable imagery or assaulted them with screaming sounds. Occasionally a few of the group would rouse long enough to imitate what they vaguely saw or heard, painting weird squiggles upon canvas and even upon their own bodies, or plucking crude instruments to make loud noises to which they wailed accompaniment. What they sang and shouted made little sense to those who were not drugged like themselves. Eventually they relapsed into a mumbling preoccupation, gazing raptly at their own faces in tiny mirrors which distorted their features beyond recognition until they came to resemble hairy beasts. Servomechanisms moved to those sunk in the deepest stupor and their switches were swift.

Jon continued on, vaguely conscious that he was gradually coming to know the various routes and recesses of the Maze. Eventually he chanced upon a room that seemed more inviting than the others, even though the servomechanism posted at the doorway did not exhort him to enter. Perhaps it was this that attracted him, or the fact that the mechanism wore a different mask. In place of human features there was only a surface emblazoned with a symbol. Jon recognized the curlicue and dot as something he'd seen on a screen long ago — a question mark.

Intrigued, he glanced into the room of silence. A few men sat cross-legged upon the floor, gazing at screens that were utterly blank and from which issued only a faint, deep drone. The drone was somehow soothing, but those who listened did not seem drugged or sleeping, merely contemplative.

Weary of walking, weary of peering and puzzling, Jon moved into the chamber. Almost automatically he sank down and assumed the cross-legged position, staring up at a screen. For a moment it seemed that he could see into the emptiness to catch a fleeting glimpse of something beyond. And wasn't there a voice whispering within the drone?

Concentrating with all his being, Jon strained to see, to hear. But the more he tried, the less he perceived, for such exertion only made him conscious of himself.

Finally he realized, and then it came. Making no attempt to see, he saw. Making no effort to hear, he heard. But the vision and voice came from within, and suddenly they blended into revelation.

For the first time Jon understood the Learning Maze. Completely computerized, completely controlled, it was a reasoned reproduction of the past —mankind's past, in all its aspects, recapitulated in physical form. These were the life styles constructed by men in the real world long ago, and which they had followed to their own destruction.

Those who sought sensory stimulation to the exclusion of all else were doomed. Those who pursued power, those who concentrated upon accumulating meaningless tokens of ownership, those who fought one another over differences in appearance or belief, were destined for extinction. Preoccupation with data or theory for its own sake was self-defeating, the distortion of phenomena by means of theology, pharmacology or art was meaningless.

All activity, all inquiry, all self-scrutiny and self-indulgence had its place in the scheme of things, but only in moderation and only as means to an end. The purpose of the Maze was to teach by precept and example, to pinpoint the pitfalls endangering men in their ancestral past and their own individual futures. It illustrated the myriad facets of existence and illuminated the dangers of surrendering wholly to any one phase of behavior in its extreme. The whole man knew and experienced life as a whole, but never gave himself completely to a fraction — only to totality.

In its system of rewards and punishment, the Learning Maze eliminated the weak and unfit from among those seeking to journey through it and emerge into the real world beyond.

Even contemplation such as this could become a self-limiting and self-destructive thing; awareness was granted for a purpose — for use in actual living.

It was time now to leave the Maze, and at last Jon knew the way.

When he emerged from contemplation and left the quiet drone of the chamber he no longer hesitated. The method was so simple once one grasped it. These rooms were only blind alleys set to trap the unaware; it was the corridor itself that was important. All he had to do was concentrate upon its convolutions and follow the path to the outer portals.

There was no longer any need to pause or peer or participate — he'd experienced enough of the chambers so that his curiosity was no longer aroused by them. Now he was free to direct his footsteps toward the greater goal.

It was almost as though instinct had taken over, finding the proper route for him. Ignoring sham and semblance, he moved toward substance and reality. And he came to a point where the twisted passageways merged into a single continuous corridor leading straight upward.

Now, directly ahead of him, Jon could see the actual opening and the light beyond; not the artificial light of the caverns but the light of reality.

He hastened toward it, toiling up the steep slant with renewed resolution. There was no obstacle now, nothing to impede his progress.

A servomechanism loomed up before him at the very threshold, but Jon's pace didn't slacken. He pressed forward, purposeful and determined, his body weary but his voice firm with resolve.

"Let me pass," he commanded.

The mechanism stood motionless, featureless face staring, seeming to question without speaking.

Jon sensed the question, voiced his answer.

"Why? Because I've had enough of faceless authority, of artificial motivation, meaningless routine and still more meaningless change. I've learned all you can teach me here. Now I'm ready to live in the real world."

"But you have lived all your life in the real world," said the mechanism softly. "Try to understand."

Jon tried, but there wasn't much time.

Because the mechanism was already pulling the switch.

THE MODEL

BEFORE I BEGIN THIS STORY, I must tell you that I don't believe a word of it.

If I did, I'd be just as crazy as the man who told it to me, and he's in the asylum.

There are times, though, when I wonder. But that's something you'll have to decide for yourself.

About the man in the asylum — let's call him George Milbank. Age thirty-two, according to the records, but he looked older; balding, running to fat, with a reedy voice and a facial tic that made me a little uptight watching him. But he didn't act or sound like a weirdo.

"And I'm not," he said, as we sat there in his room on the afternoon of my visit. "That's why Dr. Stern wanted you to see me, isn't it?"

"What do you mean?" I was playing it cool.

"Doc told me who you were, and I know the kind of stuff you write. If you're looking for material — "

"I didn't say that."

"Don't worry, I'm glad to talk to you. I've been wanting to talk to someone for a long time. Someone who'll do more than just put down what I say in a case history and file it away. They've got me filed away now and they're never going to let me out of here, but somebody should know the truth. I don't care if you write it up as a story, just so you don't make me out bananas. Because I'm going to tell it like it is, so help me God. If there *is* a God. That's what worries me — I mean, what kind of a God would create someone like Vilma?"

That's when I became conscious of his facial tic, and it disturbed me. He noticed my reaction and shook his head. "Don't take my word for it," he said. "Just look at the women in the magazine ads. High-fashion models, you know

343

the type? Tall, thin, all arms and legs, with no bust. And those high cheek-bones, the big eyes, the face frozen in that snotty don't-touch-me look.

"I guess that's what got to me. Just as it was supposed to. I took Vilma's look as a challenge." His face twitched again.

"You don't like women, do you?" I said.

"You're putting me on." For the first and only time he grinned. "Man, you're talking to one of the biggest womanizers in the business!" Then the grin faded. "At least I was, until I met Vilma.

"It all came together on a cruise ship—the *Morland*, one of those big new Scandinavian jobs built for the Caribbean package tours. Nine ports in two weeks, conducted shore trips to all the exotic native clipjoints.

"But I was aboard for business, not pleasure. McKay-Phipps, the ad agency I worked for, pitched Apex Camera a campaign featuring full-page color spreads in the fashion magazines. You know the setup—big, arty shots of a model posed against tropical resort backgrounds with just a few lines of snob-appeal copy below. *She travels in style. Her outfit—a Countess D'Or original. Her camera—an Apex.* That kind of crud, right?

"OK, it was their money and who the hell am I to say how they throw it around? Besides, it wasn't even one of my accounts. But Ben Sanders, the exec who handled it, went down the tube with a heart attack just three days before sailing, and I got nailed for the assignment.

"I didn't know diddly about the high-fashion rag business or cameras either, but no problem. The D'Or people sent along Pat Grigsby, their top design consultant, to take charge of the wardrobe end. And I had Smitty Lane handling the actual shooting. He's one of the best in the business, and he got everything lined up before we left—worked out a complete schedule of what shots we'd take and where, checked out times and locations, wired ahead for clearances and firmed-up the arrangements. All I had to do was come along for the ride and see that everyone showed up at the right place at the right time.

"So on the face of it I was home free. Or away from home free. There are worse things than two weeks on a West Indies cruise in February with all expenses paid. The ship was brand-new, with a dozen top-deck staterooms, and they'd booked one for each of us. None of those converted broom-closet cabins, and if we wanted we could have our meals served in and skip the first-sitting hassle in the dining room.

"But you don't give a damn about my vacation, and neither did I. Because it turned out to be a real downer.

"Like I said, the *Morland* hit nine ports in two weeks, and we were scheduled to do our thing in every one of them. Smitty wanted to shoot with natural light, so that meant we had to be on location and ready for action by 11 A.M. Since most of the spots he'd picked out were resorts halfway across the various islands, we had to haul out of the sack before seven, grab a fast

continental breakfast, and drag all the wardrobe and equipment onto a char-
tered bus by eight. You ever ride a 1959 VW minibus over a stretch of rough
back country road in steambath temperatures and humidity? It's the original
bad trip.

"Then there was the business of setting up. Smitty was good but a real
nitpicker, you know? And by the time Pat Grigsby was satisfied with the
looks of the outfits and the way they lined up in the viewfinder and we got
all those extra-protection shots, it was generally two o'clock. We had our
pics but no lunch. So off we'd go, laughing and scratching, in the VW that
had been baking in the sun all day, and if we boarded the ship again by
four-thirty we were just in time for Afternoon Bingo.

"About the rest of the cruise, I've got good news and bad news.

"First the bad news. Smitty didn't play Afternoon Bingo. He played the
bar—morning, afternoon, and night. And Pat Grigsby was butch. She must
have made her move with Vilma early on and gotten thanks-but-no-thanks,
because by the third day out the two of them weren't speaking except in line
of duty. So that left Vilma and me.

"This was the good news.

"I've already told you what those high-fashion models look like, and I
guess I made it sound like a grunt from a male chauvinist pig, but that's
because of what I know now. At the time, Vilma Loring was something else.
One thing about models—they know how to dress, how to move, what to do
with makeup and perfume. What it adds up to is poise. Poise, and what they
used to call femininity. And Vilma was all female.

"Maybe Women's Lib is a good thing, but those intellectual types, psychology majors with the stringy hair and the blue jeans always turned me
off.

"Vilma turned me on just looking at her. And I looked at her a lot. The
way she handled herself when we were shooting—a real pro. While the rest
of us were frying and dying under the noon sun, she stayed calm, cool and
collected. No sweat, not a hair out of place, never any complaints. The lady
had it.

"She had it, and I wanted it. That's why I made the scene with her as
often as I could, which wasn't very much on the days we were in port. She
always sacked out after we got back from a location and I couldn't get her to
eat with me; she liked to have meals in the stateroom so she wouldn't have to
bother with clothes and makeup. Naturally that was my cue to go into the
my-stateroom-or-yours routine, but she wasn't buying it. So during our
working schedule I had to settle for evenings.

"You know the kind of fun and games they have on shipboard. Second-
run movies for the old ladies with blue hair, dancing on a dime-size floor to
the music of a combo that would make Lawrence Welk turn in his baton. And

the floor shows — tap dancers, magic acts, overage vocalists direct from a two-year engagement at Caesar's Palace — in the men's room.

"So we did a lot of time together just walking the deck. With me suggesting my room for a nightcap and she giving me that it's-so-lovely-out-here-why-don't-we-look-at-the-dolphins routine.

"I got the message, but I wasn't about to scrub the mission. And on the days we spent at sea I stayed in there. I used to call Vilma every morning after breakfast and when she wasn't resting or doing her nails I lucked out. She was definitely the quiet type and dummied up whenever I asked a personal question, but she was a good listener. As long as I didn't pressure her she stayed happy. I picked up my cue from that and played the waiting game.

"She didn't want to swim? OK, so we sat in deck chairs and watched the action at the pool. No shuffleboard or deck tennis because the sun was bad for her complexion? Right on, we'd hit the lounge for the cocktail hour, even though she didn't drink. I kept a low profile, but as time went on I had to admit it was getting to me.

"Maybe it was the cruise itself that wore me down. The atmosphere, with everybody making out. Not just the couples, married or otherwise; there was plenty going for singles, too. Secretaries and schoolteachers who'd saved up for the annual orgy, getting it all together with used-car salesmen and post-graduate beach bums. Divorcées with silicone implants and new dye jobs were balling the gray-sideburn types who checked out Dow-Jones every morning before they went ashore. By the second week, even the little old ladies with the blue hair had paired off with the young stewards who'd hired on for stud duty. The final leg, two days at sea from Puerto Rico to Miami, was like something out of a porno flick, with everybody getting it on. Everybody but me, sitting there watching with a newspaper over my lap.

"That's when I had a little Dear Abby talk with myself. Here I was, wasting my time with an entry who wouldn't dance, wouldn't drink, wouldn't even have dinner with me. She wasn't playing it cool, she was playing it frigid.

"OK, she was maybe the most beautiful broad I've ever laid eyes on, but you can't look forever when you're not allowed to touch. She had this deep, husky voice that seemed to come from her chest instead of her throat, but she never used it for anything but small talk. She had a way of staring at you without blinking, but you want someone to look *at* you, not through you. She moved and walked like a dream, but there comes a time when you have to wake up.

"By the time I woke up it was our last night out and too late. But not too late to hit the bar. There was the usual ship's party and I'd made a date to take Vilma to the floor show. I didn't cancel it — I just stood her up.

"Maybe I was a slow learner or a sore loser. I didn't give a damn which it was, I'd just had it up to here. No more climbing the walls; I was going to tie one on, and I did.

"I went up aft to a little deck bar away from the action, and got to work. Everybody was making the party scene so I was the only customer. The bartender wanted to talk but I turned him off. I wasn't in the mood for conversation; I had too much to think about. Such as, what the hell had come over me these past two weeks? Running after a phony teaser like some goddam kid with the hots — it made no sense. Not after the first drink, or the second. By the time I ordered the third, which was a double, I was ready to go after Vilma and hit her right in the mouth.

"But I didn't have to. Because she was there. Standing next to me, with that way-out tropical moon shining through the light blue evening gown and shimmering over her hair.

"She gave me a big smile. 'I've been looking for you everywhere,' she said. 'We've got to talk.'

"I told her to forget it, we had nothing to discuss. She just stood there looking at me, and now the moonlight was sparkling in her eyes. I told her to get lost, I never wanted to see her again. And she put her hand on my arm and said, 'You're in love with me, aren't you?'

"I didn't answer. I couldn't answer, because it all came together and it was true. I *was* in love with Vilma. That's why I wanted to hit her, to grab hold of her and tear that dress right off and —

"Vilma took my hand. 'Let's go to my room,' she said.

"Now there's a switch for you. Two weeks in the deep-freeze and now this. On the last night, too — we'd be docking in a few hours and I still had to pack and be ready to leave the ship early next morning.

"But it didn't matter. What mattered is that we went right to her state-room and locked the door and it was all ready and waiting. The lights were low, the bed was turned down and the champagne was chilling in the ice bucket.

"Vilma poured me a glass, but none for herself. 'Go ahead,' she said. 'I don't mind.'

"But I did, and I told her so. There was something about the setup that didn't make sense. If this was what she wanted, why wait until the last minute?

"She gave me a look I've never forgotten. 'Because I had to be sure first.'

"I took a big gulp of my drink. It hit me hard on top of what I'd already had, and I was all through playing games. 'Sure of what?' I said. 'What's the matter, you think I can't get it up?'

"Vilma's expression didn't change. 'You don't understand. I had to get to know you and decide if you were suitable.'

"I put down my empty glass. 'To go to bed with?'

"Vilma shook her head. 'To be the father of my child.'

"I stared at her. 'Now wait a minute —'

"She gave me that look again. 'I have waited. For two weeks I've been waiting, watching you and making up my mind. You seem to be healthy, and there's no reason why our offspring wouldn't be genetically sound.'

"I could feel that last drink but I knew I wasn't stoned. I'd heard her loud and clear. 'You can stop right there,' I told her. 'I'm not into marriage, or supporting a kid.'

"She shrugged. 'I'm not asking you to marry me, and I don't need any financial help. If I conceive tonight, you won't even know about it. Tomorrow we go our separate ways — I promise you'll never even have to see me again.'

"She moved close, too close, close enough so that I could feel the heat pouring off her in waves. Heat, and perfume, and a kind of vibration that echoed in her husky voice. 'I need a child,' she said.

"All kinds of thoughts flashed through my head. She was high on acid, she was on a freak sex-trip, some kind of a nut case. 'Look,' I said. 'I don't even know you, not really —'

"She laughed then, and her laugh was husky too. 'What does it matter? You want me.'

"I wanted her, all right. The thoughts blurred together, blended with the alcohol and the anger, and the only thing left was wanting her. Wanting this big beautiful blonde babe, wanting her heat, her need.

"I reached for her and she stepped back, turning her head when I tried to kiss her. 'Get undressed first,' she said. 'Oh, hurry — please —'

"I hurried. Maybe she'd slipped something into my drink, because I had trouble unbuttoning my shirt and in the end I ripped it off, along with everything else. But whatever she'd given me I was turned on, turned on like I've never been before.

"I hit the bed, lying on my back, and everything froze; I couldn't move, my arms and legs felt numb because all the sensation was centered in one place. I was ready, so ready I couldn't turn off if I tried.

"I know because I kept watching her, and there was no change when she lifted her arms to her neck and removed her head.

"She put her head down on the table and the long blonde hair hung over the side and the glassy blue eyes went dead in the rubbery face. But I couldn't stir, I was still turned on, and all I remember is thinking to myself, without a head how can she see?

"Then the dress fell and there was my answer, moving toward me. Bending over me on the bed, with her tiny breasts almost directly above my face so that I could see the hard tips budding. Budding and opening until the eyes peered out — the *real* eyes, green and glittering deep within the nipples.

"And she bent closer; I watched her belly rise and fall, felt the warm, panting breath from her navel. The last thing I saw was what lay below — the pink-lipped, bearded mouth, opening to engulf me. I screamed once, and then I passed out.

"Do you understand now? Vilma had told me the truth, or part of the truth. She was a high-fashion model, all right — but a model for *what*?

"Who made her, and how many more did they make? How many hundreds or thousands are there, all over the world? Models — you ever notice how they all seem to look alike? They could be sisters, and maybe they are. A family, a race from somewhere outside, swarming across the world, breeding with men when the need is upon them, breeding in their own special way. The way she bred with me — "

I ran out then, when he lost control and started to scream. The attendants went in and I guess they quieted him down, because by the time I got to Dr. Stern's office down the hall I couldn't hear him any more.

"Well?" Stern said. "What do you make of it?"

I shook my head. "You're the doctor. Suppose you tell me."

"There isn't much. This Vilma — Vilma Loring, she called herself — really existed. She was a working professional model for about two years, registered with a New York agency, living in a leased apartment on Central Park South. Lots of people remember seeing her, talking to her — "

"You're using the past tense," I said.

Stern nodded. "That's because she disappeared. She must have left her stateroom, left the ship as soon as it docked that night in Miami. No one's managed to locate her since, though God knows they've tried, in view of what happened."

"Just what *did* happen?"

"You heard the story."

"But he's crazy — isn't he?"

"Greatly disturbed. That's why they brought him here after they found him the next morning, lying there on the bed in a pool of blood." Stern shrugged. "You see, that's the one thing nobody can explain. To this day, we don't know what became of his genitals."

A Case of the Stubborns

THE MORNING AFTER HE DIED, Grandpa come downstairs for breakfast.

It kind of took us by surprise.

Ma looked at Pa, Pa looked at little sister Susie, and Susie looked at me. Then we all just set there looking at Grandpa.

"What's the matter?" he said. "Why you all staring at me like that?"

Nobody said, but I knowed the reason. Only been last night since all of us stood by his bedside when he was took by his attack and passed away right in front of our very eyes. But here he was, up and dressed and feisty as ever.

"What's for breakfast?" he said.

Ma sort of gulped. "Don't tell me you fixing to eat?"

"Course I am. I'm nigh starved."

Ma looked at Pa, but he just rolled his eyes. Then she went and hefted the skillet from the stove and dumped some eggs on a plate.

"That's more like it," Grandpa told her. "But don't I smell sausages?"

Ma got Grandpa some sausage. The way he dug into it, they sure was nothing wrong with his appetite.

After he started on seconds, Grandpa took heed of us staring at him again.

"How come nobody else is eating?" he asked.

"We ain't hungry," Pa said. And that was the gospel truth.

"Man's got to eat to keep up his strenth," Grandpa told him. "Which reminds me — ain't you gonna be late at the mill?"

"Don't figure on working today," Pa said.

Grandpa squinted at him. "You all fancied up this morning. Shave and a shirt, just like Sunday. You expecting company?"

351

Ma was looking out the kitchen window, and she give Grandpa a nod. "Yes indeedy. Here he comes now."

Sure enough, we could see ol' Bixbee hotfooting up the walk.

Ma went through the parlor to the front door—meaning to head him off, I reckon—but he fooled her and came around the back way. Pa got to the kitchen door too late, on account of Bixbee already had it and his mouth open at the same time.

"Morning, Jethro," he said, in that treacle-and-molasses voice of his. "And a sad grievous morning it is, too! I purely hate disturbing you so early on this sorrowful occasion, but it looks like today's another scorcher." He pulled out a tape measure. "Best if I got the measurements so's to get on with the arrangements. Heat like this, the sooner we get everything boxed and squared away the better, if you take my meaning—"

"Sorry," said Pa, blocking the doorway so ol' Bixbee couldn't peek inside. "Needs be you come back later."

"How much later?"

"Can't say for sure. We ain't rightly made up our minds as yet."

"Well, don't dillydally too long," Bixbee said. "I'm liable to run short of ice."

Then Pa shut the door on him and he took off. When Ma come back from the parlor, Pa made a sign for her to keep her gap shut, but of course that didn't stop Grandpa.

"What was that all about?" he asked.

"Purely a social call."

"Since when?" Grandpa looked suspicious. "Ol' Bixbee ain't nobody's friend—him with his high-toned airs! Calls hisself a Southern planter. Shucks, he ain't nothing but an undertaker."

"That's right, Grandpa," said sister Susie. "He come to fit you for your coffin."

"Coffin?" Grandpa reared up in his seat like a hog caught in a bobwire fence. "What in bo-diddley blazes do I need with a coffin?"

"Because you're dead."

Just like that she come out with it. Ma and Pa was both ready to take after her but Grandpa laughed fit to bust.

"Holy hen-tracks, child—what on earth give you an idee like that?"

Pa moved in on Susie, taking off his belt, but Ma shook her head. Then she nodded to Grandpa.

"It's true. You passed on last night. Don't you recollect?"

"Ain't nothing wrong with my memory," Grandpa told her. "I had me one of my spells, is all."

Ma fetched a sigh. "Wasn't just no spell this time."

"A fit, mebbe?"

"More'n that. You was took so bad, Pa had to drag Doc Snodgrass out of his office — busted up the game right in the middle of a three-dollar pot. Didn't do no good, though. By the time he got here you was gone."

"But I ain't gone! I'm here."

Pa spoke up. "Now don't git up on your high horse, Grandpa. We all saw you. We're witnesses."

"Witnesses?" Grandpa hiked his galluses like he always did when he got riled. "What kind of talk is that? You aim to hold a jury-trial to decide if I'm alive or dead?"

"But Grandpa — "

"Save your sass, sonny." Grandpa stood up. "Ain't nobody got a right to put me six feet under 'thout my say-so."

"Where you off to?" Ma asked.

"Where I go evvy morning," Grandpa said. "Gonna set on the front porch and watch the sights."

Durned if he didn't do just that, leaving us behind in the kitchen.

"Wouldn't that frost you?" Ma said. She crooked a finger at the stove. "Here I went and pulled up half the greens in the garden, just planning my spread for after the funeral. I already told folks we'd be serving possum stew. What will the neighbors think?"

"Don't you go fret now," Pa said. "Mebbe he ain't dead after all."

Ma made a face. "We know different. He's just being persnickety." She nudged at Pa. "Only one thing to do. You go fetch Doc Snodgrass. Tell him he'd best sashay over here right quick and settle this matter once and for all."

"Reckon so," Pa said, and went out the back way. Ma looked at me and sister Susie.

"You kids go out on the porch and keep Grandpa company. See that he stays put 'til the Doc gets here."

"Yessum," said Susie, and we traipsed out of there.

Sure enough, Grandpa set in his rocker, big as life, squinting at cars over the road and watching the drivers cuss when they tried to steer around our hogs.

"Lookee here!" he said, pointing. "See that fat feller in the Hupmobile? He came barreling down the road like a bat outta hell — must of been doing thirty mile an hour. 'Fore he could stop, ol' Bessie poked out of the weeds right in front of him and run that car clean into the ditch. I swear I never seen anything so comical in all my life!"

Susie shook her head. "But you ain't alive, Grandpa."

"Now don't you start in on that again, hear!" Grandpa looked at her, disgusted, and Susie shut up.

Right then Doc Snodgrass come driving up front in his big Essex and parked alongside ol' Bessie's porkbutt. Doc and Pa got out and moseyed up to the porch. They was jawing away something fierce and I could see Doc shaking his head like he purely disbelieved what Pa was telling him.

Then Doc noticed Grandpa setting there, and he stopped cold in his tracks. His eyes bugged out.

"Jumping Jehosephat!" he said to Grandpa. "What you doing here?"

"What's it look like?" Grandpa told him. "Can't a man set on his own front porch and rockify in peace?"

"Rest in peace, that's what you should be doing," said Doc. "When I examined you last night you were deader'n a doornail!"

"And you were drunker'n a coot, I reckon," Grandpa said.

Pa give Doc a nod. "What'd I tell you?"

Doc paid him no heed. He come up to Grandpa. "Mebbe I was a wee bit mistaken," he said. "Mind if I examine you now?"

"Fire away." Grandpa grinned. "I got all the time in the world."

So Doc opened up his little black bag and set about his business. First off he plugged a stethyscope in his ears and tapped Grandpa's chest. He listened, and then his hands begun to shake.

"I don't hear nothing," he said.

"What do you expect to hear — the Grand Ol' Opry?"

"This here's no time for funning," Doc told him. "Suppose I tell you your heart's stopped beating?"

"Suppose I tell you your stethyscope's busted?"

Doc begun to break out in a sweat. He fetched out a mirror and held it up to Grandpa's mouth. Then his hands got to shaking worse than ever.

"See this?" he said. "The mirror's clear. Means you got no breath left in your body."

Grandpa shook his head. "Try it on yourself. You got a breath on you would knock a mule over at twenty paces."

"Mebbe this'll change your tune." Doc reached in his pocket and pulled out a piece of paper. "See for yourself."

"What is it?"

"Your death certificate." Doc jabbed his finger down. "Just you read what it says on this line. 'Cause of death — card-yak arrest.' That's medical for heart attack. And this here's a legal paper. It'll stand up in court."

"So will I, if you want to drag the law into this," Grandpa told him. "Be a pretty sight, too — you standing on one side with your damfool piece of paper and me standing on the other! Now, which do you think the judge is going to believe?"

Doc's eyes bugged out again. He tried to stuff the paper into his pocket but his hands shook so bad he almost didn't make it.

"What's wrong with you?" Pa asked.

"I feel poorly," Doc said. "Got to get back to my office and lie down for a spell."

He picked up his bag and headed for his car, not looking back.

"Don't lie down too long," Grandpa called. "Somebody's liable to write out a paper saying you died of a hangover."

When lunchtime come around nobody was hungry. Nobody but Grandpa, that is.

He set down at the table and put away black-eyed peas, hominy grits, a double helping of chitlins, and two big slabs of rhubarb pie with gravy.

Ma was the kind who liked seeing folks enjoy her vittles, but she didn't look kindly on Grandpa's appetite. After he finished and went back on the porch she stacked the plates on the drainboard and told us kids to clean up. Then she went into the bedroom and come out with her shawl and pocketbook.

"What you all dressed up about?" Pa said.

"I'm going to church."

"But this here's only Thursday."

"Can't wait no longer," Ma told him. "It's been hot all forenoon and looking to get hotter. I seen you wrinkle up your nose whilst Grandpa was in here for lunch."

Pa sort of shrugged. "Figgered the chitlins was mebbe a little bit spoiled, is all."

"Weren't nothing of the sort," Ma said. "If you take my meaning."

"What you fixing to do?"

"Only thing a body can do. I'm putting evvything in the hands of the Lord."

And off she skedaddled, leaving sister Susie and me to scour the dishes whilst Pa went out back, looking powerful troubled. I spied him through the window, slopping the hogs, but you could tell his heart wasn't in it.

Susie and me, we went out to keep tabs on Grandpa.

Ma was right about the weather heating up. That porch was like a bake-oven in the devil's own kitchen. Grandpa didn't seem to pay it any heed, but I did. Couldn't help but notice Grandpa was getting ripe.

"Look at them flies buzzing 'round him," Susie said.

"Hush up, sister. Mind your manners."

But sure enough, them old blueflies buzzed so loud we could hardly hear Grandpa speak. "Hi, young 'uns," he said. "Come visit a spell."

"Sun's too hot for setting," Susie told him.

"Not so's I can notice." He weren't even working up a sweat.

"What about all them blueflies?"

"Don't bother me none." Big ol' fly landed right on Grandpa's nose and he didn't even twitch.

Susie begun to look scared. "He's dead for sure," she said.

"Speak up, child," Grandpa said. "Ain't polite to go mumbling your elders."

Just then he spotted Ma marching up the road. Hot as it was, she come along lickety-split, with the Reverend Peabody in tow. He was huffing and puffing, but she never slowed until they fetched up alongside the front porch.

"Howdy, Reverend," Grandpa sung out.

Reverend Peabody blinked and opened his mouth, but no words come out.

"What's the matter?" Grandpa said. "Cat got your tongue?"

The Reverend got a kind of sick grin on his face, like a skunk eating bumblebees.

"Reckon I know how you feel," Grandpa told him. "Sun makes a feller's throat parch up." He looked at Ma. "Addie, whyn't you go fetch the Reverend a little refreshment?"

Ma went in the house.

"Well now, Rev," said Grandpa. "Rest your britches and be sociable."

The Reverend swallowed hard. "This here's not exactly a social call."

"Then what you come dragging all the way over here for?"

The Reverend swallowed again. "After what Addie and Doc told me, I just had to see for myself." He looked at the flies buzzing around Grandpa. "Now I wish I'd just took their word on it."

"Meaning what?"

"Meaning a man in your condition's got no right to be asking questions. When the good Lord calls, you're supposed to answer."

"I ain't heard nobody calling," Grandpa said. "Course my hearing's not what it used to be."

"So Doc says. That's why you don't notice your heart's not beating."

"Onny natural for it to slow down a piece. I'm pushing ninety."

"Did you ever stop to think that ninety might be pushing back? You lived a mighty long stretch, Grandpa. Don't you reckon mebbe it's time to lie down and call it quits? Remember what the Good Book says — the Lord giveth, and the Lord taketh away."

Grandpa got that feisty look on his face. "Well, he ain't gonna taketh away me."

Reverend Peabody dug into his jeans for a bandanna and wiped his forehead. "You got no cause to fear. It's a mighty rewarding experience. No more sorrow, no more care, all your burdens laid to rest. Not to mention getting out of this hot sun."

"Can't hardly feel it." Grandpa touched his whiskers. "Can't hardly feel anything."

The Reverend give him a look. "Hands getting stiff?"

Grandpa nodded. "I'm stiff all over."

"Just like I thought. You know what that means? Rigor mortis is setting in."

"Ain't never heard tell of anybody named Rigger Morris," Grandpa said. "I got me a touch of the rheumatism, is all."

The Reverend wiped his forehead again. "You sure want a heap of convincing," he said. "Won't take the word of a medical doctor, won't take the word of the Lord. You're the contrariest old coot I ever did see."

"Reckon it's my nature," Grandpa told him. "But I ain't unreasonable. All I'm asking for is proof. Like the feller says, I'm from Missouri. You got to show me."

The Reverend tucked away his bandanna. It was sopping wet anyhow, wouldn't do him a lick of good. He heaved a big sigh and stared Grandpa right in the eye.

"Some things we just got to take on faith," he said. "Like you setting here when by rights you should be six feet under the daisies. If I can believe that, why can't you believe me? I'm telling you the mortal truth when I say you got no call to fuss. Mebbe the notion of lying in the grave don't rightly hold much appeal for you. Well, I can go along with that. But one thing's for sure. Ashes to ashes, dust to dust—that's just a saying. You needn't trouble yourself about spending eternity in the grave. Whilst your remains rest peaceful in the boneyard, your soul is on the wing. Flying straight up, yes-iree, straight into the arms of the Lord! And what a great day it's fixing to be—you free as a bird and scooting around with them heavenly hosts on high, singing the praises of the Almighty and twanging away like all git-out on your genuine eighteen carats solid golden harp—"

"I ain't never been much for music," Grandpa said. "And I get dizzy just standing on a ladder to shingle the privy." He shook his head. "Tell you what—you think heaven is such a hellfired good proposition, why don't you go there yourself?"

Just then Ma come back out. "We're fresh out of lemonade," she said. "All's I could find was a jug. I know your feeling about such things, Reverend, but—"

"Praise the Lord!" The Reverend snatched the jug out of her hand, hefted it up, and took a mighty swallow.

"You're a good woman," he told Ma. "And I'm much beholden to you." Then he started down the path for the road, moving fast.

"Here, now!" Ma called after him. "What you aim to do about Grandpa?"

"Have no fear," the Reverend said. "We must put our trust now in the power of prayer."

He disappeared down the road, stirring dust.

"Danged if he didn't take the jug!" Grandpa mumbled. "You ask me, the onny power he trusts is in that corn-likker."

Ma give him a look. Then she bust out crying and run into the house.

"Now, what got into her?" Grandpa said.

"Never you mind," I told him. "Susie, you stay here and whisk those flies off Grandpa. I got things to attend to."

And I did.

Even before I went inside I had my mind set. I couldn't hold still to see Ma bawling that way. She was standing in the kitchen hanging on to Pa, saying, "What can we do? What can we do?"

Pa patted her shoulder. "There now, Addie, don't you go carrying on. It can't last forever."

"Nor can we," Ma said. "If Grandpa don't come to his senses, one of these mornings we'll go downstairs and serve up breakfast to a skeleton. And what do you think the neighbors will say when they see a bag of bones setting out there on my nice front porch? It's plumb embarrassing, that's what it is!"

"Never you mind, Ma," I said. "I got an idea."

Ma stopped crying. "What kind of idea?"

"I'm fixing to take me a hike over to Spooky Hollow."

"Spooky Hollow?" Ma turned so pale you couldn't even see her freckles. "Oh, no, boy — "

"Help is where you find it," I said. "And I reckon we got no choice."

Pa took a deep breath. "Ain't you afeard?"

"Not in daylight," I told him. "Now don't you fret. I'll be back afore dark."

Then I scooted out the back door.

I went over the fence and hightailed it along the back forty to the crick, stopping just long enough to dig up my piggy-bank from where it was stashed in the weeds alongside the rocks. After that I waded across the water and headed for tall timber.

Once I got into the piney woods I slowed down a smidge to get my bearings. Weren't no path to follow, because nobody never made one. Folks tended to stay clear of there, even in daytimes — it was just too dark and too lonesome. Never saw no small critters in the brush, and even the birds kep' shut of this place.

But I knowed where to go. All's I had to do was top the ridge, then move straight on down. Right smack at the bottom, in the deepest, darkest, lonesomest spot of all, was Spooky Hollow.

In Spooky Hollow was the cave.

And in the cave was the Conjure Lady.

Leastwise I reckoned she was there. But when I come tippy-toeing down to the big black hole in the rocks I didn't see a mortal soul, just the shadows bunching up on me from all around.

It sure was spooky, and no mistake. I tried not to pay any heed to the way my feet was itching. They wanted to turn and run, but I wasn't about to be put off.

After a bit I started to sing out. "Anybody home? You got company."

"Who?"

"It's me—Jody Tolliver."

"Whoooo?"

I was wrong about the birds, because now when I looked up I could see the big screech-owl glaring at me from a branch over yonder near the cave.

And when I looked down again, there she was—the Conjure Lady, peeking out at me from the hole between the rocks.

It was the first time I ever laid eyes on her, but it couldn't be no one else. She was a teensy rail-thin chickabiddy in a linsey-woolsey dress, and the face under her poke-bonnet was black as a lump of coal.

Shucks, I says to myself, there ain't nothing to be afeard of—she's just a little ol' lady, is all.

Then she stared up at me and I saw her eyes. They was lots bigger than the screech-owl's, and twice as glarey.

My feet begun to itch something fierce, but I stared back. "Howdy, Conjure Lady," I said.

"Whoooo?" said the screech-owl.

"It's young Tolliver," the Conjure Lady told him. "What's the matter, you got wax in your ears? Now go on about your business, you hear?"

The screech-owl give her a dirty look and took off. Then the Conjure Lady come out into the open.

"Pay no heed to Ambrose," she said. "He ain't rightly used to company. All's he ever sees is me and the bats."

"What bats?"

"The bats in the cave." The Conjure Lady smoothed down her dress. "I beg pardon for not asking you in, but the place is purely a mess. Been meaning to tidy it up, but what with one thing ard another—first that dadblamed World War and then this dadgummed Proh oition—I just ain't got round to it yet."

"Never you mind," I said, polite-like. "I come on business."

"Reckoned you did."

"Brought you a pretty, too." I give it to her.

"What is it?"

"My piggy-bank."

"Thank you kindly," said the Conjure Lady.

"Go ahead, bust it open," I told her.

She whammed it down on a rock and the piggy-bank broke, spilling out money all over the place. She scrabbled it up right quick.

"Been putting aside my cash earnings for nigh onto two years now," I said. "How much is they?"

"Eighty-seven cents, a Confederate two-bits piece, and this here button." She kind of grinned. "Sure is a purty one, too! What's it say on there?"

"Keep Cool With Coolidge."

"Well, ain't that a caution." The Conjure Lady slid the money into her pocket and pinned the button atop her dress. "Now, son—purty is as purty does, like the saying goes. So what can I do for you?"

"It's about my Grandpa," I said. "Grandpa Titus Tolliver."

"Titus Tolliver? Why, I reckon I know him! Use to run a still up in the toolies back of the crick. Fine figure of a man with a big black beard, he is."

"Is turns to was," I told her. "Now he's all dried up with the rheumatiz. Can't rightly see too good and can't hear for sour apples."

"Sure is a crying shame!" the Conjure Lady said. "But sooner or later we all get to feeling poorly. And when you gotta go, you gotta go."

"That's the hitch of it. He won't go."

"Meaning he's bound-up?"

"Meaning he's dead."

The Conjure Lady give me a hard look. "Do tell," she said.

So I told her. Told her the whole kit and kaboodle, right from the git-go.

She heard me out, not saying a word. And when I finished up she just stared at me until I was fixing to jump out of my skin.

"I reckon you mightn't believe me," I said. "But it's the gospel truth."

The Conjure Lady shook her head. "I believe you, son. Like I say, I knowed your Grandpappy from the long-ago. He was plumb set in his ways then, and I take it he still is. Sounds to me like he's got a bad case of the stubborns."

"Could be," I said. "But there's nary a thing we can do about it, nor the Doc or the Reverend either."

The Conjure Lady wrinkled up her nose. "What you 'spect from them two? They don't know grit from granola."

"Mebbe so. But that leaves us betwixt a rock and a hard place—'less you can help."

"Let me think on it a piece."

The Conjure Lady pulled a corncob out of her pocket and fired up. I don't know what brand she smoked, but it smelled something fierce. I begun to get itchy again—not just in the feet but all over. The woods was darker now, and a kind of cold wind come wailing down between the trees, making the leaves whisper to themselves.

"Got to be some way," I said. "A charm, mebbe, or a spell."

She shook her head. "Them's ol'-fashioned. Now this here's one of them newfangled mental things, so we got to use newfangled idees. Your Grandpa don't need hex nor hoodoo. Like he says, he's from Missouri. He got to be showed, is all."

"Showed what?"

The Conjure Lady let out a cackle. "I got it!" She give me a wink. "Sure 'nough, the very thing! Now just you hold your water—I won't be a moment." And she scooted back into the cave.

I stood there, feeling the wind whooshing down the back of my neck and listening to the leaves that was like voices whispering things I didn't want to hear too good.

Then she come out again, holding something in her hand.

"Take this," she said.

"What is it?"

She told me what it was, and then she told me what to do with it.

"You really reckon this'll work?"

"It's the onny chance."

So I stuck it in my britches pocket and she give me a little poke. "Now sonny, you best hurry and git home afore supper."

Nobody had to ask me twice—not with that chill wind moaning and groaning in the trees, and the dark creeping and crawling all around me.

I give her my much-obliged and lit out, leaving the Conjure Lady standing in front of the cave. Last I saw of her she was polishing her Coolidge button with a hunk of poison oak.

Then I was tearing through the woods, up the hill to the ridge and over. By the time I got to the clearing it was pitch-dark, and when I waded the crick I could see the moonlight wiggling on the water. Hawks on the hover went flippy-flapping over the back forty but I didn't stop to heed. I made a beeline for the fence, up and over, then into the yard and through the back door.

Ma was standing at the stove holding a pot whilst Pa ladled up the soup. They looked downright pleasured to see me.

"Thank the Lord!" Ma said. "I was just fixing to send Pa after you."

"I come quick as I could."

"And none too soon," Pa told me. "We like to go clean out'n our heads, what with the ruckus and all."

"What kind of ruckus?"

"First off, Mis Francy. Folks in town told her about Grandpa passing on, so she done the neighborly thing—mixed up a mess of stew to ease our appeytite in time of sorrow. She come lollygagging up the walk, all rigged out in her Sunday go-to-meeting clothes, toting the bowl under her arm and looking like lard wouldn't melt in her mouth. Along about then she caught sight of Grandpa setting there on the porch, kind of smiling at her through the flies.

"Well, up went the bowl and down come the whole shebang. Looked like it was raining stew-greens all over that fancy Sears and Roebuck dress. And then she turned and headed for kingdom come, letting out a whoop that'd peel the paint off a privy wall."

"That's sorrowful," I said.

"Save your grieving for worse," Pa told me. "Next thing you know, Bixbee showed up, honking his horn. Wouldn't come nigh Grandpa, nosiree—I had to traipse clear down to where he set in the hearse."

"What'd he want?"

"Said he'd come for the remains. And if we didn't cough them up right fast, he was aiming to take a trip over to the county seat first thing tomorrow morning to get hisself a injection."

"Injunction," Ma said, looking like she was ready to bust out with the bawls again. "Said it was a scandal and a shame to let Grandpa set around like this. What with the sun and the flies and all, he was fixing to have the Board of Health put us under quar-and-tine."

"What did Grandpa say?" I asked.

"Nary a peep. Ol' Bixbee gunned his hearse out of here and Grandpa kep' right on rocking with Susie. She come in 'bout half hour ago, when the sun went down—says he's getting stiff as a board but won't pay it no heed. Just keeps asking what's to eat."

"That's good," I said. "On account of I got the very thing. The Conjure Lady give it to me for his supper."

"What is it—pizen?" Pa looked worried. "You know I'm a God-fearing man and I don't hold with such doings. 'Sides, how you 'spect to pizen him if he's already dead?"

"Ain't nothing of the sort," I said. "This here's what she sent."

And I pulled it out of my britches pocket and showed it to them.

"Now what in the name of kingdom come is that?" Ma asked.

I told her what it was, and what to do with it.

"Ain't never heard tell of such foolishness in all my born days!" Ma told me.

Pa looked troubled in his mind. "I knowed I shouldn't have let you go down to Spooky Hollow. Conjure Lady must be short of her marbles, putting you up to a thing like that."

"Reckon she knows what she's doing," I said. " 'Sides, I give all my savings for this here—eighty-seven cents, a Confederate quarter, and my Coolidge button."

"Never you mind about no Coolidge button," Pa said. "I swiped it off'n a Yankee, anyway—one of them revenooers." He scratched his chin. "But hard money's something else. Mebbe we best give this notion a try."

"Now, Pa—" Ma said.

"You got any better plan?" Pa shook his head. "Way I see it, what with the Board of Health set to come a-snapping at our heels tomorrow, we got to take a chance."

Ma fetched a sigh that come clean up from her shoes, or would of it she'd been wearing any.

"All right, Jody," she told me. "You just put it out like the Conjure Lady said. Pa, you go fetch Susie and Grandpa. I'm about to dish up."

"You sure this'll do the trick?" Pa asked, looking at what I had in my hand.

"It better," I said. "It's all we got."

So Pa went out and I headed for the table, to do what the Conjure Lady had in mind.

Then Pa come back with sister Susie.

"Where's Grandpa?" Ma asked.

"Moving slow," Susie said. "Must be that Rigger Morris."

"No such thing." Grandpa come through the doorway, walking like a cockroach on a hot griddle. "I'm just a wee mite stiff."

"Stiff as a four-by-four board," Pa told him. "Upstairs in bed, that's where you ought to be, with a lily in your hand."

"Now don't start on that again," Grandpa said. "I told you I ain't dead so many times I'm blue in the face."

"You sure are," said sister Susie. "Ain't never seen nobody look any bluer."

And he was that—blue and bloated, kind of—but he paid it no heed. I recollected what Ma said about mebbe having to put up with a skeleton at mealtime, and I sure yearned for the Conjure Lady's notion to work. It plumb had to, because Grandpa was getting deader by the minute.

But you wouldn't think so when he caught sight of the vittles on the table. He just stirred his stumps right over to his chair and plunked down.

"Well, now," Grandpa said. "You done yourself proud tonight, Addie. This here's my favorite—collards and catfish heads!"

He was all set to take a swipe at the platter when he up and noticed what was setting next to his plate.

"Great day in the morning!" he hollered. "What in tarnation's this?"

"Ain't nothing but a napkin," I said.

"But it's black!" Grandpa blinked. "Who ever heard tell of a black napkin?"

Pa looked at Ma. "We figger this here's kind of a special occasion," he said. "If you take my meaning—"

Grandpa fetched a snort. "Consarn you and your meaning! A black napkin? Never you fear, I know what you're hinting around at, but it ain't a-gonna work—nosiree, bub!"

And he filled his plate and dug in.

The rest of us just set there staring, first at Grandpa, then at each other.

"What'd I tell you?" Pa said to me, disgusted-like.

I shook my head. "Wait a spell."

"Better grab whilst you can git," Grandpa said. "I aim to eat me up a storm."

And he did. His arms was stiff and his fingers scarce had enough curl left to hold a fork and his jaw-muscles worked extra hard—but he went right on eating. And talking.

"Dead, am I? Ain't never seen the day a body'd say a thing like that to me before, let alone kinfolk! Now could be I'm tolerable stubborn, but that don't signify I'm mean. I ain't about to make trouble for anyone, least of all my own flesh and blood. If I was truly dead and knowed it for a fact — why, I'd be the first one to go right upstairs to my room and lie down forever. But you got to show me proof 'fore I do. That's the pure and simple of it — let me see some proof!"

"Grandpa," I said.

"What's the matter, sonny?"

"Begging your pardon, but you got collards dribbling all over your chin."

Grandpa put down his fork. "So they is. I thank you kindly."

And before he rightly knowed what he was doing, Grandpa wiped his mouth on the napkin.

When he finished he looked down at it. He looked once and he looked twice. Then he just set the napkin down gentle-like, stood up from the table, and headed straight for the stairs.

"Goodbye all," he said.

We heard him go clumping up the steps and down the hall into his room and we heard the mattress sag when he laid down on his bed.

Then everything was quiet.

After a while Pa pushed his chair back and went upstairs. Nobody said a word until he come down again.

"Well?" Ma looked at him.

"Ain't nothing more to worry about," Pa said. "He's laid down his burden at last. Gone to glory, amen."

"Praise be!" Ma said. Then she looked at me and crooked a finger at the napkin. "Best get rid of that."

I went round and picked it up. Sister Susie give me a funny look. "Ain't nobody fixing to tell me what happened?" she asked.

I didn't answer — just toted the napkin out and dropped it deep down in the crick. Weren't no sense telling anybody the how of it, but the Conjure Lady had the right notion after all. She knowed Grandpa'd get his proof — just as soon as he wiped his mouth.

Ain't nothing like a black napkin to show up a little ol' white maggot.

CROOK OF THE MONTH

EDISON WAS RIGHT.

Genius is 1% inspiration and 99% perspiration.

But Jerry Cribbs couldn't find the proper deodorant.

He started sweating long before the plane touched down in the Rio dawn, and continued all through Customs inspection. But the black bag preserved its secret, and he hugged it in his lap during the long taxi ride to his Copacabana hotel. Anyone who survives a cab trip through Rio de Janeiro traffic is entitled to feel relieved, but by the time Jerry checked into his room he was perspiring again. And a shower didn't help, even though he took the bag into the stall with him.

Jerry dried off, only to find himself wringing wet again in the few moments it took him to dress and shave. Then he sat soaking and waiting for the phone to ring. He held the black bag on his lap, hugging his secret — and his genius — to him for reassurance.

Why didn't the call come?

A knock on the door answered his question. Of course they'd never risk using the telephone; they'd rely on personal contact.

Or would they?

Jerry shoved the black bag under the bed and moved to the door.

A soft voice from the hall outside murmured, "Mr. Cribbs?"

Jerry flinched. He'd registered downstairs as Mr. Brown, figuring that any alias good enough for the late Al Capone should be good enough for him. And yet the stranger beyond the door knew his name. In a way this was reassuring, but he had to make certain.

"Who sent you?" he whispered.

"The Big Bird."

With a sigh of relief, Jerry opened the door.

A baldheaded black giant entered, nodding curtly. He was dressed in the ornate uniform of a Brazilian general or chauffeur—it didn't matter which, because the Big Bird could have sent either if he chose.

"Come with me, please," said the giant.

Jerry turned and started out, but a hand gripped his shoulder.

"Aren't you forgetting something?" the giant asked.

"Sorry." Jerry stooped and retrieved the black bag from its hiding place beneath the bed. The giant reached for it but Jerry shook his head.

"I'll carry this," he said.

The giant shrugged. "As you wish." He followed Jerry through the doorway and down the hall. He didn't speak in the elevator or in the lobby below, and his silence continued as he led Jerry to the huge limousine parked insolently on the sidewalk outside the entrance.

Jerry slid into the back seat and his escort got behind the wheel.

If Jerry had any doubts about the black giant being a chauffeur, they were quickly dispelled as the car weaved through Rio's noonday traffic—from the way he drove, the man was obviously a general.

Once aboard the waiting launch at the wharf he proved himself to be an admiral too. The boat raced off across the harbor and out into the open sea while Jerry crouched in the bow with the black bag between his trembling knees.

The long, sleek lines of the yacht loomed ahead, bobbing in the swell. As they pulled astern Jerry looked up at the gold-leaf lettering which identified the vessel as *The Water Closet*.

The black giant killed the engine and rose, cupping his hands. "Ahoy there!" he called.

A bearded seaman peered down from the deck above and shook his head.

"Sorry," he said. "Ahoy's not on duty today. I'm in charge."

"Never mind," the black man muttered. "Let down the ladder."

Climbing a rope ladder while holding the handle of the black bag in his teeth wasn't easy, but Jerry managed it. Once on deck he heaved a sigh of relief.

The black giant stepped before him and beckoned.

"This way," he commanded. "And take that bag out of your mouth."

"Oh, yeah—" Jerry nodded and complied.

Clutching the bag, he followed his guide along the deck, past the elegant array of staterooms; past the sauna, the private projection room, the bowling alley. And there, just beyond the outdoor bar, was the Olympic-size swimming pool.

"He's expecting you," said the black man.

Jerry squinted down at the pool. Over the stereophonic screech of raucous rock rose the shrill shrieks from the pool, where a half-dozen figures splashed and sported, stark-naked in the sunlight.

Jerry had no trouble recognizing his host; he was the only male.

"Mr. Buzzard?" he murmured.

The scrawny, balding little man climbed out of the water, scowling against the sun as a waiting attendant instantly draped a gold lamé robe over his shoulders.

The Big Bird nodded. "I'm Al Buzzard," he said. "You've met my wife." He gestured vaguely toward the naked naiades giggling in the pool.

"Oh — sure — "

"Come on, then." Al Buzzard held out both hands. The alert attendant placed a frosted full triple-martini glass in one of the hands and a lighted Upmann in the other; then Buzzard turned and led Jerry aft.

From the looks of the stateroom they entered, with its mirrored walls and ceiling and king-size circular bed covered with leopard skin, Jerry at once deduced that he was in the Captain's cabin.

The scrawny man closed the door. With a lightning gesture he disposed of his drink, then set the empty glass down on the mink carpet. He sprawled back on the bed, puffing his cigar and staring moodily at his visitor.

"Did you ever have one of those days when nothing seems to go right?" he sighed. "Just look at that!" He gestured toward the empty glass. "A triple martini with only two olives in it! As soon as we get out into international waters, remind me to have the bartender keelhauled."

"Really, Mr. Buzzard, it isn't all that bad — "

"Hah!" Buzzard snorted and sat up. "You sound just like Barabass."

"Barabass?"

"My publisher. He was out here last week. Somehow we got into a conversation during the orgy and he said to me, 'Why don't you look on the bright side of things for a change? After all, you're the world's most popular author, next to Conway Mann, that is. Ten all-time bestsellers, eight blockbuster movies, a hit television series that lasted almost an entire season — what more do you want? Why, your name is a household word — like Drano, or Sani-Flush.' That's what he told me."

"Well, it's true, isn't it?"

"No — it's a damnable lie! I'm much more popular than Con Mann. Him and his sexy romances — why, I knew him when he didn't have a plot to kiss in!"

"But you're rich and famous — " Jerry gestured at the mirrored walls. "You live on this big yacht, you have a lovely wife and — "

Buzzard shrugged. "Boats make me seasick. I have to stay on board because the minute I set foot on land the IRS will lay a suit on me for thirty-three million dollars in back taxes. And my wife isn't all that lovely — the first nine were much more attractive. Trouble is, none of them could understand me. This one doesn't understand me, and neither do any of my mistresses. The shrinks all tell me we don't have the right chemistry. So what am I supposed to do about that — go and study to be a chemist at my age?"

Sighing wearily, Buzzard rose and threw his cigar out of a porthole. When he turned back he was different man; his shoulders straightened beneath the gold lamé robe and his beady eyes matched its glitter.

"Now, to business," he said. "Have you got it?"

"It's in the bag."

Jerry held out the black, bulging bulk and Buzzard's twitching fingers closed around the handle. He carried it to the bed and scrabbled at the lock.

"The key, man!" he panted. "Where's the key?"

Silently, Jerry rolled up his trouser leg and ripped the adhesive tape from his right ankle, revealing the tiny instrument. He handed it to Buzzard, who inserted it in the lock with a vicious twisting motion. The black bag sprang open and its contents tumbled out onto the leopard skin coverlet.

Buzzard stared down at the bed, rubbing his hands together.

"How many pages?" he whispered.

"Three hundred."

"It's all there, then?"

"All but the last chapter. I expected to finish by the end of next week, but then your wire came — "

"You can knock off the ending when you get back," Buzzard said. "Just so's I get the whole thing to the publisher by the end of the month. We gotta hit the fall list before that nerd of a Conway Mann beats us to it. I hear he's got a big one coming up, but we'll show him." He paused, eyeing Jerry suspiciously. "It *is* a goodie, isn't it?"

"I think so."

"Think? I'm not paying you to think — I'm paying you to write." Buzzard made a face. "It damn well better be good. After all, I've got a reputation to live down to."

"Don't worry, Mr. Buzzard. Just read it and you'll see for yourself."

"Yeah, yeah — later sometime." Al Buzzard gathered up the pages, hefting their bulk. "Feels nice and thick, anyhow. Barabass likes 'em that way." He frowned. "Where's the carbon?"

"Home, in the safe."

"Good." Buzzard nodded. "Speaking of home, we better get you on the next flight outta here. I'd invite you to stay for lunch, but seeing as how you still have a chapter to go there's no sense wasting time. Besides, you can grab a sannich or something on the plane, right? So let's get moving — "

"Uh — aren't you forgetting something, Mr. Buzzard?"

Buzzard scowled. "I know. That's the difference between guys like you and a creative artist like I am. All you writers ever think about is money."

Sighing, he reached under the bed and pulled out a large locked metal box. "Okay, if that's the way you want it."

He fiddled with the combination until the box flew open, cascading a heap of glittering objects over the bed.

"Godfrey Daniel!" he muttered. "I told you this wasn't my day. Wrong box — I got the diamonds by mistake!"

Buzzard stooped and fumbled until he found a second metal container identical with the first. When its tumblers clicked and the lid rose, Jerry stared down at the stacks of currency.

"Petty cash," Buzzard explained. "Only fifties and hundreds." He extracted a wad of bills and began to count. "Let's see, now — three hundred pages at ten dollars a page — "

"You promised me fifteen this time, Mr. Buzzard."

"Oh — yeah — fifteen times three hundred — "

"Forty-five hundred," said Jerry.

"What's the matter, don't you think I know how to count?" Scowling, Buzzard thrust a sheaf of currency into Jerry's hands. "That's a lot of loot, fella. If you ask me, you're being overpaid."

"But it took me almost six months to write the book, Mr. Buzzard. Why, nowadays, a plumber can make that much in three weeks."

"So take some of the money and study plumbing," Al Buzzard told him. "Just so you finish up that last chapter first. Hey, there's an idea. If you got a pencil and paper, maybe you can write it on the plane."

But Jerry Cribbs did no writing on the return flight. Instead he brooded.

The plane slipped between the crowded peaks, picked a few air pockets above Latin America, then sped like a thief up the Atlantic Coast. And when it landed at Kennedy, Jerry was still brooding.

"Darling — what's the matter?"

Jerry halted at the terminal exit and stared down at Ann Remington's troubled face.

Then he kissed it. "I'll tell you later, after we get out of here."

Thanks to the marvels of modern technology, Jerry got through Customs and into Ann's car and out of the airport and through the city traffic in less time than it had taken him to fly from South America, though not much.

And it was in the car that he finally unburdened himself. "Don't you see?" he sighed. "It's the same old story."

"But it's a *good* story," Ann said. "I was reading one of your carbons, just last night. I like that hero of yours, Lance Pustule. And having him murder his parents at the age of eight — it's going to win a lot of reader sympathy, because everybody has a kindly feeling for orphans."

"Ann, please — "

"That scene where he's raped by his grandmother is terrific! And all those killings and tortures he uses to get control of the television network — you really tell it like it is! The drugs and violence and kinky sex are dynamite. By the way, what's the title of the book?"

"THE ARISTOCRATS."

"Perfect!"

Jerry shook his head. "Al Buzzard pays me forty-five hundred dollars for ghostwriting a book that will make him millions. What's so perfect about that? All he does is sit on his big fat yacht, divorcing wives and having affairs with movie stars and throwing fashion models overboard—"

"But that's why he gets all that money," Ann said. "Doing those things makes him a celebrity. His life style is front-page news, so when he writes a book, that's news too."

"Only he doesn't write any books. *I* do, and can't even earn enough for us to get married." Jerry sighed. "If I could just write my own book, under my own name—"

"Why don't you?"

"Because I can't find the time, or the money."

Ann smiled. "We could manage. There's my secretary job at the travel agency."

"I'm not going to live off your salary, and that's final."

Ann's smile faded as she gripped the steering wheel and swung the car toward the curb in front of the dingy, run-down apartment building where Jerry spent his dingy, run-down life.

"I don't understand you," she murmured. "How can a man who writes such trendy modern porn have such old-fashioned ideas?"

"Because I *am* old-fashioned." Jerry lugged his bags out of the car. "And when I do write my book, it isn't going to be trendy, either. A good novel doesn't need all that cheap sensationalism." Ann started to get out of the car, but he checked her with a gesture. "Sorry, but you'd better not come up with me. I have to get to work on that last chapter right away. The big identity-crisis scene when Lance finally discovers where his head is at—he gets rid of his wife and girlfriend and becomes a child-molester—"

"Then when will I see you?"

"I should have everything wrapped up by tomorrow night. Suppose you come around and we'll have dinner together then. Make it about seven."

They clung together for a moment; then Ann drove away and Jerry hastened upstairs to commit a statutory offense on paper.

Neither of them noticed the cross-eyed little man crouching behind the pillars before the apartment-house entryway. He stared after them—one eye following Ann's car as it moved away down the street, and the other eye on Jerry as he disappeared into the building.

"Seven o'clock," the little man whispered. "Tomorrow night."

It had been a good day's work, Jerry decided. Three thousand words, many of which were four-letter; twelve pages of solid hard-core sex and violence. Al Buzzard and his readers would be happy, and Jerry was satisfied with a dishonest job, raw but well-done.

He showered, shaved and dressed, and when the doorbell rang shortly before seven he was ready to answer its summons.

Jerry lifted the latch and the door swung open.

"Ann—" he said.

"Wrong." The little cross-eyed man stood in the doorway staring him up and down simultaneously.

Jerry frowned, perplexed. "Who are you?"

"Sorry, no time for introductions." The little man moved past him into the apartment. "You're coming with me."

"Now wait a minute—"

"I don't have a minute." The intruder crooked a commanding finger. "Let's go."

"No way," said Jerry, eyeing the stranger. Whoever he was and whatever he wanted, Jerry had no intention of being pushed around by this cross-eyed little character.

He turned, and that was his mistake.

Because a big man, who wasn't cross-eyed at all, loomed up in the doorway behind him, raising a rubber truncheon.

As the weapon descended on Jerry's skull the little man, with a mighty effort, focused his eyes on his wristwatch, then nodded approvingly.

"Six forty-nine," he said. "Right on schedule."

"Yah," said the big man, who was presently preoccupied by the task of stuffing Jerry's limp form into a large gunnysack. Grunting, he swung the sack up over his shoulder and carried it down the hall to the backstairs exit of the building.

The little man followed and they descended the steps together.

The big man scowled at him apprehensively. *"Mach schnell,"* he panted. "Maybe somebody sees us."

"Don't worry." The little man nodded. "It's in the bag."

In the bag was no place to be, and when Jerry recovered consciousness he wanted out.

Voicing these sentiments through a mouthful of burlap, he was conscious of a shuddering drone and a sound like far-off thunder, gradually fading.

Then a knife slashed through the cloth above his head, the gunnysack shredded and fell in folds about his shoulders, and Jerry emerged. He wobbled to his feet, blinking at his surroundings.

He stood in the capacious cabin of a private plane—a Lear jet, from the looks of it. Only a man wealthy enough to own such an aircraft could afford to decorate its interior with the original artwork exhibited on these walls.

Jerry recognized a Renoir, a Picasso, a Modigliani. And then, turning toward the far end of the cabin, he recognized the owner of the paintings.

There was no mistaking the identity of the bearded figure seated behind the ornate Chippendale desk, wearing an incongruously-crumpled hat and peering at him through tinted glasses. The face would be instantly familiar to anyone who had ever watched a television talk show, interview program, or *Bowling for Dollars*.

"Conway Mann!" gasped Jerry.

The bearded author nodded. His pudgy hand waved in imperious dismissal, banishing the cross-eyed minion and his sap-swinging accomplice from the confines of the cabin. Then he smiled and beckoned Jerry to a Heppelwhite chair before the desk.

"Welcome to my humble digs," he said. "I trust you'll excuse the crudity of my invitation, but I really had to see you, Mr. Gibbs."

"Cribbs," Jerry murmured.

"Exactly." The pudgy hand investigated the contents of a desk drawer, emerging with a fistful of yellow pills which disappeared between Conway Mann's bearded lips. He gulped and nodded. "I suppose you're wondering what brought you here."

"I already know," said Jerry. "Two goons and a gunnysack."

"My dear Hibbs —"

"Cribbs."

"Ah yes." The hand fumbled in the drawer once more, then rose to extend a crumpled sheet of paper. "Please be good enough to read this proof of an advertisement scheduled to appear in *Publishers Weekly*. I think it may interest you."

Jerry stared down at the bold lettering of the full-page ad.

SHOCKING! SCANDALOUS!
SENSATIONAL!

Searing sex . . . vicious violence . . . raw and raunchy . . . a novel that rips aside the last shreds of convention to reveal the hidden world of secret passions and unbridled lusts behind the locked doors of America's power-mad masters . . . as they move from boardroom to bedroom in their savage search for forbidden pleasures! Don't miss

THE TASTE-MAKERS
by
CONWAY MANN
The bestselling blockbuster of the year from
SCRIBBLER'S & SONS

Jerry put the ad down on the desk-top. "Your new novel?"

"Precisely so."

"What's it about?"

Conway Mann shrugged. "That's up to you. Because you're going to write it."

"Now hold on —"

"I am holding on, Mr. Dribbs. But I can't hold on much longer. The manuscript is due at the publisher's office by month's end."

"Let me get this straight. You mean to say you don't write your own books?"

"Why should that surprise you? That wretched Al Buzzard doesn't write his novels either."

"Then you know — ?"

"Of course. Why else would I bring you here?" Conway Mann shook his head. "Don't get me wrong. I'm perfectly capable of doing the job myself, but lately I've suffered from a writer's block."

"When did it start?"

"In 1959." The pudgy hand popped red capsules into its owner's mouth. "Besides, I have a full schedule of commitments ahead of me — Johnny Carson, Merv Griffin, *Hollywood Squares* — we bestselling authors must live up to our responsibilities, even at the sacrifice of the creative impulse. And that's where you come in."

"That's where I get out," Jerry told him.

"At forty thousand feet in the air?" Conway Mann shrugged again. "Very well, suit yourself. But watch that first step — it's a gasser."

"Now see here — you kidnapped me! That's a federal offense. I can push charges."

"You can push up daisies, if you refuse."

"But why me?" Jerry said. "Surely you must have a regular ghost writer of your own. What happened to him?"

"He refused," Conway Mann murmured softly. "Would you like to see where he's buried?"

Conway Mann wasn't conning. With his royalties and reputation at stake he might very well carry out his threat. And when his hand descended again to the desk drawer, Jerry fully expected it to reappear holding a revolver.

Instead it clutched a bundle of bills.

"Money talks," said the bearded man. "Six thousand, in advance."

"Six thousand?"

"That's more than you get from that chintzy Al Buzzard, if reports from my spies are correct." The pudgy hand extended. "Now take it and get out. You've got a deadline to meet."

"But I couldn't possibly write an entire novel by the end of the month," Jerry said.

"You can and you will," Conway Mann told him. "Unless you're awfully fond of daisies."

Jerry pocketed the bills; no easy task for trembling hands. "I'll try," he said. "Only you haven't told me what the book will be about."

"Ninety thousand words, that's what it's about." Conway Mann gestured at the proof sheet on the desk-top. "This ad doesn't bother mentioning anything about a plot, so you can suit yourself. You know what the readers expect. Behind the scenes in politics and big business, and the farther behind the better. Maybe a touch of necrophilia in San Francisco, a Black Mass at the U.N., orgies in the White House — I leave it to your discretion."

Jerry took a deep breath. "I'll do my best."

"Your best isn't good enough," Conway Mann said. "I want you to do your worst."

He rose and came around the desk, glancing at his watch. "I'll tell the pilot to take us down, and the boys will see to it that you get home safely."

"That's not necessary."

"I think it is." Conway Mann's eyes narrowed behind the tinted lenses. "They're going to be keeping tabs on you from now on until the book is finished."

"And if it isn't — ?"

"Then they'll finish you."

"I'm not afraid of your threats," Jerry said. "I can call the police — "

"That's already been taken care of. Your phone is dead. And unless you want to follow its example, you'll stay in your apartment from tonight until the manuscript is in the hands of my publishers." Conway Mann put his hand on Jerry's shoulder and smiled. "If you want to stay healthy, learn a lesson from the flowers. Daisies don't tell."

It was good advice, but Jerry couldn't take it. Not when he found Ann waiting for him outside the apartment door.

"It's after nine o'clock!" she told him. "I've been waiting here for two hours. Where on earth have you been?"

"I wasn't exactly on earth," Jerry said, glancing over his shoulder toward the car from which he'd emerged. The headlights glared, the motor growled, and its sleek black length crouched at the curb like a panther waiting to spring.

Ann followed his gaze, noting the big man behind the wheel and his small companion seated beside him.

"Who are those two nerds — Sonny and Cher?"

"Please, darling, come inside." Jerry gripped her arm and drew her through the doorway. "I can explain everything."

"It better be good."

But once inside the apartment, it wasn't good.

"Not good at all," Ann said, after she'd listened to Jerry's account of the evening. "It took you months to knock out the novel for Buzzard. And now this Conway Mann expects you to do the job for him in a couple of weeks!"

"Impossible." Jerry nodded. "But there's no way out."

"Not for you," Ann said. "But I'm free to come and go."

"Meaning—?"

"It's simple." Ann smiled. "I'm going to leave now. The minute I get home I'll put through a call to the police. They'll get over here, you tell them what happened, and you're home free."

"Dynamite!"

Ann smiled reassuringly as she moved to the door and opened it quickly. Then her smile faded as the dynamite exploded in her face.

The little man stood in the doorway, cross-eyes bulging. There was another ominous bulge where his hand rested in his pocket.

"I heard what you just said, lady. But nobody's calling the fuzz."

Ann stared at him. "You mean you intend to keep me locked up here with Jerry?"

The cross-eyed man shook his head. "I didn't say that. Somebody's got to go for groceries and it might as well be you. But whenever you cut out, I go with you. And my buddy downstairs keeps an eye on your boyfriend. Boss's orders."

Jerry faced him, frowning. "He thinks of everything, doesn't he?"

"You better believe it." The little man gave him a crooked smile. "Time for you to start thinking too, fella. You got a book to write."

The days that followed moved in a blinding blur. Ann spent most of her time in the living room, while the typewriter pounded away behind the bedroom door. Sometimes she read, sometimes she watched television, sometimes she just stood at the window and stared down at the immobile black limousine. On occasion she took brief walks or shopped at the supermarket, but always under escort. She didn't talk to the little man and he didn't talk to her. She scarcely talked to Jerry when he came out of the bedroom for meals.

One look at his haggard face told the story. He was racing the deadline, racing for his life, and she resolved not to bug him with questions.

But as the end of the month inched closer there came a moment when she could keep silent no longer.

They were seated at the kitchen table, over coffee, and the sight of Jerry's gaunt features and glassy stare was too much for Ann to bear. From her lips burst the age-old question, the question every writer dreads.

"How's it going?" she said.

Jerry shook his head.

"It isn't," he muttered.

"You mean you won't finish in time?"

"I haven't started."

"Haven't started?" Ann frowned. "But you've been in there typing night and day—"

"I type at night because I can't sleep. And I can't sleep because of what I type during the day. Page after page of new beginnings — none of them make sense, and all of them go into the wastebasket. I'm afraid it's finally happened. Just the way it did to Al Buzzard, and Conway Mann."

"What are you talking about?"

"When they started, they wrote their own stuff. Then, gradually, it got to them. No man can stand such a pace forever — a daily diet of corruption, brutality, mayhem, incest, voyeurism, sadomasochistic satyriasis, and all the other things that are so hard to spell. So they hired ghost writers, people like myself. Trouble is, now the same thing is happening to me." Jerry raised his anguished face. "All those rapes and murders — it's just too much! Even Jack the Ripper had to quit in the end."

Ann rose and moved to the stricken man. "Listen to me," she said softly. "It's not that bad. You did finish Buzzard's book, and all you have to do is get the last chapter over to the publisher. So half your problem is already solved. If you can only go on a little longer, until you do Conway Mann's novel—"

"Don't you understand?" Jerry slammed a clenched fist on the table. "It's too late now. Even if I stayed at the typewriter twenty-four hours a day, I'd never beat the deadline. There isn't time."

Ann sighed, turned, and made her way into the living room. Jerry followed. Together they stared out of the window, stared down at the street where the big black car crouched and waited. Neither of them said a word; no words were necessary. And words wouldn't help now — unless Jerry could put ninety thousand of them down on paper in the next three days.

It was Ann who broke the silence, her face and voice thoughtful.

"Maybe it's all for the best," she said.

"What do you mean?"

"Even if you could have finished on time, it wouldn't help. At first I hoped this would be a blessing in disguise. Forty-five hundred from Al Buzzard and six thousand from Conway Mann — that's ten thousand five hundred dollars in cash, enough to live on until you realized your ambition. With that much money you could finally write a novel of your own. But it doesn't matter now, does it? If you say you can't write any more—"

"I never said that!" Jerry gripped her hands tightly with his own. "All I said is that I couldn't turn out any more sex and violence. The novel I want to write is different. No sensationalism, no cheap anti-heroes, no rip-off of celebrities disguised under other names. My book would be about ordinary people, coping with everyday problems that all of us have to face."

"But would such a book sell?"

There was doubt in Ann's voice, but none in Jerry's. "Why not? At least I'd give the readers some reality, something to think about and remember. Those porno fairy tales Buzzard and Mann are credited with are just the same thing repeated over and over again — you couldn't really tell one from another, in the long run. I'm talking about real literature."

Ann eyed him dubiously. "How could you promote it?"

"An honest book doesn't need promotion," Jerry told her. "A good writer needs no notoriety. Think about it — did Thackeray have a yacht? Did Henry James wear a funny hat and fly around in a Lear jet? Did Jane Austen sleep around? Did Shakespeare ever appear on a late-night talk show?"

"I am thinking about it," Ann told him. An odd note crept into her voice. "Jerry, do me a favor. Come into the bedroom with me for a minute."

Jerry hesitated. "What did you have in mind?"

"Come along." Ann turned. "I want you to show me where you keep your files."

Together they moved into the bedroom. "Right here in this cabinet," Jerry said.

"I see." But Ann's glance strayed from the filing cabinet to Jerry's desk — the typewriter, the paper, the carbons resting under a heavy paperweight. Her eyes narrowed. "Jerry — about this book of yours. You really want to write it?"

"More than anything in the world."

"And you're sure it could sell?"

Jerry nodded, then turned away. "If I'm wrong, may I be struck dead on the spot."

It was then that Ann hit him with the paperweight.

"Dead," Jerry mumbled. "Well, I asked for it — "

"Wake up." Ann was shaking him by the shoulders. "You're not dead."

Jerry opened his eyes. The room was dark and he could just make out Ann's shadowy face peering anxiously over him.

"Why did you do it?" he said, sitting up and rubbing the lump on the side of his left temple.

"I'll explain later," Ann murmured. "Right now there isn't time. We've got to get out of here."

"What about the goon squad?"

"See for yourself."

Legs shaking, Jerry allowed her to lead him into the living room and over to the window. He stared down.

The black limousine was gone. Ann's car stood in its place.

"Come on," Ann said. "We've got to get to the airport. Your bags are packed and in the car."

"Where are we going?"

"Costa Rica."

Jerry frowned. "I don't get it."

"You will."

And once the plane took off, he did.

"What you said about writing your own novel convinced me," Ann told him. "That's when I got the idea. I'm sorry about knocking you out, but I knew you'd never agree to go through with it on your own."

"Agree to what?"

"Delivering Conway Mann's new novel to his publisher."

"But there is no novel!"

"There is now. I took one of the carbons of Al Buzzard's manuscript. All I did was go through it and change the names of the characters."

"You mean you gave both publishers the same book?"

"Including the last chapter." Ann nodded. "You said yourself that these things are all alike."

"So that's why Conway Mann's goons let us go."

"Right. Once the manuscript got to the office of Scribbler's and Sons, they took off. And so have we."

"But why Costa Rica?"

"They don't have an extradition law. Even if Mann and Buzzard find out, you can't be touched. You've got the cash, enough to keep us going for a year. And you can write your book." Ann smiled. "Besides, darling, if what you say is true, nobody will find out. Not Buzzard, or Mann, or the publishers, and certainly not the readers."

Jerry groaned. "I hope you're right," he whispered.

Ann patted his hand. "I know I am," she said.

And she was.

In the months that followed, THE ARISTOCRATS hit the bestseller lists with such force that Al Buzzard bought a new yacht, with two swimming pools, one of which he kept filled with champagne. If anything, THE TASTE-MAKERS was an even bigger success; Conway Mann was able to purchase a Jackson Pollock, a Van Gogh, a Rembrandt, and another hat.

Best of all, Jerry Cribbs finally wrote his own novel, which was duly published under his own name. You may have read it.

Then again, you may not.

It sold 148 copies.

NINA

AFTER THE LOVEMAKING Nolan needed another drink.

He fumbled for the bottle beside the bed, gripping it with a sweaty hand. His entire body was wet and clammy and his fingers shook as they unscrewed the cap. For a moment Nolan wondered if he was coming down with another bout of fever. Then, as the harsh heat of the rum scalded his stomach, he realized the truth.

Nina had done this to him.

Nolan turned and glanced at the girl who lay beside him. She stared up through the shadows with slitted eyes unblinking above high cheekbones, her thin brown body relaxed and immobile. Hard to believe that only moments ago this same body had been a writhing, wriggling coil of insatiable appetite, gripping and enfolding him until he was drained and spent.

He held the bottle out to her. "Have a drink?"

She shook her head, eyes hooded and expressionless, and then Nolan remembered that she didn't speak English. He raised the bottle and drank again, cursing himself for his mistake.

It had been a mistake, he realized that now, but Darlene would never understand. Sitting there safe and snug in the apartment in Trenton, she couldn't begin to know what he'd gone through for her sake — hers and little Robbie's. Robert Emmett Nolan II, nine weeks old now; his son, whom he'd never seen. That's why he'd taken the job, signed on with the Company for a year. The money was good, enough to keep Darlene in comfort and tide them over after he got back. She couldn't have come with him, not while she was carrying the kid, so he came alone, figuring no sweat.

No sweat. That was a laugh. All he'd done since he got here was sweat. Patrolling the plantation at sunup, loading cargo all day for the boats that went downriver, squinting over paperwork while night closed down on the bungalow to imprison him behind a wall of jungle darkness. And at night the noises came—the hum of insect hordes, the bellow of caimans, the snorting snuffle of peccary, the ceaseless chatter of monkeys intermingled with the screeching of a million mindless birds.

So he'd started to drink. First the good bourbon from the Company's stock, then the halfway-decent trade gin, and now the cheap rum.

As Nolan set the empty bottle down he heard the noise he'd come to dread worst of all—the endless echo of drums from the huts huddled beside the riverbank below. Miserable wretches were at it again. No wonder he had to drive them daily to fulfill the Company's quota. The wonder was that they did anything at all after spending every night wailing to those damned drums.

Of course it was Moises who did the actual driving; Nolan couldn't even chew them out properly because they were too damned dumb to understand plain English.

Like Nina, here.

Again Nolan looked down at the girl who lay curled beside him on the bed, silent and sated. She wasn't sweating; her skin was curiously cool to the touch, and in her eyes was a mystery.

It was the mystery that Nolan had sensed the first time he saw her staring at him across the village compound three days ago. At first he thought she was one of the Company people—somebody's wife, daughter, sister. That afternoon, when he returned to the bungalow, he caught her staring at him again at the edge of the clearing. So he asked Moises who she was, and Moises didn't know. Apparently she'd just arrived a day or two before, paddling a crude catamaran downriver from somewhere out of the denser jungle stretching a thousand miles beyond. She had no English, and according to Moises she didn't speak Spanish or Portuguese either. Not that she'd made any attempts to communicate; she kept to herself, sleeping in the catamaran moored beside the bank across the river and not even venturing into the Company store by day to purchase food.

"Indio," Moises said, pronouncing the word with all the contempt of one in whose veins ran a 10 percent admixture of the proud blood of the *conquistadores.* "Who are we to know the way of savages?" He shrugged.

Nolan had shrugged, too, and dismissed her from his mind. But that night as he lay on his bed, listening to the pounding of the drums, he thought of her again and felt a stirring in his loins.

She came to him then, almost as though the stirring had been a silent summons; came like a brown shadow gliding out of the night. Soundlessly she entered, and swiftly she shed her single garment as she moved across the room to stand staring down at him on the bed. Then, as she sank upon his nakedness and encircled his thighs, the stirring in his loins became a throbbing and the pounding in his head drowned out the drums.

In the morning she was gone, but on the following night she returned. It was then that he'd called her Nina—it wasn't her name, but he felt a need to somehow identify this wide-mouthed, pink-tongued stranger who slaked herself upon him, slaked his own urgency again and again as her hissing breath rasped in his ears.

Once more she vanished while he slept, and he hadn't seen her all day. But at times he'd been conscious of her secret stare, a coldness falling upon him like an unglimpsed shadow, and he'd known that tonight she'd come again.

Now, as the drums sounded in the distance, Nina slept. Unmindful of the din, heedless of his presence, her eyes hooded and she lay somnolent in animal repletion.

Nolan shuddered. That's what she was; an animal. In repose, the lithe brown body was grotesquely elongated, the wide mouth accentuating the ugliness of her face. How could he have coupled with this creature? Nolan grimaced in self-disgust as he turned away.

Well, no matter—it was ended now, over once and for all. Today the message had arrived from Belém; Darlene and Robbie were on the ship, ready for the flight to Manaus. Tomorrow morning he'd start downriver to meet them, escort them here. He'd had his qualms about their coming; they'd have to face three months in this hellhole before the year was up, but Darlene had insisted.

And she was right. Nolan knew it now. At least they'd be together and that would help see him through. He wouldn't need the bottle any more, and he wouldn't need Nina.

Nolan lay back and waited for sleep to come, shutting out the sound of the drums, the sight of the shadowy shape beside him. Only a few hours until morning, he told himself. And in the morning, the nightmare would be over.

The trip to Manaus was an ordeal, but it ended in Darlene's arms. She was blonder and more beautiful than he'd remembered, more loving and tender than he'd ever known her to be, and in the union that was their reunion Nolan found fulfillment. Of course there was none of the avid hunger of Nina's coiling caresses, none of the mindless thrashing to final frenzy. But it didn't matter; the two of them were together at last. The two of them, and Robbie.

Robbie was a revelation.

Nolan hadn't anticipated the intensity of his own reaction. But now, after the long trip back in the wheezing launch, he stood beside the crib in the spare bedroom and gazed down at his son with an overwhelming surge of pride.

"Isn't he adorable?" Darlene said. "He looks just like you."

"You're prejudiced." Nolan grinned, but he was flattered. And when the tiny pink starshell of a hand reached forth to meet his fingers he tingled at the touch.

Then Darlene gasped.

Nolan glanced up quickly. "What's the matter?" he said.

"Nothing." Darlene was staring past him. "I thought I saw someone outside the window."

Nolan followed her gaze. "No one out there." He moved to the window, peered at the clearing beyond. "Not a soul."

Darlene passed a hand before her eyes. "I guess I'm just overtired," she said. "The long trip—"

Nolan put his arm around her. "Why don't you go lie down for a while? Mama Dolores can look after Robbie."

Darlene hesitated. "Are you sure she knows what to do?"

"Look who's talking!" Nolan laughed. "They don't call her Mama for nothing—she's had ten kids of her own. She's in the kitchen right now, fixing Robbie's formula. I'll go get her."

So Darlene went down the hall to their bedroom for a siesta and Mama Dolores took over Robbie's schedule while Nolan made his daily rounds in the fields.

The heat was stifling, worse than anything he could remember. Even Moises was gasping for air as he gunned the jeep over the rutted roadway, peering into the shimmering haze.

Nolan wiped his forehead. Maybe he'd been too hasty, bringing Darlene and the baby here. But a man was entitled to see his own son, and in a few months they'd be out of this miserable sweatbox forever. No sense getting uptight; everything was going to be all right.

But at dusk, when he returned to the bungalow, Mama Dolores greeted him at the door with a troubled face.

"What is it?" Nolan said. "Something wrong with Robbie?"

Mama shook her head. "He sleeps like a angel," she murmured. "But the *señora*—"

In their room, Darlene lay shivering on the bed, eyes closed. Her head moved ceaselessly on the pillows even when Nolan pressed his palm against her brow.

"Fever." Nolan gestured to Mama Dolores, and the old woman held Darlene still while he forced the thermometer between her lips.

The red column inched upwards. "One hundred and four." Nolan straightened quickly. "Go fetch Moises. Tell him I want the launch ready, *pronto*. We'll have to get her to the doctor at Manaus."

Darlene's eyes fluttered open; she'd heard.

"No, you can't! The baby—"

"Do not trouble yourself. I will look after the little one." Mama's voice was soothing. "Now you must rest."

"No, please——"

Darlene's voice trailed off into an incoherent babbling and she sank back. Nolan kept his hand on her forehead; the heat was like an oven. "Now just relax, darling. It's all right. I'm going with you."

And he did.

If the first trip had been an ordeal, this one was an agony: a frantic thrust through the sultry night on the steaming river, Moises sweating over the throttle as Nolan held Darlene's shuddering shoulders against the straw mattress in the stern of the vibrating launch. They made Manaus by dawn and roused Dr. Robales from slumber at his house near the plaza.

Then came the examination, the removal to the hospital, the tests and the verdict. A simple matter, Dr. Robales said, and no need for alarm. With proper treatment and rest she would recover. A week here in the hospital——

"A week?" Nolan's voice rose. "I've got to get back for the loading. I can't stay here that long!"

"There is no need for you to stay, *señor*. She shall have my personal attention, I assure you."

It was small comfort, but Nolan had no choice. And he was too tired to protest, too tired to worry. Once aboard the launch and heading back, he stretched out on the straw mattress in a sleep that was like death itself.

Nolan awakened to the sound of drums. He jerked upright with a startled cry, then realized that night had come and they were once again at anchor beside the dock. Moises grinned at him in weary triumph.

"Almost we do not make it," he said. "The motor is bad. No matter, it is good to be home again."

Nolan nodded, flexing his cramped limbs. He stepped out onto the dock, then hurried up the path across the clearing. The darkness boomed.

Home? This corner of hell, where the drums dinned and the shadows leaped and capered before flickering fires?

All but one, that is. For as Nolan moved forward, another shadow glided out from the deeper darkness beside the bungalow.

It was Nina.

Nolan blinked as he recognized her standing there and staring up at him. There was no mistaking the look on her face or its urgency, but he had no time to waste in words. Brushing past her, he hastened to the doorway and she melted back into the night.

Mama Dolores was waiting for him inside, nodding her greeting.

"Robbie——is he all right?"

"*Sí, señor.* I take good care. *Por favor,* I sleep in his room."

"Good." Nolan turned and started for the hall, then hesitated as Mama Dolores frowned. "What is it?" he said.

The old woman hesitated. "You will not be offended if I speak?"

"Of course not."

Mama's voice sank to a murmur. "It concerns the one outside."

"Nina?"

"That is not her name, but no matter." Mama shook her head. "For two days she has waited there. I see you with her now when you return. And I see you with her before — "

"That's none of your business!" Nolan reddened. "Besides, it's all over now."

"Does she believe that?" Mama's gaze was grave. "You must tell her to go."

"I've tried. But the girl comes from the mountains, she doesn't speak English — "

"I know." Mama nodded. "She is one of the snake-people."

Nolan stared at her. "They worship snakes up there?"

"No, not worship."

"Then what do you mean?"

"These people — they *are* snakes."

Nolan scowled. "What is this?"

"The truth, *señor.* This one you call Nina — this girl — is not a girl. She is of the ancient race from the high peaks, where the great serpents dwell. Your workers here, even Moises, know only the jungle, but I come from the great valley beneath the mountains, and as a child I learned to fear those who lurk above. We do not go there, but sometimes the snake-people come to us. In the spring when they awaken, they shed their skins, and for a time they are fresh and clean before the scales grow again. It is then that they come, to mate with men."

She went on like that, whispering about creatures half-serpent and half-human, with bodies cold to the touch, limbs that could writhe in boneless contortion to squeeze the breath from a man and crush him like the coils of a giant constrictor. She spoke of forked tongues, of voices hissing forth from mouths yawning incredibly wide on movable jawbones. And she might have gone on, but Nolan stopped her now; his head was throbbing with weariness.

"That's enough," he said. "I thank you for your concern."

"But you do not believe me."

"I didn't say that." Tired as he was, Nolan still remembered the basic rule — never contradict these people or make fun of their superstitions. And he couldn't afford to alienate Mama now. "I shall take precautions," he told her, gravely. "Right now I've got to rest. And I want to see Robbie."

Mama Dolores put her hand to her mouth. "I forget — the little one, he is alone — "

She turned and padded hastily down the hallway, Nolan behind her. Together they entered the nursery.

"Ah!" Mama exhaled a sigh of relief. "The *pobrecito* sleeps."

Robbie lay in his crib, a shaft of moonlight from the window bathing his tiny face and form. From his rosebud mouth issued a gentle snore.

Nolan smiled at the sound, then nodded at Mama. "I'm going to turn in now. You take good care of him."

"I will not leave." Mama settled herself in a rocker beside the crib. As Nolan turned to go she called after him softly. "Remember what I have told you, *señor.* If she comes again—"

Nolan moved down the hall to his bedroom at the far end. He hadn't trusted himself to answer her. After all, she meant well; it was just that he was too damned tired to put up with any more nonsense from the old woman.

In his bedroom something rustled.

Nolan flinched, then halted as the shadow-shape glided forth from the darkened corner beside the open window.

Nina stood before him and she was stark naked. Stark naked, her arms opening in invitation.

He retreated a step. "No," he said.

She came forward, smiling.

"Go away—get out of here."

He gestured her back. Nina's smile faded and she made a sound in her throat, a little gasp of entreaty. Her hands reached out—

"Damn it, leave me alone!"

Nolan struck her on the cheek. It wasn't more than a slap, and she couldn't have been hurt. But suddenly Nina's face contorted as she launched herself at him, her fingers splayed and aiming at his eyes. This time he hit her hard—hard enough to send her reeling back.

"Out!" he said. He forced her to the open window, raising his hand threateningly as she spewed and spit her rage, then snatched up her discarded garment and clambered over the sill to drop into the darkness beyond.

Nolan stood by the window watching as Nina moved away across the clearing. For a moment she turned in a path of moonlight and looked back at him—only a moment, but long enough for Nolan to see the livid fury blazing in her eyes.

Then she was gone, gliding off into the night where the drums thudded in distant darkness.

She was gone, but the hate remained. Nolan felt its force as he stretched out upon the bed. Ought to undress, but he was too tired. The throbbing in his head was worse, pulsing to the beat of the drums. And the hate was in his head, too. God, that ugly face! Like the thing in mythology—what was it?—the Medusa. One look turned men to stone. Her locks of hair were live serpents.

But that was legend, like Mama Dolores's stories about the snake-people. Strange—did every race have its belief in such creatures? Could there be some grotesque, distorted element of truth behind all these old wives' tales?

He didn't want to think about it now; he didn't want to think of anything. Not Nina, not Darlene, not even Robbie. Darlene would be all right, Robbie was fine, and Nina was gone. That left him, alone here with the drums. Damned pounding. Had to stop, had to stop so he could sleep—

It was the silence that awakened him. He sat up with a start, realizing he must have slept for hours, because the shadows outside the window were dappled with the grayish pink of dawn.

Nolan rose, stretching, then stepped out into the hall. The shadows were darker here and everything was still.

He went down the hallway to the other bedroom. The door was ajar and he moved past it, calling softly. "Mama Dolores—"

Nolan's tongue froze to the roof of his mouth. Time itself was frozen as he stared down at the crushed and pulpy thing sprawled shapelessly beside the rocker, its sightless eyes bulging from the swollen purple face.

No use calling her name again; she'd never hear it. And Robbie—

Nolan turned in the frozen silence, his eyes searching the shadows at the far side of the room.

The crib was empty.

Then he found his voice and cried out; cried out again as he saw the open window and the gray vacancy of the clearing beyond.

Suddenly he was at the window, climbing out and dropping to the matted sward below. He ran across the clearing, through the trees, and into the open space before the riverbank.

Moises was in the launch, working on the engine. He looked up as Nolan ran toward him, shouting.

"What are you doing here?"

"There is the problem of the motor. It requires attention. I come early, before the heat of the day—"

"Did you see her?"

"Who, *señor?*"

"The girl—Nina—"

"Ah yes. The *Indio.*" Moises nodded. "She is gone, in her catamaran, up the river. Two, maybe three hours ago, just as I arrive."

"Why didn't you stop her?"

"For what reason?"

Nolan gestured quickly. "Get that engine started—we're going after her."

Moises frowned. "As I told you, there is the matter of the repairs. Perhaps this afternoon—"

"We'll never catch her then!" Nolan gripped Moises's shoulder. "Don't you understand? She's taken Robbie!"

"Calm yourself, *señor*. With my own eyes I saw her go to the boat and she was alone, I swear it. She does not have the little one."

Nolan thought of the hatred in Nina's eyes and he shuddered. "Then what did she do with him?"

Moises shook his head. "This I do not know. But I am sure she has no need of another infant."

"What are you talking about?"

"I notice her condition when she walked to the boat." Moises shrugged, but even before the words came, Nolan knew.

"Why do you look at me like that, *señor*? Is it not natural for a woman to bulge when she carries a baby in her belly?"

Freak Show

Goober City Fairgrounds lay out in the boondocks and came to life only during the county fair. Nothing ever happened on the premises the rest of the year, aside from a few muggings and an occasional rape.

But on this particular morning, as Sheriff Higgs drove up in the patrol car, he noticed signs of other activity.

Parked right spang in the middle of the main arena was a big red van. And standing next to it was a man.

Sheriff Higgs knew every four-wheeled contraption or two-legged critter in Mayhem County, but he'd never seen this van or man before. He pulled up about fifty feet away, climbed out, and walked over slow and easy.

The van was unmarked and had an out-of-state license, so that didn't give him much to go on. The man was nothing to write home about, either — tall, on the skinny side, dark hair and eyes — he could be young or well into middle age, depending on the face under the beard. But his shirt and pants were too clean for a hippie-type, and there just wasn't anything about him you could get a handle on.

Sheriff Higgs decided to feel his way. "Morning," he said. "Mighty warm day and fixing to get worse. Folks say it's so hot you can fry eggs on the sidewalk."

"Bad for your health," said the man. "Too much cholesterol."

"Don't worry about my health," the sheriff told him. "I'm here on official business."

The stranger smiled. "And what might that be?"

Sheriff Higgs held up a printed placard and squinted at its bright red lettering in the sunlight. CARNIVAL OF LIFE, he read. THE GREATEST SHOW ON EARTH. ADULTS ONLY — FAIRGROUNDS, TONIGHT.

The man nodded. "Went up late last night when I arrived. You'll find them on every telephone pole in Goober City. Forty-seven, as I recall."

"That's forty-seven violations," the sheriff told him. "Law says you can't post bills in public property without a permit."

"Sorry," said the man. "I thought that was merely a formality. And since my stay is short I'm rather pressed for time. But I suppose law and order is the name of the game." And he winked.

Sheriff Higgs looked him straight in the eye. "It's not a game with me. Like I said, I'm here on business."

"I agree," said the stranger. "Let's shake on it." He stuck out his hand and Sheriff Higgs took it, feeling the crisp crackle of folding-money against his palm as he slid the bill into his trouser pocket.

The man turned away. "Now that the proprieties are observed I must ask you to excuse me. There's work to be done."

"Hold it," said the sheriff. "I got to know a little something about this carnival of yours before I give you the go-ahead."

The man shrugged. "No problem. It's just a mud-show. Been doing these one-night stands for years, like Dr. Lao or Cooger and Dark."

"Never heard of them," the sheriff said. "Or you either. Mind giving me your name?"

"Fall," said the stranger. "Fall's the name—though I'm a man for all seasons, so to speak."

Sheriff Higgs cocked his head at the red van. "Where's the rest of your outfit, Mr. Fall?"

"They'll be along shortly. Once I get the tent up—"

"Not so fast. Suppose you tell me just what goes on inside that tent of yours. Handbill here says ADULTS ONLY. Is this here one of them sex shows?"

"Certainly not."

"What about gambling?"

"I'm not partial to games of chance."

"You bringing in any wild animals?"

"I have no dealings with animals."

"Then just what do you deal with?"

"It's a ten-in-one," said Mr. Fall. "What you'd call a freak show."

"What kind of freaks?"

"Come back tonight and see for yourself." Mr. Fall smiled. "I think you and the good people of Goober City will find it a most unusual attraction."

The good people of Goober City must have expected sex, gambling and wild animals, because they came swarming onto the fairgrounds right after dark.

Sheriff Higgs saw that just about everybody was there, from the folks who worked in the mill to the big wheels who lived on the hill—banker

Fence, lawyer Tudd, even Mayor Stooldrayer. Brought their wives along, too; it wasn't the kind of show they'd choose for their girlfriends.

The arena lights were on and loud music blasted from an amplifier out-side the tent. But that's all Sheriff Higgs noticed—there weren't any rides or shooting galleries or guess-your-weight outfits, no fortuneteller booths, no Keeno concessions, not even a stand where you could buy a chiliburger or a Dr. Pepper.

There was just this one tent, not all that big, either. It had a platform out front, and the sheriff spotted Mr. Fall standing on it with his back turned, putting up banners all along the side of the canvas wall. When Fall turned around, the sheriff saw he was wearing a fancy red suit that looked to be velvet, with shirt and tie to match. Even his shoes were red and he carried a red cane in the crook of his arm. He'd slicked his hair back with little puffs standing up on either side of his forehead, and with that beard of his he was a dead ringer for the label on a bottle of Pluto Water.

"Good evening," he said, coming down to the edge of the platform. "Glad you could make it."

"That's some getup you're wearing," Sheriff Higgs told him. "You look like one of those old-time stage magicians."

"All part of the act." Mr. Fall smiled. "If you mean to succeed in this world, you've got to cater to your customers' wants. And what they want most is illusion."

"What kind of tricks do you do?"

"Just the basics. No complicated gimmicks, no phony effects, no walking on water or changing water into wine. I leave cheap miracles to the opposi-tion. Experience has shown me that most people don't require much in order to be fooled. All they need is the opportunity for self-deception."

Sheriff Higgs frowned. "Well, you don't put over anything on me with that scam," he said. "Notice you still only got one tent. Where's the other stuff you said was coming?"

"Everything's inside," Mr. Fall told him. "And the show is ready to begin."

He turned away and walked to the center of the platform, pounding on the wooden planks with his cane.

The cane must have been rigged up with some kind of remote-control amplifier because it made quite a racket. And Mr. Fall's voice came through loud and clear.

"This way," he called out. "This way, ladies and gentlemen, for the free show."

The ladies and gentlemen began to gather around the platform, pushing and shoving and fighting for a place up front, the way people always do when they figure on getting something for free.

There was quite a bit of cussing, and some of the older folks got their toes tromped on, but no one was seriously hurt, from what Sheriff Higgs could see. He was right up front himself, of course; nobody gets ahead of the law.

"Good evening one and all," said Mr. Fall. "And welcome to the Carnival of Life."

"Some carnival!" mumbled a voice from behind the sheriff. "Where's the belly dancers?"

Sheriff Higgs didn't bother to look around; he knew who was speaking because he could smell his breath. Clay Tolliver, the mortician's son, always got pretty well bombed by this time of evening.

Mr. Fall smiled and nodded. "In answer to the question regarding the performers, allow me to call your attention to the pictorial displays directly behind me. In the quaint jargon of the old-time carny, they are known as 'the bloody banners.' If there happen to be any Englishmen in the audience, I trust they will take no offense."

There were no Englishmen or any other foreigners present and no offense was taken; everyone peered up at the painted panel of an enormously fat woman indicated by Mr. Fall's cane.

"Big Bertha," he said. "Five hundred pounds of pulsing pulchritude—a quarter of a ton of solid human flesh—the fattest female figure in the firmament."

Down in front, Mrs. Agatha Crouch stood bulking before the billowing poster, one hamlike hand gripping her husband's arm and the other encircling an open jar of garlic dills. Raising the jar to her gaping mouth, she snagged one of the pickles between her teeth and began to munch on it.

Mr. Crouch was a feisty little man and he swore a blue streak as a squirt of pickle juice sprayed the top of his head.

"God-diddly-damn-it!" he yelled. "You dribbling all over me!"

"Okay, then you hold it," said Mrs. Crouch, thrusting the jar into his hand and fishing another dill from the brine with her pudgy fingers.

Mr. Crouch scowled. "Bringing pickles to a carnival," he muttered. "Eat, eat, eat, that's all you ever do. Don't you get enough food at home?"

Agatha Crouch's chins quivered with righteous indignation as she popped the pickle into her mouth. "I don't get me enough of anything at home, you miserable runt! Now shut up and listen to the man."

The man was indicating another portion of the panel, where a tiny figure rested on the fat woman's lap, almost obscured by her bulging belly.

"Big Bertha's diminutive darling," he chanted. "Little Leo—a minuscule mite of mankind mated to a mountain—a marvel of mirth and merriment!"

"Haw!" remarked Agatha Crouch, squinting at the small shape lost in the flabby folds of the fat lady's lap. "Sure looks funny, don't it?"

"Yeah." Mr. Crouch nodded as he craned his neck to see the banner. But he was staring at the picture of the fat woman.

Up on the platform Mr. Fall moved to another panel. This one depicted a strangely garbed, grinning creature with a chinless face, pointed ears, pale skin and a shaved, oddly pointed skull. As a fanciful touch the poster artist had added a dozen white mice crawling over the creature's head and shoulders; a thirteenth dangled by its tail from between his teeth.

"Pooky the Pinhead!" said Mr. Fall. "Actually a microcephalic — one of Mother Nature's little mistakes. But as you can see by his smile, he's a cheerful fellow and doesn't mind playing the game of life without a full deck."

Somebody in the crowd let out a cackle, and the sheriff turned to see who was responsible. But it was only Junior Dorkin; you couldn't hardly call him responsible, seeing as how he was the village idiot and an albino to boot. He just kept laughing and pointing up at the picture, same as usual. Junior laughed just about all the time, even when he was cutting up a stray cat.

"Huh-huh-huh!" he wheezed, wiping a gob of spittle from his receding chin. "Wanna see him eat mouses — "

Now Mr. Fall was gesturing at another banner, even more lurid than the others. It showed a hulking hairy monster with apelike features, leering down at a cowering, scantily clad girl.

"Out of the primeval past," he was saying. "A bestial being emerges from the misty mystery of prehistoric time. Behold the living, breathing ancestor of human kind — Horneo Porneo, the Wild Man of Borneo!"

"Man, that's weird!"

Sheriff Higgs glanced around to see Fuzz Foskins grinning up from his place in the crowd, wearing his usual outfit of tank top and soiled jeans. Bushy hair sprouted from his head in an enormously unnatural natural, a bushy beard tangled with the matted hair on his chest. His armpits were bushy too, and from them welled a fetid scent which mingled with the reeking odor emanating from his open mouth.

Probably high on angel dust again, the sheriff figured. If Fuzz's father wasn't the county judge, he'd have been busted long ago.

Sheriff Higgs recognized the girl clinging to Fuzz's arm — Mamie Keefer, a sallow-faced little snip with stringy cornsilk hair. Worked in the mill off and on when she wasn't riding shotgun on Fuzz's motorcycle.

"Whaddya mean, weird?" she said. "Look at that built!"

"I am looking," Fuzz told her. And he sniggered at the half-naked girl on the poster. "Some built, man! This I gotta see."

Several of the older people standing nearby started to frown disapprovingly — mostly the wives, of course. Sheriff Higgs took note of it and so did Mr. Fall up on the platform. He moved along to a row of banners hanging before the entrance of the tent and gestured again with his cane.

"If you folks will kindly move in a little closer, I'd like to give you a glimpse of our more cultural attractions," he announced.

"That must be the belly dancers," Clay Tolliver murmured. "Now we're getting somewhere!"

Mr. Fall's eyes narrowed slightly, just enough to indicate that he'd heard the remark, but his smile never wavered. "All that is strange or unusual in the world derives from two sources," he continued. "The curiosities of nature originate in mystery, while the idiosyncrasies of mankind are found in history."

"What's he saying?" sniffed Mrs. Tudd.

Lawyer Tudd shrugged. "Double-talk," he said. "Sounds like one of those smart-ass civil rights troublemakers to me."

Mr. Fall didn't miss a thing. He nodded down at the solid citizens in the front row. "I assure you there is nothing political about this spectacle. Naturally I cannot reproduce the actual events of a bygone era. These are merely representations, a few simple samples of man's freakish pastimes in the past." His cane stabbed out at one of the canvas panels behind him. "May I have your attention, please? Here, from long ago and far away — King Atahualpa and the Room of Gold!"

There must have been a light behind the banner, for now its colors blazed forth so brightly that the crowd gasped.

What they saw was a regal-looking man in flowing robes, standing with arms upraised in the center of a stone chamber.

"Awful dark-complected for a king," Mrs. Fence whispered to her husband. "Looks like some kind of a nigra to me."

Banker Fence just nodded but did not reply. He was staring at the gold heaped around the figure — the glittering glut of jewelry, ornaments, plate, goblets, coins and virgin ingots crammed into the chamber from wall to wall and rising halfway to the ceiling.

"I'm sure you all remember Francisco Pizarro, the conqueror of Peru," Mr. Fall was saying. "In 1532 he captured the Inca, Atahualpa, and imprisoned him in Cajamarca. As a ransom for their king's release, his faithful followers promised to fill the prison chamber — measuring ten feet long and sixteen feet in width — with enough gold to reach the level of Atahualpa's raised arms."

"Do tell," breathed banker Fence.

Mr. Fall nodded toward the panel. "Loyal followers came from all over the land, bringing their most precious possessions to lay at the feet of the Inca, impoverishing themselves to secure the freedom of their living god. The task took many months, but at last it was completed. Never before and never since did men behold such an array of radiant riches — this roomful of glittering gold. Still, they kept their word and the bargain was fulfilled."

"Great God in the morning," banker Fence murmured. "What happened then?"

Mr. Fall shrugged. "The inevitable," he said. "Pizarro had King Atahualpa strangled to death in the marketplace. Not too long afterwards, Pizarro himself was murdered."

"Never mind the details," said banker Fence. "What became of the gold?"

"No one knows," Mr. Fall said. "Somewhere along the line it just disappeared."

"Poor security," banker Fence grunted to his wife. "Gold is a bad risk anyway. Now you know why I keep telling the kids to invest in comics."

"I'd still like to see that room," said Mrs. Fence. "With that jewelry and all, it sounds real educational."

But now the light was flickering up behind another banner, and again the crowd gasped at what appeared — a gigantic bulldozer cutting a swath through a mountainous pile of naked, emaciated human corpses.

"For those who prefer something more contemporary," Mr. Fall proclaimed. "Auschwitz — the Holocaust!"

Lawyer Tudd nodded. "Concentration camp," he told his wife. "Read about it in law school. Some monkey business of a trial over in Nuremberg, as I recall."

"Oh, how horrible!" his wife murmured. "Look at those poor people!"

"Now don't go getting so uptight. Like he says, it's only history."

"Well, in that case I suppose it's not so awful." Mrs. Tudd stared intently at the bodies, and her tongue flicked over her parted lips as her breathing quickened. "You know, I always wondered just how they did such things, all those tortures and such. I hear tell they used to make lampshades out of the skins, stuff like that."

"Legal points involved," said lawyer Tudd. "Might be kind of interesting at that."

He turned to seek Mayor Stooldrayer's opinion, but that dignitary and his wife were both gaping at another blazing banner directly over the entrance to the tent.

Mr. Fall was already pointing up at the familiar figure, bearded and nude except for a loincloth, hanging impaled upon a cross.

"No monstrosity spawned by nature, no man-made marvel, can possibly compare to the fantastic reality of divine inspiration," he said. *"Ecce Homo —* the Passion Play!"

Mrs. Stooldrayer turned and whispered to her husband. "Icky homo? Does he mean Jesus was some kind of morphodite, like? And what's all this stuff about passion?"

"It's just a play," the mayor told her.

"Well, I'm not sure I want to see it," Mrs. Stooldrayer mused. "After all, I'm working with the PTA and we're supposed to be against violence, to say nothing of gays." She hesitated. "On the other hand, we don't get a chance to see a real live play around here very often."

"That's the spirit," said Mayor Stooldrayer. "Way I figure, we're entitled to a little entertainment."

Mr. Fall must have been listening, because now he tapped his cane on the platform and nodded.

"Entertainment!" he cried. "It's all waiting for you here on the inside. Step right up, ladies and gentlemen — the show is about to begin!"

Mr. Fall jumped down from the platform and parted the curtain flaps before the entrance as the crowd began to surge forward.

"What about tickets?" Sheriff Higgs called out to him.

"Law always gets a free pass," Mr. Fall murmured. Then he raised his voice. "As you folks can see, I'm a little short-handed here and there's no one operating the ticket booth. So just keep moving, go right ahead — you can pay on the inside."

"Didn't say how much," banker Fence muttered to lawyer Tudd. "Think we ought to take a chance?"

Lawyer Tudd nodded. "No problem." He grinned. "Law says you got to establish a price in advance. We don't have to pay him a red cent if we don't want to."

Chuckling, he moved into the tent, holding his wife's arm tightly to keep from being separated from her in the jostling throng. Behind him came the banker and the mayor with their spouses, Mr. and Mrs. Crouch, Junior Dorkin, Mamie Keefer, and all the rest.

The assorted effluvia of Fuzz Foskins and Clay Tolliver mingled in the darkness of the tent's interior as the rest of the crowd pushed on inside until the tent was packed solid, wall to wall.

For a moment everyone stood silent, and then little indications of irritation began to arise.

"Hey, what gives?" somebody grumbled. "I can't see."

"Lights!" yelled Clay Tolliver.

Sheriff Higgs was always prepared for such emergencies and he responded now, pulling forth a flashlight from his pocket.

The beam played over the sea of faces scowling across the confines of the tent, then came to rest on the rear wall.

The wall was blank. Below it stood the sole object of furnishing — a bare platform.

The crowd stared and its murmurs rose to a roar.

"Hell!" someone shouted angrily. "What kind of a show you call this? They ain't no freaks in here!"

"There are now," murmured Mr. Fall, as he finished sewing the entrance flaps together from outside and poured the kerosene.

Then, smiling, he lit the match.